Please return on or before the latest date above.
You can renew online at *www.kent.gov.uk/libs*
or by telephone 08458 247 200

CUSTOMER SERVICE EXCELLENCE   **Libraries & Archives**

Kent
County
Council

00884\DTP\RN\07.07   LIB 7

C153246938

ABOVE THE HARVEST MOON

Hannah Casey and her mother Miriam have lived with her aunt and uncle since her father's death, but it is not a happy home. Hannah escapes to her friend Naomi's house whenever she can, and on her sixteenth birthday she begins to court Naomi's brother Adam, but when she flees her uncle's advances, it is the damaged, taciturn Jake, Naomi's older half-brother, who becomes her protector. Hannah has always felt tongue-tied in Jake's presence, but when he takes her to the farm where he works her feelings begin to change. Will those feelings be reciprocated ... and will Adam accept her change of heart?

ABOVE THE HARVEST MOON

ABOVE THE HARVEST MOON

by

Rita Bradshaw

Magna Large Print Books
Long Preston, North Yorkshire,
BD23 4ND, England.

British Library Cataloguing in Publication Data.

Bradshaw, Rita
    Above the harvest moon.

    A catalogue record of this book is
    available from the British Library

    ISBN   978-0-7505-2940-2

First published in Great Britain 2007 by Headline Publishing Group

Published in Large Print 2008 by arrangement with
Headline Publishing Group Ltd.

Magna Large Print is an imprint of Library Magna Books Ltd.

Printed and bound in Great Britain by
T.J. (International) Ltd., Cornwall, PL28 8RW

This book is especially for our darling grandson, Connor Joshua Thompson, as he prepares to start big school. Such a precious, comical and amazingly determined spirit in so small a body. Pappy and I love you so very much, little man.

And my Cara, already mourning the end of an era. Take comfort in the knowledge your boys love you all the world and that you and Ian are raising them to be the sort of men the world is in huge need of. I'm so proud of you, sweetheart, and the wonderful mother you are.

Out of much research material special thanks go to *Treasured Tales of the Countryside*, published by David & Charles, *A Remembered Land* edited by Sean Street and *Tommy Turnbull, A Miner's Life* by Joseph Robinson.

Contents

ABOVE THE HARVEST MOON

How often did he come to me
Beneath the harvest moon,
Take me in his arms awhile
Beneath the harvest moon,
Whisper that he loved me,
That sweethearts we'd remain,
Though all would try to part us
He'd not forget our sweet refrain.

But then the days turned colder
And I waited there in vain,
Until another came and spoke
And took away my pain.
And when I gave my heart to him
I knew he would be true,
That beneath the fire and brimstone
He was of softer hue.

Now when the harvest moon comes peeping
And sweet whispers fill the air,
I can give my love so freely
Because I know how much he cares.
The twilight holds a magic
And nature sings a finer tune
Because my love he takes me
Far above the harvest moon.

ANON

PART ONE

1898 – Suffer the little Children

Chapter 1

Rose Fletcher glanced at the clock then her mother, her voice anxious and apologetic when she murmured, 'I'm sorry, Mam...'

'Aye, I know, I know.' Her mother hugged the small child nestled on her lap and it was to him she spoke next. 'I've got to make myself scarce before your da comes home, Jake,' she said into the bright little face looking up at her. 'By, it comes to summat when I'm not welcome in me own daughter's home.'

'Aw, Mam, don't. You know how much I love to see you but Silas... Well, you know what he's like.'

Aye, she knew what Silas Fletcher was like all right. Ada Hedley said no more. Her poor lass had enough on her plate without her adding to it. She stood up and placed her grandson on his feet, whereupon he toddled over to the thick clippy mat in front of the glowing range and picked up the tin lid and wooden spoon he had been playing with when she had arrived earlier. Her voice soft, Ada said, 'He's a grand little lad, Rose, and so bonny. Bright as a button an' all.'

Rose smiled. 'Thanks for the brisket and dripping and everything, Mam, but you shouldn't. You can't afford it.'

'Go on with you. Your da's in work and there's only the two of us at home. If I can't see me only

19

bairn all right it's a poor lookout. Here.' Ada glanced over her shoulder as though there was someone else in the kitchen with them before thrusting some coins into her daughter's hand. 'Put this where he can't get his mitts on it. I bet you're behind with the rent again.'

'Mam, no, I can't take this.' Rose stared down at the two half-crowns and shilling. 'It's too much. You don't have to do this all the time.'

'Look, hinny, it fair kills me to see you taking in all that washing and ironing and working every hour the good Lord sends, while that one drinks and gambles his wage away with them pals of his. Take it, Rose. It's for you and the bairn. I know how you whittle about paying the rent.'

'Aw, Mam, Mam.'

'An' don't cry, lass. You'll upset the bairn, now then. It'll work out in the end, things always do.'

'I've been such a fool.'

'Aye, well, we can all say that at some time or other, hinny. There's not a man nor woman can say, hand on heart, they've not made a few mistakes along the road.'

'But most of them didn't have to marry their mistake.'

Both women's eyes were drawn to the child who was banging away at the tin lid with the spoon, jabbering nineteen to the dozen in baby talk. Becoming aware of their gaze, he stopped and gave them a big smile, showing his small white teeth, before resuming his game. 'You can't say some good didn't come out of it when you look at him,' Ada said warmly. 'He's the bonniest bairn I've ever seen and no mistake.'

'I wish Da would try and see it that way.'

'Lass, lass, you know how your da is. He's a proud man and it knocked him for six, especially it being Silas Fletcher. He's never had any truck with the Fletchers, thinks they're the lowest of the low, he does.'

Rose couldn't argue with this. She agreed with it. Instead she lifted her apron and dried her face, a little catch in her voice when she said, 'I don't know what I'd do without you, Mam.'

'An' me you, lass.' Ada reached out and gently touched her daughter's cheek, a rare gesture from one who was not physically demonstrative. Then, as the wooden clock on the shelf above the range chimed the hour, she pulled on her worn hat and coat, sliding woollen gloves over chilblained fingers. 'I'd better be off but you keep your chin up, hinny. Like me old mam used to say, worse things happen at sea. I'll see meself out, lass.'

Worse things happen at sea. Once the door had closed behind her mother, Rose walked across to the loose brick at the side of the range which Silas knew nothing about. She carefully withdrew it and placed the coins next to the sixpence and odd pennies in the little hollow over which the brick fitted and slid it back in place. Then she cleared away every trace of her mother's visit and set the table for dinner, her mind churning. She couldn't think of anything worse than being married to Silas. If it wasn't for Jake she would have walked down to the river months ago, like poor Emily Burns had after her three bairns had been taken with the fever within weeks of each other. All the

21

old wives hereabouts had had a field day gossiping about that, saying Emily shouldn't have done it, that it was a mortal sin to do away with yourself, but Rose had understood that life could be such that facing the Almighty's wrath in the hereafter was preferable to living.

Jake's grizzle told her he was hungry. 'I'm sorry, hinny. We're all behind with Grandma coming, aren't we?' she said softly, picking him up and putting him into the stout high chair her father had made for her when she was a baby. 'You've normally had your tea by now. Here,' she handed him a crust of bread, 'have that till Mam can feed you your bowl of broth.'

After checking the mutton broth simmering on the range, Rose hastily sliced one of the loaves she had baked earlier and put it on the table. She then filled the big black kettle and placed it on the hob, putting the teapot on the steel shelf at the side of the range so it would warm through. Outside, the January day was raw, the smell of snow in the wind, but in the kitchen the mellow light from the oil lamp increased the cosiness. All the furniture had been bought second-hand – with her mother's help – in the frantically busy days before her hasty marriage to Silas. The kitchen table with its two narrow benches tucked underneath, the stout old sideboard and massive clippy mat – so heavy it took two to lift it but which provided some comfort against the cold stone flags – had all come from the house of an elderly widow who had died. Silas's very ugly high-backed chair with a slatted back and flock cushions had been going cheap in the old market due to its condition, but after she had recovered the cushions it didn't look so bad.

Silas hadn't lifted a finger to provide so much as a teaspoon. Rose's soft mouth tightened. That should have told her something about the nature of the man she was marrying. But of course it had been too late by then. She'd been in the family way and had been grateful he was marrying her at all.

Shaking her head at the foolish young girl she had been in those days, Rose bit down hard on her bottom lip. She'd counted herself fortunate when a friend of her mother's had tipped them off about these rooms becoming vacant due to the previous tenants doing a moonlight flit. The family who lived on the top floor in the two-up two-down terrace had to lug buckets of water up a steep flight of stairs every day from the outside tap shared among four houses. At least she'd been spared that.

But there were worse things than carrying heavy buckets of water upstairs. Rose crossed her arms over her middle and her hands gripped the sides of her apron. She swayed back and forth, her eyes shut. She had been near to blurting out to her mam that it wasn't only Silas's drinking and gambling she had to put up with and she mustn't do that. Her da loathed Silas as it was; the two of them had come near to blows at the colliery because of her father's attitude to her husband – Silas had told her so. What her da would do if he knew about the indignities Silas heaped upon her when the mood took him she didn't dare imagine. Sober, Silas could be violent and unpredictable.

Drunk, his brutality took on an altogether more unnatural and depraved twist. And if it came to a confrontation with his son-in-law, her da wouldn't stand a chance. The Fletchers' reputation for dirty fighting was well known throughout Monkwearmouth.

Why had she got mixed up with Silas in the first place? she asked herself for the hundredth time. His bad-boy reputation had fascinated her, that was the thing, along with his dark good looks and glib tongue. But she had paid for the clandestine assignations.

She had only met Silas twice before he had got her drunk in the old quarries off Cemetery Road Southwick way, one baking hot summer's afternoon. He'd had his way with her right there in the open. She had been but fifteen years old to his twenty-six, and she had never tasted strong liquor before. Afterwards she had prayed and prayed there would be no result of their union but after three months she had been unable to fool herself any longer. She was expecting a bairn, Silas Fletcher's bairn. That same month she had turned sixteen. And now, two years on, she had a son who was the light of her life and a husband she hated and feared.

The sound of the back door opening brought her springing to the range. When her husband entered the kitchen from the tiny scullery moments later Rose continued stirring the broth. Her voice flat, she said, 'There's a fresh loaf on the table and I'm about to dish up if you want to sit down.'

She knew he'd sat because she heard the scraping of the bench on the flags as he'd pulled it out. She made sure his plate held three good-sized dumplings along with most of the scrag end of mutton and some vegetables, and then she ladled more broth over the whole. This left little meat for herself and Jake but it was preferable to Silas throwing his plate against the wall as he'd done once or twice when they were first married, yelling that a plate of slops wasn't a fit meal for a man after a hard day's work down the pit. When she had protested she couldn't manage on the housekeeping he gave her, a night of such torment had followed that she had never answered him back again. That had been the start of her taking in the washing and ironing to make ends meet, although they never did.

She placed Silas's plate in front of him, her gaze on the table. She could smell the coal dust thick in the air. When her father had come home from the pit he had always stripped off in the scullery and sluiced himself down before pulling on his other set of clothes. Her mother would take his work clothes out into the yard and bang the dust out of them as much as she could before hanging them over the chair in the scullery ready for morning. She had imagined everyone did this before Silas had disabused her of the notion.

He wanted his dinner on the table when he walked in, he had growled at her, and he would change when he damn well wanted to. It was her job to clean up after him and she'd better get used to it. She had got used to it. She'd had no other option.

After blowing on Jake's bowl of broth to cool it down, she fed the child his dinner and then gave him another crust to eat while she ate her own meal. Not a word was spoken, the only sound besides the odd spit and crackle from the fire that of Silas slurping at his food like a pig at a trough.

It was strange how silent the child became when his father was around, Rose thought, eating her own meal swiftly so she would be ready to dish up the semolina pudding when Silas had finished his main course. From a tiny baby Jake had seemed to sense his father had no time for him. This had developed into a wariness which kept him as quiet as a mouse in Silas's presence.

'That old biddy in New Bridge Avenue cough up for the washing this morning?'

She had been waiting for him to ask from the moment he'd walked through the door. It was always the same. It didn't matter that oft times this kitchen was as steamy as a laundry with washing strung across the ceiling and the walls running with moisture, or that the mountains of ironing which ensued meant she worked to the early hours, her red hands cracked and swollen. At the heart of him Silas still considered he had a perfect right to her money, especially if he'd had a bad week with the gambling.

Without raising her eyes from her plate, Rose said quietly, 'Aye, she did. That's what I bought the mutton with and the flour for the bread. We were right out of everything. Mr Bell dropped round a sack of potatoes an' all.'

'A sack? You didn't need to buy a sack.'

'They were cheaper that way.' Harsh experience had taught her to make it look as though every penny had been spent even if she'd hidden a bit away towards the rent. 'We needed some dripping and marg an' all, and some lamp oil–'

'All right, all right, don't go on.' He wiped a chunk of bread round his plate to mop up the last of the gravy, stuffed it in his mouth and chewed.

She could feel his eyes on her and knew he was calculating the cost of the food and oil. Her mother's two half-crowns and shilling safely tucked away, she told herself not to get rattled. When she got rattled she trembled, and when she trembled it brought the fiendish side of him to the fore with a vengeance. It was as though he fed off her fear...

She reached across for his empty plate and placed it on hers then took them out to the tiny scullery to be washed later, before taking the milk pudding out of the oven. Spooning half of it into a bowl, she added a good dollop of strawberry jam and put it down in front of Silas, then returned to the range. She still hadn't looked at him.

'So it's all gone then?'

'What?' She feigned ignorance.

'The money, it's all gone? And stop what you're doing, woman. I'm talking to you.'

Slowly she turned, Jake's bowl in her hand. Meeting the eyes that were so dark brown as to be black, she said flatly, 'Yes, it's all gone. There was nothing in the house to eat.'

'Don't take that tone with me.'

She hadn't taken any sort of tone and they both knew it. 'I'm sorry.'

'You will be if I have any of your lip.'

After staring at her for another few seconds he began to shovel the pudding into his mouth. It was only then Rose went and sat in front of the high chair and fed Jake.

She hadn't finished when Silas said, 'Leave that and fill the bath, I'm off out in a while. And lay out me other shirt and trousers while you're about it.'

As she rose to do as he bid, Jake, seeing his food about to disappear, cried out in protest.

'Shut him up.'

'He's still hungry.'

'I said shut him up. I don't work all the hours under the sun to come home to him squawking his head off. If you can't shut him up, I will.'

Hastily Rose pushed into Jake's hand the half-eaten crust he had been gnawing at before she'd started to feed him the pudding. Her voice soft, she said, 'Here, eat this, there's a good lad. Mam'll see to you in a minute.' As the chubby fingers closed over the crust, she breathed a sigh of relief.

Once she had filled the tin bath in front of the range she would get Jake to bed and out of the way while Silas had his wash and got ready to go out. No doubt it was the Times Inn in Wear Street he was aiming for rather than the Colliery Tavern where most of the miners had a pint or two after a day's work down the pit. Being a riverside pub, the Times drew in plenty of seamen, keel and dockside workers as well as men from the ship-yards, men with more money in their pockets than miners, men who weren't averse to gambling the shirts off their backs. Her da had always reckoned the pubs down by the river rivalled Sunderland's East End with what went on in their murky depths.

Keeping her thoughts to herself, Rose fetched the tin bath from where it was propped against the scullery wall and partially filled it with boiling water from the kettle which she'd refilled and put back on the hob after mashing the tea. She added several buckets of cold water from the communal tap in the backyard until the water was tepid, the way Silas liked it, and placed a ha'penny piece of blue-veined soap on top of the rough sheet of towelling she'd brought through from the scullery.

'It's ready.'

Silas was sitting drinking his third cup of tea at the table as she spoke, and as he stood up she gathered Jake into her arms and carried him through to the bedroom.

By feel rather than sight she changed Jake's nappy and got him into his nightclothes in the dark room. They only had one oil lamp and that was in the kitchen with Silas. Once the child was ready, she sat down on her bed and bared her breast for his last feed of the day. He was now almost completely weaned but she loved these few minutes with him at night, when she was all in all to him and he was held close to her heart.

Within just a short while the dark room and her gentle rocking as he'd fed had worked their spell and he was fast asleep, the small head with its dark loose curls lolling against her arm. She held him for a minute or two more, relishing the baby smell and feel of him and then stood up and carried him over to his cot in a curtained-off section of the room. As with the high chair, the cot had been hers when she was a baby. She tucked the blankets round him and straightened up but did not immediately turn and walk out into the main part of the bedroom to sort out Silas's change of clothes. Instead she stood for a few moments more, gazing down at her sleeping child.

How often had her own mam done this, looked down into this very same cot at her sleeping baby? She asked herself silently. And with her mam it must have been a bitter-sweet experience knowing she couldn't have more children. Something had gone very wrong at her birth and the resulting operation had meant further bairns were out of the question. But her mam and da had loved each other; still did. Her da worshipped the ground her mam walked on although he'd never admit it.

Biting her lip against the tears which were always hovering at the back of her eyes these days, Rose bent and stroked the small silky forehead before turning and closing the curtain behind her.

Apart from their brass double bed and Jake's cot, the room held a narrow wardrobe with a rail one side and box-like shelves the other. Jake's nappies and the items of clothing her mother had bought for her grandson filled the top two shelves; the rest of the wardrobe contained a change of clothes for herself and Silas, along with their Sunday best.

Quietly Rose sorted out Silas's spare pair of trousers and shirt, and his Sunday coat and cap. He always left the house clean and tidy when he was going to the Times, and it wasn't just the gambling that drew him there, she thought bitterly. She wasn't daft. Several times she had smelt cheap cologne on his clothes when she had put them away the next morning, and no woman but the dockside dollies used that.

She took the clothes through to the kitchen and placed them on Silas's chair in front of the range to take the chill off them, then laid the vest and long johns he'd discarded on top. His work shirt and trousers she carried into the backyard where she banged them against the wall for a minute or two, filling the icy air with a cloud of black dust. She left them folded in the scullery and she opened the kitchen door, hoping Silas would have finished his bath by now.

'Come and wash my back.' He looked up as she entered the room, his handsome face sullen. 'You could have seen to me work clothes later.'

Yes, she could. Keeping all expression from her face, Rose took the piece of flannel he held out with the soap and walked behind him. Holding her revulsion in check, she attempted to work up a lather on the flannel – no mean feat with the soap the slaughterhouse sold as a sideline – and then bent and scrubbed at the narrow back. His skin was pitted in places with the blue-black indent-ations the coal left on human flesh, his knobbly knees callused and stained from working in some of the coal seams where the roof was too low to even crawl and men had to move snakelike on their stomachs.

The sight invoked no pity in Rose. Would a bird pity the hawk that had the ability and will to tear it limb from limb? It merely increased the feeling of uncleanness any contact with him, however slight, brought to her body.

Once she had finished washing his back she

rinsed away the suds with bath water already coated with a film of black grime and then turned away, drying her hands on her apron. When Silas had left the house she would bucket the bath water away, scrub out the tub and return it to its place in the scullery, propped against the wall.

By the time Silas was ready to leave the house, Rose was sitting at the kitchen table darning a pair of socks. She heard the jingle of coins in his pocket and wondered how much he was going to lose that night. Dully, and without looking up, she said, 'We're six weeks behind with the rent.'

'So?'

'I was just saying. Fairley said he wants it this week and something off the back an' all. He was threatening the bums last week.'

'Fairley can threaten all he likes.'

'He ... he means it, Silas. Since he took over from Vickers he's had more than one family put out on the streets. And,' she paused, breathing hard, 'and he said to tell you he's checked with the colliery and knows you've been in work the past months.'

Silas made a sudden movement and Rose flinched, her voice a gabble when she said, 'I'm only telling you what he said to say, that's all.'

'Aye.' It was a low growl. 'Well, you've told me now.' He stood without moving, watching her, and Rose began to tremble in spite of herself, her fingers tightening on the sock until her knuckles shone white. When she couldn't stand it a second more she raised her eyes to his. Without seeming to move a muscle of his face, he said, 'I'll deal with you when I get back.'

'I didn't mean anything, Silas, honest,' she whispered pitifully.

He stared at her for another endless moment, then a slow smile spread across his face. His voice soft and thick now, he said, 'When I get back, Rose,' nodding his head to emphasise the quietly spoken threat.

Then he turned on his heel and walked out of the kitchen, leaving her sick with dread.

Chapter 2

The next morning when Silas had gone to work and Jake was still fast asleep, huddled under his blankets in the icy bedroom like a baby animal in its burrow, Rose stood at the kitchen window staring out into the backyard they shared with four other houses. She watched one or two women come with their buckets to the tap. The first one went away again and returned with a piece of burning paper which she pushed up the spout to melt the ice so she could get a trickle of water going. Mrs Ducksworth from two doors up disappeared into the privy with her bucket of ashes and scrubbing brush, it being her turn to clean it, and emerged far too quickly to have done a proper job. Mind, the scavengers were due the day and the week's accumulation of waste must be nearly up to the long wooden seat by now and stinking to high heaven.

These thoughts and many others moved around

the perimeter of Rose's mind but without really touching the core of it, the part that was numb with the agonies her body and spirit had suffered the night before. Once she had been sure Silas was finally asleep, she had crept into the kitchen and washed away the blood and stickiness with lukewarm water left in the kettle. Then she had gone into the scullery where the bucket full of ice-cold water was waiting for morning and had perched on that in an effort to numb the pain. All night long, as she had lain rigid and still at the side of him, she'd told herself she couldn't go on. She would go to her mam's, tell them everything. Her mam could look after Jake during the day and she could get a job so the pair of them weren't a burden on her parents. Her old room was still vacant; many times her mam had talked of taking a lodger but her da hadn't liked the idea.

How long she stood there before she heard Jake begin to stir she didn't know. It could have been minutes or hours, such was the state of her mind. But when she walked into the bedroom and drew back the curtain from around the cot, her son was standing with his arms already lifted to her and it broke the trance-like stupor. She gathered him into her arms and held him so tightly he began to wriggle in protest.

'Oh, Jake, Jake...' Swaying back and forth and with tears streaming down her face, she nuzzled her chin into the dark-brown curls. She couldn't leave Silas, and not just because she was terrified of what her da would do if he discovered what had been going on. Silas would come after her, he wouldn't have her making him a laughing stock, which is how he would look at her going. And knowing him as she did, he would claim the child just to spite her if she didn't go back to him. That, or worse. She wouldn't put anything past him. And whereas it didn't matter what he did to her, if he hurt Jake...

Taking the child through to the warmth of the kitchen, she placed him in his high chair with his pap bottle of milk while she divided the last of the porridge she'd made earlier for Silas into two bowls.

People had no idea what Silas was like. His mam and da and brothers had a reputation for being rough and ready and well known to the law, but she could have coped with that if he had been kind to her. And she didn't mind his family, not really, even if they did swear and fight and carry on something awful. They weren't like him. He was ... inhuman, fiendish. Beneath that handsome face and the charm he could turn on and off like a tap, something was terribly wrong, but she knew no one would believe her if she said. No one except her mam and da, that was. Oh, what was she going to *do?*

It began to snow heavily mid-morning, the sky so low and heavy it seemed to rest on the roof-tops. The daughter of one of the women Rose washed for had delivered two big bags of soiled laundry just after breakfast. When she had got the boiler going in the wash house in the yard it took some violent scrubbing and pummelling and plenty of work with the poss stick to get the stains out. Eventually the washing was hung from wall to wall in the kitchen and she sat down at the table for a cup of tea, her back breaking and her hands aching so much she found it difficult to hold the cup.

The weather worsened during the afternoon, a thin wind moaning against the window as it rattled the glass and drove the snow further and further up the pane until it was impossible to see out. Jake had developed a cough during the day, whether the result of the damp atmosphere due to the steaming washing she wasn't sure, but her worry about him took her mind off her own physical condition. By the time Silas returned home, Jake was already in bed, having missed his afternoon nap due to his cough, and for this Rose was thankful. Silas had no patience with illness of any kind. She had already planned to bring the child into the kitchen if he woke during the night, lest his coughing should disturb and anger his father.

She was dreading Silas's homecoming, but in the event it was something of an anti-climax. He demanded his bath immediately he walked in the door and left the house again within the hour in spite of the foul weather, having gobbled down his dinner in record time. She knew the signs. He had a special game on, something he wasn't about to miss come hell or high water. He rarely won and if he did she never saw any of his winnings, although once or twice in the very early days of their marriage he had flung her enough money to clear any back rent.

Since Silas was out, she was able to get on with the ironing and fold the laundry away ready to deliver first thing the next morning. She'd just walked into the kitchen after putting the flat iron on the scullery shelf to cool when she heard Jake start coughing and soon he was crying for her. She carried the baby through into the warmth of the kitchen, sitting him on her lap and soothing him by singing gently when he refused a drink. He quietened after a while although his cough was still bothering him and when she placed her hand on his little back she could feel the phlegm gurgling. She would buy a pot of goose grease to rub on in the morning, she promised herself, and perhaps a camphor block too. It would mean less money for Fairley when he called but she couldn't help that. Hopefully she would still have sufficient to pay this week's rent along with something off the back, maybe even a couple of weeks' worth.

On impulse she stood up with Jake in her arms and walked over to her hidey-hole, mentally calculating the price of the goose grease and camphor as she removed the brick and felt inside for the pile of coins. And she was standing like that, Jake in the crook of one arm and her other hand fumbling for the money when the kitchen door swung open and Silas walked in.

Rose froze, petrified with fear. Perhaps if she had been able to think she might have salvaged something from the impending disaster. As it was, her terror at Silas's sudden appearance robbed her of the ability to move or reason.

Silas stared at her, his eyes narrowing to black slits. She watched as comprehension dawned and with it a cold fury that twisted the handsome features into something ugly.

'What have we here?' He moved towards her, shoving her roughly aside so she stumbled and almost fell. He thrust his hand into the cavity and the coins chinked as he withdrew them.

Rose's legs were threatening to give way. She stumbled over to the table and sat down on the bench, holding Jake against her breast. 'It's for – for the rent,' she stammered. 'He said he'd turn – turn us out onto the st-streets.'

'You've been keeping this from me.' There was a touch of incredulity in his tone. 'Salting money away.' He swore, not loudly but softly and obscenely and as he approached her she shrank back, crouching over the child in her arms. Flinging the money onto the table, he ground out, 'Where's the rest?'

'What?'

'Don't tell me this is all of it. You're crafty enough not to have put all your eggs in one basket.'

'No, no. There's no more. My mam knew I was worried about the rent and she–'

He hit her so hard across the face she slammed against the wall and fell back onto the floor, cracking her head on the flagstones, her feet up on the bench. She had been able to make no move to save herself because of Jake in her arms.

As the child began to scream in fright, she scrabbled her feet free and huddled against the wall, bringing her knees up to try and protect Jake. Silas heaved the table and bench away, sending the coins spinning to the floor, and then stood in front of her.

'Get up.' Again he didn't raise his voice but the softness was more menacing than any shouting. 'Get up or so help me I'll kick you senseless.'

Her ears still ringing, she struggled to her feet and stood swaying slightly as Jake clutched at her in a paroxysm of crying.

'Thought you'd make a monkey of me, is that it?' He was pulling his belt free of the loops of his trousers as he spoke, his eyes never leaving her white, terrified face. 'You an' your mam and da. Never thought I was good enough for their precious little lamb, did they, eh? Their pure little lamb. But you weren't so pure by the time I'd finished with you and that's stuck in your da's craw enough to choke him ever since. Scum like me having his daughter. Well, let me tell you, there's scum and scum in my book, and your da's the worst of the lot. Thinking he's above the rest of us. An' your mam sniffing about and reporting back, I know, I know. An' I tell you, if she sets foot through this door again I'll do for her and you an' all, you hear me?'

As the buckled end of the belt came down, Rose instinctively twisted to protect the child in her arms, taking the force of the blow across her shoulders. He was going to hurt Jake. He was going to hurt Jake. It was the only thing on her mind through the searing pain. She almost threw her son onto the floor away from her and then sprang towards the range, grabbing at the massive black frying pan. Silas followed her, the belt whistling through the air. The buckle ripped across the back of her neck this time but then she swung round with the frying pan in her hand, catching him a resounding blow across his arm as he raised it to shield his face. He staggered backwards with a shriek of pain, the belt falling from his fingers as he landed against the sideboard.

For the rest of her life Rose was to remember every moment of what followed. Silas's screaming curses, his groping hand searching for something to throw at her and finding the base of the oil lamp standing on the sideboard. Jake beginning to toddle towards her, still wailing. Her spring towards her son, then the oil lamp missing her by a whisker only to smash down on the flagstones at her feet where the shock of it caused Jake to plump down on his bottom as he lost his balance. As the thick glass reservoir shattered and sprayed its contents over Jake, there was one infinitesimal moment when she took comfort from the fact the lamp hadn't hit him. But then the lighted wick did its devastating job of igniting the spilt oil, turning her baby into a human torch.

Her screams mingled with those of the writhing child, but she retained enough presence of mind to leap into the scullery and grab the bucket of ice-cold water she had placed there for the morning. She tipped the whole lot over him, dousing the flames, and gathered him up against her breast, pulling her skirt up and round him so as to cocoon him.

He was gurgling horribly in his throat, the smell of burnt flesh and hair in her nostrils as she held his convulsing body, screaming for someone to help her. She was aware that Silas had gone, presumably by the front way, and now she stumbled into the scullery, shouting for Mrs Murray who lived next door. She came face to face with that good lady as she opened the door into the backyard.

'Landsakes, hinny, what's wrong?'

As Rose fell into Mrs Murray's arms, she was aware of her neighbour yelling for her husband at the top of her voice and then more people surrounding them. Rose fought the enveloping faintness with all her might, struggling to stay conscious for the sake of her child, but then the rushing darkness took over and she knew no more.

Chapter 3

Silas's rage was still uppermost as he left the house, pulling on his cap and tucking his muffler into the neck of his jacket. He walked along the dark snowy street rubbing his bruised arm and calling Rose every name under the sun. She'd taken him for a mug, that's what she'd done, and he'd have sworn on oath before this day she wouldn't dare defy him, let alone salt money away. It would have made all the difference to that last game; he could have won the lot, damn her. As it was, he was even further in over his head with the McKenzies, and they'd made it clear before he left this evening they weren't going to wait much longer for their money.

He ground his teeth, wishing his hands were round Rose's neck. And now this with the kid on top of everything else. Would she keep her mouth shut and say it was an accident? He doubted it, she was besotted with the brat, besides which she'd see it as the perfect opportunity to set man and beast against him.

Damn it, how had he let himself get saddled with her and the bairn? It wasn't as if she had ever held any attraction for him. She was too thin and scrawny and quiet. He liked his women big and busty with a bit of fight in them. He had only taken her down in the first place to get one over on Donald Hedley, the bumptious upstart. What was her da but a miner like himself and yet he dared to look down his nose at him and his da and brothers. Aye, it'd been sweet knowing he had Hedley's daughter eating out of the palm of his hand but he hadn't expected the rest of it. She had gone and got herself pregnant and when she'd come blubbing to him and he'd told her to sling her hook, she'd let on to her father and all hell had broken loose.

Without conscious thought, Silas made his way to North Bridge Street, turning off into the grid of streets which led to the river. He had to *think*. He had to work out what he was going to do and say. His da would skin him alive if he thought he'd hurt the kid. Mind, it was his da who'd got him into this mess. When old man Hedley had come shouting the odds, it had been his da who had insisted he marry Rose, threatening he'd break his legs if he didn't get wed sharpish. For all his drinking and fighting, his da could be a soft touch and his mam was fair barmy about Jake. He didn't understand that because the only endearment he and his brothers had ever got from his mam was a cuff round the ear or worse.

As he walked, the enormity of his predicament fully dawned but it was more the threat of the

McKenzies that had him gnawing on his bottom lip than anything else. He knew how the Mc-Kenzies handled bad payers. They started with a knee-capping and progressed from there, and more than one body found floating in the docks had the McKenzie stamp on it.

It had started to snow quite heavily by the time he reached Williamson Street at the back of the ship-repairing works. Silas knew this area well, he was in the habit of visiting a certain bawdy house here. For a moment he was tempted to see if Vera was available. She was game for anything, was Vera, if he paid her enough, but therein lay the problem. He was skint.

Cursing under his breath, he stood for a moment, hands thrust in his pockets as he watched a few seamen leave the White Swan pub. He wished he'd chosen a seafaring life instead of following his da and brothers down the pit. Them sailors had a woman in every port, whereas he was lumbered with a wife and bairn. And a frigid stick of a wife into the bargain.

Hell, I need a drink, he thought. He sorted through the few pennies in his pocket, his brow furrowed. He should have stopped long enough to pick up her little hoard, it was his by rights anyway. He had enough for a couple of pints but that was all and he needed a drop of the hard stuff. Cursing again, he walked on round the wharf, passing the warehouse where he'd bet on the outcome of a cock fight the previous week, and turned into an alleyway which divided the warehouse and a shipbuilding yard on his right.

He had taken no more than a step or two when

through the driving snow he became aware there was a fight in progress in front of him. He flattened himself against the slimy wall of the alleyway, aiming to make himself invisible. He had enough on his plate without getting mixed up in anything more and from the look of it the man on the ground was getting a good kicking from his two assailants. The grunts and pants which had alerted him to trouble were all coming from the two men on their feet; the other one was making no sound as they laid into him with a viciousness that excited Silas. Violence of any kind always had this effect.

After a minute or two the men rifled the pockets of the third man, speaking to each other in a language Silas didn't recognise. It could be Dutch or perhaps Swedish, some Nordic tongue.

Whether something alerted them to his presence he wasn't sure, but one of the men looked his way and said a few words in a different tone before the two of them took off, immediately lost to sight in the whirling snow. Silas let out his breath in a sigh of relief. He hadn't known how things would go there for a moment. Waiting to make sure they had really gone before he moved, he carefully made his way to the inert body on the ground, intending to see if they had left anything which might be worth taking.

He stood for a moment staring down at the man who was lying on his stomach. He jabbed at the body with his boot but there was no sign of life. He realised why when he turned the body over. The lolling head was a pulped mess with half his skull gone and his brains showing. They'd done for him all right. Silas knelt in the crimson snow and began a thorough search of the body. The trouser pockets were empty but he'd expected that, and he thought he'd seen one of the men unhook a pocket watch, certainly something which had shone momentarily anyway, before they had made themselves scarce.

The man's clothes were of good quality, a cut above the norm, Silas thought. He could have been a well-to-do merchant or perhaps the captain of a ship. Certainly his attackers could have been foreign sailors, the way they'd spoken. Maybe the dead man was their captain and they'd got a grudge against him. Whatever, they'd done a thorough job on him; even his own mother wouldn't recognise him.

A moment later Silas's hand froze. He'd worked his way under the man's jacket, shirt and vest and his fingers had found what felt like a money belt. His heart beating fit to burst and keeping a constant lookout for anyone approaching, he pulled off the jacket and undid the shirt buttons to see what was what. A few seconds later he sat back on his heels, the cloth pouch in his hands. Shaking with excitement, he opened the bag and then let out a soundless whistle. He drew out a thick wad of notes. There must be all of thirty pounds, maybe more. A small fortune. Enough to pay the McKenzies what he owed and then some. But wait, how was he going to explain coming by it? And what if someone knew the dead man was carrying a muckload of cash? If his death got in the paper, that someone could well put two and two together and make ten. And ten could hang him.

His fingers tightened greedily on the small pouch. He wanted this money; he'd had nothing to do with the man's death and what was the point in looking a gift horse in the mouth?

He continued to sit for a few moments more, his mind racing. An idea came to him, an idea so beautiful, so perfect, he marvelled it hadn't occurred to him immediately. He began to strip the clothes from the figure on the ground until the man was as naked as the day he was born. Then Silas hastily divested himself of his own clothing, shivering as he pulled on the dead man's underwear and then his other garments. The shirt was badly stained with blood as was the collar of the jacket, but if he knotted his muffler round his neck it'd do for now until he could get somewhere quiet and rub the stains out in the snow until they were faint enough. He'd take his cap too, it didn't look as though the man had been wearing a hat of any kind, something which again suggested he might be a foreigner.

Dressing the body in his own clothes was much more difficult than he'd thought, but eventually it was done. When he tried to fit his boots on the dead man's feet, though, he ran into a problem. His boots were a good couple of sizes too small. He hadn't noticed that when he'd pulled on the other boots – they were calf length, of a fine good leather and infinitely superior to his hobnailed ones. They'd slipped onto his feet like a lass's caress.

He frowned. The body would have to be boot-less. It wouldn't matter. The law would assume someone had made off with them.

46

When he'd finished, he was panting slightly. He now had to drag the body to the landing near the wharf and shove it under the platform as far as it would go. With any luck it would bob about there for days before it was discovered, and with every hour it was in the water it would deteriorate, which was all to the good.

The last thing he did was the most important for his plan to succeed. From a lad he'd had a lucky rabbit's foot on a small chain which he always carried with him, making sure it was in his pocket for everything from the odd tinpot game with his father and brothers to the real gambling schools like those with the McKenzies. He'd had his name carved in the pewter base surrounding the foot by one of the travelling engravers at the annual Michaelmas fair years ago, earning himself a good ribbing from his family in the process.

'You make your own luck in this world, lad,' his father had scoffed, 'and it's nowt to do with a dead rabbit.'

But his father had been wrong. This piece of luck was everything to do with a dead rabbit. Smiling to himself, Silas knelt beside the dead man and made sure the rabbit's foot was still in the pocket of his coat and that the clip was holding to the material inside. The rabbit's foot was going to confirm he was dead while at the same time buy him a new life. A life that would start with plenty of money in his pocket, good clothes on his back and a fine pair of boots on his feet. No matter they were too big, they were of the finest quality and that's what he intended to have from now on. No wife, no squawking brat hanging on his coat-tails. He was a free man again. It felt heady, euphoric.

Once the body was in the water under the landing, Silas returned to the alleyway, thanking his lucky stars the night was such a raw one with the snow reaching blizzard proportions. This area right on the waterfront was always quiet once the engine works and rope works and other extensive industry lining its banks closed for the night, but some of the streets nearby had one pub to every half a dozen houses and the dockside dollies who frequented such establishments often brought their customers to just such a secluded spot.

The big fat snowflakes were starting to hide what had occurred in the alley although here and there red stains were still visible. But it wouldn't be long before all evidence was under a layer of snow and it was unlikely anyone would come this way now. Silas picked up his hobnailed boots and tucked them under the thick warm jacket which was like nothing he had owned before. Glancing around one last time, he pulled his cap low over his eyes and made off, keeping his head down.

He walked swiftly, his only desire to put as much distance between him and Monkwear-mouth as he could. He had already made up his mind to go down south, Sheffield maybe or even further afield. If the weather had been better he would have walked all night, he felt so good.

Mind, if the weather had been better, he reminded himself in the next instant, likely there would have been more folk about and he wouldn't have found himself in this position. The dead man might still be walking about with his money belt in place. No, he certainly wasn't knocking the weather, far from it. It had served him well the night.

He reached North Bridge Street without meeting a soul apart from one or two scurrying figures in the distance. The bridge into Bishopwearmouth was equally deserted, the weather and the late hour having driven most Wearsiders indoors.

Walking wasn't easy in the blizzard but the unaccustomed luxury of the expensive, richly lined jacket and thick trousers meant he was as warm as toast. He cut through the town and veered east towards Hendon where he slung his hobnailed boots into the back of the cricket ground. Someone would find them in due course and it would be finders keepers and no questions asked.

His fingers caressed the money pouch which now resided in the pocket of his jacket as he walked, and every so often he grinned to himself. He'd walk as far as Ryhope and then find a barn or something to hole up in for the night. Come morning he'd try and hitch a lift on a farmer's cart to the next village and work his way down the country like that. If it was too slow-going with the weather and all, he might even take the train. He had never ridden on a train before but he was a man of means now, he had money in his pocket, and he intended to see it remained that way.

He stood for a moment, raising his face to the starry snowflakes tumbling to the ground in their thousands, and it was like that, with his head thrown back to the heavens, that he laughed out loud. It was a joyous sound, without restraint, ringing in the dark night like the sound of bells on a Sunday morning.

And then he began walking again.

PART TWO

1925 – Entanglements

Chapter 4

'Don't be so gormless, girl. You've got eyes in your head, I shouldn't have to tell you everything that wants doing. You know your aunt's been bad this week and I've been run off my feet. I was banking on you coming straight home after church and helping me. Where have you been anyway? As if I didn't know.'

Hannah stared at her mother. It was on the tip of her tongue to say, 'Why ask then, if you know?' but she knew she would be playing into her mother's hands. Her mam was itching for a row. She'd been the same for the last week, since Christmas Day in fact. Hannah felt her bad mood might have something to do with the bracelet her aunt and uncle had given her for Christmas. Her fingers instinctively felt for the silver charm bracelet on her wrist as she took off her coat and she moved it under the sleeve of her dress. She'd seen the way her mam's face had changed when her uncle had put the little box in her hands. But her aunt and uncle had given her mam a lovely big box of chocolates with a picture of a thatched cottage on the ribboned lid, along with a pair of fine gloves, so she didn't understand why her mam was vexed. Or perhaps it wasn't that. There was no telling with her mam.

'Well, miss, answer me.' Miriam Casey's thin face with its sharp-pointed nose displayed her

53

irritation in deep lines either side of her mouth, making her appear far older than her thirty-six years. 'And none of your cheek, mind. Not unless you want to feel the back of my hand. You're getting too big for your boots lately.'

'I called in at Naomi's for a few minutes,' Hannah said flatly. 'She wanted to show me the kittens.'

'*Kittens?*' It was disparaging. 'There's nine of them crammed in that place as it is and then the cat has kittens. I'd have thought Rose would have drowned them at birth.'

'Naomi's mam wouldn't do that,' Hannah said indignantly. 'She's already found homes for all the kittens but one.'

'Has she indeed?' Miriam's pale blue eyes narrowed. 'Well, don't run away with the idea you're having it, girl. I've told you before, there'll be no cats in this house. Filthy creatures cats are, full of fleas and disease.'

'Naomi's cat hasn't got fleas.'

'No, well, it wouldn't have, would it? Not with everything being so perfect within those four walls, according to you.' Miriam glared at her daughter. Flapping her hand an inch from Hannah's face, she said, 'I've been waiting an hour for a scuttle of coal. Make yourself useful now you're back. And you can see to the taties after. I've been in and out to your aunt all morning while you've been gallivanting. I'm fair worn out.'

Fair worn out, that was a joke. Hannah turned on her heel and walked through to the bedroom she shared with her mother in the flat above the shop in Wayman Street, close to the Wearmouth colliery. She didn't want to risk dirtying her Sunday clothes when she fetched the coal. She didn't immediately begin to change however, but walked across to the sash window, peering out at the patch of grey sky above the rooftops opposite.

The small protesting voice deep inside which had got louder and louder of late brought her soft full mouth into a tight line. Her mam worn out! That would be the day. Her mam enjoyed the life of old Riley and they both knew it. Half the time she sat about like Lady Muck, drinking tea and reading magazines or one of the novels she borrowed from the town library.

Turning abruptly, she took off her Sunday dress and pulled on her weekday skirt and blouse, her mind churning. All her mother had to do all day was to see to poor Aunt Aggie who tried to be as little trouble as possible, and cook and clean these four rooms above the shop. Whereas she worked from seven in the morning until eight at night in the shop – half past ten on a Saturday – and even then her mam expected her to see to the ironing and help with the household chores. Every Sunday morning there was a list as long as her arm of the jobs her mam had lined up for her for the day.

On leaving the bedroom, Hannah collected the coal scuttle from the sitting-room hearth. Her mother was sitting in an armchair reading *Good Housekeeping*, one of the newer magazines her uncle stocked in the shop below, which Miriam brought upstairs to read before putting it back on the shelf to be sold. Even in her present state of burning resentment, Hannah had to smile to herself. Her mother wasn't a natural homemaker, she loathed housekeeping of any kind and cooking still more.

Hannah went downstairs to the backyard. This area was full with packing cases holding this and that, the privy and boiler house, and the brick-built coal-hole. Besides the four rooms in the flat above the shop premises – a sitting room, two bedrooms and kitchen – there were two rooms behind the shop. One was a large and useful scullery-cum-kitchen which had an inside tap, and the other was a storeroom holding all kinds of produce from tubs of butter and sacks of flour to large sides of bacon and cured ham. Her mother had told her that once her uncle's shop and flat had been two separate houses which had been knocked into one. When Hannah had been a child her mother used to help out in the shop for a few hours most days, and her uncle had employed a full-time assistant too. The assistant had been given notice a couple of weeks before Hannah had left school at fourteen, nearly two years ago now, and her mother had gradually stopped working in the shop over the last twelve months.

Hannah began to fill the scuttle using the long-handled shovel which stood at the side of the coal-hole. She frowned to herself as she worked. In spite of the saving her uncle had made in paying out wages, she received no regular income. He merely slipped her a shilling or two when he felt like it. Her mam had explained the arrangement by saying she ought to be thankful she had a way of repaying the kindness she'd received by way of free board and lodging since they'd come to live here when she was a babe in arms. Her father had died from a disease of the stomach shortly after she had been born, and but for his elder brother taking them in, her mother assured her they would have been destitute and consigned to the workhouse.

And she *was* grateful to Aunt Aggie and Uncle Edward, Hannah thought now, shivering in the icy wind. She really was. But she wished she didn't have to work in the shop nonetheless. It wasn't that she didn't get paid even, but more... She screwed up her face for a moment as she tried to find words to describe the feeling which assailed her of late when she was alone with her uncle.

It was starting to snow again. As a starry snow-flake landed on her eyelashes, Hannah shook her head at her muddled thoughts, grabbed the coal scuttle – which was now heavy – and carried it into the house. Her aunt and uncle were good, they were. They often said they looked on her as the daughter they'd never had. Maybe her mam was right, perhaps she was an ungrateful little madam who didn't know which side her bread was buttered.

She shut the back door behind her and walked across the shop kitchen, keeping her gaze away from the far corner of the room where two dead pheasants were hanging on a hook by a piece of string secured round their feet. Billy Hogarth had been out with his traps again by the look of it. He always dropped off a couple of birds or a rabbit or two for her uncle on his way home and because this room was used for any mucky jobs and as an overflow from the storeroom, Hannah was never sure what she would find. It was daft, she knew that, but she hated seeing the beautiful pheasants hanging limp and lifeless when earlier that morning they had been gloriously alive. She didn't like seeing anything dead but it seemed worse somehow, them being wild birds. She could never bring herself to eat pheasant, a strong bone of contention with her mother. At those times Miriam always took pleasure in pointing out how good she had it compared to Naomi.

As she carried the scuttle up the stairs which led to the flat, Hannah's thoughts turned to her friend. With just a few days between them in age they had been best friends since they could toddle, and she loved Naomi's mam. Mrs Wood always made her welcome in their house, slipping her a shive of stottie cake or a teacake whether Mr Wood and Naomi's two older brothers were on short time or not. Not that she stayed long if Mr Wood was in. He was a dour man and she found his presence intimidating. But with four younger brothers still at school, things were constantly tight in her friend's house, so maybe Mr Wood had something to moan about. Naomi had told her she gave all of the wage she earned at the jam factory to her mam each week, and whereas her mam had once given her half of it back, she now got only her tram fare and a few pennies for herself.

Hannah opened the front door of the flat and walked into the sitting room, placing the scuttle on the hearth. Her mother didn't look up from her magazine. Hannah had reached the door again before Miriam said, 'Your aunt could do

58

with a cup of tea. Put the kettle on before you start on the taties.'

There was no doubt in Hannah's mind who it was who wanted the tea but she said nothing, continuing through to the kitchen. There she found the kettle and bucket empty, not an unusual occurrence. Gritting her teeth, Hannah retraced her steps down the stairs and filled both the kettle and bucket before lugging them back up the stairs. Once the kettle was on the hob she started peeling the potatoes, her thoughts again returning to Naomi's family. She didn't know how they'd manage without Naomi's eldest brother, Jake, bringing Mrs Wood a load of stuff each week from the farm where he lived and worked.

She paused, her hands becoming still for a moment. Well, he was Naomi's half-brother really, which was strange, because she thought Jake Fletcher was just like Mr Wood. Much more like him than his own children were. Not in looks, but then with Jake having had that awful accident when he was a bairn and being so scarred, he wouldn't be, would he? But Jake was every bit as dour and taciturn as Mr Wood and she didn't know which of the two scared her more. Whereas Adam... Her eyes became dreamy. There wasn't a lass for miles around who didn't long to walk out with Adam Wood.

The boiling kettle brought her back to reality. She quickly made the tea and left it to mash while she finished the potatoes, adding them to the juices of the joint sizzling in the range oven.

After taking her mother a cup of tea she placed her own and her aunt's on a tray with a plate of ginger nuts. She crossed the hall and knocked on her aunt's door before opening it and smiling at the woman sitting propped against a mountain of pillows in the double bed facing the window. 'I've brought you a cup of tea, Aunty. You feeling any better?'

'I'm all right, lass.' It was her aunt's stock answer unless she was very ill indeed. 'How was church?'

The bedroom was larger than the one Hannah shared with her mother and well furnished. There was a wardrobe and chest of drawers, several woollen rugs on the polished floor and two chintz armchairs either side of the window. Hannah ignored these, perching herself on the end of the bed and handing her aunt a cup of tea and the biscuits, before she said, 'Church was the same as usual. Father Gilbert sends his regards and says he'll look in tomorrow afternoon, all being well. And Mrs Mullen and Mrs Chapman are coming on Tuesday afternoon.'

Agatha Casey did not comment on this. What she did say was, and in an undertone, 'Did you get to see the kittens?'

Hannah nodded. 'It's all right, Mam knows. She went on and on when I got in so I had to tell her where I'd been. I was only fifteen minutes or so in Naomi's but I think Mam puts a stopwatch on me when I leave the house. She doesn't seem to realise other girls go out in the evening sometimes or on a Sunday afternoon.' And then, as if her words might be taken for a criticism of her aunt and uncle, she added hastily, 'Not that I mind most of the time.'

Agatha nodded, her voice soft when she said, 'Don't worry, lass. I know how four walls can press in on you.'

Immediately Hannah was filled with contrition. Reaching forward in the warm impetuous way she had, she said, 'Oh, I'm sorry, Aunt Aggie,' squeezing her aunt's arm as she spoke. 'Here am I rabbiting on when you have to lie in this bed all day every day and never a word of complaint.'

'Go on with you, lass. I'm no saint, nor do I pretend to be. Besides, you're young, it's the most natural thing in the world to want to spread your wings a bit. It doesn't mean you're not thankful for what you've got.'

Hannah smiled at her aunt. Aunt Aggie always understood. For as long as she could remember she'd harboured the secret wish that it could have been her aunt who had borne her rather than her own mam although she would never voice it.

Agatha smiled back into the young face. If she had but known it her thoughts were on a par with her niece's. If one of her many pregnancies had gone full term and she had been able to bear a child of her own, she would have liked it to be exactly like the young girl in front of her. It wasn't so much that her niece showed promise of great beauty with her warm creamy skin, heavily lashed dark-brown eyes and dark chestnut hair with its hint of red, it was Hannah herself who was captivating. Her warmth, her kindness, her brightness.

Agatha took a sip of her tea. How Hannah had come from the body of her sister-in-law she'd never understand, because if ever two personalities were at opposite ends of the spectrum,

61

Hannah's and her mother's were. Did Miriam really think she was unaware of what was going on between her and Edward? More likely she didn't care, truth be known. How she would love to confront them both but where would that leave her? Part of her felt Edward had been manipulated into the affair, that it wasn't of his choosing, but that could be wishful thinking on her part. She just didn't know any more. Her husband was most solicitous on her behalf, one could say almost overwhelmingly so, and since she had been confined to her bed the last eight years he had never once shown any irritation or annoyance that *that* side of their marriage was over. But then he wouldn't, would he, if he was getting what he wanted elsewhere? And Edward had been a very physical man in the early days of their marriage, exhaustingly so.

'...suits her to say that.'

'I'm sorry, hinny?' Agatha realised her niece had been talking and she hadn't heard a word. 'What did you say?'

'I said Mam was going on again about me not having one of Naomi's kittens, not that I'd asked for one anyway. She said it's because of the shop downstairs but I don't think it's anything to do with that. She just doesn't like animals, any animals. She says they're all dirty and full of fleas and take too much looking after.'

Aye, she would. Miriam spent most of her days with her legs up on the sofa reading magazines she'd borrowed from the shop and drinking endless cups of tea, only to spring into action once Edward made an appearance. She knew, oh yes, she knew. She might be confined to this bed most of the time but that didn't mean she was half sharp. Keeping her thoughts to herself, Agatha said, 'Your mother has never had anything to do with cats or dogs, that's the thing. What folk don't understand they're often nervous of.'

Her mam nervous about anything! Hannah could have laughed out loud. Instead she said quietly, 'Perhaps. But she needn't have said Mrs Wood should have drowned them when they were born. They're such bonny little things, Aunty. So helpless and small.'

'She said that?'

Hannah nodded. They stared at each other for a moment, Agatha shaking her head slowly, and then they continued to drink their tea without further conversation.

Hannah was just leaving her aunt's room with the tray a few minutes later when her uncle came in from his Sunday morning visit to the Oak Tree in North Bridge Street. He smiled as she passed him, his voice soft as he said, 'You been looking after your aunt, lass? There's a good girl.'

Before she could say anything, Miriam appeared in the doorway to the sitting room. 'There you are, Edward. Dinner will be a little while but I've poured you a glass of beer and put your slippers by the fire. Come and sit down.' Her gaze switched to her daughter. 'Turn the roast potatoes and check on the Yorkshire pudding while you're in the kitchen.'

Edward stared at his sister-in-law. For a moment he seemed to be about to say something but then he walked across the hall and joined her in the sitting room where he sat down before the fire and picked up the newspaper. He hadn't spoken and he did not do so now, settling back in his chair and beginning to read.

'Here.' Miriam knelt at his feet, his slippers in her hands. 'Let me take your boots off and you put these on.'

He submitted to her ministrations with merely a grunt, the newspaper held in front of his face, and after she had fitted the slippers on his feet, Miriam stood up and looked at him for a moment. When he continued to read, she bit her lip and then returned quietly to the seat she'd vacated when she heard him come in.

Edward Casey was a large man in breadth as well as height. He had a rough, pockmarked complexion, thick grizzled hair and a bulbous red nose, the result of a penchant for several glasses of port of an evening and beer throughout the day. It was his wide, thick-lipped mouth that dominated his features and revealed the sensual nature of Hannah's uncle.

The fact that his wife had been unable to give him a son or daughter did not worry Edward unduly. He had married Agatha because as the only child of a well-to-do shopkeeper, a shop-keeper who was reportedly in ill health, he'd thought he was on to a good thing. And so it had proved. His father-in-law had died within twelve months of their marriage and, Agatha's mother having died some years before, his wife inherited the shop and flat and a nest egg into the bargain.

He had been grateful to his wife for providing him with a living which had taken him out of the pit. It was a living he considered comfortable and easy, and one in which he could freely indulge his love of food and drink. Moreover he liked Agatha and she had always been obliging in the bedroom. Until the last miscarriage, that was, after which she'd become confined to bed most of the time.

When Miriam had made it plain she was eager to provide what Agatha could not, he had gone into the affair willingly, for by then he had been desperate for the release only a woman could give and it had been either Miriam or visiting a brothel. He had wished many times since he had chosen the latter. Miriam had become like a leech and her body had started to hold less and less attraction for him. And with its demise, another desire had grown...

Chapter 5

'Ask your mam, just ask her. She might say yes.'

'She won't.'

'You don't know for sure if you don't ask. And it's not like her an' your uncle an' aunt ever do much on New Year's Eve apart from having Mrs Mullen and Mrs Chapman over. Go on, ask, Hannah. I'd love you to come round. We always have such a laugh on New Year's Eve at home.'

Hannah stared at Naomi. She would like nothing more than to see the New Year in at her friend's house, but her mother would never agree to it. As she heard her uncle coming through from the storeroom where he had been weighing sugar out of a sack into blue paper bags, Hannah pushed Naomi towards the shop door. 'All right, I'll ask but don't expect me,' she said under her breath. 'You know what she's like.'

The shop bell tinkled Naomi's departure as her uncle appeared. 'Who was that?'

'Naomi. She called in on her way home from work.' She didn't say why. Her friend often stopped a few minutes for a chat in the evening.

Her uncle nodded, turning and placing the bags of sugar in the box he was carrying into their appropriate spot on the shelves behind the long wooden counter. With his back towards her, he said, 'She's quite a young woman now – you both are. Has she got a lad yet?'

Hannah swallowed. It was daft but she always felt funny when her uncle talked like this and he was doing it more and more often of late. Saying she was so grown up, that there must be lots of lads after her, things like that. Not that there was anything wrong with it, but... She couldn't explain the 'but' to herself. Swallowing again, she said flatly, 'Her mam said she can't walk out with a lad until her sixteenth birthday.'

'Very wise, very wise.' He turned from what he was doing, a bag of sugar in his hand. 'You don't want to go messing about with lads, Hannah,' he said softly. 'Take it from me, I know what I'm on about. Young lads won't treat you right.'

The creeping sensation in her flesh was making itself felt again, not so much because of what he said but the way he said it and the look on his

66

face. She stared dumbly, her heart beating so hard she felt it in her throat. 'I ... I don't. I mean I haven't got a lad. I don't want one.'

'They'll tell you one thing and do another. That's the way it is with youth. And you don't want that, do you? You don't want to find yourself in a pickle.'

'No.'

'I'm talking sense, lass.' He was red in the face and perspiring although it wasn't warm in the shop – it was bitingly cold outside with a high wind blowing that spoke of snow. 'And you're worth more than that, all right? So you mind what I say and keep yourself to yourself. Will you do that for me, lass?'

She nodded and then almost jumped out of her skin as the door behind her opened and her mother walked into the shop. She was carrying a bag containing her aunt's medicines which she had fetched from the chemist.

'What's the matter?' Miriam's eyes flashed from her daughter to Edward.

'The matter?' The thick trembly note had gone from her uncle's voice. Now he sounded faintly belligerent. 'Why should anything be the matter?'

'I don't know' Miriam didn't look at Hannah again but kept her gaze on her brother-in-law. 'So there's nothing wrong?'

'Not that I know of.'

Miriam slanted her eyes and inclined her head, a sharp movement. 'Good.'

'You got all Aggie's stuff?' Edward said heartily.

'Aye, it's all here.' Miriam's voice was expressionless.

'I'll be shutting bang on time, it being New Year's Eve, so if you want to dish up for half eight we'll be up then. And after dinner we'll all have a nice little drink together, eh? See the New Year in in style. Now this young lady is nearly sixteen I reckon it's high time we faced the fact she's all grown up and treated her accordingly.'

There was something in her mother's face that made Hannah want to reach out and take her arm and for a moment she forgot her own concerns. She didn't understand what was wrong but she hadn't seen her mother look this way before. But she resisted the impulse, suspecting her mother would slap her hand away. Instead she found herself saying by way of a diversion, 'Naomi has invited me round theirs tonight, Mam. Can I go?'

'What?'

As her mother brought her gaze away from her uncle and looked at her, Hannah said again, 'Naomi has invited me round theirs to see the New Year in. They always have a bit of a do. Can I go?'

Miriam straightened her back. She looked at her daughter's heart-shaped face, at the unlined, baby soft skin which carried the silky glow of youth. She was holding on to the shopping bag so tightly her knuckles were showing white and bleached through her flesh. As Edward began to say, 'I don't think that's a good idea, lass,' she cut in tightly, 'Yes, you can go.'

'I can go?' Hannah thought she had misheard.

'Aye.' Miriam nodded, looking at Edward again as she said, 'You'll likely want to be with people your own age.'

Hannah was so surprised it was a moment or two before she could say, 'Well, yes.'

'That's settled then.' Her mother's voice was clipped, cold. 'I'll have dinner ready for half eight and you can go once you've eaten. I'll sort out a plate of something for you to take round. You can't go empty handed.'

Hannah glanced at her uncle to see if he was as amazed as she was but he was staring at her mother. After a moment he turned back to the shelf behind him and her mother disappeared upstairs.

'She let you come!' It was Naomi who answered Hannah's knock at the Woods' back door later that evening, shrieking with delight when she saw her friend. Pulling Hannah into the scullery, she said, 'Me an' Mam are doing the sandwiches for tonight, the others are in the front room. You can help if you like. Oh Hannah, I told you to ask, didn't I? You see?'

They were both laughing as they entered the kitchen, but when Hannah saw that Naomi and her mother weren't alone and Jake Fletcher was sitting at his mother's kitchen table, she was taken aback.

Nervously now, she said to Naomi's mother, 'Mam sent this fruit cake round, Mrs Wood, and a tin of biscuits for tonight.'

'Did she, lass? That's right nice of her.' Rose smiled at her daughter's friend, thinking the while, how on earth did she manage to get out of that prison, poor lass. It had long been her private opinion that Miriam Casey was a nasty bit of work. 'Grab a knife, hinny, an' start buttering that stack of bread. Once everyone arrives these sandwiches'll melt away like the morning mist before the sun.'

'Thank you for letting me come, Mrs Wood.' Hannah was painfully aware of the big dark man watching her. She hadn't looked at him directly, she never knew quite what to do if he was at Naomi's. She didn't want him to think she was gawping at him. He must have people do that all the time, poor thing.

And then, as Jake said, 'Hello, Hannah,' she did glance at him, forcing a smile as she answered, 'Hello, Mr Fletcher.'

'So you're going to let your hair down the night?' He turned his gaze to his sister. 'Just you watch Naomi, that's all I'd say. I have it on good authority she was tiddly last year.'

'Oh you, our Jake.' Naomi feigned indignation. 'I wasn't, was I, Mam?' It was Adam and Joe who were three parts to the wind.' Catching Hannah's hand, she added, 'Oh, I forgot to tell you. Jake is going to have the last kitten at the farm 'cos no one will take her. I said he's got to call her Buttons because that's what you and I named her. He's taking Polly too' – Polly was the kitten's mother – ''cos Da told Mam to get rid of her now everyone's on short time.' She grimaced eloquently, letting Hannah know what she thought of her father's hard–heartedness.

'Oh, right.' Hannah smiled awkwardly, wishing she could be herself in front of Naomi's half-brother. She could normally converse with any-

70

one but Jake Fletcher was different, and it wasn't just his scars, bad as they were. It was only the left side of his face which was affected, the puckered lumpy skin emerging from under his hairline and running right down his face and into the collar of his shirt. The eyelid was half closed, giving his face a faintly malevolent expression, and the ear was badly distorted. In contrast, the good side of his face which was only marked with a couple of tiny scars was unusually handsome. Perversely this only increased the slightly sinister effect. But the main thing which always tied her tongue in his presence, certainly for the last little while, was that Jake Fletcher was such an altogether *masculine* man. Big, broad shouldered, powerful. Adam and Joe had their father's slight build and Naomi's four younger brothers were small for their ages. Jake was the odd one out in more ways than one. And he scared her.

Her thoughts brought hot colour into her cheeks and she busied herself with buttering the slices of bread stacked on the table, her head down. The atmosphere in the kitchen changed abruptly a minute or so later when the door to the hall opened and Adam Wood came in. Glancing over them, Adam's eyes narrowed on his half-brother. 'You still here then?'

'As you see.'

The two men stared at each other for a moment longer and then Adam turned and spoke directly to Hannah. 'The old witch let you out then? Never have there been such days.'

Hannah forced a smile but she felt uncom-fortable. Adam's boyish good looks hid a tongue that could be as sharp as a knife on occasion, and although she might share her resentment about her mother's treatment of her with Naomi, she didn't like Adam calling her mam a witch.

'You staying to see the New Year in then?' he asked when she said nothing, reaching for a slice of the bread she'd buttered and folding it in half before biting into it. At her nod, he grinned. 'That's a turn-up for the book. What've you promised the old witch to persuade her to let you come then?'

'*Adam.*' Rose's voice held a note of admonition.

'What?' Adam's blue eyes were laughing. 'We all know what Hannah's mam is like. I'm only saying what everyone else thinks.'

'Perhaps your mother is suggesting you're embarrassing a guest.' Jake had risen to his feet as he spoke. He reached for his overcoat and pulled it on.

'Huh.' The smile slid from Adam's face. Flinging the half-eaten slice of bread on the kitchen table, he said to Hannah, 'Have I embarrassed you?'

His eyes like black marble, Jake said, 'Shut up, Adam.'

'Shut up yourself.' Like David squaring up to Goliath, Adam glared at the older man. 'Just because you come here playing the big man and bountiful benefactor doesn't mean you own the place.'

'I never said I did but I dare say you're not above having your share of what I bring your mam, eh?'

'Hark at him. Dead easy you have it compared

72

to the rest of us, and you know it. You want a few shifts down the pit and you'd soon see what was what.'

'You didn't have to go down the pit any more than I did,' Jake said quietly. 'I looked for work elsewhere, you could have done the same, but you chose to follow your da. Don't gripe about it now.'

'Who are you to tell me anything, you freak?'

'*Adam!*' Rose had sprung in front of Jake as he made a sudden movement towards the younger man. Holding on to Jake but speaking to Adam, she said, 'You talk like that again and so help me you'll be looking for somewhere else to lay your head. And get out of my kitchen.'

Jake's face was bereft of colour, his jaw clenched and his eyes blazing, but he could not push his mother aside without being rough, so tightly was she clinging to him. 'I'll see my day with you, boy,' he ground out, the threat soft but deadly as he looked at his brother.

'You and whose army?'

The defiance in the words belied the expression on Adam's face. Hannah had seen him jump when Jake had made to get to him and she knew he was frightened. She didn't blame him. He was half the size of his brother. She lowered her eyes again, not wishing to add to his humiliation. Then ten-year-old Stephen came rushing into the kitchen, saying, 'Mam, Mam, the Father's just arrived,' and she experienced a feeling of deep relief as the tension broke.

As Adam left the kitchen with Stephen, Rose turned to Jake who was now pulling on his cap and muffler. 'I shall have to go and say hello to Father Gilbert.'

'Aye, you go, Mam. I told you I was only staying for an hour.'

'Thanks for all the stuff, lad.' Rose's voice was low, apologetic. 'And for dropping by. It wouldn't have been the same if I hadn't seen you although that's daft in a way. New Year's Eve is only a night like any other.'

'Aye, mebbe.'

'Lad, about Adam–'

'Leave it, Mam.' And then as though to make up for his brusqueness, Jake said quietly, 'It's all right, don't fret. I've had folk say worse and it's water off a duck's back. You go and enjoy yourself the night. If anyone deserves a bit of jollification, you do.'

'You sure you won't stay?' And as her son lifted his eyebrows, she bit her lip. 'I'm sorry, lad.'

The catch in his mother's voice brought a tenderness to Jake's face. 'I've told you, don't fret.' Turning to Naomi who, like Hannah, was keeping her gaze fixed on the sandwiches they were making, he added, 'You make sure your mam enjoys herself tonight. All right, lass?'

'Aye, all right, Jake.' Naomi's face had brightened. The fight had been averted. Jake wasn't going off in a strop which would have meant her mam would have been miserable the whole night long. All was well.

Jake walked across the room but before he stepped into the scullery and left by way of the backyard, he turned. 'Happy New Year.'

Hannah added her voice to those of Naomi and

Mrs Wood, but when after a moment or two Naomi said, 'I wish Jake could have stayed for once, Mam,' she remained silent. She was glad he had gone.

In the back lane Jake stood for a moment breathing deeply with his eyes shut. Then he drove his fist into the brick wall with a sickening thud, not so hard as to break bones but enough to relieve some of the murderous rage inside him. At least, that's what he told himself he was feeling – rage. Never for a moment would he allow himself to term it pain.

The cocky little snot. He flexed his bruised hand, wiping the blood from his knuckles with his handkerchief. Showing off in front of the Casey lass.

It was a fine night, the snow crisp with a coating of frost beneath his feet and the air as sharp as a blade. He looked up into the black sky. It was high and star filled, beautiful, and for once the stench of the privies was absent. Nevertheless, the sensation which always assailed him when he came into town to visit his mother, that of being hemmed in, enclosed, was as strong as ever.

He hated the town. The gridiron acres of Sunderland's narrow streets with their back-to-back terraced houses and heaving humanity, and the tight-packed industries bordering the river were stifling, choking the life out of their inhabitants. As a lad he'd sometimes walked along the river bank, past the factories and workshops, roperies, glassworks, potteries, limekilns, ironworks and shipyards, all the time wondering what he was going to do when he was grown up because even then he'd known he couldn't stomach the colliery.

His mother had always insisted his fear of being shut in had come from the months he'd been in hospital as a little bairn. He unconsciously touched the left side of his face. He didn't know about that. What he did know was that living in the warren that was Monkwearmouth was not for him. He didn't fit in, in more ways than one. He smiled grimly. And he hadn't wanted to fit in.

He began to pick his way down the narrow lane, careful of the ice underfoot which made walking treacherous. There were more lights than usual in the windows, it being New Year's Eve, and once he'd emerged into Southwick Road there were more folk about too. He'd already decided not to take a cab and continued down Southwick Road into Sunderland Road, but it wasn't until he'd walked a couple of miles and North Hylton Road stretched before him that he began to breathe more easily. This area was more open, with just the odd house and farm dotted here and there, and by the time he had reached the old quarries at the back of Hylton Red House, the lights of the town were far behind him.

It was only then he permitted himself to acknowledge the truth which had been gnawing at him since he had left his mother's house. That little lass in the kitchen had been scared to death of him. He'd noticed before she was nervous and on the quiet side but he hadn't been sure if it was him or whether she was the same with everyone.

76

But tonight when she had looked at him he had known. He disgusted her. Why it should bother him when he had been used to a similar reaction from people most of his life he didn't know. But it did. Damn it, it did.

He stood for a moment staring over the white fields in front of him before turning off the main road and into the narrow lane which led to Clover Farm. The night was quiet and still, every twig on every tree and bush in the hedgerow either side of the winding lane outlined in silver tracery against the moonlit sky. The frozen tufted grass was especially lovely, each blade encrusted and edged with filigree frost-work. It brought the mingled pain and pleasure that beauty always produced in his chest and he shook his head at what he considered shameful weakness. He would rather cut out his own tongue than confess that such things – the sun setting like a ball of fire in a copper sky, shimmering films of mist rolling over a field in the pearly light of dawn, even a nightingale's song – had the power to create a rhapsody in his soul. He was different enough already without adding to it.

He could remember the very moment he discovered he wasn't like everyone else. He had been five years old and the day had started when his mother had set him on her knee and ex-plained he was going to have a new da along with a new brother and sister. Their own mam had died, like his da, but now they'd be one family again. That'd be nice, wouldn't it? He'd thought so. Grandma Hedley had never let him play out in the street with the other bairns and the thought of playmates had been exciting. But his new sister had screamed with fright at the sight of his face and had had to be taken home early.

There had been no mirrors within his reach at his grandparents' house where he and his mother had lived since he'd returned from the infirmary just after his second birthday. Later that afternoon he'd crept away into his grandmother's hallowed front room, used only on high days and holidays or when the priest or doctor called at the house. He had pulled a chair over to the small black-leaded fireplace which held a dried flower arrangement and peered into his grandma's brass-framed mirror above the wooden mantelpiece holding two candlesticks and a clock.

He had stared at his reflection for a long time. When he had finally climbed down and wiped his eyes, restoring the chair to its place by the door, he had understood why the pretty little girl who had come to the house had been so frightened. The very next week he had started school and the limited but happy world within the four walls of the house was gone for ever. There were folk who labelled the animal kingdom as cruel. He had discovered animals couldn't hold a candle to humankind.

There were no lights in the windows of the four labourer's cottages built in a terrace at the end of the lane, but he hadn't expected there to be. Everyone would be in the barn Farmer Shawe had ordered to be swept and cleared out for the end of year feast and celebrations to welcome the New Year in. No doubt the revelry was well underway by now and everyone would be making merry on homemade wine and beer and cider. Seamus Shawe was a good master in plenty of ways and progressive in his views, treating man and beast well, and he always provided plenty of food and drink.

Once past the cottages which had no gardens at the front but long narrow strips of land at the back where each labourer's wife and children cultivated their own crop of vegetables, the lane divided into two wide tracks. One led to the large sprawling farmhouse with its massive farmyard to the front and enclosed garden to the rear, with a wash-house and separate privy and beyond that an overgrown tangle of lawns and flower beds. The other snaked past a number of barns, the stables and other buildings, including the pigsties. It wound along at the side of fields enclosed by drystone walls until it came to the edge of a steep quarry. Here all the human excrement from the privies at the farmhouse and cottages was dumped weekly by a farm cart kept specially for that purpose. Jake had visited other farms with Seamus and he counted himself fortunate there were no foul, stinking cesspools at Clover Farm. In some places the smell from the human waste far exceeded that of the animals.

Taking the right track, he walked along the frozen ridges of dirt and snow to the back of the farmhouse which he entered by way of the kitchen. This room was enormous and the heart of the three-storey building which had been built towards the end of the seventeenth century by an ancestor of the present farmer. As well as the kitchen, there was a pleasant dining room and study on the ground floor, a sitting room and two bedrooms on the first floor and three bedrooms at the top of the house underneath the attic, but it was showing signs of severe neglect. Dust was thick, the stone-flagged floor didn't look as if it had been scrubbed in weeks, and the black-leaded range was caked in fat and grime. Nevertheless the smell of bacon and burning wood was comforting; it meant home to him.

Jake had first come to live at Clover Farm as a lad of fourteen, initially residing with an old couple in one of the labourers' cottages before moving to the farmhouse itself shortly after the Shawes' son was killed at the Somme in 1916. In those days Bess, Seamus's wife, had been alive and the whole farmhouse had been as clean as a new pin. Enid Osborne, one of the labourers' wives who cooked and cleaned for the two of them now, was not so particular.

'You're back then.' Seamus was sitting smoking his pipe in front of the glowing fire, his slippered feet resting on the fender and a glass of whisky in one hand.

'Aye, I'm back.' Jake smiled down on the shining bald head of the man he thought of as a father. The man who had been instrumental in lifting him out of the suffocating hell of the town, and into what he privately termed as heaven on earth.

He'd come across Clover Farm as a lad of ten one Sunday afternoon. As was his wont, he'd escaped the town to walk the countryside. Skirting any buildings to avoid human contact and the inevitable staring, he'd stopped to drink at the brook which fed the farm with water. He had noticed a horse lying on its side at the edge of the bank some distance away, and what looked like a new-born foal half in and half out of the water.

Realising something was seriously amiss, he'd pulled the foal onto the thick grass by its mother and then raced across a couple of fields of waving corn towards the barns he'd seen, shouting as he went. He was brought up short as he rounded the corner of the first barn by a man grabbing hold of his arm.

'Hey, what you think you're up to, trampling my corn and hollering like that?' the man had shouted in his ear, shaking him like a terrier with a rat.

He'd gabbled his story, upon which the man, who had turned out to be Seamus himself, had called for a couple of men in the distance and the lot of them had returned to the brook, Seamus keeping hold of his arm when he'd tried to disappear. The mare, a favourite of the farmer's, was already dead, but thanks to his prompt action the foal was saved, and that had been the start of his friendship with Clover Farm. Seamus had offered him a weekend job cleaning the cow-houses and stables, working in the fields, feeding the animals and the hens and turkeys which made a substantial profit at market come Christmas. When he had completed his schooling he had gone to live at the farm and begun work properly.

It wasn't an easy life. In winter the wind could be like a carving knife, cutting hands and cheeks until they bled, and when added to driving snow it had the ability to turn coats, mufflers and gloves into frozen boards. The fourteen-hour-plus days, longer at harvest time, tested strength and stamina, but Jake had taken to the life like a duck to water.

The farmer and his wife and son had always treated him differently to their other employees, but for the first time in his life the distinction had been a good one. They had looked beyond his face, and everyone else on the farm had taken their cue from their master. Consequently he had found a contentment bordering on happiness. The feeling of belonging had grown when, after his son's death, Seamus had made him his manager and invited him into the farmhouse to live.

'I told them we'd put in an appearance a bit later,' Seamus said now as Jake took his coat off and sat down in the other big armchair at the side of the range. 'We needn't stay long, they'll be dancing and carrying on until the early hours most likely.' He pushed a second glass to Jake, along with the bottle of whisky. 'There'll be a few sore heads in the morning, sure as eggs are eggs.'

'I dare say.' Jake poured himself a good measure, knocking back half of it in one swallow before relaxing in the chair and stretching out his long legs. Drinking was the least of the shenanigans that went on at times like these. After the last harvest supper, young Herbert Lyndon had come cap in hand to Seamus to announce he was going to wed Florence, one of the other workers' comely sixteen-year-old daughter, a mite sharpish. Seamus had given his blessing and the wedding had gone ahead forthwith, and both mothers were already knitting baby clothes.

The two men sat talking for some time in front of the fire, their conversation easy and punctuated by comfortable silences. It was after one of these that Seamus straightened in his chair, saying, 'I want to talk to you about something, lad, and tonight is as good a time as any, it being the end of one year with a new one about to come on us. How do you see Daniel fitting in here?'

'Daniel? Daniel Osborne, Jack's lad?'

'Aye, him.'

'In what way?'

'You think he's brighter than average?'

Jake stared at Seamus. He didn't understand where the conversation was going. Nevertheless, he considered the question for a moment or two before he said, 'Aye, Daniel's a canny lad, but more than that he's one of them you can give a job to and know it'll be done come hell or high water and done well.'

Seamus nodded. 'I want you to start giving him a bit of responsibility over the others. He can take the load off your shoulders to some extent which'll give you time to take on the accounts and office work.'

'You do the office work.'

'Aye, I know. Now I want to show you what's what.' As Jake went to speak, Seamus held up his hand. 'Look, lad, I went to see the old quack afore Christmas after that last turn I had.'

'That was indigestion. You'd just polished off one of Enid's baked jam rolls single-handedly.'

'Aye, well, I hadn't let on to you but that wasn't

the first time I'd felt bad. Anyway, he says there's something wrong with my ticker. Now don't look like that, lad. I'm not about to pop my clogs, but I want to set certain things in order, just to ease my mind. For that reason I want you to know everything there is to know about the financial side of things, just in case you have to step in sharpish at any time. And if Daniel's coming up alongside to do the sort of job you do now, a manager so to speak, it'll be plain sailing rather than everyone disappearing up their own backsides. I can't abide disorder. You know that.'

Jake's face was ashen but his voice was quiet when he said, 'Tell me exactly what the doctor said.'

Seamus took a swallow of his whisky. 'Like I said, he reckons my heart's none too good. Mind, I'm getting on a bit, like I told him. I'm no spring chicken.'

Jake didn't return Seamus's smile. 'You should have told me before.'

'Not at Christmas, lad. That'd have put a damper on things. But while we're sitting quiet like this there's something else an' all. I want to tell you now so you're prepared. I've made a will, it's with me solicitors in Bishopwearmouth, Appleby and Jefferson, and I did it just after our Terence bought it at the Somme. You get the lot, lad. Farm, bit in the bank, the lot. Just so you know and there's no mix-up. All right? I've got that nephew that came sniffing about when Terence died and I wouldn't put it past him to try something. I told him then and I'll tell you now, from early on I thought of you as a second son.

You don't always have to sow the seed that lands in your field.'

The burning in Jake's eyes became unbearable and as the tears ran down his face he was aware of movement in the chair opposite. He felt the old farmer's arms go round him and hold him tight. For the first time in his life he knew what it was to be hugged as a beloved son.

Chapter 6

Hannah was enjoying herself. The feeling of achievement that her mother had agreed to let her see in the New Year at Naomi's was heady. Naomi's four younger brothers were in bed but several of the neighbours were present, along with Larry and Hilda, Mr Wood's children from his first marriage, and their spouses. Everyone was very merry, their jocularity only partly due to the beer and whisky which had been consumed. There was also a kind of defiance to the gaiety. Times might be bad, they might be in the grip of a slump that was worsening by the month with dole queues lengthening and a quarter of the country's miners out of work, but they still knew how to enjoy themselves. The coal owners didn't own their souls.

The front room was crowded and laughter filled the house. Mr O'Leary from three doors up had brought along his accordion and was doing requests. As one of the hits of the previous year,

'Fascinating Rhythm', bellowed forth from a number of throats, Rose and Hannah smiled at each other. They were in the kitchen making up yet another batch of sandwiches, the third of the night.

'It ought to be Naomi doing that,' said Rose, waving at the pile of ham sandwiches Hannah had prepared. 'You're a guest when all's said and done, lass.'

'I like helping, Mrs Wood.' She did like to be useful but she liked being with Naomi's mother even more.

'I don't know what we'd have done without them joints of ham and beef Jake brought, and the ham and egg pie. He's a good lad, my Jake.' Rose was deftly slicing Hannah's fruit cake into small squares as she spoke. 'The lot's gone now though but it's nearly midnight, things slow down after that. Go and find Mr Fraser, hinny, and remind him he's first-foot. Tell him to come an' get the coal and bread and his bottle, I've got it here ready. It's time he got himself away. I don't want him rushing and ending up flat on his back on the ice with everyone waiting in the hall for his knock at the front door.' Rose made a face and they both laughed.

Hannah was still smiling as she left the kitchen with the plate of sandwiches in one hand and the fruit cake in the other. She nearly dropped the lot when she was grabbed from behind and Adam's voice whispered in her ear, 'I was wondering where you'd got to.'

As he turned her round to face him, his flushed cheeks and bright eyes told Hannah he'd had more than a few beers. Quickly she said, 'I've got to take these through and your mam wants me to tell Mr Fraser–'

'Blow Mr Fraser.' He took the plates out of her hands and put them on the bottom tread of the stairs. Then he pulled her against him as he said again, but under his breath now, 'Blow Mr Fraser.'

Hannah's heart was beating so violently she could hardly breathe but she didn't resist as he lowered his head and took her lips. She wanted Adam to kiss her. She'd dreamt of this so many times and it was actually happening. His mouth was warm and firm on hers, his hands moving up either side of her face as he murmured, 'Oh, Hannah, Hannah, you're bonny. And sweet, so sweet.'

The front room door opened and brought them jerking apart. As Mr Fraser lurched past them making for the kitchen, Hannah let out a silent sigh. Her first kiss and she had liked it. She had liked it very much. 'I'd ... I'd better take the sandwiches and cake through,' she said shyly, knowing she was blushing scarlet.

'Aye, all right. I'll help you.'

Adam's voice was soft, like his eyes. Hannah blinked, then as Adam smiled at her she returned the smile. *Adam Wood had kissed her.* She felt as though she was floating a foot above the ground as he followed her into the front room.

When the stout wooden clock on the mantelpiece began to chime midnight and the ship's whistles down in the docks along with myriad church bells rang out, everyone began to embrace each other. The men shook each other's hands or clapped each other on the back and everyone said, 'Happy New Year, happy New Year.' There was some laughing and hugging and one or two of the women were crying but not in a sad way.

Hannah drank it in. This was lovely, lovely. Everything was lovely and Adam had kissed her.

When the clock struck for the twelfth time they heard a loud knocking at the front door. As though no one had any idea it was going to happen, there were shrieks and cries as Mr Fraser came into the house, grinning widely and shouting, 'First foot! First foot!'

'Happy New Year, Hannah.' Naomi was laughing loudly and the two friends hugged each other for a moment before Naomi moved on. Then Hannah was in front of Joe who, at seventeen, was two years younger than Adam. She liked Joe, everyone did. Adam's brother was the soul of gentleness and much quieter than Adam, she had never heard him raise his voice or argue with anyone.

'Happy New Year,' he said a little shyly.

She smiled at him and said, 'The same to you, Joe.'

The next moment Joe was pushed aside by his brother but good-naturedly and the two grinned at each other before Joe turned away. 'A happy New Year, Hannah.' Adam didn't kiss her, he didn't even touch her. His eyes holding hers, he said, 'When are you sixteen?'

Her heart raced. 'March the tenth.'

He nodded slowly. 'I'll have to be patient till then.'

Hannah stared at him. She was shivering inside,

not with cold but exhilaration. She felt she could drown in the vivid blue of his eyes. And then Mrs Fraser bustled between them, stopping to say, 'Happy New Year, lass, happy New Year,' and when she had gone Adam was hugging his mother.

For the rest of the night she was aware of exactly where he was even though they didn't talk again. She sat and chatted to Joe for a little while once everyone had calmed down. He startled her somewhat by saying quietly, 'What do you want out of the new year, Hannah?'

'Want out of it?' She shrugged. It wasn't the sort of question folk asked. 'I don't know. Happiness, I suppose. Doesn't everyone want that?'

He didn't answer this directly but even more quietly said, 'I'd like to get out of the pit but I can't see that happening.'

'Why not?'

'I'm a miner. Da's a miner, Adam is and I suppose Stephen and Peter and the twins will follow suit.'

'But you don't like it?'

There was a look on his face she hadn't seen before when he said, 'I hate it. I mean, no one really wants to be underground but...' He shook his head, looking down at his hands which were resting on his knees. 'I hate it.'

'But you don't have to go down the pit just because your da does surely?' She searched her mind for something positive to say to take the look of desolation away. 'I mean your brother, Mr Fletcher, decided to do something else. Couldn't you work at the farm with him? There might be a job there.'

Joe looked at her, a long look. 'Adam wouldn't understand it if I did that.' It ended the conversation.

Just after one o'clock Hannah left the house. It was so cold outside it took her breath away. There was the odd light still burning in one or two houses as she picked her way along the frozen pavement. She let herself into the shop as quietly as she could and then stood with her hands pressed to her cheeks. Adam Wood wanted her for his lass, he'd all but said so. She couldn't take his remark about him waiting until she was sixteen any other way, could she?

The shop's normal rich blend of smells – smoked bacon and mature cheese, coffee, peppermint and liquorice – washed over her. From a small child she had loved being in here, often creeping down without her mother knowing. At those times her uncle had slipped her a penn'orth of bull's eyes or a big fat bar of Fry's chocolate cream.

She glanced round the interior, breathing deeply. Lately, since she had been working alone here with her uncle, the shop had lost its allure but tonight the magic was back. She walked across to a row of big glass jars of sweets and unscrewed the top of one containing love-hearts. Drawing out a handful, she sorted out one but couldn't make out the little message inscribed on it in the dim light shining in from the street lamp outside.

Popping it in her pocket she passed through the shop and climbed the stairs leading to the flat.

Her mother had promised to leave the flat front door unbolted for her return. On entering the hall she placed the key for the shop on the small table by the front door so her uncle could open up in the morning. All her actions had been silent, she didn't want to bring her mother's wrath down on her head for waking them. Not after the wonderful night she'd had. Neither did she want to talk to anyone. She just wanted to get to bed and think of Adam.

She was about to creep along the hall when she caught the murmur of voices from the sitting room. The door was slightly ajar but as far as she could see there was no lamp lit. Frowning to herself, she paused. And it was then she distinctly heard her uncle say, 'I don't know what's the matter tonight but I can't perform to order. I'm sorry but there it is.'

'You've never had any problem before.' It was her mother's voice, thick and wobbly. 'Is it me? Have ... have I done something wrong?'

'Don't be silly, it isn't that. It's me. Look, I'm tired, lass. That's all. It's been a long day.'

There was silence for a moment or two and Hannah had actually taken a couple of tentative steps towards the bedroom, her brow wrinkled as she tried to sort out what had been said and what it meant, when her uncle's voice came again, sharper this time. 'For crying out loud, Miriam, leave it. I've told you.'

'You don't love me any more.'

'I just want to get to bed, is that a crime? What if Aggie wakes up or Hannah comes back?'

Now her mother's voice was more in the nature

of a low hiss as she said, 'How can you say that with the risks you've took at times? Couldn't get enough of me in the early days, could you? Morning, noon and night you wanted it.'

'Aye, well, you were willing. More than willing.'

'I still am. It isn't me who's changed.'

'How many times do I have to tell you, woman? I'm tired, that's all. It's all right for you, you just have to lie back and enjoy it. It's different for a man.'

'Oh aye, it's different for a man all right.'

She heard her uncle swear and then her mother say, 'No, don't go, Edward. Please. Not like this. Please, Edward.'

Hannah sped along the hall and into her bedroom, shutting the door soundlessly and divesting herself of her clothes with frantic haste. She pulled her nightdress over her head, slid into bed and pulled the covers up to her chin. She felt physically sick. *Her uncle and her mam.*

Her feet were as cold as ice and she was shivering, her mind replaying every word she'd heard. Poor Aunt Aggie. For her uncle to do that and with her mam. Did her aunt know? And then she answered herself immediately with, of course she didn't. She hadn't known, had she, so why should her aunt? Aunt Aggie was confined to bed most of the time.

Her heart was drumming in her ears as she waited for her mother to enter the room but when after a minute or two nothing happened, her heartbeat gradually returned to normal and she began to relax. Curling herself into a little ball under the thick eiderdown to get warm, she tried to take in the enormity of the fact that her mother was carrying on with her Uncle Edward. Suddenly a hundred and one small incidents in the past took on a new significance.

They were horrible, the pair of them. To treat her Aunt Aggie like that. It didn't matter that she didn't know, it was still awful, disgusting. And her mam... Only last week she'd gone on and on about that woman from Swan Street running off with the milkman, she'd called her everything. And yet she was living in her aunt's house and supposedly looking after her. *Her own sister-in-law.*

Her eyes wide, Hannah stared up at the ceiling. Trust her mam to spoil everything. She had been so happy when she came in tonight and now it was all ruined. And then she felt guilty for being so selfish in view of how her aunt was being treated.

After a few minutes of tossing and turning she sat up in bed. She reached for her coat which she had slung on the chair next to her bed along with her other clothes and delved into the pocket and found the comfit. Her bed was situated under the window and now she knelt up, pulling the thin curtains aside so the light from the street lamp spilled over the window sill.

'Let this say what Adam's thinking,' she prayed softly. 'Let it be a sign. Please.'

Manoeuvring the little heart so she could read the tiny words, she peered down at the inscription. 'Will you be mine?'

He wanted her for his sweetheart. Sighing, she held the sweet close to her chest for a moment, the blood racing through her veins. Then she slipped it back into the pocket of her coat and slid down in bed again after closing the curtains.

He was going to wait until she was sixteen, knowing what Mrs Wood had told Naomi about no lads before her birthday, but then he would ask her. And when he did, she would say yes. He'd had lots of lassies after him, Naomi had told her that, and he had courted a few for a while, but then he was nineteen going on twenty. Lots of lads got married at twenty. She hugged her knees in sudden ecstasy. She'd marry him tomorrow if he asked.

She wanted to leave this house. She was sorry for Aunt Aggie and she hated what her mam and uncle were doing behind her aunt's back, but it wasn't as if she could make any difference if she stayed. And if she got married she'd still come and see her aunt regularly. It had been bad enough before but now she knew about her mam and uncle it was ten times worse. She felt dirty. Just knowing made her feel as if she was in on the conspiracy but she couldn't tell her aunt. It would break her heart. Oh, how could her mam *do* that to another woman?

She was still wide awake when her mother entered the bedroom nearly half an hour later. Hannah shut her eyes and became as still as a mouse as the door opened, and she was aware of her mother crossing the room and standing looking down at her before she went to her own bed and began to get undressed. She heard the creak of the bed springs and then silence for a while, but just as she was drifting off to sleep she heard her mother sniff and then the unmistak-able sound of a stifled sob.

Her mam was crying. The shock of it brought Hannah rigid. She had never once known her mam to cry, not even when she had slipped on the ice a couple of winters back and broken her arm. In spite of herself she felt a softening effect flood through her spirit and her face screwed up as though she herself was in pain. There was a pressure in her throat, the feeling would not allow her to swallow and she continued to lie stiff and straight until eventually the muffled sounds across the room died away and all was quiet.

Had they quarrelled? Maybe even ended their ... well, she supposed the word was affair, incred-ible though it still seemed for her mother and uncle to be doing that. If so, she didn't think it was what her mother wanted, not from what she had heard in the hall. She continued to chew everything over for a little while longer and by the time she eventually drifted off to sleep she was sure about one thing. Her uncle hadn't played fair with either her aunt or her mother and he wasn't the man she'd thought he was. And she wished, she did so wish she didn't have to work in the shop with him every day.

Chapter 7

'We're out.' There was a note of exultation in Wilbur's voice as he marched into the kitchen, closely followed by Adam and Joe. Slinging his bait can onto the kitchen table, he surveyed his wife. 'They've closed every pit in the country and locked us out because we wouldn't crawl to the blighters.'

Rose stared at her husband. She'd known it was coming, everyone did. The last few years most of Britain's workers had had to accept reduced pay packets – those that still had jobs, that was. But this last stroke of the colliery owners, that of insisting wages be cut again and the minimum wage agreement of two years before abolished, was too much, especially when combined with the 'temporary' increase in the miners' working day from seven to eight hours. Brushing a wisp of hair from her face, she said flatly, 'And you think the TUC will back you?'

'To the last man. They know that all working men's jobs, their wages and conditions, are under threat. What happens to us miners today will be what happens nationwide if they don't stop the rot.'

She wished she could believe it. There had nearly been murder done in this kitchen a week ago when Jake had been listening to Wilbur and Adam rant on that the government would be broken by working men's solidarity. He had proferred the opinion that they'd be sold out within a matter of weeks if not days if a general strike came about, and it was only Wilbur and Joe restraining Adam and she hanging on to Jake like a limpet that had prevented the half-brothers coming to blows. And the thing was, she was with Jake on this. The Alliance had sold them out in 1921, they'd do the same now. But she couldn't say that to her husband and sons.

Quietly, she said, 'I'll make a pot of tea.'

'Not for me, Mam. I'm just going to let Hannah know what's happening.'

Adam was out the back door in the next moment and she watched from the window as he strode out of the backyard. His step was jaunty; his head held high, and he looked elated. All three of them did. And she understood why. Years of short time, pay cuts, being treated as less than muck under the mine owners' feet had caused a resentment that was bitter and deep rooted. Now they could actually do something, fight back. Of course they wanted the strike. *Please God, please let it turn out right. Don't let them be broken. Let the country back them. Jake was sure the rest of the country's workers wouldn't put their necks on the line for the miners. Let him be wrong.*

'Him and Hannah are courting strong.' Joe sat down at the kitchen table as he spoke. 'I haven't seen him so keen on a lass before.'

Rose nodded but again she kept her opinion to herself. She loved all her children but she wasn't blind to their weaknesses, and lassies were Adam's. From when he could toddle they'd been after him and he loved every minute of their attention. But perhaps it would be different with Hannah. Maybe he wouldn't mess her around like he had the others. She hoped not. She loved that little lass like one of her own.

Joe drank his tea down and then looked at his father. 'The lads are having a meeting at the Tavern. You coming?'

'Mebbe later. You go.'

When Joe had left they had the house to themselves, the other children being at school, and Wilbur said, 'I'm not sorry it's come, Rose. Can't you at least pretend to be for it? The other wives are backing their men to the hilt.'

'That's not fair, Wilbur.'

'The hell it's not. You'd have me working for nowt, that's what you'd do. According to the coal owners and their friends in Parliament we're the "New Red Threat" and "worse than the Hun". You've read the papers, you know what they're saying about us. And why? Because honest working men want a wage that'll support a wife and bairns.'

'I know, Wilbur, I know.' He was working himself up into a state and she didn't want that. She hadn't seen him lose his temper until they had been married six months or more, but although it happened infrequently she had learned to fear it. She had also learned how to deflect it most times, a knack she'd never managed with Silas. Not that you could compare her first husband with Wilbur. Her voice placating, she said, 'I've just made some teacakes. You want a couple with your tea? And I've got a nice bit of brisket for dinner.' She didn't add the latter had been courtesy of his stepson.

'Aye, I'll have a bite.' He settled back in his chair, satisfied his point had been made.

As Rose glanced at him she experienced an echo of the old tenderness that had persuaded her to marry him. He could be childlike at times. When she had first met him he had been struggling to cope with two young children on his own, and he had needed her. He still needed her. And he was a good father, as far as his own bairns were concerned anyway; Wilbur and Jake had never hit it off. That had grieved her more than a little. In the early days of their marriage she hadn't known how to handle Wilbur, and the fact that Jake had seen him raise his hand to her once or twice had forever set her son against his stepfather. They'd never spoken of it, she and Jake, but she knew. And it was a shame. Wilbur had his faults but there were worse than him as she knew only too well.

Her thoughts made her voice soft when, setting the plate with the teacakes in front of him, she said, 'The bairns are at school all day now, I could take washing in for a while. Just till you and the lads are back at work,' she added hastily as her husband's face darkened.

'Don't start.' Wilbur glared at her. 'I've told you before, no wife of mine works.'

Rose didn't point out that with three grown men, Naomi and four little ones to cook and clean and wash for, she was on her feet from dawn to dusk and what was that if it wasn't work?

'I can just hear that son of yours if you did something like that. Crow about it all the way to

Newcastle, he would, me not being able to support me own family. Well, I can support you, all right?'

Rose bit her lip. It was always there below the surface, this antipathy towards Jake. And it wasn't fair. Jake was so good to them. Quietly, she said, 'He knows you can and he wouldn't take it like that–'

The crash of the plate as it smashed against the wall of the kitchen, spraying fragments of teacake in a wide arc, caused Rose to jump violently. Her hand to her mouth, she shrank against the table as Wilbur stood to his feet, glowering at her. 'You're not taking in washing or owt else. Get that through your head once an' for all. The day that happens'll be the day after they put me six foot under an' I can't do owt about it. Until then I'm master in this house. Me. Not him, all right?'

He glared at her before grabbing his cap and stuffing it on his head. Rose said nothing as he left the house by way of the back door, but once he had gone she drew in a deep shuddering breath. He was all of a two-an'-eight and no wonder, what with the lockout and what it might mean. He wasn't daft, Wilbur. He knew the coal owners and the government would fight dirty. Whenever a group of workers protested about poor living standards or dangerous working conditions, the same old labels were bandied about in the papers. 'Organised menace.' 'Wicked and treacherous.' She plumped down on a hard-backed chair, reaching for her own cup of tea with a shaking hand. 'Where will it all end?' she murmured to herself. 'And when?'

Adam was saying much the same thing to Hannah in the kitchen at the back of the shop but in contrast to his mother his voice was bright and animated. 'I don't know how it'll work out, lass, but I do know we'll be a sight better off at the end of it than we are now. All the lads know that the government, especially Churchill and his gang, together with the coal owners and the owners of every other industry in the land, want to destroy the unions once and for all. But there's more of us than there are of them, that's what they're forgetting, and if we all stick together we can come out of this smelling like roses.' He grinned. 'Would you like that? Me smelling of roses?'

She didn't care how he smelt and her eyes told him so. He kissed her, long and hard, and then held her close as he said, 'I'll come round later once you've had your tea. Do you think your mam will do the last hour or two so we can go for a walk before it's dark?'

'I'll ask.' This latest from her mother, offering to work in the shop in the evenings so she could see Adam, was only one of the surprises of the last weeks. She had thought there would be ructions when Adam had come to the house on the afternoon of her sixteenth birthday and made his intentions plain. Instead her mam had been all sweetness and light, immediately agreeing they could start courting. It hadn't improved her mam's attitude to her the rest of the time, in fact she was more snappy and prickly than she had ever been, but where Adam was concerned, everything was hunky-dory.

'I'll come just after six.' He kissed her again, his hands wandering up under the swell of her breasts before Hannah caught them and brought his fingers back to her waist. He accepted the silent reproof without comment, he always did but she knew he would try it on again. After a moment he raised his head, saying, 'I'd better get going. There's a meeting at the Tavern.'

She walked through into the shop with him and saw him out. Her uncle was tied up with a customer and didn't look their way, and she returned to the job she had been doing before Adam's arrival – stacking tins on the shelves. Once the customer had left, her uncle began to clean the counter with a damp muslin cloth, working it round and round the wood for what seemed to Hannah an inordinately long time.

'I don't want him coming in here at all times of the day and night. This is a working environment. Does he understand that?'

'What?' She turned and looked at her uncle. He was red in the face and obviously in a tear about something. 'Adam came to say the miners are out,' she said quickly by way of explanation. People had talked of little else but the impending showdown for the last week.

'Be that as it may, I don't want him in here unless he's buying.'

Her face changing, Hannah straightened. 'I see.'

'And don't take that tack with me. You wouldn't expect to be able to go and see him at the pit, would you? Or visit the shipyard or the glass-works for a nice little chat? Just because this is a shop it doesn't mean every Tom, Dick or Harry can waste your time.'

He was angry, furiously angry, and she didn't understand why. People called in all the time for a gossip, it was part of the going-on, and they didn't always buy something. Her temper rising, Hannah said, 'Mr Routledge was in here half an hour yesterday talking about the match on Saturday and he didn't buy anything.'

'Mr Routledge is a friend of mine.'

'And Adam's my friend.'

'This is my shop, are you forgetting that? And you and your mother live under my roof.'

'No, I'm not forgetting that.' She faced him squarely, her eyes flashing. 'Neither am I forgetting that you get your money's worth out of the pair of us.' She wasn't sure this applied where her mother was concerned but it suited her to ignore that for the moment. 'Mam takes care of Aunty so you don't have to have a housekeeper or a nurse, and I work for nothing, remember? I could leave here tomorrow and get a job in a factory or somewhere and you'd have to pay out for an assistant or even two. And you know it.'

'You ungrateful little scut. Where do you think you'd be now if I hadn't took you and your mother in? Eh? You answer me that. I've looked after the pair of you for years.'

She stared at him, at his greasy face and big fat wobbly belly and it came to her that any affection she'd once had for her uncle had died, the death knell having rung on New Year's Eve. Quietly now, she said, 'Anything you've done, you've done because it suits you. And I am grateful that you took us in, whatever you might think, but it doesn't mean I'm beholden to you for life.'

She expected more angry words and it took her aback when he just stared at her and seemed to deflate. Suddenly he seemed to lose inches. 'I don't want to argue with you, lass,' he said, his voice low. 'I've never wanted that. You know how much I – me an' your aunt – think of you. But that Adam is not the one for you. He's too much of a lad where the lassies are concerned. I know the type.'

For a moment she was sorely tempted to throw her knowledge about him and her mother in his face. Only the thought that it would make living at home impossible and that her aunty might get to know about the affair stopped her. She was almost sure it was over; certainly there was a coolness between her mother and uncle these days, and she didn't want to be the one to cause her aunt unnecessary pain. But for her uncle to criticise Adam after how *he'd* behaved. Stiffly, she said, 'I like Adam Wood and he likes me.'

The look she hated came over her uncle's face and his voice held the soft thickness that went hand in hand with it when he said, 'You're a bonny lass, you could have anyone. You don't want to throw yourself away on a miner, now then. And not one like him who's had umpteen lassies that I know of–'

'Stop it.' She actually stamped her foot. 'I won't listen to this. I'm seeing Adam and that's that. And I trust him, I trust him absolutely. He would never do anything to hurt me.'

'And you think you could stomach being a miner's wife? If it came to that? Scrimping and scraping and never having a penny to your name? One bairn after another until you're an old woman at gone thirty?'

He was angry again but she preferred that to the squirmy creepiness that always made goose pimples prickle her skin. 'If necessary.' She was ramrod straight. 'But it won't be like that. After the unions win, the miners will get a decent wage and everything will change. Adam says so.'

'Adam says so, does he?' Her uncle nodded his head. 'Well, we'll soon see if Adam is right, won't we? But I wouldn't hold your breath.'

When, three days later, the General Strike began and workers in almost every industry laid down their tools and walked out, Hannah refrained from saying 'I told you so' to her uncle. Buses and trains stopped, factories were silent, docks deserted and offices empty. Britain's workforce united.

Nine days later it was over. But not for the miners. As the rest of the country returned to work, Lord Londonderry, the Durham coal owner, vowed he would smash the pitmen's union from top to bottom and he meant it. The miners were now on their own.

Hannah sat in Rose's kitchen listening to Wilbur, Adam and Joe talk, and although she didn't understand all that they were saying, she knew they would be fighting long and hard. She glanced at Naomi who was now the sole breadwinner in the house. She was listening with rapt attention to the menfolk. Then Hannah met Rose's gaze. They stared at each other for a moment until Rose's eyes dropped to the sock she was darning.

Hannah continued to look at Naomi's mother for a second more and then she, too, lowered her gaze. What she'd read in that brief unguarded moment had shocked her. Surely Mrs Wood thought the miners were right to stand out against the pit owners? The lodges in every district of every coalfield were determined to raise money and they'd already organised fellowship dinners where the mining families were sure of a good meal while the men discussed ways and means of making ends meet. Adam had told her all sorts of things had been discussed – brass band concerts, athletic contests, dances, boxing matches, talent competitions, coconut shies. Practically everything you'd find at a fairground. And the weather was good now for May and they had the whole summer in front of them. It had been a shock when the other trade union leaders had welshed on the colliery workers, but it had strengthened the miners' resolve, if anything. They were standing up for what was right, for their wives and bairns; couldn't Naomi's mam see that?

It was another half an hour before Adam stood up, holding out his hand to her as he said, 'Fancy a walk, lass?'

She nodded, pulling on her coat and straw bonnet as they left the kitchen to a chorus of 'Ta-rahs' from Naomi and her mother and Joe. Mr Wood said nothing but he smiled at her.

There were still a few bairns playing outside in the street as they emerged from the back lane, several involved in a game of hopscotch with an old boot polish tin, and a little group playing mothers and fathers with a real bare-bottomed baby who kept crawling away from his five-year-old 'mother', much to her very verbal annoyance. Hannah glanced down at the dribble-nosed infant who was demonstrating his considerable lung power in protest at being confined in one place. She knew his mam. Amy Stamp was only eighteen months older than her and she was already expecting again. The rest of the children were the baby's young uncles and aunties. Amy's mother had a bairn regular as clockwork every twelve months. Since Amy had wed and her husband had joined the family, there were well over twenty folk crammed in the two-up, two-down house.

She didn't want to live like that. The thought sprung into being and she acknowledged it had been at the back of her mind since the row with her uncle. She didn't want to have one bairn after another as decreed by the Catholic church. She didn't want a life forever fighting the thick mud from the back lanes and the dirt from the town's filthy industrial chimneys either. No privacy, no time or energy to do anything but get by.

'Penny for 'em?'

Adam was peering at her. Shaking herself mentally, she forced a smile, taking his arm as she said, 'It doesn't matter.' Adam wouldn't understand. He was very much like his father in the way he saw things. She had heard him rib Joe when his brother had made everyone a cup of tea one day after Naomi's mother had sprained her wrist. Adam would have expected Naomi or even her to do it. Women's work was women's work. Men brought in the wages, provided for their families and therefore didn't lift a finger in the home.

She had mentioned the incident to him once they were alone, asking why he had teased Joe for helping his mother. 'Helping Mam?' he'd said in surprise. 'That's Naomi's job. The trouble with Joe is he's as soft as clarts and Naomi can be a lazy little madam when she wants to be.' End of conversation. No matter that Naomi worked hard at the jam factory and brought in a wage too.

The May evening wasn't cold but Hannah shivered. Adam put his hand over the one she had through his arm and said, 'Come on, we'll walk up Newcastle Road and cut through Grange Park Avenue to the back of the cricket ground. They've got a couple of benches where we can sit and it's out of the wind.'

The further they walked, the more open it became. They were in the outskirts of Southwick now and there were some very nice houses with a garden at the front and rear to be seen. They came to the spot Adam had spoken of, which was a small park area with rows of elm trees bordering it. It had been a fine day and the sky was still blue, the clouds snowy white. The scent of May blossom from the trees in the park drifted in the air and the wind had died down to a breath, the area being sheltered. Hannah wondered how many other lassies Adam had sat with here as he put his arm round her and drew her against him. And then he kissed her and it didn't matter.

There weren't many people about, just a young family at one end of the park and another couple like themselves sitting on a bench some twenty yards away. When Adam raised his head, he settled her into the crook of his arm. 'The strike won't last for ever, you know that, don't you?' he said softly. 'And once I'm earning again we can go to the pictures or dancing at the Pally.'

Hannah nodded. She didn't care where she went as long as she was with Adam. They sat for a minute or two watching the father of the young family kicking a ball with his son, who couldn't have been more than four or five, while his wife sat watching with a little baby on her knee. The man was in a suit and they looked well-to-do.

'Do you ever think about leaving the pit and moving away, perhaps down south?' She hadn't meant to say it, it had just popped out as she watched the young husband.

'What?'

'Well, all this with the strike and everything and the pit being so dangerous, I just wondered if you'd thought about doing something else.'

Adam stared at her as though she was talking double Dutch. 'I'm a miner.'

'I know. I just wondered...'

He smiled. 'You're a funny little thing at times, you know that?' And then his voice grew husky as he murmured, 'But bonny, so bonny. Aw, Hannah, you've no idea what you do to me. There's not a lass in the country can hold a candle to you. I'm the luckiest man alive.'

She melted when he said things like this. He kissed her again but when his hand slid under her coat and cupped her breast, she drew back quickly. 'Don't. Someone'll see.'

She watched his white even teeth drag at his lower lip for a moment, then his right shoulder moved upwards in a gesture that held irritation.

'We've been seeing each other over eight weeks now and I'm not made of wood.'

'I know.' She didn't mind him touching her on the rare occasions they were alone, once or twice in his mam's kitchen when everyone else had gone to bed and another time when he'd walked her home and stood in the darkness of the back alley. At least not much. At first it had just been a light touch on the outside of her clothes but the last time he'd tried to lift her jumper and his hands had been hard and insistent. She knew it was wrong. Her mam hadn't told her much about the birds and the bees when she had started her monthlies two years ago, but she had been very clear that one thing led to another and that *that* had to be avoided at all costs. Quite what *that* entailed she wasn't sure, but she knew it could lead to the worst fate that could befall a lass, that of having a baby without being wed.

'I'm not going to do anything to hurt you. You know that, don't you?' Adam's face had softened when he saw her distress. 'But I've been used to–' He stopped, waving his hand as he said, 'It doesn't matter. But I know a thing or two. You wouldn't have to worry, that's what I'm saying.'

She stared at him in silence, then moved her lips one over the other before she said, 'I'm sorry.' She didn't want them to quarrel.

'Aye, well, we'd better be getting back.' And then, as she still looked at him with a troubled face, he smiled, drawing her into his arms again but this time just kissing the tip of her nose. 'Don't worry. I know you're a nice lass. I wouldn't be walking out with you otherwise, would I? We'll take it slow if that's what you want, all right?' He kissed her again, warmly.

Relieved, she kissed him back, and then as he drew her to her feet, she said again, but without really knowing why, 'I'm sorry.'

'It'll be better once the strike's over,' he said, as though that had a bearing on the situation. 'And you'll love the Pally, they have some right good bands there on a Saturday night. By, some of the lads' eyes'll pop out of their heads when I walk in with you on my arm.'

Her smile was more natural now. He was himself again. Everything was all right.

'Aye, once the strike's over we'll paint the town red, lass. That'll show 'em.'

She wasn't sure who it would show but she laughed anyway and they went home arm in arm.

Chapter 8

Over the next weeks it became clear there was going to be no easy resolution to the lockout. And a lockout was what it was, in spite of most of the miners calling it a strike, maybe because that way it seemed as though they were in charge, as if it was the working man taking the action instead of the employers. Gradually it became commonplace to see miners fixing roofs and cleaning chimneys and grooming dogs or ponies, or digging gardens.

Adam and his father decided to try their hand

at a spot of painting and decorating and went knocking on doors in Fulwell and Roker and the more well-to-do part of Southwick, but as they were competing with many other miners, jobs were few and far between. Joe had a little more success collecting fish and vegetable scraps from the market and from people's bins which he sold to folk who kept hens or pigs. The four younger children thought it was great fun to go out with shovels and buckets and follow the carthorses, picking up their manure, which they sold to the big houses on the outskirts of town for their gardens. As the strike dragged on into August, it was clear to Hannah that without Jake Fletcher's help in the way of the sacks of food he brought to the house each week the Woods would have been in dire straits.

It was this very thing that caused the first serious disagreement between Hannah and Adam late one Sunday evening at the beginning of September, a disagreement which was to have repercussions neither of them could have dreamt of. It had been a fine day and Hannah had joined the Wood family for a picnic on the beach. At least that was the way everyone referred to the hours spent picking winkles and looking for crabs and sea coal. The week before, Adam and his father and brother had earned a few shillings fetching sand from the beach, washing it in buckets and selling it to a local builder. This source of income had been short-lived. The builder had told them kindly there was only so much sand he could use and he wouldn't be needing any more for a week or two. But the three men had noticed women and children foraging for anything the tide left behind. Hence the Sunday outing.

It was close to sunset when they walked home to Wayman Street through the hot dusty streets. People were sitting on their doorsteps or gossiping over their backyard in the dying sunshine, the smell of the privies overpowering in some places due to the heatwave they'd been enjoying the last weeks.

Hannah and Adam trailed behind the others, who walked ahead in a small group, Joe and his father carrying the five-year-old twins, Matthew and Robert, on their backs. Rose was holding a bucket full of winkles and Naomi one containing a few crabs, while Stephen and Peter were pulling the wooden packing case on wheels Mr Wood had made to transport the sea coal and seaweed which would be dried out and used on the range fire. No one glancing at the family group would have guessed the growing desperation within its ranks. The summer was all but over, autumn was upon them and winter loomed round the corner with its ice and snow and raw winds. They were weeks behind with the rent, the twins had ringworm and impetigo and no matter what their mother tried she hadn't been able to get rid of the infections, and all the family were pale and washed-out looking.

As Hannah and Adam turned the corner into Wayman Street, they saw the others approaching the tall dark figure of Jake Fletcher who had obviously been waiting outside the house for their return. Adam swore under his breath. 'What's he doing here? Come to gloat.' He swore again, a base oath, and Hannah blinked against it. 'Why me da doesn't tell him to stuff his charity where the sun don't shine, I don't know.'

'He's family, Adam. He's only trying to help out.'

'Help out?' Adam stopped and looked at her, shaking his head. 'Don't you believe it. He's rubbing our noses in it, that's what he's doing with his sacks of this an' that. I'd rather starve than take anything from that scum.'

But he didn't. He ate the spuds and turnips and other vegetables Jake brought each week, along with a joint and the odd round of cheese and butter. Quietly, she said, 'Why do you hate him so much?'

'Because he's an upstart. Thinks he's better than the rest of us. You can see it in his eyes, and all because he got lucky. He's managed to pull the wool over Farmer Shawe's eyes and work his way in but he'll come a cropper one day.'

She stared into Adam's face, at the clear fresh skin and handsome features. 'It must have been hard for him, looking the way he does.'

'Don't you believe it. He's canny, he's used it to his advantage. How else do you think he's got where he is? By rights he should be here with the rest of us, doing what his da did and his granda afore him. Instead he chickened out and took the easy road.'

Such animosity. 'Perhaps it's not the easy road, just a different one.'

Adam's face stiffened. 'You sticking up for him?'

The look on his face warned her to say no more

but lately she had bitten her tongue more than once. 'I'm only saying people don't necessarily have to follow what their parents do, that's all. Just because his da was a miner and yours is, it doesn't follow Jake or you have to be one. Everyone should be able to make their own destiny and aim for what they really want.'

Adam's expression didn't alter. 'You're talking rubbish.'

'I don't think so. If folk want to better themselves—'

'Oh, so he's better than us now, is he? Here's the truth of it. You think he's better than me.'

'Of course I don't. I didn't mean that. I was talking generally.'

'Generally my backside.' He was livid. She could see it. 'Maybe you think you're too good to walk out with me, is that it? All this talk about leaving the pit and going down south.'

Her expression altered to one of angry surprise. 'I said that once, just once.'

'Maybe it was once too much.'

'You mean I can't discuss anything with you? Can't have an opinion? I've got to be like your mam and most of the women hereabouts, treating the man of the house as lord and master and worshipping the ground he walks on? Well, I don't think I'm like that, Adam. So there you have it.'

There was a telling silence while they stared at each other, Adam's face red with fury and Hannah's chalk white. But she wasn't going back on what she'd said, much as she loved him. He was like his father in as much as he didn't think anyone could have a different opinion to him, certainly not a woman anyway. And she hated that about him.

'If that's the way you want it...' He turned and marched away from her down the street towards his front door. The others had gone indoors.

For a moment she couldn't believe he'd left her like that and she stood still, expecting him to turn any second and call for her to catch up with him. She watched him reach his front door and without pausing he went into the house. He did not look back.

The air went out of her like a deflated balloon and she felt the colour sweeping over her face with the urge to cry. Did this mean he'd finished with her? She wouldn't be able to bear it if he had. Oh, why had she said those things? What did any of it matter compared to Adam? How could she have been so stupid?

She walked the twenty-odd yards to the shop on leaden feet, praying Adam's head would appear round his front door any moment and he would come towards her. Inside the shop, she stood for a minute or two. She didn't want to go upstairs yet. She needed a little while alone to compose herself. She took off her straw bonnet and coat and left them at the foot of the stairs, and carried on through to the shop kitchen and backyard. Outside, the warm muggy air hung like a blanket within the brick confines of the yard and she walked across and sat on top of a stack of empty orange boxes. She had managed to secrete one or two into Adam's house over the last weeks but she'd had to be careful her uncle didn't catch wind of what she was about. She didn't have to worry now. She could hardly go round to Naomi's if she and Adam weren't speaking, let alone walking out.

With the thought came the tears. She was still sniffing and in the process of drying her eyes on her handkerchief when her uncle's voice from the doorway of the house brought her off the orange boxes with a start. 'What you doing out here?'

'Nothing. I was just coming up.' She pushed her handkerchief into her pocket as she spoke but did not move towards him. He was blocking the way into the house and she didn't want to have to squeeze past him. Lately there seemed to have been too many occasions when he'd engineered just such a situation and the feel of his flabby body made her nauseous. This last thought and the funny way her uncle was looking at her caused her to say flatly, 'Where's Mam?'

'Your mother has a headache. She's lying down.' He stared at her in the gathering twilight, the setting sun turning her thick chestnut hair fiery red. Licking his lips, he said softly, 'What's the matter? You've been crying.'

'Nothing.'

'It's that Wood lad, isn't it? I told you. I told you how lads are but you wouldn't listen. You've only yourself to blame, letting him take liberties and then wondering why he starts messing you about.'

'It's not like that.' Indignant, her chin rose.

'No?'

'No.'

'I don't believe you. I know how lads and lassies

are. You're not in the family way, are you?' he added as the thought struck.

She could smell the alcohol on his breath from where she was standing. These past few months he had been drinking more than he used to; not getting blind drunk, but having just enough to make him either awkward or maudlin. Her chin rising even higher, she snapped, 'Don't you talk to me like that. I haven't done anything to be ashamed of.'

'I don't doubt you're not ashamed. Brazen you are, like the rest of your kind.' And then his attitude changed in the blink of an eye and he mumbled, 'Aw, lass, lass, don't look at me like that. I don't mean it. You make me say these things. Look, don't hanker after the Wood lad, he's not worth it. You want someone who can treat you nice, buy you things, eh? He'd never have been any good for you, not a miner. Even when they're in work they don't make enough to keep body and soul together. You want different to that.'

He had been slowly approaching her as he talked and now a terror like nothing she had felt before froze Hannah's vocal chords. She didn't know how to describe what was in his face, she'd never before seen blind lust, but as he had advanced she had retreated until now she felt the hard wall of the yard behind her back. Her eyes, wide in a petrified stare, held the bloodshot ones of her uncle, and from somewhere she found the strength to stammer, 'St-tay away from me.'

'I'm only asking for a bit of kindness, Hannah, that's all, and for that I'll treat you like a princess,

118

you'll see. Anything you want, anything. You know what's what, you can't have messed about with the likes of Adam Wood without learning a few things, and I wouldn't let you down.'

'*No.*' As his hand came out tentatively, she smacked it away and immediately he grabbed her, pinning her against the wall with his bulk as his mouth fastened over hers in a wide wet kiss that had her choking. Struggling violently and half mad with fear, she kicked and struck out, the acid smell of his sweat thick in her nostrils. She managed to wrench her mouth from his and give one strangled scream but then he slapped her across the face and her head hit the wall behind her hard enough to make her see stars.

He had one hand over her mouth and nose and she could hardly breathe, which only added to the dizziness caused by the bang on her head. When she found herself lying on the dusty stone slabs she continued to struggle, but it wasn't until she felt his nails scratch her skin as he hoisted her skirt up to her thighs that she found the energy from somewhere to kick out.

There wasn't a great deal of power in her legs but straddled as he was above her, one hand fumbling with his trousers, it was enough to knock him off balance and onto his side. As she rolled over and away from him, he caught her foot, grunting obscenities, but now that she could breathe again, panic and fear renewed her strength and this time when she kicked she jerked herself free. Scrambling away on all fours, she reached the back door and hoisted herself to her feet. She didn't look behind her. He was

119

swearing and cursing as she stumbled through the kitchen and into the main area of the shop, making for the front door and the street, her only thought to get away.

She heard him lumbering after her as she wrenched open the door and fell into the street – straight into the arms of Jake Fletcher. He caught her as she fell, almost losing his own footing in the process, and his startled exclamation of, 'What the hell?' was followed by, 'Hey, hey, it's all right, I've got you.'

'He–he tri–' Clasping hold of Jake and sobbing hysterically, her legs gave way, and the next moment she was whisked up into his arms. Expecting her uncle to appear at any moment, she clung to him, gasping, 'He's coming after me.'

'No one is coming after you and if they do I won't let them get you, OK?' It was almost dark now and helplessly Jake glanced about him, but apart from a couple of women at the far end of the street, it was deserted. 'You're safe, don't cry,' he said as her sobs mounted.

What on earth had happened in there? He thought there had been someone behind her but the shop door had swung to and with the blind down it was impossible to see in. Something had scared her half to death though. Making a snap decision, he turned and retraced his footsteps.

It was Naomi who answered his knock, her eyes nearly popping out of her head as she took in Hannah in her brother's arms. Rose was sitting in the kitchen and she was alone; the four younger children had gone to bed, and Wilbur, Adam and Joe had gone straight to the Colliery Tavern after returning from the beach.

Rose jumped to her feet as her son walked in and for a few minutes all was flurry and commotion. When Hannah was sitting in Wilbur's armchair in front of the range, with Rose and Naomi kneeling either side of her comforting her, she managed to tell them something of what had happened. Jake's face became dark with rage. 'Her uncle?' He glanced at his mother who was grim faced. 'The filthy dirty swine.'

Naomi and Rose had their arms round Hannah who was still shaking and sobbing, but as Jake turned to leave, Rose sprang to her feet. 'Wait up, lad. Don't go in there by yourself.'

'Don't go in there? I'm going to give him something he'll remember for a long time.'

'No, lad, no. Look, I'll come with you. The lass'll be all right with Naomi for a minute or two. We don't know what's what yet.'

Jake glanced at Hannah. Her coiled hair had become loose and strands of it fell in wild disarray about her shoulders. One side of her face was flaming from her uncle's handiwork and her blouse had several buttons missing and was gaping open, showing her petticoat. His voice guttural, he growled, 'Look at her, Mam.'

'I know, I know.' Rose agitatedly smoothed her hair and reached for her shawl. She bent and whispered something in Naomi's ear before straightening and saying to Jake, 'Come on then, but please keep calm, lad. We don't want more trouble, I've enough on me plate as it is.'

In the street, Jake caught hold of his mother's arm. 'What did you say to Naomi?'

'I asked her to find out if there could be possible consequences to what's happened.'

'Dear gussy.' Jake stopped dead. 'You don't think he managed to...'

'I don't know. That's why I asked her to find out while it's just the two of them.'

Jake shook his head. 'He wants stringing up from the nearest lamp post.'

'Aye, maybe, but not by you and not tonight.' They had reached the shop and it was Rose who stepped forward and rang the bell. She had to repeat this twice before the door was opened. Miriam Casey looked at them, her thin face unsmiling.

'Where is he?' Jake said grimly.

'If you are referring to my brother-in-law, he is upstairs having his supper.'

She knew. It was in every line of her face and body. Wondering what kind of a woman Hannah's mother was, Jake said, 'You'd better get him down here pretty fast.'

'I don't think so, Mr Fletcher. He's rather upset.'

'He'll be more than upset if I have to go up and drag him down.'

'You've been listening to Hannah's lies, haven't you?' Miriam's voice was low but without a tremor in it; in fact, unbelievable though it was, Jake could have sworn there was a touch of elation in her tone. 'Edward told me exactly what happened earlier. Were you aware your son and Hannah have quarrelled?' she added, turning to Rose. Without waiting for an answer, she went on, 'And she came in upset and Edward tried to talk sense

122

into her. He reprimanded her admittedly, told her to have some pride and to stop chasing Adam, but that was all. And then she went mad.'

'So mad she slapped her own face and tore her clothes?' Jake's voice made Rose shiver. 'Let me make myself clear, Mrs Casey. If your brother-in-law isn't down here in thirty seconds flat I'm raising the street. All right? And I'll tell them exactly what transpired and show them the lass to prove it.'

Miriam raked Jake with her cold eyes before stepping back a pace. 'You had better come in.'

Once they were both standing within the aromatic confines of the shop, Miriam said shortly, 'I'll fetch him but please keep your voices down. My sister-in-law has been unwell today and he doesn't want her distressed.'

'I bet he doesn't.'

As Jake glared at her, Rose spoke. 'How could you take his part, Miriam? Against your own child, against Hannah? You must know what he tried to do to the lass and she wouldn't make a thing like that up. Not Hannah.'

'What do you know about it?' Miriam stared at the woman she would once have termed a friend, certainly in the early days when she had first come to live with her brother-in-law and Hannah and Naomi had been two little bairns playing together. Many a time she had sat in Rose's kitchen and bemoaned her lot but she had not visited the house in years, not since she had first begun sleeping with Edward and had assumed the rights of mistress of his house. 'You think butter wouldn't melt in her mouth, don't you?

Oh, I know she's got you twisted round her little finger all right, Rose. But she's not what she seems.'

'I find that difficult to believe.'

'Aye, well, like I said, she's got the lot of you on her side.'

'I think you had better fetch your brother-in-law, Mrs Casey,' said Jake flatly. He couldn't take any more of this. The woman wasn't normal, to talk about her own daughter like that. And a daughter like Hannah. You only had to look at the girl to see she was a nice little lass. But all this about her and Adam falling out was news to his mam, he'd seen her expression when this venomous old shrew had spoken. If his brother had been here he'd have agreed with him about one thing, probably the first time he'd agreed with Adam about anything: Hannah's mother was a witch and a spiteful one at that.

It was a good five minutes before Edward made an appearance; Jake was just about to go to the foot of the stairs and holler when Hannah's uncle opened the door and walked in, positioning himself behind the counter.

He didn't wait for them to speak. 'I didn't touch her, whatever she's been saying. I gave the lass a bit of a dressing down about getting herself into a state about Adam and she went for me. Claws, teeth an' all. It ought to be me creating. Took her in when she was nowt but a baby and this is the thanks I get.'

'You're a liar,' Jake said, his tone deep with anger. His gaze moved to Miriam who had come in behind her brother-in-law and was now stand-

124

ing with one hand on his arm. 'And you know he's lying.'

'Who are you calling a liar?' It was Miriam who spoke, her stance aggressive. 'He's her uncle, for goodness sake. He wouldn't do anything like she's suggesting.'

'How do you know what she's suggesting?' Jake said softly. 'Neither my mother nor me have said anything, as I recall. We merely said we wanted to speak to Mr Casey.'

'It's obvious, isn't it?' Edward was blustering, his face scarlet. 'A young lass runs screaming from the house in a two-an'-eight. What else could it be?'

'A hundred and one things, Mr Casey.'

'Don't talk to him in that tone. Who do you think you are?' Miriam said tightly. 'You come in here all holier than thou. You've got no idea what she's like. Flaunting herself every minute she gets, giving him the eye, leading him on. I've seen it. *I've seen it.* She deserves everything she gets, the little strumpet.' She stopped abruptly.

Jake's voice was hard and flat, holding a wealth of disdain when he said, 'You disgust me. Do you know that? You disgust me. How Hannah ever came from the likes of you is beyond me. How long have you two been at it, eh? How long? Long enough for you to come to understand the type of man he is, that's for sure, because if ever the green-eyed demon shone from a pair of eyes, it shines from yours. And you,' he turned to Edward, his eyes blazing, 'I'll see you go down the line for this, you mealy-mouthed bit of scum, you.'

Rose was looking from one to the other of them in naked bewilderment, her face expressing a variety of expressions as the truth dawned. And when Jake suddenly moved forward, doubling his fist and punching Hannah's uncle full in the face, she said not a word. Edward sprawled backwards and onto the floor, Miriam screaming shrilly, and it was into this ear-splitting sound that Jake said, 'That was for Hannah, you dirty swine. You come within a mile of her again and see what you get.'

'He wouldn't touch her with a bargepole.' Miriam was now kneeling at her brother-in-law's side and like a child he had buried his face in her flat bosom. 'And I'll have the law on you, you see if I don't. This is assault.'

'You do that.' Jake's voice was quiet now, as though with the venting of his anger a pressure had been released. 'I'll be waiting for them, make no bones about that. And what I'll tell them will fill their notebooks from end to end. But for now, you,' he pointed to Miriam, 'you get all the lass's things, everything. She'll not step foot in this place again unless it's of her own choosing, which I doubt.'

Miriam stared at him for a moment, then turning to Edward she said, 'Come on, come on out of it.' She helped him to his feet and led him to the door, supporting him with her arm as though he was weak and infirm. She turned at the door to say, 'I'll bring her things round later.'

'You won't.' Jake's voice was harsh. 'You'll get 'em now and be quick about it, and if you leave something she's fond of out of spite I'll be back when the shop's full shouting the odds. Just so you know.'

The look Miriam cast upon him was so vitriolic Rose caught her breath. When they were alone, she said shakily, 'By, lad, I can't believe it. Her and him. I'd never have thought it in a month of Sundays. Poor Aggie.'

Poor Aggie? Jake stared at his mother for a moment. The little lass in his mother's kitchen had been pawed and slobbered over by that swine and she was thinking of his wife. And then he caught the anger and irritation. The wife was to be pitied for sure, bedridden as she was and cared for by that one who had stated her claim on her brother-in-law as brazenly as if she'd voiced their goings-on, but to his mind the lass had the whole of her life in front of her and something like this could put a blight on it the like of which she wouldn't recover from. If he'd had her, if there had been penetration, he would be back here to take it out of his hide no matter what his mother said.

'I'd best get back and see how Hannah is while you wait for her things.' Rose glanced at her son before clearing her throat. 'To be truthful, lad, I don't know what to do with her. You know how on top of each other we are with the lads upstairs and me and Wilbur in the front room and Naomi on the desk bed in the kitchen. And all that apart, there's always the chance she'll run into one or the other of them if she stays round here and that's enough to make the lass as skittish as a pony. She needs to put some distance between her and them to my mind.'

'You're asking me to take her to the farm?'

127

'Would you?' Rose said eagerly. 'It'd be the perfect answer for the time being. She'll be well out of the way and it'll be easier for her all round. She's without a job now, without a home and–'

'All right, all right.' Jake raised a hand, silencing his mother. 'But there's a couple of things you're forgetting. Adam won't take kindly to her coming with me and, more to the point, she might not want to. Added to which, if he did manage to interfere with her there might be a bairn at the end of all this.'

'Oh, lad, don't say that. Not a pure young lass like she is.'

'Aye, well, she still might be pure but if she's not then likely the law'll be involved and that's a whole new ball game.'

'I see that.' Rose nodded. 'But if she's all right and she wants to get away for a while? You'll take her?'

'There's always work to do on a farm and she could stay with Frank Lyndon and his wife. Since young Herbert married Florence there's only been the two of them in their cottage. Likely she'll need a woman to talk to after this lot and Clara is a motherly soul.'

'Thank you.' She reached out and squeezed his hand. 'You're a good lad, none better. Look, I'll get back and see how things are and you come when you can. I just hope Wilbur and the lads don't come back before she's gone.'

His mother was talking as though Hannah was definitely accompanying him to the farm. He didn't voice this, saying instead, 'Why?'

'She's a bit of a lass, Jake. This must have been

awful for her and she'll be so ashamed.'

'She's got nothing to be ashamed of,' he said sharply.

'Aye, well, likely she won't see it like that for a while.'

Once his mother had gone, Jake stood exactly where he was in the middle of the shop floor, his brow furrowed. His mother was one of the kindest souls on God's green earth but she had talked of Hannah being ashamed as though it was inevitable, even as though she should be. And while his mam might not think that at the heart of her, he knew plenty round these streets who would point the finger if they got to know of tonight's events. But there was no reason they should, not if Hannah came to live and work at the farm for a while until she found something else. No one had to know anything.

When Miriam entered the shop carrying a bulging cloth bag and Hannah's coat and hat over her arm, he was still in the same spot. He watched as she placed the bag and other things on the counter and then stood back a pace. He walked over and picked them up and when their eyes met, he said quietly, 'You'd better pray he wasn't able to do what he'd got in mind.'

Miriam said nothing until he reached the front door. Then her voice came low and harsh. 'You tell her from me that from this day forth I've got no daughter and she's got no mother. You tell her that from me, the ungrateful little madam.'

He turned and gazed at her. She was still determined to keep up this game of pretence she was playing. Her effrontery was amazing. When, and only when, she dropped her eyes, he said, 'It seems to me that Hannah has never had a mother, Mrs Casey, but then you'd know more about that than me.'

Out in the warm claustrophobic street, he stood for a moment, annoyed at the position he found himself in through no fault of his own. The last thing he wanted was to cart that young lass back to the farm with her in a state worse than China. And she likely wouldn't want to go with him either. He touched the side of his face, running his fingers down the lumps and bumps. All in all he wished he'd stayed home the night and had been well out of it.

His mother must have been looking out for him because she opened the front door as he reached the doorstep. 'He gave her a fright, that's all,' she whispered as he stepped into the brown-painted hall. 'She managed to get away before any real harm was done.'

'Thank God,' he said, and he meant it. 'How is she now?'

'Better.'

His mother led the way into the kitchen and when Jake entered and his gaze went to the young girl sitting in the dilapidated armchair he saw she had dried her eyes and was sipping a cup of tea. She gave him a wan smile but her voice was unfaltering when she said, 'Thank you for helping me, Mr Fletcher. I'm sorry to have been such a trouble.'

She'd got a bit about her, had Hannah. He liked folk who fought back. His thoughts made his voice warmer than usual when he said, 'No trouble, lass.'

'Mrs Wood told me what my uncle, and mother said.' She swallowed hard but again her voice did not tremble. 'It's not true, Mr Fletcher.'

'I never thought it was.'

'Thank you.'

His mother had gone to the range and was fiddling about with the kettle behind Hannah. She now inclined her head meaningfully. He knew what she meant. Clearing his throat, Jake said quietly, 'My mother was thinking you might like to get away for a bit until you've had time to decide what you want to do. Unless you feel you could go back home.'

Hannah shuddered, shaking her head.

'It's entirely up to you of course, but if you would like to get out of the town for a bit there's an old couple who live and work on the farm where I'm employed who would be glad to offer you board and lodging.'

She stared at him, her eyes wide. Rubbing her nose in a childish gesture, she said, 'But what would I do? How could I pay them? I don't have a job.'

'There's plenty of work to be found on a farm so don't worry your head about that. Since Farmer Shawe's wife died, one of the women has been helping out at the farmhouse, cooking meals and cleaning a bit, things like that, but she would be better employed in the dairy where she used to work. You could take over in the farmhouse until you decide otherwise.'

'But what if Farmer Shawe doesn't agree? He doesn't know me.'

'I know you.'

'And ... and it wouldn't get you into trouble?'

Jake smiled. 'No, it wouldn't get me into trouble.'

Hannah bowed her head for a moment, then she rose from the chair and stood taking in a deep breath. He saw her eyes were glittering with un-shed tears and realised she wasn't nearly as composed as she was trying to make them believe. But then who would be after something like that?

'This is very kind of you, Mr Fletcher,' she said in a low voice. 'And if you're sure it'll be all right with Farmer Shawe, I'd like to accept your offer. But ... but if he doesn't like it or something goes wrong, please don't think you can't tell me. Just ... just to get away for a little while will be...'

Her lips were trembling as her voice trailed away, and it was Rose who spoke into the embar-rassed silence, saying briskly, 'Well, that's settled then and there's no time like the present. You and Jake go now before it's as black as pitch out there. You've a way to walk, lass.'

'I'll get a cab,' Jake said immediately.

'No, no.' Hannah brought out a protesting hand to Jake and then dropped it by her side as sharply as if she had actually touched him. Her head again bent, she said, 'I'd rather walk if that's all right with you.'

Rose and Jake exchanged a glance over Hannah's head but Naomi stepped into the breach, hugging her friend and saying chokingly, 'Oh, Hannah, I'll miss you not being close. You'll still come and see us, won't you?'

'There's nowt to stop you coming to the farm,'

Jake interposed quickly before Hannah could reply. 'Perhaps that'd be better for the time being.'

'Aye, all right.' Realising she'd been less than tactful, Naomi nodded. 'I will. I'll come next Sunday, shall I?'

'You do that.' Only Rose understood what a concession Jake was making when he added, 'And bring whoever you like with you. All are welcome.'

He meant Adam.

Hannah bit down hard on her lower lip to prevent the tears Jake's kindness was causing from falling. Would he come? To her knowledge, none of Jake's family had ever visited the farm.

The goodbyes were awkward but eventually they left the house, Jake carrying the cloth bag and Hannah wearing her bonnet and coat, the latter covering her torn blouse. Hannah walked quietly alongside him with her head down but her eyes dry. She felt very small and lost, but this was less to do with the bulk and height of the man beside her than her mother's betrayal. When Naomi's mam had told her what her mother had said, she had been stunned, even though her mother was like she was. Her mam had chosen to take her uncle's word against hers. She was not only surprised and hurt to the core but also furiously angry. Her body ached in various places and as she walked, the tops of her legs stung where her uncle's fingernails had torn her flesh. She wanted nothing more than to stand in a bath of hot water and scrub and scrub at her skin to take the sick feeling of being dirty away.

The cloying, tainted air in the terraced streets

began to smell fresher once they were nearing the outskirts, and although the night was dark, the moon was high and the sky starlit. They hadn't spoken for some time, and they were in sight of the North Hylton Road when Jake said, 'You should have let me find a cab.'

He didn't add, 'After what you've been through,' but she knew what he meant, and it was in answer to this that she said quietly, 'I needed to walk.' It was also less embarrassing, less intimate than riding in a cab with him somehow. Now the shock of her uncle's attack was beginning to abate a little, she felt mortified she had collapsed in Jake Fletcher's arms like that. She hadn't been thinking straight at the time but she remembered now the effortlessness with which he had picked her up and carried her, and the muscled strength in the big male body. If it had been anyone but him, anyone, she wouldn't feel so strange about it. Or perhaps she would. She didn't know. She felt so muddled, so all at sea, but surmounting everything was a feeling of humiliation and degradation.

'Do you like the country?'

He was trying to make conversation but she wished he wouldn't. Rousing herself Hannah said, 'I don't know. I've only ever gone for walks on a Sunday afternoon as far as the edge of Southwick and I've never stepped foot on a farm.'

'Then perhaps my question should have been do you like the town?'

She hesitated for a moment, glancing at him and looking away again. The good side of his face was towards her and as she had done on other occasions, she thought, it must be worse for him, looking in the mirror and knowing he could have been so handsome but for the accident. There were fields stretching either side of the road now and the warm night air carried the scent of sun-drenched meadows and corn. Hannah breathed in the fragrance before she said, 'I've never really thought about it but now you ask I don't think I do. Monkwearmouth is so dirty and smelly.'

'A farm can be pretty dirty and smelly too.'

'But not in the same way.'

She didn't raise her eyes but his voice told her he was smiling when he said, 'I couldn't agree more. Nevertheless, when you're up to your eyes in mud and the wind's enough to cut you in two, you might find yourself longing for solid pavements under your feet and the shelter of the streets.'

'Do you?'

This time he laughed out loud. It was a husky sound as though he didn't do it very often. 'Never,' he said softly. 'Coal is the lifeblood of the north, I know that, and it provides the basis of other industry, even the railways, but I hate the sight of the colliery chimneys sending their black columns of smoke into the sky. That's not to say I don't respect the men who risk their lives every day working under tons of rock, whatever Adam might have told you to the contrary.' He glanced at her but she didn't look at him. After a moment, he said, 'Anyway, I'm the wrong shape for a miner. Ideally you need to be small and wiry to work those tunnels.'

'Was your father small and wiry?' She didn't

know why she had asked that because she knew no one talked about Mrs Wood's first husband. It was common knowledge he'd disappeared on the night of Jake's accident, only to be found a week later wedged under the landing at the docks. A double tragedy, everyone had said, the father getting murdered like that on the very night his bairn pulls an oil lamp on himself. But that was the way of things sometimes – it never rains but it pours. And at least the doctors managed to save the bairn.

He didn't seem bothered by the question. 'Aye. I understand he was. I'm obviously a throwback to someone in the past.'

'My da died when I was a baby.'

'Oh aye? Then we've something in common.'

They walked in silence after this until they came to the lane which led to the farm. Hannah's heart was thumping so hard she was surprised he couldn't hear it. Had she done the right thing in coming here? She didn't know anything about how things were done on a farm after all, and what if the farmer decided she couldn't stay? What if this old couple didn't want her in their cottage?

'Don't worry.'

Startled, she glanced at Jake and saw his eyes were on her. 'I'm not,' she lied.

'You don't have to stay here if you don't want to but it'll give you a breathing space, I think that's what my mother thought. And there is no need to be frightened of me.'

'I'm not,' she said again. Another lie.

They were in sight of the labourers' cottages

136

now and she thought she heard him sigh before he said quietly, 'You'll be staying with a couple called Frank and Clara Lyndon. The last of their four sons married a short while ago and moved in with the in-laws, so Frank and Clara have a spare room. They're a nice couple, you'll like them, and Clara is the sort to put you right about anything you don't understand. I'll tell them I've decided to get a housekeeper in and you're a friend of the family, that's all, OK? It's up to you if you want to say more. Get a good night's sleep and I'll come down to the cottage some time tomorrow and take you up to the farmhouse to see Farmer Shawe.'

She nodded. She felt petrified but was determined not to show it.

When they reached the small row of cottages she could see they weren't the kind of thatched affair you might see on a picture postcard or chocolate box lid. They were built of brick with three steep steps directly from the lane to the front door. She couldn't see much else by the meagre light of the moon. Jake rapped smartly on the front door. The cottage, like the ones either side of it, was in darkness, its occupants obviously in bed. It was a minute or two before a flickering light showed and then a second later the door opened.

'It's me, Frank.'

'Jake?' The large burly man holding the oil lamp peered at them. 'What's wrong, man?'

'Nothing's wrong, not really. Look, this is Hannah Casey. She's going to do for us in the farmhouse for a while and I thought she could stay with you and Clara now you've got a room free. I'm sorry about the hour but she couldn't come any earlier.'

Hannah stared at Jake's dark profile. He had made it sound as if it had all been arranged for days.

'Ee, don't stand there on the doorstep. Come in, the pair of you, come in.' A woman had come up behind the man, her grey hair in two long plaits and her plump little body wrapped in a faded brown dressing gown.

Jake stood aside for Hannah to precede him and when she climbed the three steps and entered the cottage she found herself in a small but comfortable sitting room. She watched as the man pulled down an oil lamp that hung on a chain from the ceiling and lit it before pushing it back up out of the way of their heads. His wife had taken the lamp he had been holding and placed it on a small round table covered with a fancy lace tablecloth.

'That's better.' The woman beamed at them, her rosy-cheeked face shining. 'Now you say you want the lass to stay with us? That's grand. Our Herbert's room has been going begging for months, as you know. All I'll have to do is make the bed up. I keep everything aired and shipshape.'

Hannah didn't doubt it. In the golden light from the lamps she could see that the cottage was as clean and bright as a new pin.

'Thanks, Clara.' Jake placed Hannah's bag on the floor which was covered from wall to wall with coconut matting, and then straightened. 'I'll come and see you in the morning and sort out about her board and all.'

'Don't worry your head about that, there's no rush.' Smiling at Hannah, she said, 'You're more than welcome to stay as long as you like, lass, and I mean that. It'll be nice to have another woman to talk to sometimes.'

'Thank you.' Hannah told herself she couldn't cry now, not in front of them all. She hadn't expected such a warm reception and it was weakening, undermining her resolve to put a brave face on things. Whether Clara sensed something was amiss Hannah didn't know, but suddenly the little woman was all bustle, instructing her husband to get Jake a drink while she and Hannah sorted out the room upstairs.

It wasn't a small room but it wasn't large either and, like the sitting room, it was immaculately clean. The old floorboards had been scrubbed to a bleached anaemic colour and the curtains at the sash window were blanched, a faded pattern just visible. A thick clippy mat at the foot of the double bed provided a splash of bright colour in the neutral surroundings, and the bed itself consisted of a thin flock mattress on an iron frame. Besides the bed, the room held a small chest of drawers and a studded trunk in one corner, and two rows of pegs on the far wall took the place of a wardrobe.

Clara placed the oil lamp on the chest of drawers and opened the lid of the trunk and took out linen and blankets.

'I can make up the bed, Mrs Lyndon.'

'Ee, call me Clara, lass. We don't stand on ceremony, me an' Frank. You make up the bed then

139

and I'll bring up your bag when I've had a word with Jake. I'll leave you the lamp. The privy's at the end of the garden if you want it, there's a path at the side leading to it. Each cottage has its own so it's nice and clean.'

'Thank you, and thank you for letting me stay.'

'Like I said, you're more than welcome, lass. There's another pillow or two if you want 'em in the trunk. In the old days when all my lads were at home they topped and tailed. High jinks we had then but they were happy days. Still, I've got me grandchildren now. Six at the last count and one on the way. Two little lassies and four lads an' I see plenty of 'em so I count meself fortunate.'

Once she was alone, Hannah did not immediately begin to make up the bed. She stood for a moment in the middle of the room looking around her. It seemed incredible that she was here at the farm that she had heard Naomi speak of so often and that Jake Fletcher had brought her to this place because her Uncle Edward had tried to rape her. She shut her eyes tightly. The word had been at the back of her mind since her uncle had attacked her but she hadn't been able to give heed to it before. If he had succeeded, if he'd overpowered her out there in the backyard...

But he hadn't. She opened her eyes. That was what she had to concentrate on. And whatever it was like here, however good or bad things were, it would be better than staying in the vicinity of her uncle and her mother. What would they tell her Aunt Aggie? She screwed up her face as though in pain. Whatever it was, it wouldn't be the truth. But then how could she tell her aunt the truth anyway?

She couldn't. So perhaps it was best left alone. And Adam. What would he say when he discovered what had happened to her? Would he be sorry they had quarrelled or wouldn't he care?

She crossed her arms, her hands gripping her waist, and swayed for a few moments, the lost feeling swamping her. From the room below she heard voices and then the front door opening and closing. Jake Fletcher had gone. She should have thanked him again.

Forcing herself into action she began to put the sheets and blankets on the bed. They smelt of lavender, fresh and wholesome. When Clara brought her bag up a minute or two later, Hannah was sitting on the made-up bed, her hands in her lap and her feet on the floor.

'You all right, hinny? Would you like a hot drink to go to bed with?'

'I'm all right, Mrs Lyndon.' She couldn't bring herself to say Clara. It didn't seem right, not with her being young enough to be the woman's granddaughter. 'But if I'm going to stay in your home I think there's something you ought to know. It's only fair. And then if you don't want me to have your spare room that'll be fine.'

Clara didn't interrupt while Hannah told her what had occurred that evening but at one point during the telling she came and sat on the bed and put her arm round the shoulders of the young girl Jake had brought to the house. Hannah was shaking by the time she had finished but she wasn't crying. She didn't do that until Clara said, 'Lass, I perhaps shouldn't say it but your mam wants a good kick up the backside in my opinion.

141

As for that uncle of yours, it's a pity men like him aren't placed in line when the veterinary comes to geld the bullocks.'

'You believe me then?'

'I believe you, lass, and so would anyone else. Now I'm going to get you a nice warm glass of milk and a little tot of a sleeping draught I have now and again when my leg is playing me up. What you need is a good sleep and everything will be different in the morning. You jump into bed and I'll be back in two shakes of a lamb's tail.'

Hannah did as the little woman suggested, taking off her skirt and blouse and stockings and climbing into bed in her petticoat. She would unpack her things in the morning.

The sleeping draught was bitter. She drank it down along with the milk to please Clara although she was sure she wouldn't sleep. Her mind didn't seem to be able to stop replaying the scene in the backyard.

When Clara left, taking the oil lamp with her, Hannah lay down, the soothing scent of lavender enveloping her and the faint hoot of an owl in the distance comforting in that it told her she was far away from her uncle. She was asleep within two minutes.

PART THREE

1926 – Piecrust Promises

Chapter 9

When Hannah awoke the next morning after a solid night's sleep, it was to a room filled with sunlight. She lay for a moment or two with her eyes open but her mind hovering somewhere between sleep and consciousness, the sleeping draught blanketing her thoughts. And then she remembered. Sitting up in bed, she looked round the room, seeing it clearly for the first time without the shadows and flickers of the oil lamp distorting things.

It was nice. She glanced at a posy of lavender which had been dried and fixed to the wall above the chest of drawers, the pale, slightly mauvish blue standing out against the whitewashed wall. Her mam would turn her nose up at these spartan surroundings, no doubt, but she would far rather be here than in the flat above the shop. *Her mam.* Her mouth thinning, Hannah threw back the covers and climbed out of bed, padding across the sun-warmed floorboards to the window. Her uncle had been horrible, vile, but her mother was even worse. She didn't care if she never saw the pair of them again in the whole of her life.

Refusing to acknowledge the surge of hurt in her chest, she pushed up the sash window and stuck her head outside. Her room faced the narrow strip of back garden, and beyond that were corn fields, bright and golden in the sunshine.

The sky was high and blue and the sun was hot on her face and she smiled. Yesterday she had thought she would never smile again but this morning the joy of life was welling up again, so did that make her shallow? Frivolous? Her mother had often called her frivolous. Well, she didn't care if she was. She was glad to be here. Glad to escape working with her uncle in the shop. Not that she was afraid of hard work, and she'd prove it to everyone here. In spite of not being one of them, she would work her socks off. She'd do anything and she would pay her way or her name wasn't Hannah Casey.

She began to rummage through her bag so she could get dressed, promising herself she'd have a wash later when she found out how things were done here. She pulled out her other workday blouse; the one she had been wearing the day before would have to be mended before she could put it on. She'd like to throw it away, it felt contaminated, but of course she couldn't afford to do that. The bruises on the tops of her arms from her uncle's grip on her were already turning different colours and the scratches on her legs had an area of bruising round them too. She was glad she could cover all the marks with her clothes; at least the evidence of the attack would be hidden when she met the farmer.

When she was dressed she made her bed and then brushed the tangles out of her hair. With no mirror in the room she didn't attempt to put her hair up in its normal coils on top of her head; she simply wove it into a single plait and then pinned it firmly to her scalp. She wanted to look neat

146

and tidy when Jake came for her. It was important the farmer saw her as a respectable woman in view of the circumstances which had brought her here. She hadn't led her uncle on, she *hadn't*, despite what her mother had said but somehow she felt as though part of this was her fault. What had made him think he could treat her like that?

Taking a deep breath, she told herself not to think about it for now. She had to go downstairs and begin to fit into her life here as best she could.

Clara was in the kitchen and she turned as Hannah entered, smiling as she said, 'There you are, lass. The sleeping draught did its job then. Never fails, that doesn't. Breakfast is long since past and I've just taken Frank his mid-morning bite, but help yourself to a cup of tea, I've just made a brew. And there's a shive of stottie cake and some cold bacon on the slab in the pantry.'

'I've overslept.' Belatedly Hannah realised how late in the morning it was. Hardly an auspicious start. 'Has Mr Fletcher called?'

'Jake? No, lass, don't worry your head about him. I saw him crossing the yard on my way back from Frank and told him I'd given you something to help you sleep. He'll be down at some point, never fear.'

Hannah nodded, sitting down at the kitchen table. This room was not what she had expected. There was no range as such, but a fire was burning in the deep hearth, above which hung a black kale pot suspended from a thick chain attached to a crossbar an inch or two below the chimney opening. Just above the fire a large square steel

147

shelf formed of bars like a grating had a big black kettle standing on it, and to one side of the hearth and built into the wall was what looked like an oven.

There didn't appear to be a scullery attached to the cottage. Clara was busy washing a number of pots and pans in a stone sink set beneath the kitchen window and either side of this were two tables obviously used for preparing food and storing crockery and dishes to be washed. The table Hannah was sitting at was of better quality with a leather-covered top. Further along one wall were several racks of open shelves holding everything the kitchen required, and at the far end of these, next to the back door, a tin bath stood propped on its side.

Again everything was spotlessly clean. You could have eaten your dinner off the stone-flagged floor.

After Hannah had poured herself and Clara a cup of tea and declined anything to eat, the small woman dried her hands and came to sit at the kitchen table. 'I'm to show you round the farm when you're ready,' she said after taking several sips of the strong tannic brew. 'Not the farm-house of course, but the rest of it. You might find the farmhouse a bit of a mess when you first go in, lass,' she added, lowering her voice although there was no one in the cottage but the two of them. 'Enid, her who does for Jake and the master, she's not too particular. You know what I mean? And to be fair she's got her own family to cook and clean for and she helps out in the dairy when she can. To my mind they've needed a proper housekeeper long before this but as I understand it the master was a bit funny about another woman coming in and doing much. Fond of his missus, the master was.'

Oh great. Her face must have showed her consternation because Clara smiled, her voice hearty when she said, 'But you'll be fine, lass. Don't worry about that. You can cook, hinny?'

'Yes. Well, a bit. I can make bread and pastry and stews, things like that.' But she had never cooked on such basic devices before. The range in the flat had been a prestige, up-to-date one.

'Then you're halfway there. Fill a man's stomach and they're as happy as pigs in muck. That's what I say.'

Hannah smiled weakly. She was beginning to realise Clara was something of a character.

When they had finished their tea, Clara took her on a tour of the farm. It was pleasant in the hot sunshine with a breeze blowing, but Hannah was too nervous about the coming meeting with the farmer to appreciate the fine weather. Her inward agitation increased tenfold when it dawned on her how extensive the farm was. The byres and barns, stables and store sheds, big harness room, rows of pigsties – it seemed to stretch forever, and surrounding all of it were rolling fields of corn and beet and turnips and the like. And the cattle. Acres and acres of fat cattle.

'Grand, isn't it?' Clara beamed at her, as proud as if the credit was all hers. They finished their walk close to where Frank and another labourer were working in the fields. Clara raised her hand to her husband who waved back before resuming his task. 'He's cutting the green meat,' said Clara by way of explanation.

Hannah looked at Frank from under her straw bonnet. His scythe didn't look to be cutting any meat, green or otherwise.

Clara noticed her puzzlement. 'Ee, sorry, lass. I'm not doing very well at telling you what's what, am I?' She laughed, her rosy cheeks like little apples. 'The green meat is what we call the tares an' clover and triflomen, that's the red kind of clover, you know?'

Hannah didn't but she nodded anyway.

'Some of it they'll save and mix with the hay chaff and the wheat chaff – there's little goes to waste on a farm. Waste not, want not, eh, lass?'

Hannah nodded again. There were a hundred questions she wanted to ask but she thought a good deal of them might sound silly to Clara. As they began to walk back to the cottage, she voiced one which she considered perfectly reasonable. 'How many people are there at the farm?'

'How many? Let me see. I'll start with the ones who live here, shall I? Well, there's me an' Frank, as you know, and my Herbert and his wife Florence live with Florence's parents next but one, along with Florence's two younger brothers. Rascals, Caleb and Peter can be, but their mam an' da, Sybil and Neville, are salt of the earth. Herbert and Florence had a bairn at the start of the summer and he's the bonniest baby you've ever seen.'

She chuckled and Hannah smiled. Clara's pleasure in life was infectious.

'Then next door to us there's the Osbornes, Jack and Enid and their brood. Daniel, he's twenty-five and as bright as a button; John, he's twenty or thereabouts, and then there's the three lassies, Grace, Anne and Dora. Isaac Mallard's in the end cottage, he's a miserable old devil, is Isaac. His wife died years ago and they had no bairns. Jake lived with them for a time when he first come to the farm but then the master had him up at the farmhouse. Merciful release, I should think that was.'

Hannah's head was reeling but Clara wasn't finished yet. They had left the fields and were now approaching the farm from a back road which was so narrow it was little more than a single-file track for the cattle to walk down. Trying to avoid the cow pats in their path was taking all Hannah's concentration.

'Then my other three lads, they live in the next village, they come of a morning. They've all got their eye on Isaac's cottage when he goes, but I've said to 'em, they'll have to fight it out among themselves and the master might have other plans for it anyway. And then there's the casual labour the master employs at harvest and so on, tinkers mostly, but they work well and keep themselves to themselves. That's it, lass.'

Hannah was wishing she hadn't asked, she felt more confused than ever. 'Do any of the women work on the farm?'

Clara glanced at her, her face expressing that this was a strange question. 'Aye, of course, we all do, an' the bairns when they're back from school. And the master's fair, not like on some farms I could name. Even the bairns get their wage, same as the rest of us. On some farms it's just the men who get paid and their families are expected to

151

muck in for nothing. Course the farmers say the man's wage reflects what their families do, but don't you believe it. No, lass, it's not just the miners who are abused and played on, not by a long chalk, but what can the poor folk do with jobs being so scarce? It's that or the workhouse for most of 'em.'

Clara shook her head, the thick bun at the back of her neck wobbling. 'But like I say, we're in clover here.' Her laugh rang out again. 'Clover, I said, an' this being Clover Farm. The master encourages book-learning and all that, an' again there's many who don't. Daniel Osborne, he took to reading and arithmetic like a duck to water and he's not been penalised for it, just the opposite. Not like at Dobson's farm over the quarry. He's a nasty bit of work, Farmer Dobson.'

Clara continued to chatter as they made their way to the cottage, filling her in on how this was done and that. They met Enid Osborne and two of her daughters going into the house next door and Clara introduced them. The three were pleasant enough but without Clara's warmth, and Enid's eyes were penetrating as they looked her up and down.

In Clara's kitchen they sat at the table and began shelling peas. Hannah said softly, 'Thank you for making me so welcome, Mrs Lyndon.'

'Go on with you, lass, why wouldn't I? And the bees had told me to expect you so it was no surprise.'

'The bees?'

'Aye. I had a big dumble-dore pay a visit yesterday for most of the afternoon so I knew a stranger would call before midnight. I made him welcome until such time as he took his leave so I knew the newcomer would bear no ill will.'

Clara had spoken so matter-of-factly it was clear the omen was a well-known one among farm folk, although Hannah had not heard it spoken of in the town. 'A dumble-dore is a bumblebee?' she guessed out loud.

'Aye, that's right, hinny.'

It wasn't only practical things she was going to have to learn but a whole new language, including folklore. 'I didn't know that about the bees,' she admitted.

'No?' Clara was amazed. 'But you know to make a cricket welcome with a drink of moist tea leaves if it should venture in, to ward off hearing bad news?'

Hannah shook her head.

'Ee, hinny.' Clara stared at her. 'What do they teach the bairns in the towns? Well, if you hear an owl hoot in the day you get yourself to the church mighty quick an' light a few candles or else there'll be a death in the family for sure. And if you come across the little folk in the woods, don't stare at them unless you want a face full of warts.'

Hannah wanted to laugh but she could see from Clara's face that she was in deadly earnest. 'All right,' Hannah said solemnly.

They continued to talk as Clara got Frank's lunch ready, a huge slab of baked bread pudding full of fruit and brown sugar and a chunk of cheese, to be washed down with a bottle of cold tea. As Frank was eating out in the fields, Hannah offered to take it to him and she set off at midday,

Clara's big wicker basket over her arm.

Once past the pigsties the air became heavy with the sweetness of warm grass, the breeze carrying the scents from the surrounding fields and hedgerows. Hannah walked quickly, she didn't want anyone to think she was taking her time, but all the while she breathed in great gulps of the fragrant air. She glanced up into the high blue sky where a few white clouds drifted lazily, then moved her gaze to the panorama of the surrounding fields, If only everything was all right with Adam, if he still cared for her and wanted her to be his lass, she felt she could be happy here. But she'd die if he didn't want anything more to do with her, she wouldn't be able to bear it. She loved him so much. What had he thought when his mam had told him about her uncle? And her coming to the farm with Jake Fletcher? He wouldn't like it, she knew that, but would he understand she'd had no option? That she'd had to get away? Please, please, let him still love me, she prayed as she walked. Please, God, let him come with Naomi at the weekend.

'Hello there.' She had reached the gate leading into the field where Frank was working, and as she went to open it a young man coming along the path called to her. 'You must be Hannah. I'm Daniel Osborne.'

She waited until he was standing in front of her before she said politely, 'How do you do?'

Smiling, he said, 'Nice to meet you,' and held out his hand.

Shyly she took it. His grip was firm but he did not prolong the contact, shading his eyes with his hand as he said, 'Jake told me this morning he's hoping you'll work in the farmhouse.'

Remembering the woman who presently worked there was this man's mother, Hannah nodded uncomfortably, even as she thought how nice it was of Jake to present things that way, as though it was her doing them a favour rather than the other way round. Hannah stared into Daniel's ruddy, fresh-looking face. He had light brown eyes and even lighter brown hair and he did not resemble the sharp-eyed woman she had seen going into the cottage next door to Clara's. Remembering how Enid had looked at her, she said, 'Do you think your mother would mind if I took the job?'

His brief hesitation confirmed what she'd suspected, even when in the next moment he said, 'Mind? Of course not. She used to help out when the mistress got middling so it was the natural thing for the master to ask her to do a bit more when the mistress died, but he never said it was for ever. Besides, what with helping out in the dairy and looking after the lot of us she's got enough on her plate.'

'Couldn't one of your sisters have taken on the job?'

'In the farmhouse?' Again he hesitated before shaking his head. 'My mother's always maintained the master wouldn't like it but I don't suppose she's ever asked.'

Hannah nodded, feeling awkward. It was possible that Farmer Shawe wouldn't want her as his housekeeper but if he did, she wouldn't want to cause any ill feeling by taking Enid's job.

As though he was aware he'd said too much; Daniel's voice was overhearty when he said, 'I'd better get on, we're due to start bringing the harvest in the morrer and I've people to see.'

She watched him for a moment as he strode away and then she turned and opened the gate into the field. His words had caused the brightness of the day to fade a little.

Hannah was weeding between the runner bean stakes in Clara's garden, one of the little woman's sunbonnets on her head because her straw hat kept falling off when she bent over, when Jake came to the cottage. She heard his voice first as he talked with Clara in the kitchen. As she straightened her aching back, he came out of the back door. Smiling at her, he said, 'Making yourself useful, I see.'

The usual nerves constrained her voice and for the life of her she couldn't smile back. She felt terribly embarrassed after everything that had transpired the previous night. All day she had found herself wondering what he'd really thought when her mother had said what she had. She knew her voice was stilted when she said, 'Yes, Mr Fletcher.'

'Good, good.' The smile had left his face. 'Well, Farmer Shawe is ready to see you but perhaps you'd better wash your hands first.'

'Oh yes, yes.' Visibly flustered she followed him into the cottage, and washed her hands in the deep sink with a little warm water from the kettle while Jake talked with Clara in the sitting room. She took off Clara's sunbonnet, smoothed her hair and put on her own hat, checking her skirt and blouse to make sure they weren't mucky. Her boots were dusty from the dry earth and she hastily wiped them with a damp rag before walking through to the sitting room. She stood inside the door, waiting for Jake to finish his conversation with Clara.

'Ready?' There was a flat note in his voice now.

Hannah nodded, glancing at Clara who smiled encouragingly.

As she followed Jake out of the house she realised one of the things she found intimidating about him was that he wasn't dressed like the rest of the men. Frank and the others she had seen thus far were wearing corduroy trousers which were subdued by long use to the colour of the earth and tied with string under the knees. Their bleached shirts, faded waistcoats and hard, heavy boots denoted their station in life. Naomi's brother, on the other hand, was clothed well, even smartly. In spite of the hot weather, he wore a jacket that sat full and square on his big frame, his shirt and tie were of fine material and a gold pocket watch and chain showed on his waistcoat. Even his cap, which matched the charcoal grey of his coat, was of good quality. Suddenly she could understand and sympathise with Adam's antipathy towards his half-brother. There was Adam and his father and brother unable to go to church on a Sunday because their suits were in pawn, and suits bought second-hand from the tallyman at that, and yet Jake Fletcher could afford to walk about dressed like one of the gentry, and on a weekday. Unbidden came the recollection of being held close to his body, the faint aroma of

157

tobacco and another smell – a pleasant almost scented fragrance which was a composite of fresh linen and clean skin – very real in her nostrils.

Lost in her thoughts, she started and almost fell over her own feet when he said, 'We're going to begin harvesting tomorrow so I'm afraid you've been thrown in the deep end somewhat. All the old hands are needed at the plough.'

He meant Enid. To confirm this, she said, 'Even the women?'

'Just so. Of course Farmer Shawe's wife didn't work in the fields,' he spoke as if she would know this, 'but she would see to the lunch for the workers.'

Hannah stared at him in alarm. 'What did she bring them?'

'Ham and egg pie, bread and cheese, fruit loaves, nothing fancy. And Farmer Shawe always makes sure there's plenty of beer and cider for them that want it, along with milk for the bairns.'

Feeling as though this was some sort of test, Hannah was determined not to let her agitation show. 'Right.' She nodded as though she was perfectly used to cooking for umpteen hungry adults and bairns. 'I can do that.'

Jake glanced at her out of the corner of his eye. She had more than her fair share of gumption, he'd give her that. He'd noticed it the night before and it was more apparent today. She'd need every ounce of it the mood Seamus was in. Mind, if it hadn't been Hannah coming in, it would have been someone else, because he for one couldn't stand Enid's slipshod ways a day more. Seamus hadn't liked it last night when he'd

158

said Bess would turn in her grave if she could see the state of the house, but it was true right enough. And no one was aiming to take Bess's place, this little lass least of all.

As they approached the farmhouse by way of the kitchen, Jake stopped on the threshold, his voice low as he said, 'Farmer Shawe knows you've had a falling out with your uncle and mother but that's all, all right? It's up to you if you want to tell him what occurred last night but he won't hear it from me, it's your business.'

Her cheeks flaming, Hannah nodded.

'And ... and he's got out of bed the wrong side this morning so don't be taken aback if he's a bit sharp. It means nothing.'

Hannah stared at him. She had been right. The farmer didn't want her here. The sunlight was falling on the damaged side of his face, highlighting the puckered skin so it looked worse than usual. Swallowing hard, she said softly, 'I haven't made things difficult for you with Farmer Shawe, have I?'

He did not answer for a moment but stared at her. Then he said equally softly, 'Don't worry your head about that, lass. Seamus and I get on well and he trusts my judgement.' He opened the door into the kitchen and allowed her to precede him into the house, almost treading on her heels as she stopped abruptly.

Turning, her manner completely natural for once, she said, 'This is lovely, lovely. I expected... Well, something like the cottages I suppose, but not this? Her gaze moved over the room which in her eyes was enormous. The huge range with two

159

ovens and hobs, the long wooden mantelpiece holding brass ornaments and candlesticks, the massive oak table with eight hard-backed, flock-cushioned chairs, a high dresser containing china of every description – she could barely take it all in. In front of the range were two well-padded armchairs, a rocking chair with matching padding standing in a corner of the kitchen next to a cooking table. One wall had shelves holding fancy plates with country and hunting scenes painted on them, and next to the range in an alcove was a fitted unit stacked with pots and pans and all manner of cooking utensils. The floor was flagged but the biggest clippy mat Hannah had ever seen was in front of the range, and two cats were lying on it. They raised curious eyes before sauntering over and twining themselves round Jake's legs, purring loudly.

'Oh, is this Buttons and Polly?' Hannah crouched down, stroking Buttons' sleek grey fur. 'Buttons was always my favourite kitten, Naomi's too. Although she was the runt of the litter she was such a funny, determined little thing. She seems very happy here.'

'She should be, the pair of them have the life of old Riley. We tried them outside with the other farm cats when they first came but that didn't work, they were always waiting on the doorstep to nip into the house. The others earn their keep mousing and ratting but these two...' Jake shook his head in disgust, but Hannah noticed he bent down and fondled Polly's head before walking to the far door. 'They wouldn't have been allowed in when Bess – Mrs Shawe – was alive. She had a couple of budgies she was fond of. She was very houseproud, was Bess, but there was never a word said about all their feathers and seeds puthering everywhere.'

He smiled and Hannah smiled back. She thought to herself that the farmer's wife would have had something to say about the state of the kitchen it she could see it now. The brass didn't look as though it had been cleaned for years, the black-leaded range was as bad, dust coated every surface, and the floor was filthy. Her fingers itched to spring-clean everything.

'Farmer Shawe's in the study.'

Hannah left Buttons and followed Jake into the hall, passing a stone step into what appeared to be a scullery on the right side of the kitchen as she did so.

The hall was a narrow passageway with two doors on the opposite side to the kitchen. The first Jake passed, saying, 'In there's the dining room,' before stopping at the second. 'This is the study. The sitting room is on the first floor.' At her look of surprise, he added, 'The layout seemed a little strange to me at first but that's how the house was built a couple of hundred years ago.'

Hannah glanced at the substantial staircase leading to the upper floors. Like everything else in the house, it needed a good polish but the open treads looked solid and strong. It was grand. The whole house was grand. But neglected. It needed a woman's touch. She could see now that Jake hadn't just been being kind when he said they needed a permanent full-time housekeeper.

This thought was heartening but her stomach

still turned over when after knocking on the study door Jake opened it, saying, 'Seamus, I've brought Hannah to see you,' before standing aside for her to enter the room.

A stout, bulbous-nosed individual was sitting facing the door behind a large mahogany desk. A crackling log fire was blazing in the fireplace despite the hot day. The farmer looked up from the papers in front of him. 'All right, come and sit down.' He nodded at a straight-backed chair positioned at an angle to the desk. As she walked across the room and sat down, Jake shut the door, leaving the two of them alone. 'So.' Blue eyes as hard and clear as glass looked her over. 'Jake tells me he's offered you the job of housekeeper.'

As she stared into the creased face, Hannah deliberated whether to say yes or not. After a moment, she said cautiously, 'Mr Fletcher said there might be a job available, that's all.'

'That's what Mr Fletcher said, is it?' Seamus nodded. He had been more than a little put out when Jake had told him what he'd done, it was so out of character for one thing. He was convinced there was more to this than met the eye. This lass was a friend of Jake's sister; had she decided that Jake would be a good meal ticket? Was that it? She was pretty enough to turn a man's head, especially with Jake looking as he did. He didn't have lasses falling over themselves to walk out with him. And that was all well and good, but what if she decided to give him the old heave-ho after a while? Break his heart most likely. But he was running away with himself here. He needed to find out a few facts. 'How old are you?' he asked abruptly.

'I was sixteen in March.'

'And what have you been doing since you left school?' And then he answered his own question by saying, 'Working in a shop, Jake tells me. How do you think that qualifies you for taking on a housekeeping post?'

He didn't like her, thought Hannah. Well, that was all right because she didn't like him. Her body held stiffly, she said, 'It was my uncle's shop and my mother and I lived above it in a flat with my uncle and aunt. My aunt's bedridden and from an early age I've been helping out with the cooking and things like that.'

'Helping out?' Seamus snorted. 'That's a mite different to taking on the running of my house, let me tell you. Did Jake mention you'll be seeing to the lunches for the workers during harvest?' Hannah nodded. 'And there's plenty of other things you'll be expected to do. Washing and ironing our clothes, mine and Jake's; seeing to the hens, stocking the storeroom off the scullery – you know how to make jam and preserves?' he finished sharply. 'Crab apple jelly, gooseberry chutney, rhubarb jam?'

Hannah looked at him. She could lie but she wasn't going to. 'No, we had things like that from my uncle's shop but it doesn't mean I can't learn to make my own.'

'And when we kill a pig, what about making the sausages and brawn and what have you? You ever boiled a pig's head and made brawn?'

He knew full well she hadn't. 'No.'

'And when Isaac Mallard drops by a few

rabbits his whippets have caught, can you skin and gut 'em for the pot, along with plucking a pheasant ready for the oven?'

Hannah's eyes narrowed on this thoroughly objectionable man. 'I can learn to do the rest but I won't pluck a wild bird,' she said flatly. And if that statement lost her the job, so be it.

'You won't, eh?' He peered at her. Then he said quietly, 'And why is that then?'

She raised her head a fraction higher. 'Because there's enough food on a farm without killing birds, wild ones. Or at least that's the way I see it.'

Seamus settled back in his seat. 'You've never gone hungry, lass. I can see that.'

'You're right, Farmer Shawe, I haven't.' She swallowed. 'And I've nothing against folk doing whatever it is they have to do when they have bairns to feed and nothing in the cupboard. But like I said, a farm like this one doesn't need to put wild birds on the table.'

Seamus stared at the young bit of a lass Jake had brought in. She was bonny. Bit too thin perhaps but then she hadn't the curves of full womanhood filling her out yet. 'You're no country lass, that's plain to see.'

Hannah had no reply to this and so she remained silent.

'My wife was from the town too, did Jake tell you that?'

'No.'

Seamus made a sound in his throat that could have meant anything. He reached for his pipe and filled it from a pouch of tobacco he brought

164

out of the pocket of his jacket. When the pipe was lit to his satisfaction and he had puffed away for a few moments, he said, 'Well, she was, and like you she'd got some funny ideas. It was her who insisted on us having a garden at the back of the house. Not for vegetables or owt like that, but for flowers. *Flowers,*'he emphasised. 'She got the lads to make some seats an' so on and a bird table or two. She liked seeing 'em come to feed. Daft, I called it.' His voice had softened, belying his impatient words. And then it changed again as he asked aggressively, 'I suppose you'd disagree?'

'That it was daft? Yes, I would.'

'Aye, I thought so. Never mind that the farm cats got wily enough to make sure they had a change from mice in their diet now and again, I suppose?'

Hannah blinked. She really, *really* disliked this man.

'Got me building a contraption at the end of the garden, she did, all netted round so the cats couldn't get in. Laughing stock I'd have been if anyone had found out. Didn't think of that though, did she?' He scowled at her. 'Course it's got all overgrown since she went. Haven't got time for such things on a farm.'

She stared at him, wondering how her feelings could change in the space of a second. Softly, she said, 'I'm sorry your wife died, Farmer Shawe.'

His scowl deepened. His voice little more than a growl, he said, 'What's made you want to leave the town and come to work on a farm anyhow?'

She hesitated. She didn't have to tell him, Jake had told her she didn't. But somehow, as with

165

Clara, she felt she had to. Quietly she told him the bare outline of what had occurred, her hands tightly gripped between her knees and her head bent. The silence stretched for some moments after she had finished. Then he fiddled with his pipe, which had gone out, before standing up and walking over to the window where he stood looking out into the stone-flagged yard, his back towards her. 'Aye, well, you'd better get Jake to show you where everything is,' he said gruffly. 'I haven't got all day, you know.'

'You mean I've got the job?'

'Aye.' He turned. 'And it'll be no easy ride, mind. Tomorrow least of all. We'll start proper once the harvest is finished. It'll be enough for you to do to see to the lunches midday and get a bite for me an' Jake come nightfall till then.'

'Thank you, Farmer Shawe. Oh, thank you. I'll work hard, I promise.'

'Promise, do you? Aye, well, we'll see. Like my old mam used to say, some promises are like piecrust, made to be broken.'

'Not mine,' said Hannah strongly.

The shadow of a smile touched the tough old face but his voice was still brusque when he said, 'It takes more than words to dig a ditch, lass. Still, like I said, we'll see. One thing's for sure, you're no businesswoman. You haven't asked what wage I'm offering yet.'

She stared at him. It had been the last thing on her mind.

'What did your uncle pay you for working in his shop?'

'I didn't get a wage as such. He'd taken me and

166

my mother in when I was a baby and so I was sort of repaying him...' Her voice trailed away at the look on the farmer's face.

'By, lass, your uncle's a wrong 'un in more ways than one. I can't abide a skinflint at the best of times. Strikes me he's long overdue a good hiding.'

'Mrs Wood, Mr Fletcher's mother, she said Mr Fletcher hit him last night.'

'Did he? Good on him.' They looked at each other for a moment. 'Well, as you'll be living in, shall we say ten shillings a week to start with? We'll see how you do 'cos one thing's for sure, you've plenty to learn.'

'Living in?' Hannah repeated uncertainly. Something made her think he didn't mean she would be staying with Clara and Frank.

'Aye, here, in the farmhouse. If you're going to take on being the housekeeper proper I don't want you back and forth umpteen times a day. I might as well keep Enid otherwise. Me and Jake have got rooms at the top of the house but there's two bedrooms on the first floor an' all. Take your pick out of them. The wife had the whole house done up when she first came here, liked things just so, she did. We thought there'd be bairns to fill every room but in the event we only had our Terence.'

He paused, sitting down at his desk once more. His head bent, he began to sort through the papers in front of him. 'You'd better get Enid to talk you through everything, she knows what's what, all right?'

Sensing the interview was at an end, Hannah walked to the door. She opened it before saying, 'Thank you,' but apart from a grunt the farmer did not speak or raise his head.

In the hall, Hannah stood for a moment. Her heart was racing and she put her hand to her chest. She was going to be the housekeeper in this beautiful farmhouse. Could she do it?

The steady ticking of a grandfather clock to one side of the enormous front door brought her eyes to its benevolent face. Nearly three o'clock on the first day of her new life. And that was what this was, a new life, and she would make it work no matter what she had to do. It might take a while but she'd have this place spick and span, and she'd sort out Mrs Shawe's garden too. She would work till she dropped to make sure Jake didn't live to regret bringing her here.

Chapter 10

'I don't understand why she's took off like this, that's what I'm saying. Miriam's gone on at her more times than I can remember but it's never caused the lass to walk out and stay away.'

'Aye, well, perhaps this was one time too many.'

'But to leave without saying goodbye to you and me? Something isn't right, Edward. Are you sure Miriam's telling us all of it?' Agatha stared at her husband. He was hiding something. She knew him far better than he thought she did and she'd bet her bottom dollar he was hiding something. She had sensed something was afoot last night when he'd come to bed. There had been a lot of what she could only term coming and going before he had come into the room, and then he had been strange, over-solicitous. She always knew when he'd been with Miriam because he acted in a similar way, but this had been different. If it wasn't ridiculous she could have imagined he was frightened. And all this about having tripped over a crate in the yard and banged his face. She wasn't sure if she believed that either.

'Miriam told you they had an argument, didn't she? That's as much as I know. Apparently Hannah got so worked up she walked out and went round Naomi's, and the next thing Jake Fletcher is on the doorstep demanding her things and saying she's going to work at the farm. She's over sixteen, Aggie. I couldn't stop her now then.'

'No, I see that, but are we sure it's all above board, him taking her to that farm? She's a bit lass, Edward, an' a bonny one at that.'

'It's a farm, lass, not a house of ill repute.' Edward smiled, but when he saw his wife wasn't having any of it, he added quickly, 'Now come on, Aggie, stop worrying. Hannah's not a bairn any more and she's more than capable of taking care of herself. She knows where we are if she wants us.'

'I don't like it.' For once, Agatha had the bit between her teeth. 'And I'd like to know exactly what Miriam did to make the lass leave like that. She's never been what I'd call a mother to Hannah, you know that.'

'Aye, well, they're still mother and daughter and what went on is between them, the way I see it. I know you've always been fond of the girl but

169

she can be a handful at times. You don't see it, confined to bed as you are. She always puts on a good show for you.'

Agatha looked at him in such a way he moved from one foot to the other and rubbed his nose with his thumb. He turned and walked to the door. 'Now you sit and read that *People's Friend* I've brought you. You're following the serial, aren't you? And don't worry about Hannah. Likely she wants to spread her wings a bit, it's only natural at her age. Just let things be and they'll work out all right.'

Outside the room, Edward leaned back against the bedroom door for a moment, his eyes shut and his teeth clenched. Straightening, he walked through to the sitting room where Miriam was sitting waiting for him. 'Well?' She arched her thin eyebrows. 'Still going on about Hannah, is she? She's given me gyp all day on and off, driven me mad. Thinks more about that madam than you or me, that's for sure.'

Edward didn't miss the covert message in the words. Miriam had him over a barrel and he knew it. He also knew his mistress was fully aware of the truth of what had occurred in the backyard and was choosing to ignore it – for a price.

This was confirmed when Miriam stood up and draped her arms round his neck. 'Don't fret,' she said softly. 'Hannah's gone, and Aggie thinks it's because of a row with me like we decided. Even if someone said otherwise, if you and I keep to our story it'll be all right. I love you, Edward. You know that.'

He swallowed hard, wishing he could extricate

170

himself from her embrace but knowing he didn't dare. 'I didn't touch the girl,' he mumbled weakly.

'I know, I know.' She smiled. 'Of course you didn't. Why would you, when you've got me? And I'll always do what you want, you know that, because we love each other. We do, don't we, Edward? We love each other.'

'Aye, aye.'

'Say it. Say we love each other.'

Again he swallowed. His voice flat, he said, 'We love each other.'

'And we'll forget all this with Hannah. She's gone now, she's out of our lives and she can rot at that farm, for all I care. You can get someone else to help you in the shop, a lad this time, I think. There's so many out of work, after all. Young Bart Crawford's just left school, you could have him. Yes, Bart will do very well, I think. I'll have a word with his mother tomorrow. She'll be pleased, what with her husband and Bart's brothers being laid off from the pit months now. Aye, all in all, Hannah going is no bad thing, Edward. Look at it like that. Now come and sit down and put your feet up and I'll get you a beer. Dinner will be ready in half an hour and it's your favourite.'

Edward sat down. In his mind's eye he could see the years stretching out, full of evenings like this one. Him and Miriam. Together.

A few yards down the street Hannah was also the topic of conversation in the Wood household. The twins were already in bed in the room they shared with Stephen and Peter, but the rest of the family were sitting round the kitchen table. The evening meal had been sparse and had consisted of a broth made with a ham shank and vegetables Jake had brought at the weekend. Even the thick wedges of stottie cake had been baked using flour from the farm.

It was Adam who was saying, and for the umpteenth time, 'I still don't see why she had to go with him, that's all.'

Rose stared at her son. If he said that once more she would box his ears, big as he was.

'And you needn't look at me like that, Mam. She could have bedded down with Naomi in the kitchen.'

'The desk bed isn't big enough for one let alone two, and how would I feed another mouth? The chances of her picking up work just like that are few and far between and you know it. And it was me who asked Jake to take her, I've told you. Apart from anything else she needed to get away from her uncle.' Rose glanced at Peter and Stephen as she spoke before her eyes returned to Adam. The younger children knew nothing of the circumstances that had caused Hannah to leave.

Sulkily, Adam said, 'He'll love this, playing the big man. And I'm supposed to go to the farm, cap in hand, and ask to see her?'

'*Give me patience!*' Rose stood up abruptly, her voice sharp as she said to her two younger sons, 'Get yourselves away to bed and don't wake the twins. I want no playing about the night.' Not that the poor little devils had much energy for playing up, she thought in the next moment. Everybody was skinnier and quieter these days and her lads were no exception.

Once the two boys had left the kitchen, Rose stopped clearing the table. Speaking to Adam but intending her words for Wilbur too, she said, 'I'm sick and tired of you griping about Jake. There's no way we could have had Hannah here the way things are. Have you looked in that cupboard lately? Have you? Well, don't bother, there's nowt in it. And you might not like to hear it but if it wasn't for your brother you'd likely be going to bed on an empty stomach.'

'That's right, rub it in. It's not my fault we're locked out.'

'I know that.' She was conscious that Wilbur had kept his head down and had remained silent. More than anything else in the last weeks and months, it brought home how bad things were. 'I know that,' she repeated more softly. 'But it wouldn't hurt you to show a little gratitude now and again. He's never once made a show of what he brings and you know it, Adam. And what he gives keeps our heads above water, make no mistake about that. Fanny Boyce's youngest has just died with pernicious anaemia and there's two or three others in the street with it. They've stopped the free school dinners for the bairns and folk are eating stuff that's only fit for pigs. Whole families are going into the workhouse and last week another man jumped off the Wearmouth bridge—'

She stopped as Wilbur got to his feet. Not that the movement was abrupt, in fact it was slow and measured and seemingly without heat. Without looking at anyone, he reached for his cap and put it on his head, and again the action was un-

173

hurried, even leaden. When he walked out of the kitchen into the scullery, Rose remained standing where she was, and it wasn't until they all heard the back gate swing to in the yard that she rounded on Adam, saying, 'Now look what you've done.'

'Me? I haven't done anything.'

'Joe, go with him.' Rose glanced at her son. 'You too, Naomi. Talk to him, lass. Tell him something funny that's happened at work. Make something up if you have to.' When Adam made to stand with the others, she added, 'You, wait a minute. I want a word.'

'What?' Once they were alone, Adam's voice was defensive.

'I've not asked before because it's none of my business but this last going-on changes things. How serious are you about Hannah?'

She could see her son was slightly taken aback and his voice stammered a little when he said, 'W-w-what do you mean?'

'You know what I mean and I want a straight answer. Is she the same as Flora Upton and Dolly Weatherburn and some of the other lassies you've walked out with in the past? Or does she mean more to you? If she doesn't, now is the time to leave well alone. She's going to have enough to cope with at that farm without you adding to it if you've no intention of playing fair with the lass.'

'That's good, that is. I thought mothers were supposed to think the best of their bairns.'

Rose stared at him, a hard look. 'Don't act the injured innocent, not with me. And I'm not blaming you for sowing your wild oats, it's natural enough, especially with the lassies throwing themselves at you. But Hannah's a good girl. You know that. And she's still only a bit lass. You're her first lad.'

'I know, I know.'

'Aye, well, just so long as you do. She's not like Dolly or that last one you knocked about with for a while, what was her name?'

'Lily Hopkins.'

'Aye, her. Got a name for herself, she had, but Hannah's a different kettle of fish. So, I say again, are you serious about the lass or is it just her bonny face that's the attraction?'

'What difference does it make with things the way they are? It'll be a long time before I can take on a wife and family.' Adam glared at her as though the current situation was her fault. 'Anyway, it takes two, don't forget that. You asked Hannah how she feels? No, I thought not.'

Ignoring Rose's call to stay put, he stamped out of the kitchen, banging the door behind him.

Rose stood with her hands leaning on the kitchen table staring after him. He hadn't answered her question and that bothered her. She loved her son and on the whole he was a good lad; even when he'd been in work he hadn't been one for the drink and he always spoke civilly to her and with affection. But that was Adam, charming and easygoing when he was getting his own way and everything was rosy. But his weakness was the lassies. And she didn't altogether blame him, no, not when some of them were brazen in their encouraging. That Lily Hopkins had stood waiting for him at street corners for weeks after he'd finished with her, even waylaying him outside the church of a Sunday morning once or twice.

Sighing heavily, Rose began to clear away the dirty dishes, reflecting bitterly that they barely needed washing, so clean had they been left. The broth hadn't been thick enough to stick to her family's ribs, that was for sure, and there was no way Wilbur and the lads would bring anything in this week. Nobody had any money left to give for any odd jobs, even the big houses on the outskirts had been pestered to the point they were locking their gates. Privet hedges had been cut so many times they were bald, scissors and knives worn away with sharpening and re-sharpening, tea cosies and doorstops and clippy mats were piled up in the houses of folk who'd been kind enough to buy and keep buying, and anyone who wanted a bit of painting and decorating undertaken had long since had it done.

Had she said enough to Adam to make him consider how he saw the future with Hannah? She hoped so. And him saying he wasn't sure how the lass felt was rubbish. You only had to look at Hannah to see she was fair barmy about him.

A squall of rain against the kitchen window brought Rose's head turning and she shivered. It wouldn't be long before the nights began to set in and the weather changed, and there was still no end to the lockout in sight.

Naomi reappeared, shaking the drops of water from her hat. 'It's raining, Mam.'

'Really? And there was me thinking you'd had a bath with your clothes on.'

'Oh you, our Mam.'

They smiled at each other.

'Where's your da?' Rose asked, no longer smiling.

'He's all right. He's with Joe in the Tavern.'

Another precious few pennies gone on beer.

As though Naomi had read her mind, her daughter said, 'I gave Da the extra the fore-woman slipped me when I stayed behind and cleared up after that vat leaked today. It was only a bob, Mam.'

A shilling. Enough for some cow heel and tripe and a bit of black pudding for tomorrow's dinner. She always thought in terms of food these days. Life revolved around thoughts of food.

'I ... I thought he needed a jar the night, Mam.'

Rose looked at her daughter. Naomi stumped up her wage good as gold each week and the last little while had flatly refused to keep back so much as a penny or two for herself. Her arms were sticking out of her coat which was far too small for her and her boots needed mending before the winter. Her voice soft, Rose said, 'You're right, lass, he did.' She pulled Naomi into her, holding her tightly for a moment before she pushed her away, saying, 'Put the kettle on, hinny, and we'll have a brew.'

Chapter 11

By the end of the week Hannah felt she knew what it was like to cook for an army. After moving her things into one of the lower bedrooms on the day she had seen Farmer Shawe, she had been grudgingly given the lowdown on where everything was and how things were done by a disgruntled Enid. The next morning Hannah had risen before it was light to see to the two men's breakfast and begin baking for the workers' lunch, which had taken the whole of the next six hours. Jake had come down first, standing in the kitchen doorway and smiling as he said, 'You must have been up at the crack of sparrows.'

She had been taking a batch of fruit buns out of the oven and had been too busy to feel nervous of him. 'There's lots to be done,' she'd said by way of answer, adding, 'Where do you and Farmer Shawe normally eat your meals? In the dining room? The porridge is ready and I'll do the eggs and bacon once you're eating that.'

'Aye, the dining room'll be fine,' said Jake, glancing at the kitchen table which was laden with flour and dried fruit and numerous tins and dishes. 'I've asked Clara to lend a hand in here each morning, by the way. She'll put you right on how much is needed and so on.'

'Thank you.' She flashed him a quick smile.

In a short while when Clara appeared it became

clear to Hannah that Enid had been sparing in her instructions. But for Clara's help, the amount of food would have been meagre, to say the least. As it was, the twelve large plates of pastry made with pig's fat and filled with chunks of ham and egg, the bread and cheese, baked jam rolls, fruit buns and several tins of bread and butter pudding sticky with sugar and dried fruit went down a treat if the empty plates and dishes were anything to go by.

It wasn't until the end of that first day that it occurred to Hannah that perhaps Jake had suspected Enid might attempt to make her look foolish and inexperienced which was why he'd sent Clara to her aid. She climbed into bed so tired she couldn't keep her eyes open, and she considered the matter for all of thirty seconds before she fell asleep.

The rest of the week passed in a frantic whirl, culminating with the preparation of food for the harvest supper on the Saturday evening. Clara had told her the supper was an important event in the farm calendar. One of the big brick and tiled barns was swept out, the cobwebs brushed down from the rafters and a row of trestle tables set down the middle of the building after the floor had been covered with rush matting.

Plenty of beer, cider and blackberry wine was brought in, along with lemonade and ginger pop for the youngsters. Several huge joints of roast beef and pork provided the main part of the supper. Each one had filled its oven and tested Hannah's strength when she lifted them in and out. The whole week had tested her strength, along with her stamina and ingenuity She didn't know what she would have done without Clara's advice and help each morning.

But she had got through without any howling mistakes. She glanced across the barn from where she was pouring lemonade for some of the bairns, her eyes sweeping over the assembled company. Everyone who lived at the farm was present, from Florence and Herbert Lyndon's little babbie to old Isaac Mallard, along with the farm workers and their wives and families who lived in the next village. It was like one massive family and even the young children spoke of the farm as 'theirs'. She had been surprised to learn that from the age of seven or eight the lads were doing jobs like scattering manure in the ridges of soil after ploughing, feeding the animals and cleaning out the pigsties, hen crees and stables, while the little lassies were introduced to milking, collecting the eggs from the hens and ducks, and other numerous jobs once they were home from school. There didn't seem to be much time for playing, but all the bairns appeared perfectly content with their lot. They were certainly plumper than the town children, their rosy cheeks and bright eyes testament to their good health.

When the meal was over, Farmer Shawe made a little speech thanking everyone for all the work that had been done, and immediately after that Daniel and John Osborne struck up a tune on their fiddles to start the singing and dancing. It was at this point Hannah began to feel uncomfortable. Everyone seemed to know how to dance, even the youngsters found a partner and formed a line, moving along it in turn as the dance progressed. Not that everyone was dancing. The farmer and Jake were sitting talking to Isaac and smoking their pipes, and Florence was dangling her baby on her knee, a smile on her face as she watched her husband dance with his smallest niece, a little tot of five.

Hannah began to clear the remnants of the food, glad to have something to do, but after a few minutes Daniel tapped her on the shoulder. 'Leave that.' He was smiling. 'You've done enough work this week keeping us all fed and watered. Come and dance.'

'I can't.' She glanced across to where his brother was still playing. 'I really can't.'

'Course you can. I'll help you clear later.'

'I don't mean that. It's just that I've never... I don't know the steps.'

'You've never been to a barn dance afore?'

Hannah shook her head. She had never been to any sort of dance before but she wasn't about to tell him that, she felt silly enough as it was.

'Well, there's got to be a first time for everything and if I say so myself, I'm a canny teacher.' He grinned at her, took the plates out of her hands and put them down on the table before pulling her towards the dancers.

Aware she would make a spectacle of herself if she tried to disentangle her hands, but worried she would make even more of a spectacle of herself if she attempted to join the long line of men, women and children, Hannah said urgently, 'I'd prefer to watch for a while if that's all right.'

'Nonsense. You've got to participate to get the hang of it. Trust me. And no one is going to be looking at whether you get it right or not anyway, everyone's too busy enjoying themselves. Folk won't laugh at you.'

Hannah wasn't too sure about that, but once she had joined the line she found it wasn't as hard as she expected. Daniel's brother was calling out instructions to the dancers as he played his fiddle, and owing to the fact that more than a few of the adults were a little tiddly, even old hands were getting it wrong, which caused much hilarity. Slowly she began to relax and enjoy herself.

It was over two hours later in a break from the dancing that Daniel said, 'Come and sit a while, Hannah. Tell me about your life before you came to the farm. What made you leave the town?'

She had known someone would ask eventually and she had her answer ready. Shrugging nonchalantly, she kept her voice light when she said, 'My mother and I lived with my uncle and aunt above his shop which is where I worked too. It was too ... constricting, I suppose. And I don't really like town life much, so when I had a disagreement with my mother I decided it was time to spread my wings a bit. Mr Fletcher said he and Farmer Shawe needed a live-in housekeeper and so it seemed the perfect answer.'

'I think so.'

Something in his voice made her continue, 'Mr Fletcher's sister, Naomi, is my friend and I've always lived a few doors away from the family. Her brother and I were walking out before I came here.'

He nodded slowly. 'Are you still walking out?'

She stared at him, her flushed cheeks not altogether due to the dancing. 'I – I'm not sure.' That sounded so silly she said quickly, 'It all happened in a rush, my coming here, and I'm not sure how Adam will see things, me being so far away.'

'Monkwearmouth isn't so far away. I'd walk twice as far if I–' He stopped abruptly, rubbing his chin before he said, 'They're starting the dancing again, come on.'

'No.' Her voice was firm. 'I need to clear away and see to things in the farmhouse.'

'I'll help you.'

'No.' She softened her refusal by adding, 'But thanks anyway. Look, your brother needs a break, doesn't he? So he can dance? I think it's time you took your turn.'

'Aye, maybe.' He seemed subdued.

'But thank you for teaching me the steps. I've enjoyed it.'

'Have you?'

His face brightened but when he opened his mouth to say more, Hannah rose quickly to her feet, saying, 'I'd best get on now.'

In the farmhouse kitchen she placed the dishes on the table and stood for a moment, gazing around her. She was going to make changes here, clean things up and get everything shiny like it had been in the days when Farmer Shawe's wife was alive. There hadn't been time to do anything but cook this week but now the harvest was gathered in and the feast was over, she'd have a chance to do a bit more. Everything was dusty and dirty, the covers on the sofa and chairs in the sitting room needed washing and all the curtains in the house. 'But don't worry, there'll still be

183

room for you two,' she said to Buttons and Polly who were curled up in one of the armchairs looking at her with green eyes.

She brought her gaze away from the cats as Jake and Seamus walked into the kitchen with more dirty dishes. It was Seamus who said, 'Don't do these now, lass. There'll be time in the morning for getting straight. An' you've done all right this week, all in all.'

She knew him well enough by now to know this was high praise indeed, and her voice reflected this when she said, 'Thank you, Farmer Shawe,' her eyes shining.

'Aye, well, I'm off abed, I'm a mite tired the night.' Seamus clapped Jake on the back. 'You coming up, lad?'

'In a while. I want to make sure Isaac gets home first.'

'Aye, he was packing it away the night. Mortalious by now and the drink always makes him crabby.'

The two men went their different ways and when she was alone again Hannah carried everything through to the deep stone sink in the scullery where she put the dirty dishes to soak for morning. When that was done, she tidied the kitchen and prepared the porridge for morning, leaving the oats in a big pan soaking up the creamy milk. She preferred the way porridge was done here, she thought. Her uncle, having been born into a mining family, had his porridge made with water and stiff with salt, and until she had come to the farm she had assumed everyone had it that way. Few mining families had money for several pints of milk for their breakfast.

Her thoughts brought Adam to mind. Would he come to the farm with Naomi tomorrow afternoon? Her heart began to thud. Did he still look on her as his lass? Or had their silly quarrel spoilt everything? The only thing wrong with the farm was that she was so far away from Adam and couldn't even catch a glimpse of him passing by, as she had done when working in her uncle's shop. But if he didn't want anything more to do with her, perhaps that was the best thing.

No, no it wasn't. She bit hard on her lower lip. She wouldn't be able to bear not seeing him.

Jake reappeared, his arms full of logs for the range, which he stacked at the side of it. 'Isaac's going to need a few raw eggs in the morning,' he remarked.

'I'm sorry?'

He straightened. 'Raw eggs. You know raw eggs straight from the shell and beaten in a drop of milk are the best thing out for a headache after having a load?'

It sounded horrible. Hannah couldn't repress a shudder. 'No, I didn't.'

'Aye, well, likely you've never needed it.'

He smiled and she smiled back, and it said a lot for how relaxed she had become around him that she could say, with a twinkle in her eye, 'Have you?'

He threw back his head and gave one of his rare laughs. 'Now and again,' he admitted.

She couldn't imagine him drunk. In fact she couldn't imagine him being anything but always in complete control. He was easily the most self-contained, assured individual she had come across. His scars didn't seem to bother him at all, he seemed unaware of them. Except... Her thoughts came to a hiccup. It wasn't often he sat or stood with the damaged side of his face to the fore. A little flustered now, she said, 'Can I get you a hot drink before you go to bed?'

'No, that's all right, Hannah. You go up. There's a couple of things I've got to do before I turn in.'

She nodded and returned to the scullery. She opened the adjoining door leading into the dairy to check that the pan of milk left for morning had been covered. This produced a thin layer of rich cream and Farmer Shawe liked it on top of his porridge. Enid and her three daughters worked in the dairy, churning, skimming and cheese-making, and the golden butter, rich cream, cheese and other produce was used on the farm and sold at market, although little had been done this week due to the harvest. It was fortunate, Hannah reflected, that there was an outside door into the dairy as well, so that Enid and her daughters didn't have to come through the house all the time. She had seen the woman's face when she was dancing with Daniel and if looks could kill, she'd be six foot under. It was better they didn't see too much of each other.

The pan was on its cold slab, along with a pat of butter and a round cheese covered with a white linen cloth, and by the flickering light of the oil lamp she was carrying, Hannah saw everything was spick and span. She closed the door behind her and silently retraced her footsteps. As she stepped up into the kitchen, she saw Jake sitting in one of the armchairs which he had pulled round to face the fire, his big frame leaning forward on his forearms which rested on his knees. He was staring into the red glow, the two cats curled up at his feet. She couldn't see the expression on his face, he had his back towards her, but the posture was one of brooding aloneness.

He didn't notice her as she slipped out of the kitchen. She paused for a moment in the hall and then walked slowly up the stairs to her room, the oil lamp casting grotesque shadows on the walls. As she sat down on her bed she felt a wave of deep sadness engulf her, but for the life of her she could not have explained why.

Chapter 12

'So you're going to the farm then?'

'Aye, I told you. Joe's coming along an' all.'

Rose stared at Adam. She wasn't concerned whether Joe was going to Clover Farm to see Hannah and Adam knew the reason why. Clearing her throat, she said quietly, 'Mrs Fraser said she saw you and Lily talking in the recreation ground at the back of Park Terrace, Southwick way, the other night when she was taking some washing back to one of her customers.'

Adam shrugged. 'Not a crime, is it?'

They were standing in the bedroom the two older brothers shared, Rose having followed Adam upstairs a minute before so she could

187

speak to him alone, and now she glanced over her shoulder before saying even more quietly, 'You haven't taken up with Lily Hopkins again then?'

'Course I haven't, what do you take me for? You know what she's like, forever trailing after me. I can't help but run into her the way she is. Sometimes I think she watches the house to see when I come and go.'

Rose said nothing to this. She knew what Lily was like but the recreation ground was a well-known meeting place for courting couples and it wasn't too far to open fields and the old sand pit from there. Oh, what was she thinking? Did she have a mucky mind or was it instinct that was telling her Adam had been up to something with Lily? The girl had a reputation for being no better than she should be and she'd been after Adam for years before he took up with her the last time. If he was seeing her again behind Hannah's back... 'If you go to the farm this week, Hannah will expect you to go again. You know that?'

Adam met his mother's eyes. 'Aye, I know that and for crying out loud stop worrying about her, Mam. Sometimes I think you think more of Hannah than the rest of us put together. She's sixteen years old, she's no bairn, and now she's working away we'll have to see how things go. She might meet a big strapping farmhand and give me the elbow. Ever considered that?'

No, and neither had he seriously. Her son was well aware of the effect he had on women and on Hannah in particular. It would do him the world of good if a lassie didn't want to look the side he was on but she couldn't see it happening.

'Look, I'm going to the farm with Joe and Naomi, leave it at that, Mam. Tomorrow there's a march over the bridge and likely the law will be there again coming the big fellows and arresting a few of us. Worry about that if you want to worry about anything. The last time I ended up with a bruise on my back the size of a cricket bat from their batons and Joe's broken fingers are only just beginning to let him sleep at night, and all we'd done was walk the public roads an' peacefully. The owners are bringing in blacklegs to work the pit from miles around and we're expected to stand by and raise our caps to 'em. There'll be murder done one day, you mark my words. Everyone's had enough.'

Rose stared at the angry face of her son. He wasn't telling her anything she didn't know. Tempers were getting worse all round and people were so hungry and frustrated they had either become apathetic or so full of rage the slightest thing would spark them off. The Miners' Hall had been giving out second-hand clothing from the beginning of the lockout but Wilbur had forbidden her to ask for anything or take anything that was offered. Which was all very well but the twins were running around in bare feet now because they'd long since grown out of their shoes and winter was round the corner. She stared at Adam a moment more and then turned silently away. She walked down the stairs into the kitchen where Naomi and Joe were sitting. Wilbur had taken the four youngest lads blackberrying in the fields at the back of Fulwell but she doubted they'd find much. The hedgerows were picked clean these days. She hoped Jake would send something back with Naomi and the lads when they went to the farm today, although how Adam would feel about accepting something first-hand she didn't know.

'Is Adam coming, Mam?'

Rose nodded at her daughter but she spoke to Joe when she said, 'How's your hand the day?'

'All right.'

Of the lot of them she was the most worried about Joe. He had never been as strong as his father or Adam, and the cough that had been with him since the winter before and which he had never shaken off was worse these days. 'Why don't you have a kip this afternoon?' she said quietly. 'It's over three miles to Jake's farm.'

'It's not Jake's farm.' Adam had appeared in the doorway to the kitchen as she'd spoken and his voice was sharp. 'He works there, that's all, like any of the other labourers.'

'I'll be all right, Mam.' Joe spoke quickly into the tense pause. 'We'd best get going, the nights are dropping in and it'll be better to come home in the light.'

'Bye, Mam.' Naomi was fairly hopping from one foot to the other in her impatience to see her friend again.

'Bye, hinny.' Rose watched the three of them leave, Joe's cough echoing in the backyard as they walked out into the back lane. Adam hadn't met her eyes when he had come downstairs and the niggling feeling he was seeing Lily Hopkins on the sly was stronger.

She would have loved to go with them to the farm. Rose plumped down on a hard-backed chair, resting her elbows on the kitchen table. Jake had asked her many times to visit him there but she never had although she knew how much he would like her to. She rubbed her brow wearily. But how could she go, knowing how much such an outing would upset Wilbur? Not that they had ever discussed it of course, but she knew how it would affect him if she went.

The animosity that had grown between her husband and Silas's son the older Jake had become was as fierce as ever. For her part, she had accepted Larry and Hilda as her own bairns from the beginning, but Wilbur had never tried to break through the reserve which Jake used as a defence mechanism. And that was all it was. Why couldn't Wilbur see that? Instead he had become surly and uncommunicative with Jake after the first few years, and had acted as though it was a personal insult when her son had announced he had no intention of working down the pit. Worse, he'd bred in Adam the same antagonism until now there was something bordering on hatred between the two half-brothers. It was all Wilbur's doing.

And yet no, that wasn't fair. She stood up and walked over to the window where she looked out into the backyard. The heat shimmered on the stone slabs. There was no bad blood between Joe and Jake so why between Adam and her firstborn?

She caught sight of her reflection in the window pane and maybe because it was unexpected, she surveyed the face staring back at her as though it was someone else's. The hair was almost completely grey now but thick and strong, she always had trouble securing every last strand into the bun at the back of her head in the mornings. It was the only thing in the reflection that bore any evidence of vitality and life. She looked older than her mother had when she had passed on and her mam had been all of sixty-six, a good twenty years older than she was now. She touched the lines that ran in furrows across her forehead and bit deep from her nose to the corners of her mouth, wondering how long she had looked like this. She looked old. She felt old.

Rose straightened her shoulders and turned away from the window. It was no use standing here thinking, that wouldn't help anything or anyone. And whatever Wilbur was, he wasn't like Silas had been and that was something to be thankful for. She had long since stopped praying to the Holy Mother for forgiveness for the joy she had felt when they had found Silas's body. She'd done her penance and she only had to look at her lad's face to know there was no power on earth or above it that could make her feel differently. It was fear of what Silas might do to her or Jake that had made her tell the doctors that Jake's burns had been an accident, that he'd pulled the lamp on himself. And then when they had found Silas's body she'd kept to her story but for her son's sake. What bairn wants to grow up knowing his own father had done such a thing?

She walked over to the range and put the kettle on before taking out a basket of mending and sitting herself down again. Maybe Wilbur and the lads would bring back a nice pound or two of blackberries. Maybe Jake would send a sack of vegetables and a piece of meat or two. And maybe, just maybe the lockout would end soon. Although if it did, would Joe survive working underground again? He had never been as strong as Adam and now with this cough having taken a hold...

Rose sighed. In the long stretches of the night when she couldn't sleep, tired as she was, she would lie at the side of Wilbur and imagine all sorts of things. It might be daft – she prayed daily to the Holy Mother it was just her being silly – but right from when Joe was a baby she'd felt he wouldn't make old bones. He'd caught every childhood ailment going and the measles had weakened his chest when he'd been four years old so badly they'd thought for a time they would lose him then. But he'd pulled round.

She closed her eyes, the basket of mending in her lap and her hands limp as she prayed, 'Let him find something else, don't let him go underground again. It'll be the death of him, I know it. But I can't ask Jake to take him on. Wilbur would know and he'd never forgive me and Adam would go fair mad. But somehow make a way where there is no way.'

The kettle was boiling and she rose, tipping a little hot water onto the mound of tea leaves in the teapot which had been left from earlier. These days she tried to make them do for three or more brews before they went onto the fire, even though the resulting liquid was as weak as dishwater.

Once seated again she began on the mending, her hands busy but her thoughts miles away as in her mind's eye she walked the route to Clover Farm with her children.

'By, Adam, it's no two-farthing place, this. I hadn't realised it was so big. Had you?'

Adam didn't answer his brother for a moment. He and Joe and Naomi were standing at the end of the lane just past the labourers' cottages, looking towards the farmhouse. They'd had a merry walk from the town, laughing and joking with each other, but of one accord the three had become silent since entering the lane leading to the farm. Adam's voice flat, he said, 'It's not that big.'

Naomi opened her mouth to contradict him but fortunately she was forestalled by a tall young man who emerged round the corner of a barn on the opposite track to the farmhouse and called, 'Can I help you?'

'We've come to see Hannah Casey.' Adam eyed the man up and down as he approached. 'She's expecting us.'

'Oh aye, you're Jake's family, aren't you?' The young man was smiling but Adam's face remained straight.

It was Joe who said, and quickly, 'Aye, that's right. This is my brother, Adam, and my sister, Naomi. I'm Joe.'

'Daniel Osborne.' Daniel's eyes lingered on Adam for a moment and then he said, 'It was the harvest supper yesterday so things are a bit quiet, even for a Sunday. A few aching heads, you know? Come with me and I'll take you to the house and–'

He was interrupted by Hannah running from the direction of the farmhouse, her face aglow as she shouted, 'I saw you from the sitting-room window. I've been waiting for ages. Come on, come and have a cup of tea and then I'll show you round.'

Adam and Joe remained standing where they were but Naomi sprang forward to greet Hannah. The two girls hugged and laughed and in so doing passed over what could have been an awkward moment. As Daniel said goodbye, the four of them made their way towards the farmhouse, but it wasn't until they reached the kitchen door that Adam caught hold of Hannah's hand. 'I'm sorry about everything that's happened,' he said in a low voice.

Hannah wasn't sure if he meant their quarrel or how her uncle had behaved or all of it, but now he was here it didn't matter. By way of answer, she said, 'I'm glad you've come.' They smiled at each other before she led the way into the farmhouse kitchen.

'Oh, Hannah.' Naomi was immediately over-awed. 'It's bonny.'

'It will be when I put everything to rights. The woman who was looking after things didn't have time to do anything but get meals and see to the washing and ironing.'

'You're staying then?' Adam stared at her. He and Joe were standing just inside the door but Naomi had spied the two cats on the mat and was down on her knees fussing them.

Hannah nodded. 'For the time being at least. Come and sit down and I'll get some tea. Farmer Shawe and ... and Jake' – she always referred to their half–brother as Mr Fletcher but she felt Adam would take umbrage if she showed such respectful formality towards Jake – 'have gone for a ride and they won't be back for an hour or two.' She had the feeling Jake had organised this so that if Adam accompanied Naomi, he and the farmer would be out of the way and things would be less awkward.

Naomi rose from the mat with Buttons in her arms. 'You've dropped on your feet here, lass,' she said without a trace of envy. She sat in one of the hard-backed chairs and settled the cat on her lap. 'I wouldn't want to ever leave if I was you.'

Hannah said nothing to this. She got everyone a cup of tea and a plate of blackberry tarts which vanished in moments. She fetched another plate holding a large fruit cake and while the three ate, she filled them in on the week's happenings and then took them on a tour of the farmhouse before they went outside. Arm in arm with Naomi, the lads following, she led them round the farm and all the outbuildings, stables, pigsties and barns before they climbed a ridge some distance away and stood gazing out on the great expanse of land to the boundaries of the farmer's property. The air was thin and clean, carrying the scents of a late summer's day, and the soft blue smoke of a twitch fire created a haze over the distant view, mellowing the horizon.

'This is grand, Hannah.' Joe's eyes were hungry as he took in the view. His nostrils dilated as he smelt the air, for all the world like a wild animal savouring its unfettered surroundings.

Remembering her conversation with Adam's brother on New Year's Eve, Hannah said softly, 'Aye, it's bonny, Joe.' They exchanged a glance of pure understanding.

'Be a devil in winter.' Adam sat down, clasping his hands round his knees, and the others followed suit. 'Working in the open air is all very well when it's warm and sunny but come the bad weather it's a different story.'

'The mine's no picnic whatever it's like up top.'

Adam stared at his brother. 'Aye, I know that, man,' he said. 'I was just saying, that's all.'

A silence fell on the four of them for a minute or two. Then Hannah said, 'Do you want to come and see the orchard now? Farmer Shawe said you could pick some apples and plums to take with you if you want and there's a sack of stuff in the kitchen from Jake.'

As Joe and Naomi stood to their feet, Adam pulled Hannah up, keeping his arm round her waist as he said to his brother and sister, 'You go to the orchard, we're going for a walk. We'll see you later, all right?'

The twilight was stretching shadows across the path as Joe and Naomi went one way, towards the farm buildings, and Adam led Hannah down the slope and into one of the fields which had been harvested. Hannah glanced after the others nervously. 'Farmer Shawe and Jake will be back by now, they'll likely be wanting something to eat.'

'They can wait.' He pulled her towards a haystack at the edge of the field. 'I want some time alone with you.'

She wanted that too. The air was intoxicating, carrying the scent of hot dry grass, and a blackbird was singing in one of the trees bordering the field. The evening was still, the warmth of the dying sun coating everything in a golden blanket

197

and from somewhere near a bullfinch began to compete with the blackbird in song, the metallic sweetness as piercing as a fife.

Adam pulled her against him when they reached the stack of hay, his back against it as he kissed her hard. 'I've missed you,' he said throatily. 'Have you missed me?'

'So much.'

'I could have killed your uncle when I heard what he'd tried to do.'

'It doesn't matter.' She didn't want to talk or think about her uncle, it would spoil this wonderful moment.

'I love you, you know that, don't you?'

Her reply was smothered as he kissed her again and they swayed together, their mouths joined, for long minutes. Eventually, when he raised his head, she whispered, 'I won't be here for ever, I promise.'

'I know that.' The darkness was dropping fast now the sun had set. 'And I can wait for you. Promise me you won't look at another man. Promise.'

'I promise. And you won't see anyone else?'

'How could I when I've got you?'

'Promise me, Adam.'

'I promise.' He moved her slightly from him, looking down into her flushed face. 'I can't pretend I like you being so far away and with him, of all people, but I can see you couldn't very well stay where you were. That Daniel Osborne,' his eyes were very intent, 'does he know about me? That we're walking out?'

'Daniel? Aye, he does. Everyone does.'

He smiled. 'Good.' He pulled her roughly

against him again and pressed his mouth on hers and when they sank down onto a bale of hay she made no protest, not until his hand slid up under her dress. Then with a wriggle she drew away and stood up.

'I want you, Hannah.' His voice was thick and his face looked red and hot. 'Now, today, I want you.'

'I want you too, but not until...You know. I'd be frightened.'

'There's nothing to be frightened of.' He stood up, holding her as he whispered, 'There's not, I promise. You're my lass, I don't want anyone else and one day when I'm working again we can start saving up. You can start putting away your bottom drawer now, can't you?'

'Oh, Adam.' She stared at him, her eyes shining, but when the hands holding her moved down to her buttocks and she felt his body stir as he pressed her to him, she said, 'I can't, Adam. I daren't. Even the first time things can happen.'

'You mean a bairn? I wouldn't let it.'

'You say that but it might. I love you, I do, but I don't want a bairn out of wedlock. I want everything done proper in the church.'

'You're holding me to ransom?'

'No.' Her indignant voice had the ring of truth. 'I don't mean it like that, I'm just trying to explain. It's not right if you aren't married, you know that as well as I do.'

'Nothing would happen, not once.'

'There's plenty of girls who've ended up in the workhouse who were told that.'

'You think I'd do that to you? Let you down?'

'No, but things happen. You could have an accident, anything, like when Beattie Irvin's lad fell under the tram.'

'If you loved me you'd want to do it as much as I do.'

'That's not fair. I do love you, you know I do.'

'All right, all right, don't start crying.'

'I do love you.'

'Aye, I know.' He took off his cap and ran his hand through his hair before stuffing it on his head again, saying, 'Come on, we'd better get back to the others. Wipe your eyes or else they'll wonder what's been going on.' He passed her a handkerchief from his pocket. When she handed it back to him he touched her cheek with his fingers, his voice gentler when he said, 'Once I'm back at work things'll be easier.'

She couldn't see how Adam being in work would make this particular thing easier but she didn't say so. She didn't want to start them quarrelling again. Her voice deepened by the catch of tears, she said, 'I couldn't bear it if we weren't together.'

He put his hand under her soft chin and lifted up her mouth, kissing her full on her half-open lips. 'Aye, all right, don't fret. We'll work this out.'

'And you'll come again next Sunday?'

'Aye, if you want me to.'

'I do, I do.' For a moment she was tempted to give in and do what he wanted but the fear of what the priests preached, and not least the terrible stigma of falling for a bairn, proved stronger than her desire to please him. A woman could rise above anything except having a bairn when she wasn't married. It was the only thing you were really looked down on for, and no decent man would look the side you were on once it had happened. Beattie Irvin had been a bonny lass with lovely golden hair but after her mam and da had thrown her out, she'd been forced to go into the workhouse and now she was stuck in there until the bairn was fourteen years old. 'I love you,' she said again.

'An' I love you so everything's all right, isn't it?'

Was it? She hoped so.

They walked back to the farmhouse arm in arm and as they neared it, Hannah saw Jake talking to Joe and Naomi at the juncture where the lane split. Joe had a large sack at his feet and Naomi was holding a basket of fruit and they were all laughing. Hannah felt Adam stiffen at the side of her and it caused her voice to tighten when she called, 'All ready to go?'

'Aye, it'll be dark soon.' Joe answered her but he was looking at Adam, and it was to his brother he said, 'Jake's sorted Mam a few things.'

Adam said nothing to this. His gaze went from Joe to Jake who was standing silently surveying them. 'You've been riding then?'

'Aye.'

'With the boss, I understand.'

Jake said, 'Aye,' once more in the same flat tone but his dark eyes had narrowed at the note in Adam's voice.

'Don't the others mind?'

'The others?'

'The rest of 'em who live and work here, the ones who were around long before you turned up on the scene. Don't they mind you being the blue-eyed boy?'

Jake stared at his half-brother a few moments more before turning to Joe at the side of him. 'Tell Mam I'll call by on market day once I've finished the farm business. And mind you take all of that medicine I gave you, all right? That cough's hung about too long.'

'I'll do that, Jake.'

'Thanks for all the stuff, Jake.' Naomi grinned at him, then said, 'Come on, Adam, else it'll be too dark to see where we're going. Bye, Hannah. I'll see you next week.'

'Bye,' said Hannah a little lamely as Adam left her side without a word and joined the others, whereupon they all turned and began to walk off. 'See you next week,' she called after them but it was Joe and Naomi who turned and waved. Adam marched ahead, his back stiff.

As the three disappeared from view Hannah said quietly, 'I'll see to the tea now.'

'Aye, all right.'

'I'm – I'm sorry about Adam.'

He looked at her, the eyebrow on the good side of his face quirking. 'Why are you apologising for him? He's *my* brother.'

'But he wouldn't have come today but for me being here.'

'And you think that makes you responsible for his attitude.' Adam's a big boy now, Hannah, and so am I. You know as well as I do that there's no love lost between us and nothing he does or says affects me so don't worry your head on that score.'

'He's all worked up with the strike having gone

202

on so long.'

'Possibly.'

'I'm not making excuses for him—' She stopped abruptly. That was exactly what she was doing and they both knew it.

They stared at each other for a moment and what she read in Jake's eyes humbled her. He had extended the olive branch in allowing Adam to come here and had virtually been slapped round the face with it but there was only kindness and a kind of grim humour in his expression. She found herself wondering how she could ever have been frightened of this man.

'You said something about tea,' he reminded her. 'My stomach's thinking my throat's been cut.'

She smiled as he had meant her to, and together they walked to the farmhouse.

'What's all this "I'll do that, Jake" and "thanks for all the stuff, Jake"?' Once they were out of sight of the farm, Adam stopped dead and confronted his brother and sister, his face red with anger. 'Lick his boots while you're about it, why don't you?'

'Aw, give over, man.' Joe's voice was conciliatory. 'We were only being civil, weren't we, Naomi?'

Naomi nodded, her small full mouth set in a straight line. She was sick and tired of Adam acting up every time Jake was around and considering they were at the farm, Jake's territory, she thought her brother had got a real cheek. And all the food Jake had given them too. Adam could at least have shown some gratitude.

'He acts as though he's God Almighty and you two were encouraging it.'

'We were just talking, that's all,' Joe said quietly.

'Talking, huh!'

'Aye, talking. People do talk, you know.'

'And what's this medicine he's given you? Why can't you get something in town?'

'He's had medicine from the apothecary, you know he has,' Naomi said, 'and it's done no good. Neither has that mixture that old Ma Tollett rustled up, apart from make him gag every time he swallowed it.' Naomi glared at her brother. 'And medicine costs money, don't forget that.'

'So what's so special about this Jake's given him?'

'Don't talk about me as though I'm not here.' It was rare Joe got angry and now Naomi and Adam both turned and stared at him as he said tersely, 'It's a brew the old woman Hannah stayed with when she first came to the farm makes up. She bakes something called a wurzel, a vegetable the animals have, with honey and special herbs and sloes and a whole host of bits and then you drink the juice of it. It cures the worse coughs, so Jake says. It's a recipe handed down through generations. She gave me a couple of spoonfuls when Jake took us in to see her and collect a bottle while we were waiting for you and Hannah and it's helped already.'

'All getting very friendly then.'

'Don't be daft, man.' Joe's voice was low and harsh and again Adam and Naomi were taken aback. For as long as they could remember, Joe had followed where Adam led; with only twenty months separating their births, the two brothers had always been very close and Joe had somewhat hero-worshipped Adam.

'I don't think I'm being daft.'

'He heard me cough and he was trying to help, that's all. And there's enough food in this sack to keep us going a couple of days and more, and don't tell me we don't need it. The least you could have done was thank him.'

'Me thank him? Why should I thank him when you two were slobbering all over him?'

'It wasn't like that.'

'Oh aye, an' pigs fly.'

'There's no reasoning with you when you're like this.' Joe began walking again, the sack slung over his shoulder, and after a moment Naomi and Adam followed.

After a silence which lasted until they reached the Sunderland Road, Adam said, 'You still coming on the march tomorrow?'

'Course I'm coming on the march.' Joe looked at his brother. 'Why wouldn't I?'

Adam shrugged. 'Didn't know if you wanted to be in my company with the poor opinion you've got of me.'

Joe hesitated. There had been real hurt in Adam's voice. 'Look, man, you're my brother and I think a bit of you, you know that, but fair's fair, that's all I was saying. But it's not worth falling out about, nowt is.' He held out his hand and after a moment Adam took it and the two of them shook hands.

'Thank goodness for that.' Naomi was red in the face from carrying the big basket of fruit. 'Mam's got enough on her plate without you two acting up. Here,' she held out the basket to

Adam, 'my arms are six inches longer. You carry it the rest of the way.'

'I can't, I'm not going straight home, I'm meeting someone.'

'Who?'

'None of your business, madam.' His good temper restored by Joe's capitulation, Adam took one of the apples out of the basket and bit into it with strong white teeth. 'I'll see you both later, all right?'

As they watched Adam walk away, Naomi turned to Joe. 'Who's he meeting, do you know?'

Joe shrugged. He had a good idea and he felt bad about it but with Naomi being Hannah's best friend, she was the last person he could tell. 'You know Adam, it could be anyone.'

Chapter 13

The weather changed drastically over the next few weeks, northerners paying dearly for the hot Indian summer they had enjoyed. October came in with hail and icy sleet and after days of incessant rain, Hannah felt she was drowning in a sea of mud. She had thought the back lanes in the town were bad enough, but they were nothing compared to the oozing sludge that seemed to cover every square yard outside the farmhouse. When, after repeated requests for Jake and Seamus to scrape their boots on the massive cork mat inside the kitchen door Jake forgot for the umpteenth time and left a trail of mud on the newly scrubbed floor, she erupted.

It was midday on a bitterly cold morning in the last week of October and as usual she had been up at six o'clock to prepare the men's breakfast before beginning the baking for the day and tackling a huge basket of ironing. The afternoons she always tried to leave free for scrubbing and cleaning and polishing and already the farmhouse was beginning to look a different place. She had transformed the kitchen first, it being the place that had niggled at her the most, and now it was bright and gleaming; The lustrous blackleaded range, the sparkle on the dishes and pots and pans, the shining brass on the mantelpiece and the freshly laundered covers on the old armchairs and rocking chairs all contributed to the impression of loving care. The floor was spotless – or had been until Jake's feet had trodden in clumps of mud – and the clippy mat had been shaken and beaten until its teeth had rattled. Every corner of the room was bright.

'How many times do I have to tell you?' Hannah stood in front of the big broad figure of Jake like a small virago. 'It doesn't take long to rub your boots clean and if you can't be bothered, your slippers are there, *there*,' she emphasised, pointing to the men's slippers at the side of the mat. 'Just put them on, Jake. It's simple, it's so simple!' She paused for breath and as she did so the temper which went with her chestnut hair and which neither Jake or Seamus had seen before began to subside. Aghast, she realised she had screeched at him like a fishwife and furthermore so forgot herself as to use his first name.

Seamus, who had followed Jake into the house but had remained on the mat, was the first to speak. 'By, lass,' he said, 'you remind me of my Bess. She used to go for me an' our Terence like that and for much the same reason.'

But Bess had been the farmer's wife and she was just their housekeeper. Blushing furiously, Hannah brought her eyes from Seamus's astonished face to that of the man in front of her who had said not a word. 'I'm sorry,' she said weakly.

Jake glanced over at Seamus and he was grinning. 'I told you she had a temper,' he said mildly, before looking into Hannah's red face. 'Do I take it this has finally broken the ice and you can bring yourself to call me Jake? If so, it was worth a roasting.'

'An' while we're on the subject, you can do away with the Farmer Shawe an' all, lass,' Seamus put in from the mat. 'That's all right for them out there but I can't do with it in me own house. The name's Seamus.'

Hannah didn't know what to say. She nodded at them both before saying again, 'I'm sorry for flying off the handle.'

'Nowt to be sorry for, lass,' said Seamus as he took off his boots and put on his slippers, handing Jake his with a wide grin. 'I like a lass with a bit of spirit meself. My Bess could curdle milk with a flash of her eyes when she was in a fratch with me. The thing is, me an' Jake had got used to behaving like pigs in muck since Enid starting doing for us.'

'I wouldn't exactly say that.' Jake's voice

reflected his distaste for the comparison and Hannah couldn't help smiling.

When she had dished up the meat roll and vegetables that was the lunchtime meal, she sat with Jake and Seamus at the kitchen table. This practice had begun once the harvest was over when Jake and the farmer had declared the kitchen was good enough for everyday meals and the dining room could be kept for Sundays. At first she had felt awkward and shy eating with the two men but this had soon passed, and the shared mealtimes had gone a long way in helping her to get to know them both. They usually continued to sit in the kitchen once the evening meal was over these days too, smoking their pipes and chatting in their armchairs in front of the range while she busied herself with clearing away the dishes and washing up, and then preparing the breakfast for the next morning. Sometimes she sat with a pile of mending at the kitchen table or finished the day's ironing, other times she would pore over Bess's old recipe book she'd come across recently, one of the cats on her lap. She did think it was a shame the sitting room wasn't used except for Sundays because it was beautiful, or it would be once she had a chance to get to it and clean and polish everything. She had seen to the kitchen and Seamus's study now, and the next room was the dining room. Only then would she move upstairs.

Jake and Seamus had been to a neighbouring farm that morning on business. Once they had finished their meal they disappeared to the study to look at some accounts and, being short of eggs for a fruit cake she wanted to bake before she began on the dining room, Hannah collected her basket and put on her coat and boots.

At the hen crees she collected a dozen warm eggs from the boxes and while she was doing so, a cold, late-autumn sun began to shine through the ragged fringes of the thunderclouds. After all the·rain and storms of the previous weeks, it was enchanting, and in spite of her desire to begin to tackle the dining room which stood under layers of dust and grime, Hannah didn't immediately return to the farmhouse. Instead she continued round the stables, past the pigsties and barns, and emerged on the path she had walked with Adam, Joe and Naomi some weeks previously. She walked to the same ridge they had stood on then and tarried for a while, surveying the delicate play of light and shadow on the fields and hedgerows in front of her. Every blade of grass and inch of ground at her feet was soaked with moisture but there was none of the thick cloying mud which had proved such a burden lately. The route the cattle took from the fields to the farmyard was below her.

As she watched, a double rainbow slowly climbed the sky in the far distance, its colours vibrant against the steely grey. Would Adam come tomorrow afternoon? If not it would be the third Sunday in a row he hadn't made the journey to the farm. The first week Naomi and Joe had said he was involved with strike business and last week Joe had been alone, both Naomi and Adam apparently laid low with bad colds. She believed Naomi was poorly but she wasn't so sure about Adam. It hadn't been so much what Joe had said but the look in his eyes when he said it. He wasn't a good liar, Joe. She bit her lip, shutting her eyes tightly for a moment. Joe could come to the farm every week so why couldn't Adam? And yet when he did come he swore he felt the same about her, that she was the only lass for him, so why was she worrying?

'Bonny, eh?'

She had been so lost in her thoughts she hadn't heard or seen Jake's approach on the path below, and now she jumped so violently she almost dropped the basket of eggs.

'No, don't come down,' he said when she made to move. 'Enjoy the sun for a minute or two, it's going to pour again from the look of that sky.' He climbed up the ridge to where she was, shading his eyes as he stared in the direction she was looking. 'Rain, rain, rain,' he said softly, without glancing at her. 'It happens like that sometimes in October and the winter is worse. Do you think you're going to be able to stand it?'

'Of course.' She looked at him in surprise, amazed he could ask.

'Of course,' he repeated in a way she didn't quite understand. 'You work from dawn to dusk, you have to fetch water from the well when you've been used to a tap in the yard, you have big galoots walking all over your clean floor with muddy boots–'

'But then I can come up here and see the rain smiling from the hills when the sun's shining,' she interrupted solemnly. 'It makes up for the big galoots.'

'Really?' He glanced at her out of the corner of

211

his eye and she grinned at him, whereupon they both laughed out loud.

'Seriously, Jake, I can't thank you enough for giving me a chance.' It was something she had been meaning to say for a while but now seemed the right time. 'And I like it here, I really do. The farmhouse is beautiful and I want to make it nice, and all the food for cooking... Well, anyone would like it. And I can't believe I get paid too.'

He smiled. 'You should come into town with me the next time I take the horse and trap, treat yourself to something.'

'Could I?' she said eagerly. 'I'd like to buy some material and make a couple of new dresses.' Her clothes were so worn she had felt embarrassed when Farmer Dobson and his daughter had called to see Jake and Seamus the other day.

Jake's eyes were intent on her face. 'We'll go next week. Tuesday or perhaps Wednesday. How about that?'

She nodded, and then because the sky had become overcast again they made their way back to the house. Thunder rolled in the distance.

Much later that day, when the evening meal was over and Hannah was sitting at the kitchen table mending the sleeve of one of the farmer's shirts, Seamus got up from his armchair opposite Jake and left the room. When he returned he was carrying an armful of clothes which he dumped on the table in front of her. 'There's a few of my Bess's things,' he said gruffly. 'She was a one for clothes, was my Bess, and she had an eye for a good bit of cloth. Likely you'll have to be busy with your needle, she was a slip of a thing when we first wed

212

but she'd have made two of you later on.'

'But...' Hannah glanced from Seamus – who had resumed his seat in front of the range – to Jake, and then back to the farmer. 'But I can't take these. They're your wife's. You...' She couldn't very well say, 'You would be upset to see me in her things,' so she altered it to, 'You don't have to do that.'

'I know I don't have to, lass.' Seamus appeared very busy attending to his pipe and did not look at her. 'But I've a feeling Bess wouldn't like 'em to go on gathering dust and getting moth-eaten when you could have some use out of 'em. Hated waste, my Bess did. There's a canny little sewing machine she used to use somewhere in the loft, I'll look it out tomorrow and you can have that an' all.'

Hannah stared into the rough old face and then looked at Jake who was smiling. She glanced down at her faded blouse and skirt which had had the hem let down twice, and then fingered the rich thick material of the dress on top of the pile. They were so kind, the pair of them. They were like the father and brother she had never had. Her lips trembling, she voiced this, and it was Jake who said, 'Then as your big brother I command you not to get upset, all right? That's an end to the matter. Right, Seamus?'

'Right enough.'

'Thank you.' Knowing how much the farmer hated any show of emotion, Hannah gathered up the clothes and disappeared to her room, and when she returned a few minutes later no one commented on her pink-rimmed eyes or red nose.

That night Hannah did not extinguish her oil

213

lamp once she had retired to her bedroom. She stood gazing round the interior for some moments, her eyes taking in the comfortable bed, chest of drawers, small dressing table and wardrobe the room contained, and – luxury of luxuries – the glowing fire in the grate. Jake and Seamus scorned a fire in their rooms on the floor above, but as soon as the weather had turned chilly they had insisted wood and coal be brought upstairs for her every day. She was glad of it, the bedrooms were very draughty and when the wind was in a certain direction the curtains at the window in her room blew as though it was open a crack.

Pulling a blanket from the bed round her shoulders, she positioned herself on the clippy mat in front of the fire and took up the dress she had decided to alter that night with her sewing box. She couldn't wait for Seamus to find the sewing machine, she wanted to be wearing something new and bonny when Adam came the next day. She knew she would be up most of the night; every seam needed unpicking and re-sewing once she had trimmed the material with her scissors. Seamus hadn't been exaggerating when he had said Bess had been twice her size. But the material was beautiful. She stroked it reverently. Thick and smooth and the colour of cornflowers. She would never have been able to afford cloth of this quality but now she could use her money for a pair of shoes. She would continue to wear her ugly old boots for weekdays but oh, to be able to have a pair of pretty shoes for Sundays and high days. She hugged herself, grinning like a Cheshire

214

cat, and then began work on the dress.

It was an hour before dawn when she finished and she didn't bother to go to sleep. She was too excited anyway.

After Sunday lunch Hannah left the two men at the table enjoying their glass of port and nipped upstairs to change into her new dress. When she walked back into the dining room, their reaction was all she could have desired. The amazement on both faces turned to smiles and Seamus said, 'Well, I don't know how you've done it so quickly, lass, but that dress fits you like a glove. By, you're a bonny one and no mistake. What say you, Jake?'

Jake looked at the girl who up until a moment ago he had thought of as little more than a child. The dress showed the slim young figure off to perfection and above it the face, with its cream-tinted skin and enormous eyes shaded by long dark lashes, was more than bonny. She was a beauty, a real beauty, and she was still only sixteen. What was she going to be like when she was eighteen, nineteen? For some unknown reason he felt a constriction gripping his throat. It was a second or two before he realised it was the painful emotion which always welled up in him when confronted by pure unspoilt beauty. Swallowing hard, he managed to say, 'You look lovely, Hannah.'

'Thank you.'

Her youth was brought to the fore in the next moment when she twizzled round in the manner of a very young child, saying, 'See how it flares out? It's so beautiful, Seamus. I can never thank you enough.'

'Aw, go on with you. It was Jake who put the idea in my head if you must know.'

'I thought it might be.'

Her sparkling eyes thanked him and he said, 'Even the weather seems to have conspired to fall in with you. The sky is as blue as your dress.'

'I know.' She had hugged the knowledge to herself all morning. After the fierce storms, this Sunday was the sort of nutty autumn day when it was good to walk in the tawny sunlight. He would come. She was sure he would come and then he would see her in the new dress and... Well, he would see her in the new dress. That was enough. She glanced down at her hands which were chapped and red and wished for a moment they were soft and white like a lady's. But that was daft. He wouldn't expect that.

Joe had arrived early the week before because the days were short now, but by three o'clock there was still no sign of anyone. Hannah had prepared a sack of food as usual – Jake left it up to her what she gave. She checked the bag of potatoes, stone of flour, tea, sugar, cheese and whole ham as though something would have changed from the last time she looked through the sack half an hour before.

They had to come. Apart from anything else, it was only the food Jake gave that was standing between the family and starvation now. She glanced at the basket next to the sack which contained a dozen eggs and a big slab of butter. Naomi's mam would need this. She walked to the kitchen window and peered out, and saw Jake and Joe walking towards the house.

Adam hadn't come. For a moment the disappointment was so acute she wanted to burst into tears. Then she pulled herself together. Naomi wasn't with them either. Was she still ill? Was Adam ill?

She hurried to the door and was standing in the open doorway when Jake and Joe reached the house. 'You look bonny the day, Hannah.' Joe's voice was cheerful but his face was strained and Jake wasn't smiling.

Sensing something was seriously amiss, she waited until they had both scraped their boots clean before quietly saying, 'I'll make some tea and help yourself to some seed cake, Joe.'

'Ta, thanks, Hannah.' Instead of sitting down and taking a wedge from the plate on the kitchen table, Joe raised his eyes and looked straight at her as he said, 'Adam's not coming, lass. Neither's Naomi, but she's still bad. The cold's gone on her chest...' His voice dwindled away and he glanced helplessly at Jake.

'Adam's in a spot of bother.' Jake had been standing by the range and now he took the teapot out of her hand before she could fill it with water and put it on the steel shelf next to the hob. He led her to the table and pushed her down on a chair. 'It seems he has been accused of something which he is denying.'

'It's a lass, Lily Hopkins. She says she's expecting a bairn and it's Adam's,' Joe said in a rush. 'Mam an' Da have gone round hers with Adam this afternoon. There's been ructions...'

Hannah stared into Joe's troubled face. She had heard him, the words had registered, but strangely she was feeling numb. 'Is the bairn Adam's?'

'He says not. He says she's not too particular who she goes with and it could be any one of a number of blokes.'

'What do you say, Joe? Has ... has he been seeing this girl?'

Joe's hesitation was all the answer she needed. Hannah rose swiftly from her seat and left the kitchen. When Joe stood up and opened his mouth to call her, Jake said quietly, 'Leave her a while, Joe. She'll come back when she's ready.'

'He's a fool. He's the biggest fool out.'

'Aye, we're agreed on that.'

'It's like a sickness with him, the lassies. From when he was thirteen or fourteen he's been messing about with this one and that. The daft thing is, I think he does love Hannah in his way. He's always acted as though she's different to the rest.'

Jake's voice was grim when he said, 'He obviously doesn't love her enough, Joe. You don't treat a nice little lass like Hannah the way he's done.'

'No, I know.' Joe shook his head. 'By, Jake, the roof nearly went off the house when Lily's mam an' da come round. Mam went barmy at Adam, I thought she was going to belt him one. According to Lily's mam, her an' the da came back from her sister's the other night and found Lily with her head in the gas oven. It was touch and go for a time. Then it all come out about Adam and the bairn and how he'd told her he didn't want to know. Lily's mam was bawling her eyes out and her da wanted to string Adam up from the nearest lamp post when he said the

218

bairn could be anybody's. It was all me and Da could do to hold him. Now Father Gilbert's got involved and you know what he's like. He'll have the pair of them wed or my name's not Joe Wood. He could persuade the Pope himself to walk down the aisle, could Father Gilbert.'

'Aye.' Jake smiled wryly but more to himself than Joe. He'd had one or two run-ins with this particular priest when he had stopped going to his church shortly after coming to the farm. Father Gilbert had been beside himself when he'd told the priest he couldn't do with all the pomp and ceremony and incense-swinging, and not least the tales of purgatory that frightened little bairns to death and had their mams and das terrified as well. Father Turner or Father Mc-Haffie from the Fulwell Church were a different kettle of fish; you could talk to them, discuss things without it turning into fire and brimstone. He might have continued in the Faith if he'd gone to their church but Fulwell was too far by half and so he had forever damned himself in Father Gilbert's eyes by attending the Methodist chapel in Castletown now and again.

'Course Mam's frantic at the thought of Adam marrying Lily Hopkins but at the same time she can't see any other way with a bairn on the way. As if she hadn't got enough to put up with the way things are.'

Privately Jake thought Lily Hopkins would be getting the worst of the deal and if it hadn't been for Hannah's distress he would have been shouting for joy she was rid of Adam. Knowing how much Joe thought of his older brother he didn't voice this, saying instead, 'No change with the lockout then?'

Joe shook his head. 'Things are really bad. And what makes it worse is that the rest of the world is going along on its own sweet way. Nobody's interested in the dispute any more, it's gone on too long. They've got coal coming in from abroad and for them coal is coal. They don't care if it comes from our old enemy the Germans or Timbuktu. There's bairns in rags with no shoes on their feet, pigeons have been let go, hens have stopped laying and been eaten and even the bairns' pet rabbits have gone the same way. I tell you it's as bad as it could get, man.'

Jake shook his head. He had feared things would come to this but he would gladly have been proved wrong, if only for his mam's sake. He nodded to the sack and basket. 'There's some bits to take with you when you go.'

'Thanks, man. Mam'll be grateful. That last lot of logs you dropped off a couple of weeks ago has nearly gone.'

Jake took the hint. 'I'll bring some more this week. Tell her, would you?'

'Aye, I'll do that, Jake. I tell you, every last speck of coal has long since gone from the tips. Most folk have got nothing to make a fire with. No heat to warm the house, no hot water, not even to make a cup of tea with. Amy Stamp who was, her who lives across the road with her mam and married that lad, Ivor Hutton, you know?' Jake nodded. 'She lost her latest a couple of nights ago. A week old it was and it froze to death, according to the quack. Word is they were so on their uppers the bairn had blankets made out of old newspapers. Mam said she'd have had it in our house if she'd known. But folk don't say, see? They all soldier on.'

Joe raised his eyes and looked at his half-brother. 'And the thing is, Jake, the thing that eats me up...' He stopped, shaking his head and biting his bottom lip which was trembling.

'What, man? What is it?'

'In spite of all the misery and suffering and hatred, I'm glad the lockout's lasted like it has.' He gulped deeply. 'I'm scared to death about going back down, Jake. I don't know how I'm going to stand it. I'm having nightmares every night, I feel I'm going mad—'

'You're not going mad.' Jake looked into the young face. He was very fond of Joe, half-brothers though they were. Even Naomi had more than a bit of her da in her but Joe was all their mam. 'And if it helps, I know how you feel. I only went down once, when I was a lad of nine or thereabouts. Your da thought it a bright idea but as that cage descended, it was like going into hell. According to your da I made a fool of him by being sick and then passing out in the tunnel. He'd got special permission from the gaffer to let me see what was what. Well, I saw what was what and I'd have topped myself before I went down again.'

'Mam never said.'

'She doesn't know. It was your da's idea and I was bad for a week after with the skitters but he said he'd beat the life out of me if I told so I never did.'

'Why did he make you?'

221

Jake could have said, 'Because he's always been jealous of the love Mam's had for me, me being someone else's son, and he's got a nasty streak the size of Wearmouth Bridge running through the centre of him.' But he didn't. Instead he shrugged. 'Trying to toughen me up maybe? I don't know. The point is I know how you feel and you don't have to go down again. I said I'd find you work here in the first month of the lockout, didn't I? And the offer still stands. It's up to you. Like I said, you'd have to board with Clara and Frank but they're a nice old couple and she'd be tickled pink to have someone other than Frank to fuss over. I know you wouldn't want to leave Mam's–'

'It's not that, I wouldn't mind that. It's...'

'Adam.'

'And Da. They're... Well, you know how they are.'

Aye, he knew how they were all right. The pair of them wouldn't lift a finger if he was drowning except to push him further under but they ate the food he sent each week and warmed themselves by the fire his logs and coal kept going. He bit back on the hot anger, looking at Joe's unhappy face for a long moment before he was able to say, 'Well, it's up to you, lad. All I'd say is if you really think you can't go down again, the time to make a move is before the lockout ends. That way you've the excuse that you're earning money for the rest of them if nowt else. Of course farm work might not be for you–'

'It would be. It is. I don't care how hard I'd have to work, you know that, if I was up top

222

breathing the fresh air with the wind and rain and sun on me face.'

'I don't know so much about the fresh air, not near the pigsties or when the cattle are mucked out in the winter.'

'You know what I mean.'

Aye, he knew what Joe meant. Jake's expression was soft, his tone warm, when he said, 'You turned eighteen this summer. Maybe it's time to do what you want to do rather than what pleases Adam or your da. It's your life, Joe.'

'Aye, I've been thinking along those lines since you first offered me a job, to be truthful. And now this latest with Adam and Lily... It's stuck in me craw, Jake, if you want to know. I tried to warn him he'd lose Hannah if he carried on but he just laughed at me, took the mickey because I hadn't had a girl. You know.' Joe looked at his hands, his face burning, as though the admission was shameful.

Took the mickey because he hadn't had a girl, and Joe only eighteen. Jake shook his head. Wouldn't Adam split his sides if he knew that he, at thirty, was in the same boat. Oft times he'd considered visiting one of the numerous bawdy houses down by the docks when he was in town, but something in him had been repelled by going where umpteen other men had gone. Seamus had said in the past that he didn't give a lass a chance, that it was his manner rather than his face that kept them at a distance and he was probably right. Certainly there had been the odd one or two who'd made it plain they were game if he was but he hadn't been drawn to any of them.

Eliza Dobson for instance. She was neither plain nor pretty and her figure was good, but that simpering way she had was beyond irritating. And so he chastised his flesh with hard gallops on his hunter and physical work, leaving the farmhouse when everyone was asleep some nights and walking for hours to do away with the burning in his loins.

'Jake.' Joe brought his attention back to the present. 'There would be all hell let loose if I came. Are you prepared for that?'

'Me?' Jake smiled. 'It won't affect me one way or the other, believe me. I shall still go and see Mam when I want to, I assure you, and that's who I'm concerned about. The rest of them,' he shrugged, 'I can take them or leave them, to be truthful, Joe. Naomi will still come and see Hannah if I know anything about it.'

Joe nodded. 'She's tougher than she looks.'

'Anyway, think about it.'

'I've thought. I can't go back down, that's the bottom line. I – I'll tell them tonight. With all that's happening with Adam and Lily, it might, well, deflect things from me a bit.'

'You're not as daft as you look.'

'Just as well, eh?' Joe returned smartly and they both laughed just as Hannah came into the kitchen.

She looked at them. She had spent the last fifteen minutes standing at her bedroom window fighting the urge to give way to the storm of tears in her breast, knowing once she started she wouldn't be able to stop for a long time. She felt hurt, so hurt, and humiliated and stupid, and here were these two, who'd she'd thought were her friends, laughing. They cared that little about how she was feeling. Her head drooping, the urge to cry was back tenfold but then a stern voice within her said, 'None of that, don't give him or them the satisfaction.'

'Joe has just told me he's going to come and start work on the farm.'

Whether Jake had guessed how their laughter had affected her, Hannah didn't know, but his voice was gentle, so gentle it nearly undermined all she had just told herself.

'Good news in the midst of bad,' he continued softly, 'don't you think?'

'Yes, oh yes.' Genuinely pleased, Hannah smiled at Joe before walking across to the range and moving the big black kettle deeper into the fire to bring the water to the boil for the tea she had mentioned earlier. Turning, she said, 'I'm so glad, Joe. It's right for you, I know it is.'

'Aye, I think so.' Joe looked as though he had had a weight taken off his shoulders, and this was confirmed in the next moment when he said on a note of surprise, 'I feel different now I've made up me mind. I should have done it weeks ago.'

'Well, you've done it now.' She poured hot water into the teapot and brought it to the table along with four cups and saucers. When the tea was mashed she poured it out, pushing the milk and sugar towards Joe along with a huge piece of cake. Then she made up a tray for Seamus who had gone to lie down in his room a short while ago, saying he felt like a nap.

Jake offered to take the tray and when he had

left the kitchen, Joe swallowed a mouthful of cake and said quietly, 'Mam's beside herself at our Adam, Hannah. She thinks the world of you, you know. She's called him every name under the sun and so has Naomi.'

Slightly mollified, Hannah took a sip of her tea. 'I hate him,' she said flatly. 'You can tell him that when you see him.'

'Me mam said he hadn't the gumption to recognise a rose on a dung heap.'

'Did she?' Rose's support was warming. She had missed Naomi's mother more than she would have thought possible since she had come to the farm.

'Even Da said Adam wanted knocking into next weekend and he's always on Adam's side no matter what. But not over this. They think he's barmy.'

'What's she like, this Lily Hopkins?'

'Brazen,' Joe said promptly. 'She's been after Adam for ages, ever since he finished with her before.'

'He went out with her before?' Hannah didn't know why but this made everything worse. 'What does she look like?'

'She's all right.' Joe looked longingly at the cake. 'Ordinary. Not a patch on you.'

Hannah cut him another big piece of cake and watched him while he ate it. 'On second thoughts, Joe, don't say I hate him. Say it didn't bother me a bit, that – that I was out walking with Daniel Osborne when you left and you heard us laughing. Say that.'

Joe stared at her, a little bewildered. 'Aye, all right.'

She wasn't going to let Adam see that he had broken her heart, she would rather die. Her chin rose with her thoughts. He could have this Lily Hopkins and if she ever saw them out she would smile and chat as though he had never meant a thing to her. She would show him. Him and his piecrust promises.

Jake came back within a few minutes. He shook his head and said, 'He's not well, he does far too much. The doctor told him to slow down months ago but you can't tell him anything. Don't say I let on though.'

The three of them sat and chatted about this and that for an hour or so, Hannah forcing herself to appear natural and unconcerned about Adam's betrayal in front of Joe and Jake. For once she was relieved when Joe stood up to go. She gathered up the last of the seed cake and put it in the basket with the eggs and butter, saying, 'Are you sure you can manage the sack and basket by yourself? It's a long walk home.'

'Lass, I'd walk ten times as long for what's in them.'

They both accompanied Joe to the end of the lane, waving until he'd disappeared out of sight. Hannah stared after him. She wouldn't see Adam walking down there again. Adam. Oh, Adam, Adam. The pain in her heart was so bad she didn't know what to do with herself.

'You were great.' Jake's voice was very deep and very soft at the side of her. She glanced at him and what she saw in the handsome marred face caused the dam to break. Shaking with sobs she made no protest when he took her in his arms, holding her

227

against his massive chest as she cried and cried while he made soothing noises above her head. His tweed jacket smelt of pipe smoke. It was comforting, as was the warmth of another human body.

It was a long time before she could pull herself together sufficiently to raise her head, and then a large white handkerchief was pushed into her hand. She wiped her eyes and blew her nose, pushed a few damp wisps of hair from her face before managing a wobbly smile. 'I'm sorry, I didn't mean to do that.'

'I'm glad you did, it's better out than in.' His voice was calm and matter-of-fact and it helped ease the embarrassment that was now uppermost. 'But I'll say one thing before we put this behind us. Adam might be family but he's not worth a single tear, lass.'

She looked at him. These days she found she didn't have to try to focus on just the normal part of his face, she could take in the whole without worrying he was thinking she was staring at the terrible scars. 'I – I can't see that right now,' she said honestly.

'You will.'

Would she? She hoped so, she did so hope so because she didn't want to feel like she was feeling now for months or years. Taking a deep breath, she said, 'It's got dark while we've been standing here, Seamus will wonder where on earth we've got to if he comes down.' She smiled at him, squaring her slim shoulders beneath the cornflower blue of the dress. 'And I'm freezing.'

'Here.' He took off his jacket and put it round

her shoulders. 'Let's go and have another cup of tea.'

And it was like that, with the smell and warmth of him all around her, that they retraced their steps to the farmhouse.

Chapter 14

Joe arrived back at the farm the next day. He was white-faced and stiff-lipped as a result of the row which had blazed between him and his father and brother when he'd announced his intention to work for Jake. He didn't go into detail as to what had been said and Jake did not ask. When Jake delivered the logs for the family later in the week, both Wilbur and Adam were present but they said not a word, not about Joe, nor about Adam's fall from grace. The pair of them left the house shortly after Jake arrived and did not return before he left.

Three weeks later, on the same day that Adam married Lily Hopkins in a hasty ceremony presided over by a grim-faced Father Gilbert and which only the two sets of parents attended, the six-month coal dispute finally ended, although in Durham most of the miners stayed out for another month. It was generally acknowledged the miners had been starved into submission. To add insult to injury they were forced to concede the principle that agreements on wages and conditions should be negotiated locally and not nationally. When they returned to the collieries, lists of names were posted on the noticeboards at the pit gates. If a man's name was there, he worked. If it wasn't, he didn't. Adam's name was on the gate. His father's was not. Those men who were allowed back swallowed their pride and went for the sake of their families. On the evening Lily took up residence with Adam in the room Joe had recently vacated, she announced she was feeling too exhausted to continue working at the northern laundry. This did not improve relations between Lily and her mother-in-law.

As Christmas approached, Hannah deliberated over whether to go with Jake and Joe when they visited the house in Wayman Street. Jake had told her it would be for an hour or so on Christmas Day afternoon. Although she was aching to see Rose again – and Naomi too, who had been unable to come to the farm since she'd been ill – the thought of facing Adam and his new wife was daunting. The wound was still raw and she was worried she would make a fool of herself. Eventually, though, the decision was taken out of her hands. Seamus suffered a mild heart attack just before Christmas and the doctor confined him to bed, insisting he had to remain there for at least a week. As neither Jake nor Hannah trusted the irascible old man to do what he was told if he was left in the house alone, it was agreed Hannah would stay behind and keep an eye on him.

She waved Jake and Joe off after Christmas lunch with a determined smile, watching the horse and trap until it was out of sight. Willing herself not to cry, she returned to the kitchen and cleared away the remains of the meal. She filled the cats' bowls with chopped-up turkey and watched them eat the treat as she tried to sort out her feelings. She was relieved she hadn't gone but at the same time achingly disappointed.

Telling herself not to be so silly, she put the kettle on the hob to make a cup of tea. It was a bitterly cold day but bright, the driving snow and wind of the last weeks having subsided. Everything was frozen outside but she didn't mind that. It was infinitely preferable to the acres of mud of the autumn when her legs had been constantly whipped by the wet hem of her coat and her face blotched and numb with cold.

She stood for a moment at the kitchen window. Plumes of smoke rose from the chimneys of the labourers' cottages but no one was about. The animals still had to be fed and cared for even on Christmas Day and she knew everyone had been up at the crack of dawn as usual, but for now Seamus's men were enjoying the luxury of a Christmas afternoon doze in front of the fire after their turkey lunch. Come evening they would turn out again.

After mashing the tea she took Seamus a cup, leaving it on the little table at the side of the bed when she saw he was asleep. She stood for a moment looking down at him before she left the room. She had been shocked when Jake had told her of Seamus's heart condition, she had thought the farmer fit and well on the whole, in spite of Jake mentioning the doctor had told him to slow down months before. But all old folk slowed down. She hadn't realised there was anything more sinister to it than that.

She would look after him now she knew. She nodded mentally to the thought. He had been so kind to her, as had Jake, and she would make sure he didn't do too much once he was on his feet again, even though he'd probably get irritable and fractious with her because of it. Smiling ruefully, she left the room and returned to the kitchen. She had actually sat down with a cup of tea in her hand when a voice from the direction of the scullery said, 'Hello, Hannah,' causing her to jump out of her skin and send the tea splashing onto the table.

'I'm sorry, I didn't mean to frighten you. I came in the kitchen and then I heard footsteps so I thought I'd better make myself scarce in case it was the farmer.' Adam came fully into the kitchen, his eyes never leaving her shocked face.

'What – what are you doing here?' She'd risen to her feet, her hand at her throat, shocked he'd entered the house without being invited.

He returned her stare for some seconds before he said, 'Isn't it obvious?'

'Jake and Joe aren't here, they've gone to–'

'I know where they've gone, I watched them leave. Mam said last night they were coming over this afternoon. That's why I'm here now.'

His manner wasn't what she would have expected. She had always imagined, in the moments she let herself think of him, that if they met he would be shamefaced, sheepish, even remorseful. His cool effrontery worked like a shot of adrenaline and now her voice was stronger when she

232

said, 'I don't understand why you have come, Adam, but I think you ought to leave.'

'Just like that? The snow's feet deep in places and I've walked over three miles to come and see you.'

'Well, you shouldn't have. You have a wife, a bairn on the way–'

'You don't need to tell me that.' The look on his handsome face was aggressive. She had never imagined in her wildest dreams she would be frightened of Adam but she had prickles of fear running up and down her spine. 'If anyone knows that, I do. And all this is your fault, you know that, don't you? You've brought it on yourself, on both of us. I didn't want it this way, you know I didn't. But would you be kind to me? No. You drove me to the likes of Lily, damn you. I saw her so we could be all right when we were together, that's all. Nothing would have come of it, I'd have waited for you, but she had to go and fall. I think she did it on purpose. In fact I'm sure she did.'

'I don't want to know.'

'I don't want her, Hannah. I never have.'

She could hardly believe he was here saying these things, that he was blaming *her* for his unfaithfulness. 'She's expecting your bairn so how can you say you never wanted her?'

'Oh that, that's nowt. Any lass would have done for that, it was just that she pestered me day and night. But it's you I love, you know that. And you love me, you know you do. All this about Daniel Osborne don't hold no water. Our Joe can't lie to save his life. I know you still love me.'

'I want you to go, Adam. Right now. Just go.'

'Listen to me, hear what I've got to say.' His voice low now, he said, 'I'm sorry, Hannah. I didn't mean for things to turn out the way they have. If she hadn't tricked me, you'd be none the wiser. I'd do anything to alter things but I can't.'

So it was Lily's fault now. First hers, now Lily's. Anyone's but Adam's. For the first time since Joe had told her about the other girl, she found she could think about her without her stomach clenching with jealousy and hate.

Whether Adam mistook her silence for encouragement she didn't know, but the next moment he took a step or two towards her, his voice holding the beguiling note he did so well as he said softly, 'We could still meet sometimes, Hannah, just the two of us. No one need know. I wouldn't expect anything, not a thing, but we could talk and that. I love you and you love me, we can't let anything stand in the way of that. And who knows what the future might bring? Only last week a young lass up the street died having a bairn, it happens.'

Appalled into speech, she said, 'Stop it, stop that talk right now. You're a married man and there is nothing between us now, nothing, nor will there be even if you became free tomorrow.'

'You don't mean that. You're just saying it to punish me and I can understand that, it's natural. But the odd hour sometimes wouldn't hurt anyone. Come on, lass, say you will. You know you want to. It can't end like this. You don't want that any more than I do.'

His absolute confidence in his power over her robbed her of speech for a moment. He stood scrutinising her through lowered lids and she noticed he had dressed up. He must have got his suit out of pawn, probably for Christmas Eve Mass. Such was her complete disillusionment she didn't fool herself it was specially to see her.

'I don't want you any more, Adam.' It came out more baldly than she'd intended and she saw he was taken aback. 'Whatever was between us, it's gone. Dead. I don't know what it was, to be truthful, not in view of what's happened. All I want is for you to go back to her, to your wife.'

'I know you don't mean that.'

But he was uncertain, she could read it in his eyes. He'd begun to realise he couldn't sweet-talk her.

'I do mean it,' she said flatly, praying her voice wouldn't tremble. 'I wouldn't want you to touch me now. I'd feel mucky, dirty.'

'Because I'm married?'

'Not just because of that.'

He stared back at her. 'Is it because of him, that Daniel Osborne? The first time I saw him I knew he wanted you. Have you been carrying on behind my back?'

His audacity was amazing. 'There is nothing between Daniel and me, if you want to know. Is that the only reason you can come up with for me not wanting you, that I'm seeing someone else? Well, I'm not. This has nothing to do with anyone except me and you. I really don't want you any more, it's as simple as that. You're a liar and a cheat. You must have been carrying on with Lily Hopkins for weeks and weeks, likely others as well. You disgust me, Adam Wood. All right?'

He swore, the profanity harsh. 'I've risked plenty to come here today like this.'

'No one asked you to.'

'And that's your answer?'

'Aye, it is.'

'You smug little piece. There's a side to you you've kept hidden. You've a hard streak running through you, I see it now. It makes me wonder what really happened that night with your uncle. Did you lead him on, was that it?'

She gulped, not because she didn't know what to say but because his words had hurt her so much. She felt the colour sweeping over her face and she had the urge to walk across the kitchen and smack his face, but somehow she knew that was what he was expecting. He'd turn it to his advantage somehow. It would show weakness and she mustn't do that. 'Get out.' She raised her chin in a gesture that was characteristic of her. 'And don't come back.'

'And if I don't want to?'

She didn't really think he would go so far as to try and attack her. Nevertheless she said, 'I was taking Farmer Shawe a cup of tea when you hid in the scullery.' His face reddened. 'He's in the sitting room and these days there's always a shotgun to hand since we've been having trouble with poachers.' This last had the advantage of being true. 'I would suggest you leave now and quietly. He wouldn't take kindly to someone breaking into his house. I only have to call and he'll be down.'

'I didn't break in.'

'Well, you weren't invited so how else would you term it?'

He stared at her for one moment more and then stalked past her, his face black with rage. It wasn't until the kitchen door had banged and silence had reigned for some long seconds that Hannah let out her breath in a shaking sigh and dropped onto one of the hard-backed chairs.

The things he had said, the way he had tried to blame everything on her. Of a sudden she jumped up and hurried to the door, sliding the bolts at the top and bottom before gathering Buttons in her arms and sitting in Jake's armchair. She held the cat's soft, warm body to her and cried and cried.

How could she have imagined she loved him? How? But she had. She had thought he was her sun, moon and stars.

Her eyes felt sore and her face was swollen after the bout of crying was exhausted. Telling herself she mustn't let Jake or Joe know Adam had come to see her, she bathed her face for ten minutes in cold water before going to her room and brushing out her hair and fastening it once again into a bun at the back of her head.

What a Christmas Day! Every other Christmas Day afternoon she had spent with her Aunt Aggie, sitting on her bed while they read her aunt's magazines and ate sugared almonds and chocolate. Had her aunt received the letters she had written since being at the farm? She hadn't replied, so maybe not. Oh, why were people so horrible? Human beings could be so much worse than the animals. She had said this to Jake in the aftermath of finding out about Lily, and he had agreed with her.

She stuck the last pin in her hair and stared at her reflection in the spotted mirror of the dressing table. She didn't ask herself at this moment which human beings belonged in this category but she knew Adam was only one of them. She felt tired, very tired but it wasn't a physical thing.

But there were good folk too. She nodded to the girl in the mirror. Look how Clara and Frank treated Joe as one of their own, and Daniel had gone out of his way to show Joe the ropes. And then there was Jake. The thought of his big broad-shouldered figure made her wish he was home. She felt safe when he was around.

She would have a word with him about her Aunt Aggie. See if he could come up with a way she could make sure her letters got to her aunt. Perhaps Jake would agree to go round and put one in her aunt's hand himself.

No. She immediately dismissed the thought. She couldn't ask him to do that. It would be too much of an imposition. But neither could she go. It wasn't the possibility of seeing her uncle and mother which deterred her. She could grit her teeth and cope with that, unpleasant though it would be. But if she saw her aunt face to face there was a chance the truth about her abrupt departure from the house might come out, and it would break Aunt Aggie's heart. All in all, perhaps it was best to leave things as they were. But what must her aunt be thinking?

She shook her head at her muddled thoughts. Why did everything seem so complicated? Sometimes she felt her life was a battleground governed as much by her thinking as events. But she was not going to let her uncle and mother, or Adam either, spoil her life here. It was up to her how much she let past happenings dwell on her mind and she wasn't going to give any of them the satisfaction of crumbling. This was a new life, a new start. She had to look at it like that and make the most of it.

She turned from the mirror and walked to the door. She was going to make a fresh pot of tea and sit in front of the fire with the cats for company and read the latest copy of the *Woman's Weekly* Jake had bought her a few days ago when he'd gone into town. Admittedly there were a hundred and one things needing her attention but this was Christmas Day after all. Perhaps her aunt was reading the same magazine. 'Happy Christmas, Aunt Aggie,' she murmured, walking down the stairs. 'Know I'm thinking about you today and that I love you.'

In fact Hannah had been on Agatha's mind all day. As the weeks had gone on, Agatha had become convinced an argument with Miriam wouldn't have prevented Hannah from contacting them or at least writing. No, there was more to this than met the eye but with Edward and Miriam seemingly content with the current state of affairs, there was little she could do, bedridden as she was. But if she could just see Hannah, talk to her, she was sure she could convince her niece to come back home.

She said as much to Edward when he brought her an afternoon cup of tea but in a roundabout way. The last weeks had taught her her husband was touchy about the lass's departure. She rather thought Edward looked at it as a personal insult, as though Hannah had thrown all their love and concern back in their faces.

Once he had seated himself at the side of the bed with his own tea, she let him take a couple of sips before she said, 'I've been thinking about Hannah. She was right pleased with that bracelet you picked out for her last Christmas. Do you remember?'

'Bracelet? Oh aye, that's right.'

'I wonder if she still wears it. I mean it's not as if she fell out with us, is it? Just her mam.'

His eyes were staring at her now and he said quietly, 'Likely she looks on the three of us as one and the same.'

'I shouldn't think so.' There was a note of indignation in Agatha's voice. 'I for one always got on with her extremely well and so did you, didn't you? She helped you in the shop, you worked together and never a cross word.'

'I suppose so.'

'So doesn't it seem strange to you that she hasn't at least written to us if not her mother?'

'Strange? Not really.'

'Well, it does to me.'

'Aggie, we've had this conversation more times than I've had hot dinners.' He paused, turning his eyes from her and looking to the other side of the room as he went on, 'If Hannah doesn't want to see us or write, that's up to her. You have to accept that.'

'Well, it seems to me you've certainly had no difficulty accepting it,' she said sharply. 'Perhaps

240

I can't write folk out of my life so speedily as you.' It was rare, almost unheard of for her to speak to him in such a fashion and for a moment the look on his face made her want to put out her hand and smooth his hair back from his brow and tell him it didn't matter. But it did matter, and since she had become convinced Miriam was more to her husband than merely his sister-in-law, the tenderness she'd felt for him, a tenderness which had formed a large part of her love and which had been faintly maternal in its substance, had withered and died. And so she continued to sip her tea before she said, 'I don't believe Miriam, Edward. There, I've said it. You know I've thought it for weeks and now I've said it and you can think what you like. Miriam isn't what she seems in more ways than one.'

His eyes shot to her face with the last words. 'Now, now,' he blustered, 'don't take on. I know Miriam can be a funny one at times but we'd have been hard pressed without her, lass. Fair's fair.'

Aye, you might well look like that, thought Agatha. That's put the wind up you, hasn't it? 'I don't think we would have been hard pressed as you put it. What does she do that a part-time housekeeper couldn't? I can wash myself and you see to the disposal of the chamber pot and things of that nature. For years Hannah helped out in the shop, and now you say Bart is doing well enough. You're surely not run off your feet down there, Edward. Not with the way things are at present. No one's got any money to throw about, that's for sure. To put it bluntly, sometimes I think Miriam imagines she's your wife. Not me.'

Now she had really rattled him; she could see him wondering what she knew. Edward paid great store by his reputation as a comfortably well-off shopkeeper and pillar of the community; she knew he had been angling to get on the town council for years. One whiff of scandal and that would be put paid to, along with half their business most likely.

'That new doctor that's taken over from Dr Heath, Dr Clark, you know,' she waited for him to nod his head, 'I might do what he suggested and see one of them consultant people at the infirmary in the new year. Dr Heath would have been content for me to stay in this bed for ever as long as he had his payment each month when he called, but this one is a different kettle of fish. Young, up to date with all the new advances and what have you. He seems to think they might be able to do something for me. It would be a long job, he said, with me having been bed-bound for so long, but he reckons once the bleeding and pain is seen to I'd find myself with a new lease of life. What do you say about that?'

She stopped speaking and looked him straight in the eye. He returned her glance but paused before bringing himself to say, 'Why – why haven't you mentioned this before? I – this is the first you've said about an operation.'

Yes, because she had wanted to choose her moment. She knew what Miriam had had in mind – for years. The woman was like a vulture willing her to die so she could pick the bones of everything that made up her life – her home, the business and not least her husband. Oh yes, she had Miriam's measure. And this was her Christmas box to her sister-in-law.

She watched her husband trying to conceal his agitation. She had never thought herself to be a vindictive woman. Until the last few years she would have labelled herself nice, forgiving, even overly softhearted, but since Dr Clark's visit two weeks ago when she had caught a glimpse of a way out of this soft, comfortable hell, she had been forced to recognise she hadn't known herself very well.

Becoming aware Edward was waiting for an answer, she roused herself. 'Why haven't I mentioned this before?' She shrugged. 'I suppose I wanted to get it clear in my mind first whether I was prepared to go the route of an operation. It's no good seeing a consultant unless I'd do what he might say, is it?'

She waited to see if he would swallow the explanation.

'I see.' His lips moved one over the other as if he was sucking something from them. 'And you are quite sure you would?'

'Oh yes, Edward. Quite sure.'

Even at this late stage if he had reached out and taken her into his arms, said something encouraging along the lines that of course she must take the chance and he would be with her all the way, even then she might have found it in her heart to try and love him again. As it was he continued to drink his tea before rising and saying, 'We'll speak to Dr Clark again, you and I together so I can hear what he says. These young doctors are all very well with their modern ideas but not everything new is necessarily beneficial. An operation carries a high degree of risk and is not something to be undertaken lightly.'

If she had been wavering, this would have made up her mind for her. But she was already sure. She marvelled he knew her so little after twenty-two years of marriage. But at the moment she was still stuck in this bed and at the mercy of them both and so she nodded and said, 'Quite.' She had said enough to Dr Clark for him to suspect her husband might be awkward to deal with. He was a canny lad, Dr Clark.

'Would you care for another cup of tea?'

She nodded again, letting him reach the door before she said quietly, 'The next time Rose Wood calls in the shop, ask her to come up and have a word with me, would you?'

'Rose Wood?' He swung round, his voice high with surprise.

'She's Jake Fletcher's mother and likely she has news of Hannah if she's still staying with him at the farm.'

She saw his eyes blink rapidly for a moment. 'Mrs Wood rarely comes into the shop, they can't afford much these days. Like some others I could name, that family does most of its shopping at the market late at night when stuff's marked down. But ... but if I see her passing I'll ask.'

Aye, and pigs fly. Agatha let her eyes rest on her husband for some seconds before she said, 'Thank you, Edward.'

He hesitated, looking as though he was about to say something more but then he nodded and left the room, closing the door gently behind him.

He did not walk through to the kitchen to pour his wife another cup of tea but instead joined Miriam in the sitting room. She was slouched in an armchair, a half-full box of chocolates at the side of her and a magazine in her hand. 'What's the matter?' She stared at him as he stood just inside the room.

'I'll tell you what the matter is. You should have let her have Hannah's letters like I told you. There was nothing in them she couldn't have read.'

'Well, we didn't know that till I opened them, did we? And once I'd done that we couldn't very well give her them then.'

'She's like a dog with a bone, she never lets up.'

'She will, don't fret.'

The irritation her casualness invoked came through in his voice when he said, 'Do you want to know what she's just told me?'

'What?' Miriam sat up in the chair. 'What's up?'

'Her, or likely to be. This new doctor that's took over, him that's all bright eyed and bushy tailed, he's told her to see a consultant at the hospital with a view to having some kind of operation. He reckons it'll make a new woman out of her.'

Miriam stared at him. 'That's ridiculous, she's as weak as a kitten. Look how that cold she caught in October nearly finished her off. How does he think she could come through an operation?'

'I'm just telling you what she said.'

'And she'd do it? She'd have the operation if they asked her to?'

'Oh aye, she'd have it all right.'

'Then let her.'

'What?'

Miriam did not look at him but took her time selecting a chocolate from the box beside her. 'Let her have the operation if she's set on it,' she said flatly. 'If that's what this consultant she's going to see recommends, let her have it. You couldn't very well stop it anyway.'

Edward stood staring at her, an empty cup and saucer in either hand. 'I thought...'

As his voice trailed away, Miriam looked up. 'You thought I wouldn't want her to have it?'

'Well, aye. Aye, I did. If she was up on her feet again it'd mean... Well, what I mean is, it'd be nigh impossible for us to...'

'I don't think there's much likelihood of Agatha getting on her feet again, operation or no operation. And before that happened she would have to come through the anaesthetic. From what I understand, you have to be as strong as a horse to withstand that.'

There was a long pause. 'Then ... then I should talk her out of it.'

'Oh, don't be so stupid, Edward.' Miriam stubbed the words at him. 'Not to mention hypocritical. You know as well as I do her days are numbered. Look at her, she's skin and bone. And the bleeding, it's worse than ever. What difference does it make if she goes quickly in an operation or lingers for months in the state she's in now? An operation would be ... merciful. Aye, merciful. That's all I'm saying.'

In the ensuing silence, Edward watched as she

246

took another chocolate and popped it in her mouth. She picked up the magazine from her lap, saying, 'If you're getting another cup of tea, I'd like one.'

He said nothing more before he left the room but once in the kitchen he stood with his hands palm down on the table and his head bent. He was caught between a rock and a hard place. Miriam on the one hand and Aggie on the other. Did his wife know about Miriam? It seemed impossible she did or she'd say something, and yet... He wasn't so sure. The Aggie who had spoken to him in the bedroom a few minutes ago was not the lass he had married or the invalid of the last years. Dear gussy... He groaned softly, shaking his head from side to side. If she did know and she got better, she'd make his life a living hell, any woman would. But on the other hand, if she didn't come through the operation he'd have Miriam to contend with. He'd rather cut off his right hand than marry her, but she was a nasty bit of work, Miriam. Who knew what she'd do if she felt she was a woman scorned. He wouldn't put it past her to approach Hannah and persuade the lass to tell tales out of school and then his name hereabouts would be mud. All in all he thought he'd rather take his chances with Aggie...

It was getting dark by the time Hannah heard the horse and trap return. Outside, the weather was thickening, the earlier sunshine having been overtaken by more storm clouds.

She had lit the oil lamps in the kitchen and hall and Seamus's room, and was busy making

247

sandwiches with the last of the Christmas turkey and baked stuffing when Jake walked in the kitchen, shaking the snow off his cap.

She smiled at him as he said, 'We're in for another packet right enough, it's coming down thicker than ever. Old Isaac said we were in for a bad winter and he's never wrong.' He rubbed his boots on the cork mat and walked over to the red glow of the fire in the range, holding out his chilled hands to the warmth.

'Isaac is always pessimistic,' Hannah said indulgently. 'In all the time I've been here I've never heard him predict anything good.'

'That's true.' Jake turned his head, grinning. 'And in that case I suppose he's got to be right at least some of the time. It just seems like all the time but that's probably because he isn't shy about reminding you when things turn out the way he foretold.'

She was so glad he was home. To hide the emotion which had flooded her breast, she said quietly, 'How did you find them all when you got to the house? Did your mother like the cake I sent? You did tell her it was specially from me?'

'Those were the very words I used.'

Hannah had sent Rose one of the big round Christmas cakes Clara had helped her make at the beginning of November. She had made three in all, crammed with fruit and each one holding a good measure of cooking brandy. She had also loaded Jake up with a large slab of golden butter, a cold joint of cooked beef and several other goodies, and Jake had added several bottles of cider made from the farm's apple trees. The best eating apples were laid out on newspaper in the attic ready for eating all through the winter months, but there were plenty of sour ones which were crushed in Seamus's cider press and treated with yeast and other ingredients before the juice was put into barrels. Apparently Clover Farm's cider was known for miles around for having a kick like a mule.

'So how was everyone?' she asked again.

'About as you would expect.' Jake took off his coat and the new muffler she had bought him for Christmas. She had bought a similar one for Seamus too, and in return the two men had presented her with a silver bracelet engraved with tiny flowers. She had left the charm bracelet her aunt and uncle had bought her at the flat and her mother hadn't included it with her belongings. Not that she had worn it after she realised why her mother had been so put out when her uncle had bought her the gift.

Jake walked across to the table and reached for a morsel of turkey. He swallowed it before he said flatly, 'It's not a happy household, Hannah.'

No, she didn't suppose it was. 'Perhaps it will be better when things pick up again workwise. Less of a struggle, you know.' She couldn't bring herself to mention Lily.

Jake shook his head. 'I can't see Wilbur working again. He's had his card marked as a trouble-maker. He was a puffler the last few years.' At her look of inquiry, he said, 'If any of the men's wages was docked unfairly or they felt they should've been paid for wet work or gassy work or whatever, he was designated as the one who'd go and see the deputy, even the overman if needs be. He had some right rows with them about whether the gas was bad enough to affect the men's breathing and how many lamps it'd put out, things like that. All very laudable, but Wilbur being Wilbur, he got under their skins. It's one of the reasons they haven't put Adam back at the face, if you ask me. The face is where the money is. As it is, Mam said he's earning seventeen shillings and thruppence doing the sort of labouring work you do as a young lad. Fetching and carrying, passing stuff and tidying up after the skilled blokes, even shovelling pony muck. They'll let him stew and get the message he's going to have to keep his mouth shut, unlike his father, before he gets face work again.'

If it hadn't been for this afternoon she would have found it in her to feel sorry for Adam. 'Seventeen shillings and thruppence and Naomi's bit to support the whole lot of them?'

'And Joe's wage,' said Jake mildly, sitting at the table.

'But that's not much after he's paid Clara his board.' All the men and women, the bairns who earned something too, would stand in line each week for their wages from Jake. As an inexperienced newcomer to the farm, Joe would be lucky to get half of what someone like Daniel would receive.

Jake glanced at her. 'It's not too bad.'

He was putting in money from his own pocket before he gave Rose Joe's wage packet. Hannah didn't know how she knew but she was sure of it. And although she knew he would be doing it

250

purely for his mother and to alleviate her worry, it would also mean Wilbur was saved the indignity of having to go to the Guardians because they couldn't manage on what was coming into the house. She stared at Jake. Quietly, she said, 'Does Joe know you add to it each week before you hand it over?'

His eyes narrowed momentarily, then he smiled. 'Not much gets past you, does it? Aye, Joe knows. It's our little secret.'

'And your mother?'

'Joe's wage packet is Joe's wage packet as far as she's concerned. There's no need for her to know different. If it slipped out and Wilbur got to know...' He shrugged. 'Let's just say it'd make life difficult for my mam. Not that he'd tell her to stop accepting it, mind.' He stopped, shaking his head, and the words came slow and deep as he said, 'Why she ever married him is beyond me. She didn't have to. We lived with her parents and my grandmother looked after me while she worked.'

'Perhaps she missed your father.'

'She had her parents and me.'

'But she might have been lonely for... Well, a partner. You know?'

It was some seconds before he answered, 'Aye, I know,' and he stood up as he did so. 'I'll go and have a word with Seamus before I have my tea. Do you want me to take a tray up for him?'

'I haven't mashed the tea yet. You go up and I'll bring his tray shortly.'

When Jake had left the kitchen, Hannah stood biting her lip and berating herself for her thoughtlessness. That had been a silly thing to say, why didn't she think before she spoke? He was the last person on earth she wanted to upset. But if she said anything now, it would make things worse.

She began to busy herself with setting the table for the two of them and seeing to Seamus's tray, her movements jerky with her agitation and the encounter with Adam relegated to the back of her mind. Trying to justify herself, she thought, it wasn't as if he *had* to be by himself. It was his choice. Since Joe had begun work at the farm he'd told her it was common knowledge among the farm folk that Grace Osborne had liked Jake for ages. Apparently Grace had cried buckets when Farmer Dobson's daughter had made it plain how she felt about him, only pulling herself together when it became apparent Jake had no intention of responding to the farmer's daughter's overtures either.

Hannah had been surprised at first by what Joe had said, but the more she had thought about it, the more she'd acknowledged that Jake did have something about him in spite of his scars. Or perhaps because of them. Oh, she didn't know. And she couldn't think about this now, her head felt as though it was going to explode. One thing was for sure, she wouldn't be sorry to see the end of this year once Christmas was over. Whatever happened in 1927 it couldn't be as traumatic as 1926.

PART FOUR

1927 –The New Life

Chapter 15

It was now August 1927 and life had gone on quite smoothly on the whole since Christmas. True, Seamus's health had deteriorated and he was confined to bed permanently, but he was reasonably cheerful about it most of the time. Shortly after Christmas he had suffered another heart attack and Jake had taken the decision to convert the dining room into a bed-sitting room for the farmer. This had been partly so Seamus could feel he was still part of the day-to-day life of the farm – the view from the dining room's large windows, next to which Seamus's bed had been placed, encompassed the lane which led to the pigsties and barns and was always a hive of activity – but also because it was more practical for Hannah who had taken on the daily care and nursing of the elderly man. She had done this willingly, glad she could repay the farmer in some measure for his kindness to her, and her attitude had gone a long way to settling Seamus.

He attended to his own toilette each morning, Hannah bringing in a bowl of warm water, soap and a towel and then leaving him to it for half an hour before she returned to collect the items. And Jake had acquired a commode after Seamus had flatly refused to continue using the bedpan for any foreseeable amount of time. On the whole the arrangement worked well. Seamus had a large brass bell for use in case of emergency, although to date it had not been necessary.

Jake had now taken over the running of the farm completely, and Daniel Osborne became his manager. The two men got on very well and Daniel had taken Joe under his wing which had proved invaluable for Joe's inclusion in the life of the farm, both workwise and socially.

The only cloud on the horizon, at least as far as Hannah was concerned, was that she knew the day was coming when she would have to speak frankly with Daniel and dash his hopes. He had gradually made it clear after hearing about Adam's hasty wedding that he liked her, and although she had given him no encouragement he didn't seem to take her gentle rebuffs for what they were. She didn't want to hurt him, he was a good, nice man, and Jake and Joe, the two folk she was closest to, regarded him highly, but she knew she could never think of Daniel as anything other than a friend. Thus far she had hidden behind the constant daily workload of caring for Seamus and running the farmhouse – a workload which meant she was on her feet from six in the morning until eleven at night – to put off the moment, but she knew it would come. She just hoped it didn't make it difficult for her to stay at the farm; she found it impossible to contemplate leaving.

She paused in her task of running the sheets through the mangle in the wash-house. The winter had been hard and sometimes she hadn't known what to do with herself when her chilblains had kept her awake with their itching half the night and her chapped hands had bled, however much goose fat she'd rubbed in them. But then the next day she'd visit the cowshed, warm and stickily scented with milky magic, and know she'd rather be at the farm than in the narrow confines of her uncle's shop. Spring had brought the leggy lambs running up to their mothers for short and urgent sucking sessions and May the blossoming of plum and apple trees in the farm's orchard. It had been then that she had decided to do something about Bess's long neglected garden, despite the fact she was on her feet from dawn to dusk as it was.

The garden walls were coated with lichen and everything was such a tangle of foot-high nettles, brambles, thistles and other weeds which had bitten at her for removing them that more than once she had decided the job was too big on top of everything else. But she had persevered and gradually she had uncovered a little winding path, rose arches and Bess's little paradise for birds at the rear of the gently sloping ground.

To step into the garden now, as she normally tried to do in the twilight of the summer evenings, was to be met with a glorious combination of colour and scent. Foxgloves leaned against the dry-stone walls, roses twined round the arches, their blooms heavy and drunk with perfume, honeysuckle and hollyhocks, sweet peas and lavender glowed and gleamed and exhaled a spicery of humming fragrance. Bees and butterflies vied with the birds for enjoyment of the small sanctuary. Despite all of Seamus's shaking of his head and tut-tutting when he found out what she was doing, she knew he'd been pleased with the end result when Jake and Joe had carried him out to see it a few nights back. That evening had given her the idea that had sent Jake into town that very day in the farm cart, and now, as she heard it trundling into the farmyard, she stopped her mangling and went outside.

She met him in the yard and as he jumped down from the cart, she said, 'Did you get one? Did you find one?'

He nodded, grinning as he threw back the large piece of sacking covering the object in the back of the cart.

'Perfect.' Hannah looked with satisfaction at the stout wheelchair.

'And in a while Isaac and Frank will bring round that bench they've made,' Jake said quietly although Seamus wouldn't be able to hear them from the house.

The bench had been her idea too, so that Jake or herself or any visitors could sit with the farmer in the garden when the weather was clement.

She smiled widely at him. 'This will be so good for him, you'll see.'

'You're good for all of us,' he said lightly, lifting the wheelchair onto the stone slabs. He straightened up and looked at her. 'I called in my mother's while I was in town.'

Something in his voice caused her to become still. 'Yes?'

'Lily had the bairn last night. A little girl.'

Just for a second a pang throbbed in her heart but it was gone in an instant. She was glad she was able to say with sincerity, 'I hope mother and child are well.'

'Apparently.'

'How much did the baby weigh? She was three weeks overdue.'

Male like, he said, 'Weigh? I've no idea.'

'What have they called her?'

'Mam did say.' His brow wrinkled. 'Sorry, I can't remember.'

'Oh, Jake.' It was without heat. 'Well, I'm pleased for Lily. Naomi said she's been very tearful, with the hot weather and all.'

'Do you mean that? That you're pleased for her?'

'Of course.' She knew what he was asking. And it was in answer to the unspoken question that she said, 'I feel sorry for Lily, nothing more. I can see I had a lucky escape now.'

He searched her face and what he saw there caused him to visibly relax and smile. 'Good. I wasn't sure if you'd be... But good, good.'

'I don't care for Adam any more, Jake. I haven't for a long time.' It was on the tip of her tongue to tell him about Adam's clandestine appearance at the farm on Christmas Day but she held her tongue. 'I look back now and I can't believe I was so silly. The Adam I imagined I knew didn't exist, not really. Does that make sense?'

'It does to me.'

'But I am pleased everything's all right with the bairn. Joe will be too. He thinks a lot of Adam still, you know.'

Jake nodded. 'And to be fair to Adam, if there's one person in this world he's fond of, it's Joe.'

Hannah looked at him, a straight look. 'Then he ought to be grateful to you for giving Joe a job here. But for you he'd be down the pit and hating every second.'

'He'd likely have found something else himself.'

'No, no he wouldn't, not Joe. He's ... well, he's just not like that.'

She smiled at him before going back to her mangling.

'This is getting beyond a joke.' Daniel Osborne stood staring into the massive run in front of the turkey shed, the long wooden structure which housed the birds at night and kept them safe from foxes. 'There's at least a dozen gone, I'd swear to it. Now it's one thing some poacher taking the odd rabbit and pheasant, but this. He'll be after more easy pickings, you mark my words.'

Joe stared at the man who was his immediate boss but who had become his friend over the last months. 'You think whoever it was got 'em out of the shed in the night?'

'Must have done, cheeky devil. I thought we were missing a hen or two last week, that's what alerted me. We had that trouble before Christmas, but there's been nothing much since then besides the odd passing tinker or two fancying his chance at an easy meal. Well, there's nowt for it, looks like I'm in for a couple of sleepless nights. Catching 'em in the act is the only way. If nothing else, it frightens the wits out of them. Even if you don't catch them, once a poacher knows you're on to him he'll clear off and try elsewhere. But don't say owt to anyone, Joe. I'll tip Jake the wink but it's better as few people know about this as possible.'

'You surely don't think it's anyone on the farm?'

'Course I don't, but with Frank's lads living in the village and drinking at the pub, something might let slip. They're good lads, none better, but when you've had a jar or two, tongues have a habit of wagging out of turn.'

'Me lips are sealed.'

'Good lad. I'll likely make myself a bit of a hide in that patch of scrub at the back of the shed. A couple of bales of hay should do it. Anyway, I'll be off and let Jake know. Likely he'll want to be in on the act, if I know him.'

Joe nodded, watching Daniel as he walked away. The turkeys were now happily pecking at their feed and some beech nuts and chopped stinging nettles. Joe had been at the farm long enough to understand that poachers were considered the scum of the earth. There'd be some high jinks the night if Jake and Daniel managed to catch this one. Or there might be more than one. Whatever, it would be a change from clearing and digging the ditches out which he had been doing for two weeks solid now. But he wouldn't ask Jake if he could accompany him and Daniel, he knew what the answer would be. Sometimes he thought Jake considered him little more than a bairn.

It was well gone midnight and nearer one o'clock when Jake and Daniel heard a rustling not far from their hidey-hole at the back of the shed. They stiffened in the darkness but then a voice whispered, 'Jake? Daniel? Are you there?' It brought both men turning. The next moment Joe crawled into the gap between the bales of hay.

'What the hell are you doing here?' Jake's voice

was low but full of fury. 'Damn it, Joe, I've got a shotgun here. What if I'd thought you were a poacher? Are you barmy, man? Get back to bed.'

'I want to help you.'

'Help us? The best way you can help us is by getting your backside over to Frank's. Does he know you're here?'

'Course not, I waited until they were asleep. I just thought it might be more than one poacher, that's all, and three pairs of hands are better than two.'

Jake swore softly. 'If it is more than one it's all the more reason for you to be out of it. These blokes don't play by the rules, there's no Marquess of Queensberry.'

'Who's he?'

There was an exasperated groan. 'Never mind. Just do what I say and we'll have this out tomorrow, m'lad.'

'Jake?' Daniel's voice was little more than a breath but something in it quietened the other two. 'Over there, by the bridle path at the far end. I reckon there's two of them. Can you see?'

'Aye, I can, big so-an'-sos an' all by the look of it. I'm not sorry I brought the shotgun, Dan. And you,' he pushed his head close to Joe's, 'you stay exactly where you are, no matter what happens. You hear me? I mean it, Joe.'

Joe's eyes were glittering with excitement in a shaft of moonlight but his voice was subdued when he said obediently, 'Aye, all right.'

'Promise me.'

'I promise.'

The three of them watched the two burly figures

262

stealthily make their way towards them. Even if the poachers had come from another direction, Jake and the other two would have been impossible to see, hidden as they were in deep shadow, but as it was they were largely obscured by the shed for good measure. Consequently the two men were only yards away when Jake got quietly to his feet along with Daniel and stepped out of the shadows with his shotgun held pointing in the direction of the poachers.

'Can I help you, gentlemen?' Jake said coolly.

The two men froze. One was carrying an empty sack but there was something moving in the one the other man held, and Jake surmised – rightly – that the two had already paid a visit to the hen coops. After a stunned moment or two, the smaller of the two men spoke. 'Here, there ain't no need for you to use that. We don't want no trouble.'

'Whether you want it or not, it seems to me you're in for a considerable amount.' Jake didn't take his eyes off the two figures. 'Now I suggest you put those sacks down and then we'll see about putting you somewhere nice and secure for the night until the police take over.'

What happened next occurred so swiftly that when Jake thought about it afterwards he realised this was not the first time the two poachers had been in a tight spot. Ignoring Daniel and acting as one, they launched themselves at him, taking him completely by surprise.

The shotgun went spinning away into the shadows as he landed flat on his back. One of the men who had fallen on top of him thumped him for all he was worth while the other turned on

Daniel. Momentarily stunned, Jake was at a disadvantage. The man astride him continued to use his fists but Jake managed to jab two fingers into the poacher's eyes with enough force for the man to fall aside with a howl of pain.

Jake struggled groggily to his feet before the man came at him again, then Daniel went down and didn't move and he found himself fighting the pair of them. He did his best but both men were built like brick outhouses, their squashed ugly faces suggesting they were no strangers to violence. He was knocked down once more before being dragged to his feet. The slightly larger of the men held his arms behind his back and laughed. 'Not quite such the big man without a gun in your hands, are you?' he said, before the other man drove his fist into his stomach with sickening force.

Jake doubled up, vaguely aware of Daniel still out for the count on the ground. As the big fellow hauled him straight for his companion to take another punch at him, he tried to prepare himself for the impact.

'Let go of him or I'll shoot, I swear it.'

The young frightened voice stopped the men in their tracks. At some point Joe must have got the shotgun. Jake shook his head, desperately trying to clear his mind. Joe didn't know how to use a gun, he'd never even held one before as far as he knew. He wanted to say, 'Get away, Joe, now, while you can. Go and get help, they won't come after you with you having the gun.' But he couldn't. He still couldn't get air into his lungs after the punch to his stomach.

'He's nowt but a lad.' The man who was holding Jake spoke disparagingly. 'He won't do anything. Get him, Art.'

Joe raised the gun higher. 'Stay where you are.'

The man called Art was clearly hesitating. Seizing the opportunity, Jake attempted to wrench himself free from the second poacher, causing them both to stagger forward. Whether it was this that made the first man lunge at Joe or whether he would have done so anyway was not clear. Nor could Jake determine whether the gun went off by accident or because Joe had pulled the trigger.

By now Isaac Mallard's whippets were raising hell in the end cottage, along with the three farm dogs Jake had shut in one of the barns earlier in case they got in the way of things. As he grappled with the bigger man, Jake saw the other poacher struggling with Joe. He couldn't tell whether the poacher was injured or not but the man still had the strength to tear the gun off Joe and smash him over the head with the butt. As the slight figure crumpled to the ground, there were shouts from the direction of the cottages and lights waving. This seemed to panic the man holding the gun. He went berserk, swinging the weapon at Jake and screaming at the top of his voice. The blow to Jake's shoulder wasn't enough for him to loosen his hold on his attacker who was now attempting to get away, but it knocked him off balance and he fell over Daniel who was still lying unconscious. By the time Jake got to his feet, the two poachers were running back the way they had come but they had dropped the gun, he could see it lying against the wall of the shed.

His main concern being for Joe and Daniel; Jake let them go. Daniel was beginning to groan but Joe was ominously silent. He knelt down, bending over the inert figure. 'Joe, Joe, man. Wake up. Joe.'

Jake could see a dark stain of blood covering Joe's collar and shirt. He shook Joe's arm, saying his name over and over until Daniel crawled over to them.

'What happened?' Daniel asked groggily. 'I thought you told him to stay put.'

'One of them hit him over the head with the shotgun. Joe got hold of it, he was trying to save me. Damn it, Joe.' He shook his arm again. 'Wake up.'

Frank was the first to reach them, closely followed by Daniel's father and then Isaac. 'I need to get him into the house.' Jake lifted Joe into his arms but when he tried to stand up, he nearly dropped him, slight though his brother's body was.

'Here.' Frank took Joe off him. 'The lad's not the only one who's had a bang on the head by the look of you. Jack, you and Isaac get Daniel home. John, you help Jake.'

Daniel's brother had now joined them but when he went to support Jake with his arm, Jake shook him off. 'I'm all right,' he said thickly, swaying where he stood. 'See to Daniel. And you others,' he spoke to Daniel's mother and Neville and Sybil Kirby who had come running up, 'get yourselves home. And can someone let those blasted dogs out so we can hear ourselves think.'

'Jake, I think we're going to need a doctor.' Frank's voice was quiet but his tone brought everyone's eyes to him. 'The lad's in a bad way.'

Joe was in a bad way, the worst way. His pulse was so feeble it was barely there. Hannah met them at the kitchen door, she'd had her work cut out preventing Seamus from getting out of bed to see what was happening. Her face ashen, she watched as Frank laid Joe in one of the big armchairs. Both Jake and Joe were covered in blood but beyond telling her that Daniel's brother had taken the horse and trap to fetch the doctor, Jake said nothing. He knelt by the side of Joe's chair and when Hannah tried to bathe the ugly gash on Joe's head, he brushed her aside and began to do it himself. When the gash was clean, he wound a piece of clean linen round Joe's forehead but again he would let no one touch the unconscious man but himself.

Frank went to let Seamus know what was what. When he reappeared in the kitchen, Hannah was standing by the kitchen table gnawing at her thumb, watching Jake stroke the hair back from Joe's forehead, saying over and over, 'Joe, Joe, come on. Come on, Joe. Please.'

She raised agonised eyes to Frank.

He walked over to Jake and, bending down, said quietly, 'Shall I carry him upstairs so we can lie him flat?' Surreptitiously he felt for a pulse. But even before he confirmed there was none, he had known. The lolling head and complete lack of movement had told him.

He stood up, looked at Hannah and shook his head. She stared back at him, her eyes wide, unable to believe what he was inferring. Leaning on the table for support, she watched as Frank knelt down by Jake. 'Jake, lad, come and sit down a minute, I'll see to Joe.'

'No.' Jake's voice was thick. 'No, don't touch him.'

'He's resting, lad. You can't do anything more until the doctor gets here and there's a deep cut on your head needs seeing to.'

'No.'

Frank straightened, casting Hannah a helpless glance.

She thought for a moment, trying to bring reason to mind through the whirling horror in her head. She left the room, ran upstairs and fetched a blanket. Back in the kitchen she walked across to the armchair and draped the blanket over Joe so that only his head was visible, saying, 'There, there, he's more comfortable now. Let him sleep, Jake. Come and sit down and I'll see to your head.' She could see various cuts and scrapes and his lip was split, but above his ear on the damaged side of his face the flesh had opened to reveal a two-inch gash which was oozing blood.

He looked up at her. 'He's just asleep.'

'Aye, yes, he's just asleep.'

'He shouldn't have been there. It was supposed to be just me an' Dan. I told him...'

She nodded but the pleading tone in his voice caused her to press her fingers tightly against her lip before she could say, 'Let me see to your head now, eh? Please, Jake.'

For a moment she didn't think he had heard her and then he straightened. Hannah led him to one of the hard-backed chairs at the kitchen table as though he was a child, pushing him gently into the seat. She began to clean the cut while Frank looked on, his weather-beaten face creased with concern.

Jake was feeling muzzy-headed, sick, faint, but mainly frightened, very frightened. Of what he wouldn't let himself think, he only knew there was a terrible something pressing down on him but if he didn't acknowledge it, if he gave it no room in his head, everything would be all right. Joe was sleeping, that was all, and who wouldn't after a crack on the head like that? But the doctor would be here soon, and say what you like about the fees he charged, he was a good doctor, was old Stefford. He'd been Seamus's doctor for donkey's years and he didn't beat about the bush. He liked that about Stefford. He liked straight talking.

Round and round his thoughts ran while Hannah silently bathed his head. Then she made a pot of tea and added a good measure of whisky to his. She was a good lass, Hannah. Older than her years. She didn't seem too keen on Daniel, poor devil, but lately he had thought her and Joe might get together now Joe had begun to cut the ties with Adam. Joe liked her, he was sure of it, and if it had to be anyone, he'd like it to be Joe. If nothing else, it would put paid to the secret dream that had begun to plague him. Damn it, why didn't Joe stir? But Clara always said sleep was the best medicine. Aye, that's what Clara said and she was a wise old biddy.

Frank went up to speak to Seamus once more but apart from that the three of them sat quietly waiting for the doctor in the kitchen, the soft glow from the fire in the range and the steady ticking of the clock on the mantelpiece belying the desperate circumstances.

When they heard the horse and trap, Frank went outside and met the doctor in the farmyard. Dr Stefford was a big man, robust and hearty with a booming voice, but when he came into the kitchen it was quietly and it was not to the figure draped in the blanket he looked but Jake. His voice calm and matter-of-fact, he said, 'Hear you've had trouble with poachers again then. Cunning so-an'-sos, the lot of them. Let's have a look at you, shall we?'

'Not me. It's Joe.'

'Aye, I know, I know, but we'll see to the walking wounded first.'

'No, you don't understand.'

'Aye, I do, lad.' The doctor's voice was soothing and he glanced at Hannah as he said, 'Concussion, and we'll need to stitch the cut above his ear.' Turning again to Jake as he delved into his big black leather bag, he said, 'I want you to take these pills while I look at young Joe there. All right?'

He nodded at Hannah, who had fetched a glass of water, and watched as she got Jake to take the pills and swallow from the glass several times. 'Nasty business, Jake,' he said softly. 'Did you get a good look at them?'

Jake stared at him. Why wasn't he seeing to Joe? He'd brought him here to see to Joe.

When Jake did not reply, Dr Stefford looked at him a few moments more and then turned to the slight body swathed in the blanket. After no more than thirty seconds he straightened. His tone as soft as before, he said, 'You know he's gone, Jake.'

'No.' Jake looked as though he himself was facing death. Suddenly he swung his arm violently, sending the glass and cups on the table crashing to the floor. 'No, he's sleeping,' he repeated, getting to his feet.

'Sit down before you fall down, man. Those pills I gave you would knock out an elephant.'

In spite of the doctor's words, it took both Frank and himself to force Jake down into the seat again. The tears had welled up in Hannah's eyes and were trickling down her cheeks, but she didn't know who she was crying for the most, Joe or Jake.

'He's gone, Jake,' Dr Stefford said again. 'There's nothing you or I or anyone else can do about it. I don't quite understand why because his injury doesn't look that bad, but believe me, he has gone.'

'It was one blow to the head, that's all. Just one blow.' Jake's voice was becoming increasingly slurred. 'Perhaps – perhaps he's in a coma.'

'It's no coma.' And at Hannah's involuntary movement of protest, Dr Stefford turned to her, saying, 'He has to face it now, lass, hard though it is. In a minute or two those pills will take effect and it's important he understands. I'm sorry, I'm sorry to the heart of me because I know he thought a bit of the lad but there it is.'

'It's my fault.'

'What?' The doctor screwed up his face. 'Don't be daft, man. Frank here tells me you didn't intend for the lad to be there.'

'It's my fault. I brought him here. To – to the farm.'

'Because he couldn't face another day in the mine,' Hannah put in swiftly. 'He was desperate, you know he was, Jake. If it hadn't been here it would have been somewhere else.'

'No.' His eyes were blinking as he tried to keep them open. 'No, he wouldn't have left the mine and Adam but for me. You – you said so yourself.'

'This is not down to you, Jake. Get that clear in your head once and for all.' Dr Stefford walked across and gently pulled the blanket over Joe's face before turning and saying, 'Jake?'

Jake's chin was resting on his collarbone, his eyes closed. The pills had done their work. Without further ado, Dr Stefford stitched the wound above his ear, after which he helped Frank carry Jake to his room. Leaving Frank to take Jake's boots off and undress him, the doctor spent a few minutes with Seamus who was greatly distressed by the night's happenings.

It was some ten minutes later before he returned to the kitchen. He found Hannah alone, Frank having gone home to break the news to Clara. Hannah knew the little woman would take it hard, she and Frank had been very fond of Joe.

'I'm very sorry.' Dr Stefford looked at the young girl he had come to know and like in the last twelve months since she had come to work for Seamus. 'It's a tragedy for all concerned.'

'He'll blame himself for ever.'

'No, not once he's had time to think it over. He's an intelligent man, is Jake. That's what sets

272

him apart from most of the fellows on the farm. Oh, they're good enough, don't get me wrong, salt of the earth and all that, but Jake's different.'

'We had a talk earlier.' She began to cry as her tongue loosened and she gabbled, 'I said to him that Joe would never have found another job by himself, that it was down to Jake he had come to the farm. And it was, it was, but in a good way, that's what I meant. In a good way. And Joe, he's only just turned nineteen. *Nineteen.*'

'I know, lass.'

'And now Mr Wood and maybe the others too will blame Jake. They won't remember all he's done for them. They'd be in the workhouse now if it wasn't for him.'

It was a little while before she calmed down and then she sat with her hand tightly across her mouth as though to prevent more words. Dr Stefford made another pot of tea and he was just about to pour them a cup when a tap at the kitchen door announced Clara's arrival.

'Ee, lass, lass.' Clara took Hannah into her arms, holding her tight. 'What a thing to happen, I can't believe it.' Both women's faces were wet when they drew apart.

Dr Stefford poured three cups of tea. He let Clara and Hannah drink theirs before he said, 'I shall make arrangements for the body to be collected early tomorrow morning before Jake comes to. Because of the circumstances there will have to be a post-mortem. You understand?'

Hannah nodded. Joe. Oh, Joe. Like Clara, she couldn't take in the enormity of what had occurred.

'Jake should sleep until at least midday and I should be back before then. The concussion may or may not have cleared but we'll see how things are.' Glancing at Clara, he added, 'I don't want Hannah left alone tonight.' He didn't add, 'Until the body is collected,' but both women knew what he meant.

'I shall be staying, doctor,' said Clara firmly.

He nodded. 'I shall notify the police and doubtless they will be here first thing in the morning. Now, could you direct me to the home of the other young man concerned? I would like to check him over before I leave.'

When the doctor had gone, Hannah and Clara continued to sit quietly together. The cats had made themselves scarce earlier with all the hullabaloo but now they crept into the kitchen. After circling Joe's armchair, they made for the back door, ears laid flat against their heads as they miaowed to be let out.

'They know,' Clara said as Hannah opened the door. 'Animals are far more intuitive than folk give 'em credit for. The night Isaac's wife died his whippets howled for hours, unearthly sound it was and nothing would shut them up. And then there was the time Neville Kirby turned the tractor over and was trapped underneath. Not used to it, see, it being new to the farm in them days. One of the farm dogs, nice old bitch called Josie if I remember right, she went and barked and nipped at some of the men's trousers who were working in one of the barns till they followed her to the field. Saved Neville's life she did that day. I used to see Sybil taking her a bowl of whatever they had for dinner for years after, right until the dog died.'

As Hannah reseated herself, Clara glanced at her white face. 'Why don't you go and get some rest, hinny?' she said softly. 'Likely tomorrow will be a full day.'

Hannah shook her head. 'No, I'll stay.'

'You can't do owt, lass, an' I'll come and wake you once it starts to get light.'

Again Hannah shook her head. 'I want to stay, Clara. I – I know it sounds daft, but I think Joe would want me to. I'm almost family, I grew up with them all and I don't want him to be alone tonight. Oh, I know you'd be here and he thought the world of you–'

'Don't frash yourself, hinny.' Clara patted her arm. 'You stay if you want. Look, I'll make another pot of tea, how about that?'

Hannah didn't want more tea but she knew the little woman was as upset as any of them and this was her way of coping, to be busy. 'Thank you. I – I guess it's going to be a long night. It was good of you to come over, Clara.'

'Oh, lass, lass, would that I could do more.' Clara's bottom lip trembled and she hastily rose from the table. 'It's a bad business, this. A bad business.'

Yes, it was a bad business. Hannah's mind had cleared, despite her grief and shock. It told her that, terrible though the tragedy was, the repercussions for the man presently lying in a drugged sleep upstairs would be worse. Adam and his father would blame Jake for giving Joe a job at the farm, she knew that, but if his mother added to the guilt which Jake had immediately taken upon himself, what would that do to him? Over the last twelve months since she had lived in such close proximity to him, she had come to realise he was far from being the cold, self-assured individual he presented to the world, a figure who remained aloof and untouched by the normal ups and downs which were most folk's lot. That was just his outer shell, but like a turtle he had a soft centre that was as vulnerable as the next person's – more probably, in Jake's case.

She stared at Clara who was busying herself at the range making the tea, her back to the room. Hannah's heart was beginning to thump hard; she knew that if it had been in her power she would have done anything to protect Jake from the condemnation that would undoubtedly come from his stepfather and Adam, maybe from all of them. He had had enough to put up with in his life; this wasn't fair.

Then a question came, sharp, piercing: shouldn't she be more upset about Joe's death than how Jake was feeling?

She *was* upset, she answered herself. Of course she was, terribly upset, but like Dr Stefford had said, there was nothing anyone could do about Joe. But Jake, he had to live on. And somehow she understood him like she had never understood Adam. The anguish she had seen in his eyes tonight was no passing thing. They said time healed everything but she didn't believe that. It depended on who and what – on lots of things. Some folk felt with their soul, and such depth of feeling was both a curse and a blessing.

'Here, get this down you, hinny.' Clara returned to the table and poured the tea.

'I'll take Seamus a cup first.' She knew the farmer would be in a state but she had needed to get a grip on herself before she went to see him.

'Aye, all right, lass.' Clara plumped down in her chair. 'It's a pity the master is how he is, it would have helped Jake if he was working with him every day like they used to.'

So Clara, too, knew how Jake was going to feel. For a moment the two women's gazes joined in perfect understanding. 'This is just not fair, Clara,' Hannah murmured brokenly as she stood up.

'No, hinny, it's not, but like me old da used to say when we were bairns and said the selfsame thing, neither is a blackbird's backside but he gets on with life just the same. And that's what Jake'll do, you mark my words. He's no quitter, not Jake.'

No, Jake was not a quitter, Hannah thought as she left the kitchen with Seamus's tea. And he would get on with life. But at what cost to the inner man?

Chapter 16

Rose did not blame Jake for her son's death, not even before the post-mortem revealed that Joe had been living on borrowed time for a great many years. His heart had been badly damaged, probably as a result of the attack of measles he had suffered as a child, and the doctors agreed it was a wonder he had reached manhood. Even more of a wonder that he'd endured two or three years working down a coal mine. Dr Stefford had been right. It hadn't been the blow to his head that had killed Joe but a combination of factors working together on that fateful night which had proved the last straw for his already labouring heart.

Jake heard this pronouncement from Dr Stefford at the farm. His stepfather had flatly refused to let him come to the infirmary and wait in the small side room to hear the findings.

His face continued to hold the blank look which he'd adopted since his return to the farm after visiting the house in Wayman Street on the afternoon after Joe had died two days before. He had hardly opened his mouth since then either, except to give the necessary orders to the men concerning their work. With Daniel still laid low and recovering from the beating he'd sustained, Jake was rising long before it was light and going to bed after midnight, but nothing Seamus or Hannah said could persuade him to rest more or eat properly.

'Do you understand what I've just said, Jake?' Dr Stefford stared at the man in front of him who seemed to have aged ten years since Joe's death. 'He was ill, very ill, but no one knew it. He could have gone anytime.'

'Or he could have lived on as before.' And as the doctor went to speak, Jake said, 'Don't get me wrong, doctor, I know what you're trying to say and I'm grateful. But the fact remains he worked down the mine for years and he was all right.'

'I understand from your mother that Joe was involved in a fracas with the police during one of the marches and had some fingers broken. All that kind of thing would not have helped. You have to get it into your head, Jake, that anything, *anything* could have finished him off.'

'Dr Stefford's right, Jake.' Hannah had been kneading dough at the cooking table in a corner of the room while the two men talked. Now she turned, her voice soft as she said, 'You've taken this solely on your shoulders and it's not right. You're tearing yourself apart.'

He didn't argue with her. There was silence in the kitchen for a moment and then, his voice low, he said, 'You have to be alive to tear yourself apart.'

She stared straight into the face that she no longer thought of as damaged but simply attractive and answered quietly, 'Joe wouldn't have wanted this, for you to feel like this. I know for a fact that the last months were the happiest of his life because he told me so. Not once but many times. He felt reborn, that's what he used to say. Like a bird let out of its cage and free to fly, to be what it had been born for. And I know something else too. If Joe had had to choose between the life he had before he came here and going on another five, ten, even twenty years, or these last months, he'd have taken his time at the farm and thanked you for it.'

This time the silence stretched further. It was Dr Stefford who broke it. He and Jake were sitting at the kitchen table with a glass of Hannah's homemade lemonade in front of them and he

279

took a sip before saying, 'Remember that blackbird you and Seamus had in here some three or four years back?' Turning to Hannah, he said, 'A hawk had tried to take it, damaged its wing, and Jake found it out on the bridle path. It would have been easy to hit it over the head but Jake brought it in and they put it in an old cage Seamus's wife had used for her budgerigars. Took a while, but the wing healed and in the meantime that old blackbird grew fat on a diet of worms and what have you. I remember it used to sing like a canary. You remember that, Jake? And then I came one time and it had gone. You recall what you said to me on that occasion, Jake?'

Jake stared at the elderly doctor.

'I'll remind you,' said Dr Stefford. 'I asked where it was and you said you'd let it go because it had recovered. But it was happy in that cage being fed, said I. Safe too. And you said–'

'You wouldn't have said it was happy if you had seen the difference when it flew free,' Jake put in quietly.

'Right.' Dr Stefford looked at him. 'Like the lass said, that blackbird was doing what it had been born to do and an existence in a cage, even one gilded with plenty of food and warmth, was no comparison. I asked you what you'd do if the hawk took it again and you said one day's freedom with the sun on its wings being a blackbird again was worth years as a caged bird.'

'That was a bird.'

'Aye, it was, and it chose its own destiny same as Joe did. He was no bairn, Jake.'

The story had touched Hannah to the point

where her neck muscles were tight and her throat so blocked she couldn't speak. Swallowing deeply, she managed to murmur, 'You enabled him to fly, Jake. Don't you see? For the first time in his life Joe was truly happy. But that apart, his death was not your fault. It wasn't even solely the poacher's fault. And if he hadn't gone like that, if he'd got ill and lingered, he would have hated it.'

'Don't tell me that him going so suddenly was the best thing that could have happened,' Jake said roughly.

She found herself flushing at his tone but her voice was verging on sharpness when she said, 'Why? Why shouldn't I when it's what I believe? You're entitled to your opinion, Jake Fletcher, but don't forget other people are entitled to theirs too. And everyone would agree with me and not you, I might add.'

She watched him turn his head and rub his hand tightly across his mouth. 'Not everyone.'

'You mean Mr Wood and Adam?'

He wet his lips. 'Aye.'

'They are wrong. And they've never liked you.'

'Maybe, but they did love Joe.'

'We all loved Joe. Joe was one of those people.' She was speaking softly again now, her voice scarcely above a whisper. Turning back to the dough, she began to pummel it.

It was a full minute later before the silence was broken by Dr Stefford. He stood to his feet, saying, 'I'll take a look at Seamus while I'm here and then I'll be off.'

Jake stood up too. 'Thanks for coming to let me know the results of the post-mortem, doctor. I appreciate it.'

'No trouble.'

Hannah didn't turn from her kneading as Dr Stefford left the kitchen. There was silence for a moment or two and then she heard the kitchen door click to. It was only then she allowed her shoulders to sag.

It was gone midnight and she was still awake. For the last hour she'd lain on top of the bed looking out of the window which she had opened wide before retiring.

The day had been hot and cloudless and the night was so warm it felt stifling inside. A full moon had risen high in the sky, casting its benign light over the world below. The trees and barns were clearly outlined like Indian-ink silhouettes against a background of star-speckled, midnight blue and not a breath of wind stirred the air. Every so often the melancholy hoot of a barn owl or the low moo of cattle disturbed the silence but other than that there was no sound to be heard.

She had gone over the earlier conversation with Jake and Dr Stefford a hundred times in her mind since coming to her room and cried a little. Now her skin felt tight and irritated. She swung her legs to the floor and padded over to the dressing table, clothed only in her lawn night-dress, and poured a small amount of water from the jug into its matching bowl. After washing her face she felt cooler and she walked across to the window, knelt down and stared up into the sky.

All those stars in such a vast endless expanse... Tears pricked at the back of her eyes again. And down here such heartache and misery. Every night when she'd said her prayers she had thanked God for letting Joe come to the farm and now it felt as if He had thrown it back in her face. She had only gone to Mass a few times since coming here, with the church being so far to walk; if she'd gone every week, would God have saved Joe?

Then she shook her head, suddenly angry with herself. She was being daft now, stupid. It was because she was all hot and bothered and tired.

Jumping to her feet, she decided she couldn't stay in the house a minute longer. She'd go and sit in the garden for a while, it would be cooler there and peaceful. She needed peace of mind tonight.

She pulled on her old faded dressing gown and thrust her feet into her everyday boots. All the world was asleep, no one would know and if she sat for an hour or so in the fresh air she would be able to sleep. Rather than lighting the oil lamp she made her way downstairs more by touch than sight, and once she had stepped outside, the moon lit the farm as though it was late twilight. Buttons and Polly had followed her as she had passed through the kitchen. She rather thought they looked on her as an escort who would protect them from the farm cats, most of whom were almost feral and inclined to pick on the two, given half a chance.

She made no sound as she walked to the garden. It would be harvest time soon, then would come the chill of autumn and before they knew it winter would be on them again. She had been here a whole year and in spite of what had happened with Adam, she would have said she had been happy until the last two days. Now she wondered if the farm would ever be the same again.

No, not the farm, she admitted to herself in the next breath. Jake. Would Jake ever be the same again? It was strange, and she didn't quite know how it had come about, but his grief and agony of mind were affecting her deeply. Perhaps it was because he and Seamus were such a huge part of her life. The three of them were like a small family, or that's what it felt like. And living in such close proximity what affected one was bound to concern the others, and this was such an awful, terrible thing.

The rich perfume of roses wafted to her even before she stepped into the garden. She had pruned them hard in the spring and they had rewarded her scratched and torn hands with a magnificent display come the summer. Along with gilliflowers of all varieties, giant sunflowers that always turned their broad smiling faces to the sun and a host of other flowers, Hannah had discovered Bess's little herb garden when she had started to tackle the overgrown tangle. Mint, thyme, rosemary and other plants scented the air, and she had arranged for Seamus's bench to be placed close to the herb bed. Hannah made her way towards this now, pausing to drink in the heavy perfume from a cluster of old white damask roses which wound round a trellis arch.

Immediately she sat down, the two cats jumped up alongside her. She didn't push them away, glad of the company. 'You're a fussy pair,' she said, scratching their furry heads.

'Hannah?'

As one of the shadows at the far end of the garden moved, she felt her heart jump into her mouth. Her hand at her throat, she stammered, 'J-Jake?'

'What are you doing down here this time of night?' As he made his way towards her, the moonlight caught the white of his shirt, turning him into a moving monochrome of black and white. 'Are you feeling unwell?'

She found she couldn't answer him. She wanted to, she knew she had to, but the element she had first found disturbing about him was back tenfold. His shirt was open almost to the waist, showing thick black body hair on his chest, and the thin cotton accentuated the broadness of his shoulders. The shyness she would have sworn had gone for ever was tying her tongue and as he reached her, something akin to a shiver flickered down her spine.

'Hannah? Are you unwell?' he said again.

'N-no.' She breathed in deeply through her nose. 'No, just hot. It's so warm. And ... and I was thinking of Joe.'

He nodded but didn't speak, dislodging Polly with a push of his hand before sitting down beside her. The sense of loneliness she had recognised in him months before – probably because it was something she identified in herself too – clothed him like a garment tonight. She searched her mind for something to say but before she could come up with anything, he said, 'I should have thanked you for what you said earlier, when Dr Stefford was here. It's strange because my mother said much the same thing the day I went to the house. Of course Adam and Wilbur had a different point of view.'

'I'm sorry.' The deliberate casualness in his tone told its own story. She had long since come to understand that Jake recoiled from showing his feelings.

He shrugged. 'It doesn't matter.'

'It does matter.' They were both staring ahead, not at each other, and this made it easier to say, 'Adam is more like his father than I had ever imagined. Whatever they said, it would be untrue.'

He gave a harsh laugh. 'I don't think it's a matter of truth in this particular instance, Hannah. Merely a different way of looking at what happened. They hold me responsible for Joe's death but I expected that. And I don't blame them. I can see why they would feel like that.'

'Joe's death was not your fault, Jake.'

He did not answer immediately. The warmth and scents of the garden enveloped them and somewhere in the distance the owl hooted again before he said quietly, 'I'm trying to bring reason to bear, Hannah. Believe me.'

'You must.' In her desire to get through to him she turned to face his profile and put her hand on his forearm. Hard muscles clenched beneath her fingers but he did not look at her. 'It's right to grieve for Joe but not to hold yourself responsible for what happened. Such things can put iron in your soul if you let them.'

He glanced at her, a faint smile twisting his mouth. 'That is very profound for one so young.'

'Clara said it actually.'

'Ah, that would explain it. Clara's full of such gems.'

'But she's right.' As she dropped her hand to her side, she said again, 'She is right, Jake.'

'Clara often is.' He sighed, stretching his long legs out in front of him before bending his knees again. Almost to himself, he said, 'There's the funeral to come yet.'

'You'll go, won't you?' She knew Wilbur would try to prevent it if he could, just as he had stopped Jake attending the post-mortem.

'Oh aye, I'll go. And you?'

She nodded.

'Good.'

Just one word but it warmed her.

They continued to sit quietly in the shadowed stillness and when Polly gingerly jumped onto Jake's lap he did not push her down.

Chapter 17

Rose stood gazing into the narrow speckled mirror attached to the back of the wardrobe door. She adjusted the collar of her black coat, bought hastily the day before from one of the second-hand stalls at the Old Market in the East End. The coat she'd worn for years and years was a dark bottle green but still not funereal enough. She knew eyebrows would have been raised if she had worn that. Her felt hat was a dark charcoal colour so that had been near enough.

287

She was ready and she knew the undertakers would be here any minute in their black carriage but still she did not move. She wasn't crying, she felt there were no more tears left. This day was the culmination of years of niggling worry about her bairn, her Joe, and now he was dead. She had thought he had escaped the presentiment which had been with her for so long when Jake had taken him on at the farm but she should have known you can't cheat fate. And now the waiting was over. The pain inside her caused her to bend over slightly although it was not a physical thing. No more would she see his smiling face, and he had been a smiler, had Joe. Especially the few times she had seen him since he'd gone to the farm. Different lad he'd looked. And so she had hoped...

She raised her head, meeting the eyes of the woman in the mirror. Foolish to hope. Her lips pushed together. Foolish to expect anything good. For a while she'd thought things were looking up – Joe free from the pit but still bringing in more than Adam who had been set on at the face again the last weeks, thank the Almighty. Out of habit she crossed herself. She had been able to clear something from the rent arrears and there had even been talk of the new deputy taking on Wilbur after Adam had gone cap in hand to the man, promising that his father would toe the line. Not that Wilbur knew Adam had put it quite like that.

Wilbur. Rose turned her head towards the kitchen, where her husband sat in his Sunday suit with his mouth clamped shut and his face as black as thunder. And not because of Joe, oh no, not really, but because she had insisted Jake come to the house and follow the coffin with the rest of them rather than meeting them at the church as Wilbur had wanted.

She shut her eyes tightly. Why was it Joe's death had taken the lid off the feeling she'd been fighting to subdue for a long time? And now the lid was off she couldn't pretend any more. She didn't like her husband, she hadn't liked him for years. He was an ignorant man, narrow in his thinking and capable of great vindictiveness. He had all but hounded Jake out of the house when he was a lad and was still doing the same today. And yet when she had produced the money for the undertakers he hadn't asked where it had come from. Nor would he. He was a hypocrite and she was done making excuses for him in her mind.

'Mam?' After knocking on the door, Naomi entered her parents' bedroom, her eyes pink-rimmed and her nose red. Her voice low, she said, 'They'll be here in a minute, Mam.'

Rose nodded, her stomach turning over. Her bairn in a wooden box. It wasn't right for a parent to outlive their child. For a moment the enormity of what was in front of her in the next hour or two overwhelmed her. Her hand reaching out to Naomi, she murmured, 'Stay – stay close to me today, lass. I don't feel too good.' She didn't want Wilbur or any of the lads, not even Jake, much as she loved her firstborn. Today it was her daughter she needed near. Their relationship was such that they understood each other without the need for words.

By way of answer, Naomi put her arms about her mother, holding her tightly. They stood like this for some moments until the horse and carriage carrying the coffin arrived.

As Rose stepped out into the bright sunshine, she saw that all the curtains in the houses up and down the street were drawn and a large number of the neighbours were waiting to follow. Several of the women looked as though they had been crying and when Joyce O'Leary said quietly, 'It's heart sorry we all are for your loss, lass. Heart sorry. Joe was a fine young man,' Rose almost gave way to the tears she had thought weren't there earlier.

'Come on, Mam.' Naomi took her arm and together they joined Wilbur and the lads at the front of the procession. Wilbur's children from his first marriage were there too, along with their families, and Hannah was standing next to Jake, her face ashen. Rose reached out to her daughter's friend and Hannah put her arm through hers, and so it was with Naomi and Hannah either side of her that Rose walked the half mile or so through the hot dusty streets to the church to bury her son.

'I would have thought he'd have had the decency to stay away.'

They were standing in Southwick cemetery and, the burial over, Rose and Wilbur were talking to Father Gilbert while the other mourners who hadn't already left were gathered about in small groups. Larry Wood and his wife had approached Jake a few moments before and were now deep in conversation with him, and Hannah had been standing by herself until Adam had appeared at her side. She had been conscious of him staring at her, both during the service at the church and then at the graveside, but she had ignored him. In truth, seeing him again had hardly registered on her emotions. 'I'm sorry?' she said coldly. 'I don't understand what you mean.'

'Him. Jake.' Adam nodded his head abruptly towards his half-brother without taking his eyes off her. 'Joe'd still be alive today if it wasn't for him.'

'That's rubbish.' She kept her voice low but it was vehement enough for his eyes to narrow.

'Oh aye, rubbish is it? I might have known you'd be on his side.'

'It's nothing to do with sides and I don't think you ought to be talking like this today. It's Joe's funeral, show some respect.'

He was taken aback but he recovered almost instantly. He put his head close to hers as he ground out, 'Respect? Respect you say? Joe was my best mate as well as my brother and you talk about respect? There's no one thought more about him than I did.'

'I think your mother would disagree with you.'

'I wasn't meaning Mam and you know it.'

They stood regarding one another and as Hannah looked into the handsome face she thought, how could I ever have imagined I was in love with you? Quietly now, she said, 'I know you loved Joe but none of this is Jake's fault and you're intelligent enough to understand that.'

'Intelligent, am I? Well, I suppose that's something. I'd got the impression you thought I was something less than the muck under your boots.'

Her face hardened now, and her voice too.

291

'Don't come the injured innocent, Adam. It doesn't suit you.'

'Huh.' For a moment she thought he was going to turn away but then, his manner changing and his voice low but urgent, he said, 'Hannah, don't stay at the farm, come back into town. I was a fool, I know I was a fool but I'd do anything to make things right. We could run away together. I'd do that for you, honest.'

She stared at him, hardly able to believe her ears. Glancing about her to make sure no one had overheard, she said, 'Don't be ridiculous. You're a married man with a bairn.'

'I can't stand it, Hannah. I can't stand *her*. You've no idea what it's like. She didn't lift a finger in the house before the bairn was born and now often as not she'll let it lie stinking in its own mess unless Mam sees to it. She's bone idle and it's not just me who thinks so. You ask anyone.'

Totally out of her depth, Hannah took a step backwards away from the look on his face. 'You – you're married,' she said again.

'We could go somewhere where people don't know us, down south. Change our names. And what's a piece of paper anyway? We could say we were married and live as a couple for the rest of our lives, no one would know any different.'

He must be mad. 'You're married,' she said for the third time, her voice stronger. 'You can't leave Lily and the bairn. And what we had between us was over a long time ago like I said on Christmas Day. I don't love you.'

'I think of you all the time at that farm.' It was as though he had not heard her. 'And don't tell me you like it, being nursemaid to an old man and then having to look at that freak every day.'

'Don't call him that.' Her voice had risen and conscious of one or two folk glancing their way, she moderated her tone. 'Jake is ten times the man you are, Adam Wood, and as for Farmer Shawe, he's lovely.'

'And Daniel Osborne? Is he lovely an' all?'

She stared at him a moment more and then turned deliberately away to walk over to Naomi who was talking to Mr and Mrs O'Leary. Hannah slipped her hand through her friend's arm. For him to say all that and at Joe's funeral. She wished they didn't have to go back to the house with the others, she just wanted to go home. She had felt strange enough when they had walked past the shop. The blinds had been down as a mark of respect but the door had been ajar, indicating the shop was open for business. She had thought she caught a glimpse of her uncle as she passed. She hadn't intended to look but somehow her gaze had been drawn that way. Naomi's mam had told her a month or so ago that her aunt was going to have some kind of operation, according to Mrs Mullen and Mrs Chapman. It would have been done before, her aunt's friends had said, but there had been some talk by the new doctor who was attending her aunt of building her up a little beforehand. According to him, there was a train of thought that plenty of liver and some other foods he'd said her aunt must eat would help combat the effect the constant loss of blood had on her body.

'You all right?' As Mr and Mrs O'Leary began

293

to talk to some other neighbours, Naomi squeezed her arm. 'I saw Adam talking to you. What did he say?'

'Nothing much.' She didn't intend to repeat what he had said to anyone. It made her feel ashamed he had put such a suggestion to her. 'Just saying he misses Joe mostly.'

'Aye, well, he might miss Joe but he's been as miserable as sin for months now. Lily's awful, Hannah, she drives Mam mad too and Mam's stuck in the house with her, day in, day out. She's bone idle and her back's glued to the bed some days. And I know she's been carrying the bairn an' all that but you'd have thought she was the first woman in the world to go through a pregnancy.' Naomi sighed heavily. 'Like Mam said the other day, Adam made his bed but everyone else in the house is having to lie on it with him.'

Hannah felt uncomfortable. Changing the subject, she said, 'There were lots of folk came to the funeral.'

'There'd have been more but some of his pals were scared to death to lose any time at the pit. They know there's others waiting to step into their shoes if they miss a shift.'

'Is it still difficult at home, moneywise I mean.'

Naomi looked at her. 'Awful,' she said shortly. 'In every way. And this with Joe...' She shook her head, unable to finish.

'Adam ... Adam blames Jake.'

'Aye, I know. Me da does too but it's rubbish.'

Hannah smiled at her friend. 'Thanks, lass.'

A minute or two later Jake made his way over to them. He put out his hand and tweaked Naomi's nose in greeting but his face was straight when he said to Hannah, 'Would you mind very much if we didn't go back to the house? Or you could go and I'll come back in a few hours and pick you up in the horse and trap.'

'Why?' It was Naomi who spoke and her voice was indignant. 'It's because of them, isn't it? Adam and Da. You've provided most of the food and you paid for the funeral and everything, if anyone's got a right to come back it's you.'

'It's not a question of right, lass. Adam's spoiling for a fight and think how that would make Mam feel today of all days. We've got through the service and all without anything kicking off and I'd prefer to keep it that way.'

'I'll come back to the farm with you.' And at Naomi's involuntary movement of protest, Hannah added, 'It'd be better all round, Naomi. It's a bit awkward with Adam and Lily.'

Naomi stared at them, her face woebegone. She had just started courting the Frasers' youngest son so she could imagine how Hannah felt. 'I could murder our Adam,' she said flatly.

After making their goodbyes to Rose – which was difficult because she was adamant at first they come back to the house – Jake and Hannah quietly left the cemetery. It was only a mile or so to the farm from the outskirts of Southwick where the cemetery was situated and it would have been a pleasant walk in other circumstances. As it was they walked in silence along the North Hylton Road past fields of waving corn on their right and the undulating knolls of Hylton Dene on their left. It wasn't until they'd passed the ruins of Hylton

Castle that Hannah said, 'How do you feel?'

'Like getting drunk.'

It wasn't the answer she had expected. She glanced at him. 'Would that help?'

'Temporarily.'

'Then do it.'

Now she had surprised him. 'That isn't the correct response a nice, well-brought-up lass should give.'

'No? Well, I'm nice, at least I think I am, and I was brought up properly and I'm giving it. All right?'

He smiled faintly. 'Fair enough.'

They didn't speak again until they turned into the lane leading to the farm, but as they turned a corner and the cottages came into view, they saw Frank apparently waiting for someone.

'Hello, what now?' said Jake. 'He should be in the north field.'

Frank came hurrying towards them, his lined face carrying a look of mingled relief and concern. 'You're back,' he said, stating the obvious. 'We weren't sure what time you'd stay till. Daniel's took the horse and trap and gone for Dr Stefford. The master's been took bad.'

Clara had been on duty in the house in case Seamus needed anything; now Frank said, 'Clara heard him call out, all strangled like, she said, and she went in and he was clutching his chest and couldn't get his breath. She come running for me and Daniel said he'd go for the doctor.'

'How long ago was he took ill?' Jake called over his shoulder as he started to run towards the farmhouse.

'Fifteen, twenty minutes ago. I was expecting Daniel back anytime,' said Frank as he panted after them.

In the kitchen, Jake stopped dead. Clara was sitting at the kitchen table crying and Enid and Jack Osborne were either side of her. It was Jack who said, 'H-he went a minute or two ago. There was nothing we could do.'

Jake said nothing to this, pushing past them and going through to the dining room, Hannah at his heels. He walked over to the bed and for a moment gazed down at the inert figure.

They must be wrong, Seamus looked as though he was just asleep. Dropping to his knees, Jake whispered, 'Seamus? Seamus, it's me, Jake.' He was aware of Hannah standing behind him and it was another thirty seconds before he said, 'Why now, today, when we weren't here?'

'I don't know.'

Tenderly Jake cupped the old face between his palms. Seamus was still warm and yet life had left him. This man had been the pivot of his existence for sixteen years, more if he counted the time before he had left the town to live at the farm. Initially Seamus had been Farmer Shawe, his boss, but this had quickly moved to friend and then of latter years Seamus had been the father he'd never known. He had tried to prepare himself for this day since Christmas but now it was here he knew he had not succeeded. The burning in his eyes became unbearable.

He rose from his knees and sat on the edge of the bed and took Seamus into his arms, holding him tightly. The tears came, silently raining down

297

his face as he swayed to and fro. How would he manage without Seamus, without his unconditional friendship and the companionship he valued more than he had ever been able to express? He was alone again. He had always been alone, he'd grown up being alone, but these last years he had been happy in a way. Life had become settled; he'd enjoyed the evenings in front of the fire when he and Seamus had smoked their pipes and put the world to rights.

He was vaguely aware that Hannah had moved to shut the door of the dining room. She returned to his side. 'I'm so, so sorry, Jake,' she said, and all he could do was shake his head blindly. He shouldn't be crying like this in front of her, what would she think of him?

She stood patting his shoulder, clearly at a loss to know what to do or say and this, more than anything, enabled him to gain control. After some moments he managed to say, 'He was a grand man, Hannah,' as he laid Seamus back on the pillows.

'I know.'

'I'm going to miss him.'

'We both will.' Her hand was now resting on his shoulder and when she bent and he felt the fleeting touch of her lips on his cheek his agony intensified tenfold. She had kissed the damaged side of his face. That she could bring herself to do this both amazed and humbled him, but it also brought to the fore the pain of that hidden longing. He did not respond immediately, forcing himself to breathe deeply several times and bring his emotions under control before he said quietly, 'I think I can hear Dr Stefford. Would you give me a moment more before you show him in, Hannah?'

She nodded and left the room silently. He reached into his pocket and took out his handkerchief to wipe his eyes.

Once he was alone, Jake stared down into the face of his friend. 'She thinks of me as a brother,' he murmured, 'same as she thought of you as a father. I know it, Seamus, but pray for me that I'll have the strength never to do anything to betray her trust.'

It was two weeks later and the first time Jake had gone to the house in Wayman Street since the reading of Seamus's will after the old farmer's funeral.

The harvest was in – such things could not be delayed for either tragedy or blessing – and only just in time because for the last three days violent thunderstorms had swept the north-east. Although the morning had been dry, thunderclouds had begun to gather since midday, and Jake was glad he had taken Hannah's advice and used the horse and trap when rain began to fall heavily as he reached the top of the street. He had deliberated on this for some time. He knew full well the news he was about to impart to the occupants of the house would receive mixed reactions and he hadn't wanted his stepfather and Adam to accuse him of playing the wealthy farmer before Seamus was cold in his grave. But then as Hannah had pointed out, he *was* now a wealthy farmer. Furthermore, he had had free use of the horse and trap before Seamus's death and although he had usually chosen to walk into the town, he had used the horse and trap when needs be.

Knowing Adam and Wilbur were presently working on the late shift, he had timed his visit accordingly. Owing to the rain, the street was abnormally quiet and devoid of the usual quota of snotty-nosed bairns playing their games. After tying the reins to the lamp post outside the house, he knocked on the front door. For years his mother had been telling him to walk straight in, the door was never locked, but from the day he had left to go to the farm he had always knocked.

It was his mother who answered and she looked harassed as she opened the door, but her face broke into a smile when she saw him standing there. 'Come in, lad, come in. How many times do I have to tell you, this is still your home while I've got breath in my body?' She drew him over the threshold with her hand on his arm. 'How are you? I still can't take in Farmer Shawe going within days of Joe.'

'How are you, more to the point?' He stopped her when she would have bustled ahead of him into the kitchen.

'Oh, you know.' For a moment grief thickened her voice. 'Middling at best. But come and sit yourself down and I'll make a brew.'

Once seated in the kitchen with a pint mug of tea in his hand and a plate of girdle scones in front of him, Jake said, 'I'm glad you're on your own. I've something to tell you.'

'Lily's upstairs but it'd be a miracle for her to come down. She has a morning nap and an afternoon nap...' Rose's voice died away and was little more than a whisper when she said, 'Is it good news, lad? I've been worried to death you'd find yourself out on your ear with the farmer going. What a thing to happen and on the day we buried Joe.'

'I think you'd term it good news.' Jake leant forward slightly, he had been looking forward to this moment. 'It's all mine, Mam. The farm, the land, the house. Seamus left the lot to me.'

'No.' She stared at him, her hand going to her chest as though to still her heart. 'Oh, lad, lad.'

'I knew about it some time ago but it wasn't for me to say. But now it's all official like. You are now looking at a well-to-do man, Mrs Wood, although if I could go back a month to when Joe and Seamus were alive I'd do it like a shot. If only I had had the brains to get Joe out of it that night, he'd still be alive. And if I'd been there the day Seamus died, I might have been able to do something.'

Rose stared at Jake. Silas had been a man without moral conscience, without a shred of normal human compassion come to that, and yet his son had enough for two men. Perhaps that was it, perhaps God in His wisdom had given Jake a double portion to even things out. If that was the case, God might be infinitely wise as the priests said but she didn't think much of His common sense. Her lad's thinking was a torture to him these days. Immediately her hand went to her pinny pocket for her rosary as she asked the Lord's forgiveness. She had found she was having to do that more and more lately. 'I doubt it, lad. What will be, will be,' she said softly. 'As Father

301

Gilbert said, it was Joe's time.'

'Maybe.'

The sound of the baby crying upstairs filtered through to the kitchen and as much to change the subject as anything, knowing how Jake felt about Father Gilbert, Rose said quickly, 'That bairn'll need changing again, poor little mite. Red raw her little backside is because she's never changed from one day to the next. How Lily can be the way she is is beyond me. I'll just go and tell her to see to the bairn, but,' she stood up and put her arms round Jake's broad shoulders, placing her face against his for a moment, 'I'm right glad for you, son. If anyone deserves good fortune, you do.'

Jake sat quietly after his mother had left the room. He heard her remonstrating with Adam's wife and then the sound of raised voices. How did his mother put up with it? Would life go on like this for her until she was an old woman?

The rain was lashing against the window with ever-increasing fury but the glow of the fire in the range made the kitchen cosy. He reached for a girdle scone and bit into it, and then he heard the back door open. A moment later Adam opened the scullery door into the kitchen. They stared at each other for a full ten seconds while the rain dripped off Adam's cap. Then he came further into the room, his tone aggressive when he said, 'What are you doing here?'

Rose reappeared as he spoke and before Jake could reply she said, 'I could ask you the same question. Why aren't you at work?'

Adam held up a bandaged hand in answer. 'Sliced my hand open. The deputy sent me to get

302

it stitched and said I'd have to lose a shift. So?' He looked at Jake again. 'What's brought you here at a time of day when most men are doing an honest day's work?'

Staring unblinking into his half-brother's full-lipped handsome face, Jake's eyes narrowed. Adam's tone had done away with any desire for appeasement. Taking in a slow, long breath, he delivered what he knew would be a crushing blow to the younger man. 'I'm here to see my mother and I come and go when I see fit after giving my manager his instructions for the day.'

It was as though Adam had become transfixed, every feature of his face stiffening as he visibly struggled to take in the significance of what he'd heard.

Knowing he was turning the knife but unable to help himself, Jake said, 'Daniel's turned out to be a good manager. He's come on in leaps and bounds in the last months, as his wage reflects. I wouldn't want to lose him.'

When at last Adam spoke, his voice betrayed his fervent hope that what he suspected was not true. *Your* manager? Huh! Take a sight too much on yourself, don't you?'

'Daniel is my manager, Adam. Same as the farm is mine, lock, stock and barrel.'

'It ... it can't be. You were no relation – I mean there must be others standing in line...'

'If you're asking if Farmer Shawe had family eager to take over, then the answer is yes. A nephew was always sniffing around which is why Seamus made it crystal clear in his will what he wanted. And what he wanted is for me to inherit in place of his son who was killed in the war.'

There was silence in the kitchen. Then Rose bustled forward, saying, 'Take your coat off then and sit down. I'll get a sup of tea–'

'I don't want tea.' Such was Adam's fury that he pushed his mother from him when she went to help him off with his coat.

'Don't manhandle her.' Jake stood up as he spoke.

'Says who? You're nowt here whatever you are at that farm.'

'You treat her with respect or so help me I'll make you.'

'Oh, we're really into playing the big man now, aren't we? Well, let me tell you, you don't impress no one here. Licking the farmer's boots to worm your way in. You're scum, toadying scum.'

'No, please, Jake.' Rose was between them, holding Jake back. 'I can't stand any more, I'm at the end of my tether. Please, lad.'

Looking down into her drawn face, Jake slowly relaxed his taut muscles and took a step backwards. He gathered up his coat from the back of the kitchen chair. Adam said not a word but as Jake left the kitchen by way of the hall, the two men exchanged a glance of pure hatred. Whether it was this that drew Adam into the hall as Rose was saying goodbye to her son on the doorstep or the fact that Jake inheriting the farm was a bridge too far wasn't clear. But as Jake turned to untie the horse, Adam came up behind Rose, his voice sneering as he said, 'That's it, go like the whipped dog you are.'

Jake covered the distance in one stride, grabbed

Adam by the front of his shirt and yanked him down the step into the street. It was Adam who got the first punch in but then Jake hit him with enough force to take him off his feet and into the running gutter. Adam scrambled to his feet and came back at the bigger man with fists and feet but Jake's superior height and breadth gave him an advantage, only matched by Adam's talent for dirty fighting.

The rain continued to pour down as the two men fought, deaf to Rose's entreaties which brought neighbours from several houses either side out onto their doorsteps. It ended as it had been bound to, with Adam on the ground once more but this time unable to rise. He lay writhing, his face covered with blood, as Jake stood over him. Rose pulled at Jake's arm. 'He's had enough, lad, leave him be,' she cried. 'Please, Jake, no more.'

Jake's face was bereft of colour but for the bright red of blood from a cut to his mouth and another above one eye, and his eyes were like black granite. After a moment he straightened, flexing his bruised hands. 'You talk to me like that again and I'll kill you, you hear me, Adam?'

Adam had ceased moving, lying with his arms over his face as though he feared Jake was going to kick him, but as Jake shrugged off Rose's hand and untied the reins, he sat up, nursing his stitched hand which was now bleeding heavily. As the trap began to draw away, Adam shouted, 'That's it, go back to your farm.' Taking in the watching neighbours with a sweep of his head, he said, 'He came to tell us he's the master of a big farm now, bragging how well he was set up, and to prove the point he goes for me when I won't kowtow to him. Nice, eh?'

Jake didn't hear any more, he had jerked the reins and the horse was trotting down the street away from the knot of people. When he reached the corner he looked back for one brief moment and saw that it was not his mother who was bending over Adam, another couple of women were doing that. Rose was standing watching him leave, one hand grasping her middle and the other pressed over her mouth.

'I was a fool. I knew he was trying to provoke me and I should have just come away, damn it.'

Jake was sitting at the kitchen table and Hannah was busy bathing the cuts to his mouth and eye with a mild solution of salty water. Her voice held a touch of exasperation as she said, 'Why didn't you then?'

'For the same reason I rubbed his nose in it about me getting the farm I suppose.'

'You did that? Rubbed his nose in it?'

He looked up at her. 'Aye, I did, and don't look at me like that. I've never pretended to be perfect.'

'You're certainly not perfect.' She stood back a pace. 'And did it make you feel good after?'

He glared at her. 'No. It should have because to my mind I've every right to get under his skin the way he's been, but no, it didn't. Satisfied?'

She did not answer this directly. Instead she took the bowl and cloth through to the scullery and it was from there she said, 'Your mother would have been upset.'

'Thank you for pointing that out.'

When she reappeared in the kitchen, her face was tight. 'I'll make a cup of tea.'

'I need something a darn sight stronger than tea.' He stood up, his face glowering. 'I'll be in the study if anyone wants me.'

When she was alone, Hannah let out a long irritated sigh. Jake had said he was a fool and he was right, he'd played right into Adam's hands. And this was the man who had been humming and hawing about whether to take the trap because he didn't want to appear to be bragging! Adam would make a meal out of this with the neighbours, he'd already nailed his colours to the mast by calling out what he did as Jake left the street. Everyone would think Jake had started the fight and Adam was the innocent. *Oh, Jake, how could you have been so stupid?*

Her face flushed with anger and she continued to hold herself stiffly for another moment or two before suddenly plumping down onto the seat Jake had vacated. Did it matter what the neighbours thought? Did it matter what any of them thought back in the town? Here on the farm they were in their own little world, a world where everyone appreciated Jake for the man he was. Why was she getting so het up on his behalf?

After making herself a cup of tea, her panacea for all ills, she sat exactly where she was for almost half an hour. At first she told herself she didn't know why she was making such a fuss about Jake letting Adam goad him into a fight, then her innate honesty kicked in.

No more woolly thinking. It was as though she

was having a conversation with another part of herself. She liked Jake, more than liked him. Something had slowly happened over the last twelve months, something she would have termed impossible a year ago. It didn't matter that he thought of her in the same way he thought of Naomi – no, that was silly, of course it mattered but it didn't make any difference to the way she felt.

She glanced round the shining kitchen. She could never reveal how she felt. Their relationship had developed into an easy one where they could say anything to each other; she could never do or say anything to jeopardise that. Besides which, he was now a wealthy man and she knew Farmer Dobson's daughter had been after him for ages even before this. No doubt there would be others who would be giving him the eye once word of his new standing spread.

For a moment her mind raced as she considered the possibility of Jake bringing a wife into the farmhouse. Would she be asked to stay on as housekeeper or would she be expected to leave? Could she bear to stay on and see him married to someone else? And then she shook her head, impatient with herself. She was putting the cart before the horse here. He might not want to marry. He hadn't thus far. But then he was a very private man and not given to showing his feelings. Who knew what he really wanted?

As she got up from the table, a shiver ran through her whole body. She didn't know if it was because the storms of recent days had chilled the air and suddenly everything was cold and damp, or the fact that through Jake and Adam fighting she'd been forced into admitting something she had refused to recognise for weeks now. But nothing had changed, not really. Everything could go on as before.

A day at a time. One of her Aunt Aggie's favourite sayings rang in her mind. That was the way she had to cope with this. All the fretting in the world wouldn't change anything and it wasn't as though anyone knew, her secret was her own and would remain so. The only person she could have confided in who was unconnected with Jake was her Aunt Aggie and that avenue was closed to her.

But for now there was the dinner to see to, the steak and kidney pie wouldn't prepare itself. She squared her shoulders, smoothed down her pinny and got to work.

Chapter 18

It was an unusually rainy autumn, everyone said so, and for weeks the ground outside the farmhouse resembled a quagmire. Even the animals seemed sick to death of the weather and the hens showed their displeasure by laying fewer eggs than normal. October had come in with wind and sleet showers and November was a bitterly cold month. On a particularly nasty wet November afternoon, when hail and icy sleet with a force eight gale behind them was sweeping the north-east, Hannah had a visitor.

In spite of it only being two o'clock in the afternoon she had just lit the oil lamps when a knock came at the front door of the farm-house. This was almost unheard of. Only Farmer Dobson and his daughter and one or two of Seamus's old friends stood on such ceremony, and Farmer Dobson hadn't been near the farm for weeks since Jake had made it clear to his daughter that he had no intention of availing himself of the comfort she had seemed determined to give.

Quickly discarding her pinny, Hannah smoothed her dress and patted a stray tendril of hair into the bun at the nape of her neck before hurrying through to the hall and opening the front door. 'Mam?' Her mouth fell open as she surveyed the soaked woman on the doorstep.

'I–I had nowhere else to go. She ... she's thrown me out. Just like that.'

Pulling herself together, Hannah said, 'Come in, come in.' She stood aside for her mother to step into the hall. She had been in the process of making a pot pie for their dinner when the knock had come but she didn't lead her mother to the kitchen but up the stairs to the sitting room. She lit a fire in there most days now to keep the dampness from penetrating the furniture and by mid-afternoon the room was as warm as toast.

'Come and sit by the fire.' Hannah looked at her mother but Miriam wouldn't meet her eyes. 'You're soaked through, I'll fetch some dry clothes.'

'Thank you.' Miriam put down the cloth bag she was holding which, like her, was dripping water onto the polished floorboards. 'I caught a tram as far as I could but then I had to walk the last mile.' She held out her hands to the warmth of the blaze.

Hannah said nothing more and left the room swiftly. In her bedroom she did not immediately select some clothes for her mother but stood for a moment gazing blankly ahead. Her mother. Here. She felt at a loss how to handle the situation. She wished Jake was around but he had gone into town on business and wouldn't be back for at least another hour.

When she returned to the sitting room, Miriam was standing exactly where she had left her. 'I ... I didn't like to sit down. Not wet through. Everything's so lovely...'

'Here's some of my clothes, I think they'll fit you.' Hannah placed them on an armchair with a towel. 'I'll get some tea while you change and then I'll be back.'

She took her time making the tea. Fingernails of sleet were tearing at the window and the wind was howling, but it was nothing to the turmoil inside her. Her stomach was churning and she felt physically sick. From what her mother had said, it was obvious her aunt had forced her to leave the flat. Did that mean Aunt Aggie had found out about her husband's affair with his sister-in-law?

She placed a number of jam tarts and some butterfly cakes on a plate which she put on a tray next to the tea things. She was aware she was moving slowly, delaying the moment when she would have to return to the woman upstairs.

When she walked into the sitting room, her

mother was clothed in the dress and cardigan she had given her, her wet clothes folded on top of the cloth bag. She was sitting in a chair close to the fire and immediately she said, 'I know what you must be thinking, me turning up like this, but I had nowhere else to go. I ... I wondered if I could stay overnight, just till I sort out what I'm going to do.'

'Of course.'

'Thank you.'

Hannah pulled out one of the occasional tables and placed the tea tray on it. She poured two cups of tea and passed her mother hers along with a tea plate before she offered the plate of tarts and cakes. Miriam took a small cake but did not begin to eat it; instead she crumbled a morsel in her fingers and said, 'Your aunt recently had an operation. Were you aware of that?'

'I knew she needed an operation. I didn't know she had had it.'

'Oh yes, she's had it and come through remarkably well for a woman who has supposed to have been dying for years.'

It was so bitter, the venom in her mother's voice, that it caused Hannah to blink. 'She's home again then?'

Miriam put her cup and plate on the table. She sat looking down at her hands which were joined on her lap, her bony fingers making small stroking movements between the knuckles. There was an embarrassing silence before she said, 'She came home today from an establishment in Seaburn where she's been convalescing for three weeks since leaving the hospital. Her new doctor arranged it all.'

Miriam's tone left Hannah in no doubt as to how her mother viewed this new doctor. 'I see.'

'She walked in the house, *walked* in mind, and sat herself down and told me I was no longer needed.' Miriam's voice was trembling but the look on her face told Hannah it was more with rage than anything else. 'My services were no longer required, that's what she said, and he stood behind her with his hands on the back of her chair and said not a word in my defence.'

Knowing what she knew, Hannah could think of nothing to say.

'I couldn't believe it at first. Well, you wouldn't, would you? I've worked my fingers to the bone for the pair of them and that was all the thanks I got for sixteen-odd years of servitude. I...' Miriam swallowed deeply. 'I told her I wasn't having it, that she couldn't do that to me and then ... then she accused me of all sorts of things.' Her face was burning, the colour suffusing it was almost scarlet. 'And still your uncle said nothing. He just stood there like a great lump of lard–' She broke off, visibly fighting for control before she continued, 'To be treated like this by kith and kin. Your father would be turning in his grave if he knew how his brother and wife had behaved.'

The hypocrisy was too much. Hannah stood up. She tried to speak gently because however much her mother deserved this present state of affairs, she was in a terrible state. 'I know, about you and Uncle Edward.'

Miriam's head snapped up. 'What are you talking about?'

313

'I saw you, that New Year's Eve I went to Naomi's. I came back and you didn't know I'd come in. I heard ... well, enough.'

Miriam opened and shut her mouth several times like a stranded fish before she said, 'It – it wasn't what you think. I mean...'

Ignoring this, Hannah said again, 'I *know*, Mam.'

Miriam's gaze was now riveted on her daughter. 'Did you tell her? Aggie? Was it you?'

'Of course not.'

'I don't believe you.'

'Whether you believe me or not, I did not tell her. I wouldn't do that to Aunt Aggie.'

Something in Hannah's voice must have convinced Miriam because she dropped her head, her hands working more urgently in her lap as she muttered, 'Then how did she know? She was all right before she went to the hospital and then to come back like that. She was like a different woman and I don't mean because of the operation. She stood over me while I collected my things, watching me to see what I took. It ... it was so humiliating.'

But not as humiliating as what her aunt had endured all these years if she had known about the affair. Could she have done? And kept silent? It was the only answer.

'And Edward,' her mother continued. 'He was cruel, cruel. When ... when I knew Aggie was determined to get rid of me, I admitted everything. I didn't see why he shouldn't be shown up for what he was, and he told me to get out. In front of her. He said I'd forced myself on him

314

when he was at a low point and then blackmailed him into continuing the affair by threatening to tell Aggie everything. It wasn't like that.'

Hannah stared at her mother for a long moment. 'You knew he was lying that night he said he didn't try to rape me. Why should you be surprised at anything he says or does?'

'No, no I didn't.' Her mother shook her head. 'I had no idea, I swear it. Of course I believe you now, I know what sort of man he is now, but then...'

'Even supposing you didn't know what Uncle Edward was like, which I find impossible to believe, you knew what I was like. You knew I wouldn't make something like that up, why would I? And with Uncle Edward. It was ... disgusting. You knew and you chose to protect him. I ... I can never forgive you for that. If it hadn't been for Jake I don't know what I would have done or where I'd have gone.'

Miriam's face took on a blank look. Glancing away, she said, 'Are you saying you want me to leave this minute?'

'No, that's not what I'm saying. You're welcome to stay the night, I know Jake wouldn't expect you to leave in this weather but I don't think he will want you to stay any longer than that.'

Miriam inclined her head. 'Very well.'

She was no different. Hannah stared at her mother. There was no shred of remorse in her, not for what she had done to Aunt Aggie or her, her own daughter. Her only living flesh and blood. All her mother was concerned about was herself. Her selfishness was amazing. But she knew what her

315

mother was like, she had known for some long time now, so why did it hurt so much? Stupid, but when she had seen her standing on the doorstep her heart had leapt. She had thought, she had hoped... Softly now, her voice scarcely above a whisper, she said, 'I have to go and see to the dinner. Sit by the fire and get warm and drink your tea.'

'You are joking.' Jake stared at her in jaw-dropping astonishment.

'I wish I were,' Hannah said ruefully.

'And she's up there now?'

'Yes, I told you, in the sitting room. It appears my aunt ordered her out of the house. My mother and uncle have been carrying on for years and she must have known. This operation seems to have turned her around and got her back on her feet, and she decided enough was enough, I suppose.'

'I'm sorry. It must have come as a shock to you to find out about your mother and uncle.'

'No.' She shook her head. 'I knew already. I overheard them talking one night.' Then, as something in his voice alerted her, she said, 'You don't seem very surprised.'

'I got their measure the night I punched your uncle. It was obvious what was going on.'

'But you never said.'

He smiled. 'Neither did you.'

Hannah smiled back weakly. 'It's not something you want to broadcast, is it? Not your own mother. But...' She bit her lip. 'She *is* my mother, Jake, and I told her she could stay overnight. Is that all right?'

He looked at her for a moment before replying, 'If you can show the milk of human kindness, I can. You're a nice lass, Hannah Casey.'

'So it is all right? You don't mind?'

'I'd like to kick her backside from here to Newcastle if we're speaking frankly and she sure as blighty doesn't deserve a daughter like you. I suppose it's too much to expect that she went down on bended knee and begged forgiveness for how she treated you?'

Her silence was answer enough.

He sighed. 'I'll go and have a word with her. Is she after money as well?'

'She didn't say that.'

Perhaps not, but that woman had more front than anyone he'd met. The way she had stared him out that night when the uncle had attacked Hannah was proof of that. Keeping his thoughts to himself, Jake said, 'Does she know about Seamus and how things stand here?'

'I don't know, I think she must do. I suppose it's common knowledge in the street.'

Aye, Adam would have seen to that. He had no doubt his dear half-brother had been busy spreading the worst interpretation of him inheriting the farm. He hadn't seen Adam or Wilbur the last few times he had visited his mother but he had noticed a distinct coolness in the attitude of the neighbours when he had called at the house in Wayman Street. Whereas normally they would have called out his name or asked him how things were going at the farm, folk had quickly disappeared off their doorsteps when he had arrived, or looked the other way. And he knew why. He had been branded an upstart, a money-grabber, and worse. And pack mentality demanded a closing of ranks against the one who had dared to rise above his station. Adam would be able to do no wrong and he no right. Oh aye, he knew how their minds worked all right.

His face and voice betrayed nothing as he said again, 'I'll go and have a word with her.' Then, dark amusement in his tone, he added, 'I take it we'll be eating in the dining room tonight?'

Hannah glanced at him. How did he know she had been planning to set out the dining-room table with the best of the linen and cutlery rather than them eating at the kitchen table as they'd done for the last few months? His gaze met hers and it was warm with a laughter that was not directed at her but with her. She drew her lips inward to stop herself from laughing, bowing her head slightly before tilting it to one side as if considering. 'That might be nice as we have a guest. Yes,' she nodded, 'I might do that if you think it appropriate?'

'Definitely.'

All trace of amusement had left Jake's face by the time he reached the sitting room. When he opened the door, Miriam was sitting in an armchair close to the fire but she stood up immediately. 'Good evening, Mrs Casey,' he said quietly, shutting the door behind him and advancing into the room before he added, 'I hear you're in a spot of trouble.'

Flushing, she said, 'Through no fault of my own.'

He didn't take his eyes from hers. 'That is a matter of opinion.'

'I see.' Lifting her head, Miriam said, 'She's told you.'

'We both know she didn't need to. I think I made myself clear the last time we met. Now, as to the moral standpoint,' he raised a hand to stop her when she went to speak, 'I think the old adage of we reap what we sow might be applicable. But let us put your treatment of Hannah to one side for a moment. I believe in plain speaking, Mrs Casey. No soft soap. I don't like you and you don't like me but I am happy to offer you the hospitality of my house because you are Hannah's mother. For the same reason I am prepared to assist you with a one-off payment which would enable you to live comfortably while you seek employment elsewhere. Preferably down south. Do I make myself clear?'

There was silence. Then Miriam said, 'Why would you do that?'

Jake waved a hand at the chair she had vacated and as Miriam sat down, he seated himself some distance away. 'Like I said, you are Hannah's mother and – although goodness knows why – I know she would not like the thought of you struggling. On the other hand, I'm not prepared to tolerate another visit from you.'

Miriam stiffened, her thin mouth pulling tight.

'In view of your sister-in-law's action I would imagine tongues will wag. It doesn't take much to set them going, as I'm sure you're aware. Very often the gossip round the doors is without foundation of course, but in this case...' He let the pause

319

lie on the air before he continued, 'So it would be in your interest to put as much distance between yourself and Sunderland as possible, added to which, housekeeping positions are more numerous down south. Do you agree, Mrs Casey?'

Miriam inclined her head. Her eyes were glowing with frustrated fury. Jake knew Hannah's mother would like nothing more than to fling his offer with its conditions back in his face but she was too shrewd for that. He didn't bother to hide his contempt when he said, 'I will settle fifteen pounds on you. That will be ample for your train fare and board and lodging while you look for a post. You may stay here overnight but I will take you to the train station myself in the morning. While you are under my roof, you will be civil and cooperative and you will do and say nothing to upset your daughter.'

'I wouldn't. I didn't intend–'

Jake cut her short again by raising his hand. He saw her bite hard on her lip and her eyes glowed with her hatred of him but she was helpless and they both knew it. 'You stood by and allowed Hannah's good name to be smeared by a man who isn't worthy to lick her boots. Not only that, but because of your brother-in-law's attempted rape you knew she could not return home. You didn't lift a finger to help your daughter, Mrs Casey. Dinner will be ready in an hour and until then I suggest you use the time to reflect how fortunate you are that Hannah does not resemble her mother in any way, shape or form.'

He could feel her eyes like knives in his back as he left the sitting room. After closing the door, he stood leaning against it for a moment or two and he was smiling. For right or wrong he didn't think anything had given him such satisfaction for a long time.

Chapter 19

It was three days later and the weather had changed from sleet showers and intermittent icy rain to a freezing cold with frosty nights and mornings. At long last the ground was hard and Hannah no longer had to wade through what felt like acres of mud to get to the farmhouse after she'd visited the hen crees. She had just cleared away the breakfast things and was standing gazing out of the kitchen window at the high silver-blue sky when it came to her she couldn't put off visiting her aunt one more day. Since the morning her mother had left Sunderland, she'd been trying to persuade herself nothing had changed, but it had. Irrevocably.

She had to see her Aunt Aggie. What that visit would entail she wasn't sure, she only knew she had to see her aunt and let her know she loved her and understood what she had done concern-ng her mother. The other thing that had stopped her from going before this day, the thing that had driven her from the house where she had been brought up, she'd say nothing about. Her aunt had had enough to cope with. She would keep to the story of a momentous row with her mother.

She could even say she had found out about her mother carrying on with Uncle Edward; that would be more acceptable than the truth now that her aunt knew all about the affair anyway.

Jake was sorting paperwork in his study and when she took him his mid-morning cup of coffee and piece of cake, she said, 'I'd like to go into town this afternoon. Can I have the horse and trap?'

He stared at her. This was the first time she had made such a request in all the time she had been at the farm.

'I want to call on my aunt.' She didn't wait for him to ask why she was making the journey into town. 'With all that's happened in the last days I feel it's time.'

He settled back in the big leather chair. 'What about your uncle?'

'I can handle seeing him now. It's different without my mother being there and with my aunt knowing about them.'

'She doesn't know about what he tried to do to you.'

Flushing, she said, 'I shan't mention that. She thinks I left because of a row with Mam and that's good enough.'

Jake shook his head in a show of irritation at her naivety. 'You don't think it will all come out if you see her face to face? She's already proved she's far from being a fool. You were very close to her, by your own account. She must be wondering what it would have taken to drive you away and keep you away.'

'I want to see her.'

'And I'm not saying you shouldn't, just that you must prepare yourself for what might occur.' He studied her face for a moment. 'I'll take you this afternoon. All right?'

'You needn't come.'

'If you think I'm going to let you come within a mile of that man without protection, you're wrong,' he said shortly, sitting straighter and turning his gaze to the papers in front of him. When after a moment or two she didn't move, he glanced up.

Her gaze was waiting for him. 'Thank you,' she said softly.

Warning himself to betray nothing, he smiled. 'What else are big brothers for? We'll go straight after lunch, how's that?'

She nodded. 'It's hodge podge with stottie cake.'

'My favourite.'

When Hannah had left the room, Jake remained quite still for a time, then he glanced towards the crackling fire. There was a good chance he'd go stark staring barmy before she was settled with Daniel or some other lad who caught her fancy. Dear gussy, how had it all come about? How was he in this position? Living in the same house, eating together, spending the evenings side by side in front of the fire in the sitting room.

Raking his hair back from his forehead he stood up and paced the floor for some minutes before flinging himself back down in the chair. He had to check these accounts. He had to concentrate. One hour, one day at a time and he'd get through. He had no other choice.

Hannah's heart was in her mouth as she and Jake entered the shop at two o'clock that afternoon, but it was Bart Crawford, and not her uncle, who was standing behind the counter slicing ham for Mrs Fraser.

'Ee, hello, lass.' Mrs Fraser's bright sharp gaze went from Hannah to Jake and then back again. 'We haven't seen you in these parts since young Joe's passing.'

'Hello, Mrs Fraser.' Hannah smiled but it was with some effort. She liked Mrs Fraser, she liked all their neighbours but she knew they would all be aware of her mother leaving the house and would be putting their own reasons to it. What they didn't know, they made up. That was the way of it round the streets. Before the woman could say anything more, she turned to Bart. 'Is my aunt in?'

He shook his head. 'Mr and Mrs Casey have been out since before twelve.'

'When are you expecting them back?'
The young lad shrugged. 'Any time.'

She couldn't wait, not with Mrs Fraser eager to whittle something, *anything* out of her about the goings-on.

As though in confirmation of her thoughts, Mrs Fraser bent closer to her, her voice conspiratorial as she said, 'Your mam not with you then, hinny? We wondered if she'd moved in with you?'

'No, Mrs Fraser. She hasn't.' Switching her gaze back to Bart, Hannah said, 'Would you tell my aunt I called by? I'll come back another time.'

'Only your mam said nowt to me about upping and going. I was only talking to her the other day,

324

Monday it was. I met her coming back from the library. Likes her romances, your mam.'

Hannah looked Mrs Fraser in the eye. She knew the woman did not like her mother. No one in the street did. Years ago Naomi had told her on the quiet that all the neighbours thought her mother was an upstart and full of airs and graces since her aunt had been taken ill. She'd defended her mother at the time even though she had secretly agreed with Naomi. And now Mrs Fraser was talking as though she was her mam's best friend. 'My mother received the offer of a wonderful housekeeping post down south a short while ago, and as my aunt was having the operation which would hopefully make her well, she thought it was time to make a move. Of course if Aunt Aggie hadn't recovered like she has my mother would have stayed and continued to help.'

'Oh aye?' Mrs Fraser didn't finish with 'And pigs fly', but she might as well have from the look on her face.

'Yes,' said Hannah firmly, just as the shop door opened and her aunt and uncle walked in.

Caught off guard, Hannah found herself lost for words. Her aunt looked so different for one thing. When she had imagined seeing Aunt Aggie again she'd pictured the two of them hugging, perhaps even crying, but this smartly dressed, expensively coiffured woman in front of her appeared like a stranger. She saw her uncle's gaze flash over them and he took a step backwards, presumably in shock, and then her aunt said, 'Hannah! Hannah, lass,' and opened her arms.

The next few minutes were all bustle and half-spoken sentences and no one noticed that Edward hadn't said a word. No one except Jake, that was. He hadn't taken his eyes off Hannah's uncle. Eventually Agatha led Hannah and Jake out of the shop and up the stairs to the flat, stopping halfway to shout, 'Edward? You're coming too, aren't you? I'm sure Bart can cope in the shop for a while without you, he does it all the time now.'

She didn't wait for his reply. The words had been expressed in the form of an order and it was apparent to Hannah and Jake that she was used to being obeyed.

Hannah's head was whirling as she entered the flat. Her repugnance at seeing her uncle again was partly alleviated by her amazement at the stranger who was her aunt. Gone was the vulnerable, dependent woman she had loved with all her heart and in her place was a person of authority. And her physical appearance was so changed. She looked well, her hair was cut and styled and her clothes were beautiful. Hannah glanced down at her aunt's feet. They were encased in fancy, soft leather shoes with decoration round the sides and little heels. They would have cost the equivalent of a man's weekly wage.

She had no time to dwell on this, however. Agatha turned to face her once they were in the sitting room, her voice reproachful as she said, 'I've missed you, hinny.'

'I've missed you too, Aunt Aggie.'

'Was the row with your mam really so bad that you couldn't call and see us? Not that I don't appreciate you taking care of her, Mr Fletcher,' Agatha glanced Jake's way for a moment, 'but this was your home when all was said and done.'

Hannah was aware of her uncle sidling into the doorway but she kept her eyes on her aunt as she said, 'It was pretty awful.'

'Well, sit down, sit down.' Agatha waved her hand towards the three-piece suite, and as they sat down, and without looking at her husband, continued, 'We'll have a pot of tea, Edward, and some cake and scones.'

When Edward had disappeared, Agatha, her voice soft now, said, 'Tell me about the do with your mam, lass. I take it you know she doesn't live here any more or you wouldn't be here.'

Hannah nodded. 'She came to the farm.'

'Did she now?' Agatha's face hardened. 'Brass neck, that woman. And did you give her short shrift?'

'She stayed overnight and then I put her on a train for London.' It was Jake who spoke, entering the conversation for the first time. As Agatha's eyes moved to his face, he added, 'She won't be back.'

Agatha nodded. 'No doubt she told you what a cruel woman I am.'

'I knew, Aunt Aggie. About Mam and... The row I had with Mam was all to do with that and other things. She – she said she never wanted to see me again.'

'Until it suited her.' Agatha shook her head. 'So, you know.' She let her back rest against the chair. 'Well, it might surprise you to know I had cottoned on a good few years ago. I think your mam wanted me to know, or suspect at least. She derived pleasure in emphasising she had the whip hand.' Turning to Jake, who was sitting impassively watching the pair of them, she added, 'Can you understand a woman like that? I had taken her into my home in time of need, and it was *my* home, not Edward's, I might add. My father worked hard to build up this business.' And then she made an impatient movement with her hand. 'But I'm digressing. I opened up my home and heart to her in the early days and that was how she repaid me. She is a dreadful, dreadful woman.'

Jake's voice was flat as he said, 'I agree with you, Mrs Casey.'

'But?' Agatha's eyes had narrowed.

'It takes two to tango.'

Agatha drew in a long breath. 'Aye, it does. You're right there, but men are such *physical* creatures. Edward was in a difficult position and in a moment of madness she took advantage of the weakness inherent in all men, and then virtually blackmailed him into continuing with their affair.' When Jake made no comment, she added, 'You disagree with that, Mr Fletcher?'

For a moment there was dead silence in the room. 'Does it matter what I think?'

'Perhaps not but I would like your opinion nonetheless.'

Jake nodded. 'Very well. I have no idea how the liaison between your sister-in-law and husband came about, Mrs Casey. You are right in your observation that he is a weak man but I beg to differ with the statement that all men are the same. They are not. And frankly it annoys me that he has been placed in the position of victim in all of this.'

'You don't like him.'

'I think he is a licentious, spineless excuse of a man, since you ask.'

Agatha nodded but did not comment. Turning to Hannah she said, 'If the row with your mam was concerning her and Edward, why didn't you say anything to me, lass? Why just skedaddle?'

'I didn't want you upset.' In this Hannah could speak the truth. 'What could you do about it as you were, lying in bed and so ill? I couldn't bear the thought of that being added to your suffering.'

'You're a good lass.' Agatha sighed deeply. 'And what do you think of your uncle now?'

'Honestly?' At her aunt's nod, Hannah continued, 'I agree with Jake.'

'I suppose that's natural.' Agatha leant forward slightly but did not lower her voice as she said, 'I wouldn't like either of you to be under the misapprehension that I'm a stupid woman and that Edward is getting off scot-free. I have found I am enjoying my new lease of life and I intend to buy what I want and go where I please. I shall consider no one but myself, do you understand? For the time being it suits me to have someone to fetch and carry and do my bidding and...' She paused. 'And yes, be a companion.'

She smoothed the fine wool material of her skirt. 'My father shared your low opinion of my husband, Mr Fletcher. For that reason he had the foresight to tie up my inheritance in a series of legal niceties which means my position is now a strong one. Edward was persuaded to sign papers before our marriage. Whether he was aware of their content, I don't know. He says not but that is by the by. His signature on those documents has now placed him in a vulnerable position. Strange how our circumstances have been reversed. Basically it pays him to toe the line because if we divorce or I die he gets nothing. Children of our union would have inherited everything. Failing that, the nearest living relative. Edward had quite a shock when this came to light when I had my solicitor call shortly before my operation to put my affairs in order in case the worst happened. I have to admit I hadn't realised the full significance of those papers when my father died, but I was in love then. Everything I had was Edward's as far as I was concerned. I am in love no longer, I haven't been for quite some time.'

Hannah felt a shiver go down to her toes. She couldn't equate this controlled, even cold woman with the warm Aunt Aggie she'd known from a baby. And then her aunt said, 'Don't look like that, Hannah. You have no idea what I've had to put up with since I was forced to take to my bed.'

At this Hannah rose quickly, walked across to Agatha and knelt down by her aunt's chair. 'I do know, Aunt Aggie. At least some of it. And I don't blame you, don't think that, it's just that...'

She couldn't explain what it was. But the change in her aunt was more unsettling and disturbing than she could express. It confirmed that nothing in life was straightforward, nothing turned out as you expected. She was glad her aunt had a new lease of life, as she'd put it, but with her return to full health, something had happened and it was chilling. She drew in a deep breath. 'I want you to be happy, that's all. You deserve to be happy.'

'Thank you, hinny.' For a moment there was a flash of the old Aunt Aggie and then the softness was gone. 'I intend to be. I've a mind to sell the business and travel a bit, do Europe like the toffs, you know? I've always hankered on seeing far-flung places. That surprises you, doesn't it? I can tell.'

'I suppose so.' Hannah stared into her aunt's carefully made-up face. The old Aunt Aggie would have smiled at the thought of wearing lipstick and powder. Nor would she have considered having her hair cut short in one of the avant-garde bobs that had been declared the rage earlier in the year. But it suited her. And she *was* pleased for her, how couldn't she be? Reaching up, she hugged her aunt quickly before returning to her own seat just as her uncle entered the room carrying a tray.

Agatha didn't look at her husband as she said, 'Afternoon tea, how lovely. Put the tray on the coffee table, Edward, and go and look after the shop while Bart delivers those orders on his bike. And tell him to be careful with the eggs this time. Mrs Skelton complained that two of hers were broken last week.'

As her uncle scuttled across to the table, Hannah forced herself to glance at him. He, too, had changed considerably but, unlike her Aunt Aggie, not for the better. Her uncle seemed to have shrivelled like a wrinkled prune. His clothes hung on him and it was obvious he hadn't had the benefit of a new wardrobe. He didn't look like the same man who had attacked her that frightening day fifteen months ago.

She didn't feel sorry for him. The thought was

almost aggressive, as though someone had accused her of being hard hearted. Nor would she, whatever happened. She didn't let herself think about what he'd tried to do most of the time, but she had the odd moment, often when she was tired or just about to drift off to sleep, when it was as real as the day it had happened. His hot mouth slobbering over hers, the feel of his hands and sharp nails clawing at the top of her legs, the smell and weight of him as he had crushed her into the hard ground. It could have ended so differently.

They did not stay long. Hannah was grateful Jake made an effort to keep polite conversation going with her aunt because she found herself at a loss as to what to say. She was fighting the urge to cry and yet there was no logical reason for it. Her aunt was in a better position than she had been in years so why was she feeling so desperately sad for her?

When she and Jake stood up to leave, Hannah got the impression Agatha was as relieved as she was. They had reached the small landing just outside the flat's front door when she felt her aunt's arms go about her. 'I wish you'd come before, lass. Oh, I know it would have been difficult, knowing what you knew, but I missed you.'

'I missed you too, Aunt Aggie.' The hurt in her aunt's voice brought the tears she had been fighting for the last half-hour pricking at her eyes. 'And I would have come except I was worried I might say something out of turn and you'd guess about Mam and Uncle Edward.' It wasn't the whole truth but it would have to do.

'Aye, aye, I can see that.' Her aunt continued to hold her close for another moment and then pushed her away, saying, 'Now it's all out in the open, you'll come again?'

Hannah nodded. 'I don't come into town much though. You must come to the farm too and see everything.'

As Hannah wiped her eyes, Jake said quietly, 'I second that, Mrs Casey. You'll be very welcome.'

'Thanks, lad.' Agatha smiled at the tall broad-shouldered figure. 'And I'm right glad about your bit of luck an' all by the way, inheriting the farm and everything.'

Neither Hannah nor Jake acknowledged Edward Casey as they left the shop part of the house, and it wasn't until they were seated in the horse and trap and halfway down the street that Hannah said, 'Do you think she'll come?'

'Why wouldn't she?'

'I don't know. She – she's so different, I suppose.'

'Didn't you expect her to be? After all the years of being incarcerated in that one room, her life has been turned around and it looks like she's going to make the most of it. Good luck to her, I say.'

Her eyes misted. He didn't understand. But then why would he? And how could she explain that she felt she'd suffered a bereavement? He'd think she was daft. But it was true. The old Aunt Aggie had gone and in her place stood a woman who was almost a stranger. She should have gone to see her when she was still poorly, maybe then the bond wouldn't have been broken. Or maybe she should have explained about her uncle's attempted rape. Her aunt would have understood then that she couldn't have faced going back to the house with her mother and uncle still in residence. Oh, she didn't know – perhaps nothing would have made any difference. One thing was for sure, it was too late now.

The tears gathering in her throat threatened to choke her, and she turned her head and concentrated on the view ahead as the horse and trap turned into Southwick Road. Blinking her eyes clear, she told herself fiercely she was not going to cry. Her aunt was well and healthy and making a new life for herself and her uncle had got his come-uppance to a degree. Furthermore, her mother was out of the picture. Things had settled at the farm again after the trauma of Joe's death and then Seamus's, and Naomi and her young man were coming for Sunday tea at the weekend, weather permitting. Everything was fine, or as fine as it could be after the recent tragedies. It just didn't feel like it, that was all. And still, deep inside, although she was trying not to dwell on it, she was constantly steeling herself against the day when Jake would take up with someone and the decisions she would have to face then.

PART FIVE

1929 – The Resurrection

Chapter 20

The last two years had been uneventful and mildly prosperous on the whole for the residents of Clover Farm, in spite of the increasing unemployment nationwide.

The newspapers reported the country was in the middle of a slump, something the working class were well aware of. The number of broken men, women and children entering the grim walls of the workhouses, the babies crippled with rickets, the children with ringworm and TB and a whole host of other diseases, the men who quietly ended their lives rather than see their families starve, had risen month by month since the General Strike.

It was foreign competition that was causing the problem, the newspapers chirruped, along with the Wall Street crash. The northerners' answer to that was they had been living in a slump all their lives, and what could stockbrokers jumping off skyscrapers across the ocean have to do with anything? And if things were so bad for everyone, why were semi-detached houses with bathrooms and indoor privies being built all over the hockey down south? The country had always been split in half, the men said over their pints of beer – one of which had to last all night – and the politicians and powers that be regarded northerners as second-class citizens.

So the bitterness grew. Marches to protest at

decreasing wages and lost jobs became normal, along with the violence which often ensued.

It said plenty for how desperate things had become in the Wood household that when Rose asked Jake to take Stephen on at the farm when he left school the day after his fourteenth birthday, there was no murmur of complaint from Wilbur or Adam. Wilbur hadn't worked in months, and with the cuts in the miners' pay packets, Adam's wage was almost on a par with what Naomi brought home some weeks. Wilbur's last shreds of pride were tied up with Rose not working and in this one thing she dared not defy him. But they couldn't manage on the two small wages and Jake's food parcels. And so in the autumn Stephen left for Clover Farm.

Now it was the day before Christmas Eve, and Hannah and Jake had called at the house in Wayman Street weighed down with bags of this and that for Rose, and stocking-fillers for the younger children. Outside the house was a crystal white world. The snow was thick on the ground with more to come in the heavy laden sky, but inside Rose's kitchen it was warm, the fire in the range casting a mellow glow over the old battered furniture and scrubbed flagstones.

Wilbur was there, sitting in his chair in front of the range. Each morning he ate his breakfast and left the house as though he had a shift, only to spend hours standing about on street corners with old pals who were in the same position as him. In rain, hail and snow they banded together, hands in pockets and eyes dead. Adam was now his father's connection with the pit. As long as his son was working, Wilbur felt he had a chance of returning.

Lily was round at her mother's with the baby. It appeared she was there most of the time these days. Things between her and Adam had never been good, according to Rose, but now they were at rock bottom. Rose glanced at the twins who had been forced to stay in the house rather than play with their friends, owing to the fact their boots were more holes than leather, then she put her head close to Hannah's and murmured, 'She keeps threatening to clear off for good and I wish she would, may the good Lord forgive me. But at least when she's round her mam's she's not under my feet, and her mam an' da have taken to having Sadie most weekends now.'

Hannah nodded. Rose, who loved all children, hadn't taken to her first grandchild, possibly because little Sadie was distinctly precocious and inclined to hour-long screaming tantrums if thwarted. She was also the spitting image of her mother. 'Doesn't Adam mind her being at her mam's so much?'

'He'd pack her bags himself, given the slightest chance.'

'But the child, Sadie. She's his bairn,' Jake put in quietly.

'She's Lily's bairn,' Rose said in a low voice with another glance at the twins to make sure they were not listening. Having satisfied herself they were engrossed sitting on the clippy mat sorting out the bag of marbles Jake had brought them, she continued, 'From wanting nowt to do with her when she was born, once she was crawling and talking a bit, Lily's been all over her.' She paused. 'Mind, to be fair, I can understand that, the way the marriage has gone. I suppose the bairn's a comfort.'

Jake and Hannah exchanged a glance. In an effort to divert the conversation from Adam's marital problems, Hannah said, 'And Adam? Are things any better at the pit?'

'No, an' not likely to be.' Normally Wilbur remained as silent as the grave during their visit, but now he entered the conversation with a scowl. 'He worked all of last week, and when there was a fall an' they needed extra he did a double shift, and at the end of it he come away with a pay packet with just over a pound in it. Them and their damn trumped-up fines.'

'But couldn't he say something, Mr Wood?'

Wilbur's look was pitying as he surveyed Hannah. 'One word and he'd be finished, and if he's finished now we've all had it. The blighters know that. They know how we're placed.'

Jake said nothing. His stepfather was longing to let fly at him, he knew the signs, but of late Wilbur hadn't dared. In a minute they'd have a list of Adam's virtues if Wilbur ran true to form.

'They had him shovelling on his knees for a penny farthing a yard and his legs under water from the time he went in till the time he come out, and does he whine about it? Does he heck. He's a good lad, none better, an' anyone who says different is a liar.'

'Aye, all right, all right,' Rose intervened, and as the look between wife and husband caught and held, it was Wilbur who lowered his head first. Turning to Hannah, Rose said, 'Your aunt and uncle are away for Christmas then? Somewhere foreign, I understand. I'm surprised they shut shop at what must be their busiest time.'

'Aunt Aggie's selling the business,' Hannah said quietly. 'It was all signed and sealed the day before they left so I know she won't mind me saying now. They may not return to England at all but she's going to write to me when she decides what to do.'

'Is that so? Ee, Bart's family will be hard pressed. They rely on the lad's wage.'

'The new owners are keeping him on. Aunt Aggie was insistent about that.'

They continued to chat for a few minutes more but with Wilbur sitting glowering in his chair, they didn't prolong the visit. Rose saw them out, watching Jake help Hannah into the small two-wheeled carriage and then waving as he clicked the horse into motion and they disappeared into the now thickly falling snow.

She didn't immediately return to the kitchen but stood on the doorstep for some minutes, her mind miles away. She had long since given up on the notion that had assailed her at one time after Seamus's death, that of her lad and Hannah getting together. She didn't know what had put it into her mind but once there, it had stuck for a while. Hannah was a good lass, a kind lass. If anyone could see past Jake's appearance to the man beneath, it was Hannah. As though the thought had been a criticism of Jake in some way, she followed with, and the lass would have been doing herself proud if she'd looked the side he was on. There was no one better than her lad, no one in the whole world. He wasn't just big in size

341

but in his heart as well, and there was a depth in him none of her other children had, even Naomi. But there, it hadn't happened and as the months had gone by she'd told herself it was a daft idea. One thing was for sure, the lass was so bonny she could pick and choose.

Sighing, Rose shut the door. Adam was still of the mind that Daniel, Jake's manager, meant more to Hannah than the lass let on and he might be right. They didn't know what went on at the farm after all. But Hannah wasn't walking out formally with him or else she would have told Naomi. Although the two of them didn't see so much of each other these days, they were still close. Naomi... Rose sighed again, irritably this time. She wished her daughter would see that Stuart Fraser would never be any good to her. Two years they'd been courting and he messed her about something rotten. What with Adam and Naomi, perhaps she should be thanking her lucky stars Jake hadn't got a lass and seemed content enough. But then, you could never tell with Jake. Quiet waters ran deep with her firstborn.

'Took him long enough to go.'

As she stepped into the kitchen, Wilbur glared at her but as was happening more and more these days she returned his look, saying, 'It was good of him to come in this weather and bring the bits for the bairns and the food for Christmas. There's a whole ham and one of their turkeys, along with butter and cheese and whatnot. Have you looked?'

'I don't need to look. I knew you'd tell me soon enough.'

'And why not? It's what keeps us going. The

least you could do is to be civil to him.'

'I was civil.' He shot the words at her, his voice heavy with suppressed rage as he added, 'Sure signs I'm not bringing anything in these days, the way you talk to me. Things have come to a pretty pass when there's no respect in a man's house from his own wife.'

Rose said nothing to this. She took the items Jake and Hannah had brought out of the bags and placed them on the kitchen table. The presents for the children, which Hannah had already wrapped, she put out of sight in one of the cupboards. She didn't hurry to put the food away even though she knew the sight of it was infuriating Wilbur still more. She took a brown packet from the table. 'Stephen's sent his wage packet. Do you want to open it?'

Taking Wilbur's silence for refusal, she slit the brown paper with her fingernail, her face softening as she counted the folded notes inside. Jake had told her he had given Stephen a Christmas bonus. What he had meant was she now had enough to buy the twins and Peter new winter boots, with a bit more besides.

She went across to the mantelpiece and lifted down the metal tin with a picture of the late Queen on the lid and added half a sovereign and two two-shilling pieces to the couple of coins inside. That would take care of the worry about the rent over Christmas. They would still be in arrears but when the rent man called tonight she could pay enough off the back to keep him happy. She went into the scullery and put the notes away in a small linen bag she wore pinned to the inside of the bodice of her petticoat. They hadn't a drop of beer or hard stuff in the house for Christmas, and if she knew anything about her husband and son they would put that before new boots for the bairns.

She returned to the kitchen and busied herself with the mutton broth she had simmering on the hob, skimming off the murky surface and adding a couple of dessertspoonfuls of rice, a chopped leek and some other vegetables to the scrag of mutton and bones before returning it to the hob. The evening meal seen to, she was just about to clear away the farm food when the kitchen door was thrust open and Adam came in.

Rose saw his eyes go immediately to the kitchen table and she could have kicked herself. She hadn't realised it was so late, With the bairns off school for the Christmas holidays and Jake calling in, she'd lost track of time.

'The big man's been round then?' Adam addressed his father, not her, throwing his bait can down on the table as he spoke.

'Oh aye, he's been.'

Wilbur had brightened up as soon as Adam appeared. Nowadays, even if Adam worked a double shift into the night, Wilbur would wait up for him. She had remonstrated with him at first but since she had come to understand that Adam was her husband's link with the pit Wilbur had worked in since a lad of thirteen and, more than that, his pride, she'd left well alone. She steeled herself for the inevitable question and like clockwork it came.

'So, lad,' Wilbur said, his voice as offhand as he

344

could make it, 'anything doing yet then?'

Depending on Adam's mood he would respond to the question he heard six times a week with mild impatience or downright irritation. She couldn't blame him. Since Wilbur had lost his job, six times a week added up to a fair few times her son had walked in to the same words, and there was always a note of heightened desperation after Jake had called.

Whether Adam had noticed this too and the knowledge moderated his reaction she didn't know, but her son's voice was sympathetic when he said, 'There's nowt, Da. Maybe after Christmas, eh?'

'Aye, aye.'Wilbur clutched at the lifeline. 'Things have got to ease up soon. I met Seth Todd a couple of days ago and he reckons some of the old-timers'll be set on again in the New Year. Mind, he's only working 'cos he nipped up to the colliery the day there was that accident and three men were injured and asked to be taken on. A dozen or more raced each other to the gates even as the poor devils were being carried out. If I had to get back down like that I'd tell 'em to shove it.'

Rose met her son's eyes for a moment. They both knew that if Wilbur had heard about the accident, he'd have been there with the others. Every time a man came home and said he'd been given the sack, his neighbours would slink off, shamefaced admittedly but with a thin wife and bairns crying because their bellies were empty, what could you do? Shaking off her thoughts, Rose said briskly, 'Get yourself washed and I'll have a cup of tea and a shive of sly cake ready.

345

Dinner'll be a while yet.'

Ignoring her, Adam turned to his father again. 'Hannah come with him?'

'Aye, she brought some bits for the bairns for Christmas. There's something for Sadie an' all.'

Adam's eyes were hard. 'My bairn'll have nowt that comes from him.'

Rose stared at her son, anger uppermost. Reminding herself with some effort that he had a lot on his plate what with Lily and the bairn and, not least, working down the pit for a pittance, she said nothing. She'd long since become reconciled to the fact that her eldest son and her second-born would always be at enmity with each other. She took the kettle from the hob and carried it into the scullery where she emptied the contents into the tin bowl which served for daily washing, adding most of the pail of cold water at the side of the stone sink so the water was tepid. She placed a bar of blue-veined soap and a large rough towel by the bowl, then walked back into the kitchen, saying briefly, 'It's ready.'

Adam gave no word of thanks, brushing past her with a face like thunder. Rose hurriedly cleared the table after using the remaining water in the pail to fill the kettle which she placed on the hob. When the tea was made she poured three cups, giving Wilbur his before bringing out the sly cake. Glancing at her husband, she said, 'Do you want a piece before your dinner?'

'What do you think?'

'I don't know, that's why I'm asking you.'

He glared at her, his eyes narrowed. 'One of these days...' He allowed the threat to hang in the air for a moment before he growled, 'Aye, I want a bit, why wouldn't I?'

There was silence in the kitchen until Adam came and sat down. He drank his tea in a few swallows, then pushed his mug towards his mother for a refill without speaking or looking at her. After finishing the sly cake and drinking half of his second mug of tea, he said to no one in particular, 'Hannah all right then, is she?'

It was Wilbur who said, 'Aye, far as I know, lad. She looked as bonny as ever.'

'Come clean about her and this Daniel yet, has she?'

Rose looked at her husband and he at her, and for a rare moment their thoughts were joined. Tentatively, Wilbur said, 'I think you're on the wrong tack there, lad. From what I can tell, she's one of them lasses that keeps herself to herself. Likely all that with her uncle's put her off.'

Adam leant back in his chair but it was to his mother and not his father, he said, 'Say it. I know you're thinking it.'

Rose raised her eyebrows.

'That it was me who put Hannah off, as Da terms it. Well, let me tell you, the pair of you,' his eyes briefly turned to his father before returning to Rose, 'she's pulling the wool over your eyes. She was seeing that lackey of Jake's before me and her fell out, Joe said as much back then.'

'Not to me he didn't.' Rose met her son's angry gaze and although her voice was low it was firm. 'Hannah's a good lass, she wouldn't do something like that.'

'You don't know the half.'

347

'I know enough to recognise the type of lass who behaves herself and them who don't and you got caught by one of the latter.'

'Huh!' Standing up with enough force to send his chair tottering, Adam slammed out of the kitchen.

When they heard his footsteps in the bedroom he shared with Lily, Wilbur said, 'He'll freeze up there.'

'That's up to him, isn't it?' Rose cleared away the mugs and the remains of the sly cake with jerky movements.

'We'd be hard pressed without what he brings in.'

'We'd have to manage, wouldn't we? And Stephen's wage is double that of Adam's.'

'That's not Adam's fault.'

Maybe it was the fact that for once her husband's voice was more sorrowful than angry, but suddenly Rose's irritation and resentment drained away. Plumping down on one of the hard-backed kitchen chairs, she said, 'I know, I know. And Adam's a hard worker, I'm not denying it. I just wish...'

'What?'

'It doesn't matter.' Useless to say she wished things had been different between Jake and Adam and that Adam was free of the pit and working alongside Stephen – it would be a red rag to a bull. Looking hard at her husband, she said, 'Hannah's a good lass, Wilbur. You know it same as me. And this – this *obsession* he's got about her and this lad, it's not healthy, even if he wasn't a married man with a bairn. You'll have to talk to him.'

'Me?'

'Aye, you. It's been going on for too long. I thought it'd fade after a while but you heard him tonight.'

Wilbur's head jerked to one side as it sometimes did these days. The nervous tic had started shortly after the miners had gone back after the General Strike and had got worse in the last little while. 'I'm saying nowt. He's allowed his own thoughts, even the damn owners can't take away a man's thoughts and I'm blowed if I'm going to tell him how to think.' She saw him cast her a sidelong glance. 'Anyway, like the lad says, who knows what goes on up at that farm? Jake wouldn't stand in her way if she took up with Daniel, that's for sure, he'd look at it as one in the eye for Adam.'

'Give me strength.' Rose's infuriated mutter brought Wilbur sitting up straighter but in the same moment the back door banged and a second later Naomi hurried into the kitchen, her face white and pinched with cold. In the ensuing bustle of getting Naomi's wet things off and her daughter's blue feet soaking in a bowl of hot water laced with mustard, the conversation was put to one side. But it was not forgotten, not by Rose, and the worry that had begun two years before on Christmas Day when Adam had disappeared for a large part of the afternoon and returned in a white-hot rage was stronger. She hadn't believed his explanation that he had met some pals and finished up having a row with one of them then, and she didn't now. He had been to the farm that day, knowing Jake and Joe were out of the way, she felt it in her bones, and whatever had transpired between him and Hannah had not been to his liking. And these walks he took sometimes, even in the winter if the weather wasn't too bad. Where did he go? Adam had never been one to walk. Was he trying to spy on the lass? But it was no good her saying anything.

Naomi was looking a mite better, with the colour back in her cheeks, and Rose busied herself stirring the broth and then setting the table. It was only his da who would be able to get through to Adam and with Wilbur thinking the sun shone out of his eldest son's backside, she might have known he'd do nothing to upset him.

Should she have a word with Jake on the quiet?

And then she answered herself with an immediate no. Whether she was right or wrong, Jake getting involved would be like the spark to a powder keg. No, the best she could hope for was that she was wrong. Failing that, that Adam would come to his senses by himself. But would he? Please, God, make him see sense.

She sliced the two loaves of stottie cake she had baked to go with the broth into big chunks, praying as she worked.

Chapter 21

No one looked twice at the two shabbily dressed individuals who had just climbed down from the harrier's cart at the back of the Bishopwearmouth cemetery. Even if they had, no one would have recognised the smaller of the two. The years had not been kind to Silas Fletcher. His indulgence in most of the vices known to man had stripped him of his good looks, and with the passage of time his face had taken on a sour yellowness as his thin wiry body had seemed to shrivel. Only his eyes remained the same, the permanently bloodshot whites emphasising the bullet-hard quality of the black orbs. His companion, a long lean individual with a permanent stoop, was equally unprepossessing.

It was this man who now said, 'You sure we're doing the right thing, Len?'

'Aye, I'm sure.' He had called himself Leonard Craggs when he had arrived down south and no one, not even Sid who had been a crony for over twenty-five years, knew any different. 'I told you, it's got too hot for me in London, I need to give it a bit of time to cool down with Dave Kane breathing down my neck. One warning to make meself scarce was enough.' He glanced down at his right hand and his bandaged fingers.

'Still hurt?' Sid said sympathetically.

'If you'd had your fingers broken one by one in a vice operated by one of Kane's gorillas, would it hurt?'

'You shouldn't have squealed to the law the last time you got caught. You were lucky it was just one hand. I've known Dave Kane put a man in a wheelchair for life for less than what you did. Kenneth Gray–'

'All right, all right. I don't want to hear about Kenneth Gray.' Silas swore under his breath. 'Look, I told you, I've got family round these

351

parts I can perhaps tap for a bob or two. Folk who'd rather forget I exist.'

'How do you know they're still alive?'

'I don't. That's what we've come to find out, remember?' said Silas with heavy sarcasm. 'But the main thing is we're far enough away to satisfy Kane and I know this area like the back of my hand, the old part of the town at least. Especially the East End where the action is. Stick with me an' you'll be all right.'

Sid glanced at Silas's bandaged hand. He looked doubtful.

Delving into his coat pocket, Silas counted the money he was carrying in a smart black leather wallet. 'We've a few days' board and lodging with nice grub courtesy of that gentleman's generosity back at Euston. Not that he knew he was being generous of course.' Silas smiled, showing stubs of blackened teeth. 'Not bad, considering I usually use my right hand.'

'You're a marvel, Len.'

They had begun walking as they talked and now Silas glanced up and down Chester Road. The day was bitter, the cutting edge of ice in the rain but he wasn't downcast. Like he'd said to Sid, he'd make a few inquiries about Rose and his brothers and sisters but he wasn't expecting anything from it. If Rose or any of them were alive, ten to one they'd be living hand to mouth and he wasn't about to advertise his return for a few measly pennies. His main reason for coming back to the north-east rather than going elsewhere was that he knew all the old haunts and dens, it was familiar territory which would give him an edge. Two or three months here, six at the most, and he could return south. Maybe not London though. His broken fingers were throbbing. And he'd keep his head down for a while when he left here. If Kane had wanted to put the wind up him, he'd succeeded.

He glanced at Sid trudging along at the side of him. He had tried to make out to Kane it was Sid who had ratted on him when they had both got caught peddling the drugs, but Kane hadn't had any of it. He was no fool, Dave Kane. He'd best remember that in the future.

By the time they had crossed over town and reached the East End, the weather had set in and they were soaked through. Silas was pleased to see that the East End was much as he remembered and once they had found a room in a squalid little house in a street close to the old barracks, he sent Sid out for some hot pies and chitterlings and bottles of beer. The landlady had lit a fire in the small fireplace when he had coughed up an extra bob or two, bringing up a full scuttleful with a big smile.

She might well smile, Silas thought, standing with his back to the fireplace, the palms of his hands pressed against his thin buttocks and his damp trousers steaming from the heat of the flames. Well over the odds, he'd paid. Tomorrow he'd make sure Sid got a sack of coal from some-where.

He glanced round the dirty little room, at the three-quarter size iron bed with its grey sheets and thin eiderdown and the rickety wardrobe with a broken door. A small table with a wobbly leg and two hard-backed chairs made up the sum total of furniture and the walls were damp and likely bug infested. But this would suit his purposes for the present, no one asked questions in this part of the East End.

He had learnt a lot since he'd left these parts. Funny he had returned for the same reason he'd left, because things had got a mite too hot for comfort. Full circle if you came to think about it. But the bad boys in these parts were nothing compared to the London hard cases and, like he said, he'd learnt plenty. He'd wipe the floor with them here.

Silas's amazing belief in his own ability which had carried him through some sticky situations in the past was reasserting itself after the fright he'd had when Dave Kane had had him picked up the week before. As he swayed back and forth on his heels, what passed for a smile stretched his lips in the midst of his bewhiskered face. He'd make a killing here, he could feel it in his water.

'So what's the interest in this Fletcher bloke?'

Silas turned his head and looked at Sid. They were sitting in a corner of the bar in the Friendly Tavern in Southwick Road and Silas, as he termed it to himself, had struck gold. He had long since discovered that you could learn more in the confines of a public house than anywhere else if you played your cards right. Drink loosened men's tongues and they'd tell you things they'd never dream of revealing when stone cold sober. Not that this particular thing was any sort of secret. No, it was common knowledge that

Jake Fletcher had won the jackpot by ingratiating himself with some farmer who had a nice little spread near the old quarries Hylton way apparently. And Rose had married again. Well, well, well. The pints of beer he'd bought that neighbour of Rose's had been money well spent.

Shrugging, he said briefly, 'He might be good for a bob or two, that's all.'

'You know the family then?'

'Used to, before I moved south.'

It was dismissive and said in the way Silas had, which warned Sid to lay off. For once, though, Sid was having none of it. 'Look, Len, I come up north with you, I didn't have to. The least you can do is fill me in with what's doing. You didn't pour the beer down that bloke's throat for nothing.'

'Perhaps I felt sorry for him.'

Silas hadn't meant Sid to take him seriously and now the other man laughed shortly. 'And pigs fly.'

Silas glanced about him to make sure no one was listening. The bar was full of shabbily dressed men sitting over their half pints which they made last all night. Their talk was intermittent and most of the faces were dead looking. He had noticed one or two bring out small tin boxes containing Woodbine ends which they had obviously picked up here and there. None of them was like the strong, aggressive, loud talkers he remembered from his days down the mine. He felt no pity for them, merely a mild kind of contempt. Deciding Sid would probably click on anyway, he said quietly, 'Fletcher's my kid, all right? I was married once.'

'But...' Sid's brow wrinkled. 'Your name's not Fletcher. And didn't that bloke say Fletcher's father had copped it years ago? Pulled out of the dock, wasn't he?'

'I left in a hurry. Likely someone put two and two together and made ten with me going and some bloke's body being fished out of the water. I don't know and I don't care. It suited me to disappear.' Silas took a long pull at his beer, wiping his mouth with the back of his hand before he continued. 'And now it appears me son's set up and respectable. Wonder what he'd pay for me to remain dead? Likely he wouldn't want me resurrected, what with his mam having married again and with another family. The way they are round here they'd tear her apart gossiping over their backyards. Her a bigamist with umpteen bastards to her name. Aye, if he thinks anything at all of his mam, this could be a nice little earner for us while we're in these parts.'

The cogs were still slowly turning in Sid's brain. 'So your name ain't Craggs then?'

Silas finished his pint. 'Craggs'll do,' he said shortly. He looked hard at Sid.

'All right, Len. All right.' Sid nodded. 'So do I take it we're going to pay Fletcher a visit?'

'Oh aye. Tomorrow'll do, it being Christmas Day. Little Christmas present, eh?' Silas grinned.

'What if he don't believe you, him being a baby when you cleared off?'

'He'll believe me.' It was said with quiet certainty. 'And you keep your mouth shut and let me do the talking. Better still, I'll go on me own and see him but I'll let him know there's

356

someone clocking my return. Bit of insurance in case he don't take too kindly to what's said.'

'Whatever you say, Len. Whatever you say.'

'Go and get another couple of pints in.' Silas slid some coins across the table. 'And two double whiskies to go with 'em. I've just come into money.'

Sid stood up but before doing as Silas said, he leant forward. 'What about her, your wife? You going to see her an' all?'

Silas shook his head. 'She's just the lever that works the cash till. If Fletcher's cooperative, this can remain just between the three of us.' He had no wish to open a can of worms. He hadn't had anything to do with that fella's murder years ago but it might not look like that with the rabbit's foot being found on the body. Likely his son had little knowledge of the means by which they had identified the body, him being a wee bairn at the time. He'd play it by ear when he made contact with him, but even if the lad didn't care over much about his mam, likely he wouldn't want the scandal, him being a well-to-do farmer and respectable member of the community.

Silas's lip curled as he watched Sid make his way over to the bar. Folk placed great store by respectability and his wife had been more fervent than most in that regard, probably because of the way her pious mam and da had brought her up. It had been the tool in his hands which had made her dance to his tune, and he dare bet she would have brought the bairn up the same way she'd been reared. Well, he'd soon see.

He drew a packet of Woodbines out of his

pocket and lit one, taking a deep drag and blowing out the smoke slowly, relishing the number of envious glances from the thin, drawn faces around him. When Sid returned with the drinks, Silas smiled at him. 'By the time we leave these parts we're going to look like a couple of gents, Sid. You mark my words.' He drank his whisky straight down, smacking his lips and settling back in his chair. 'Aye, I could do with some new togs, and that flea-bitten hovel we're in is fit for neither man nor beast. A nice hotel room, I think. The Grand, maybe. Fancy that?'

When Sid just stared at him, Silas's smile widened. 'You have to think big if you want to be a step ahead of the crowd, Sid. And I do that, I think big. It's what's always set me apart from the scum. I've told you, you stick with me an' you'll be all right.'

Chapter 22

Jake stood in the cow shed, gazing broodingly over the ruminating creatures but without seeing them. The lamp-lit serenity of his surroundings, the gentle puffing of the contented cattle with their turnip-sweet breath misting the cold air was lost on him. He was in turmoil.

Grinding his teeth, he sighed with a low groan, causing the nearest bovine to glance his way. He couldn't go on like this, not for another twelve months. He'd come to the end of his tether. She'd thanked him so prettily for the fur-trimmed coat and gloves he had bought her for Christmas, reaching up and touching his cheek with her lips before giving him his present of a fine leather tobacco pouch and pipe. All day his face had burnt from the contact. He could feel it still.

He was going to have to do something. But what? If he told her how he felt, ten to one she would pack her bags and disappear. But the alternative, that of further months, perhaps years, acting the big brother was beyond him. He was thirty-three years old, damn it. He wanted a woman in his bed at night, he wanted the ragings of his flesh catered for. No, not a woman, any woman. He wanted Hannah. Hell, how he wanted Hannah.

Turning, he walked over to the open door, standing with his back to the cattle as he gazed out over the snowy darkness, his breath white in the frosty air as he sighed again. He was in a cleft stick. If he said something he'd lose her for good. If he held his tongue he'd go stark staring mad. The last two years had been bitter-sweet, knowing he featured highly in her life and that she held him in affection, even love, but of the sisterly kind. She trusted him, that was the thing, and after her uncle and then Adam letting her down so badly, he didn't want to be the third man in her life to betray her trust. And how could he ask her to love him as a woman loves a man? He only had to look in the mirror to see it was impossible.

Suddenly impatient with himself, he retraced his footsteps and picked up the lamp, but as he reached the barn door again, one of the farm dogs began barking. It was probably nothing more than the scent of a fox skulking around that had set it off, but since the trouble with the poachers he'd instructed everyone at the farm to take nothing for granted. As he came round the corner of the barn, he was just in time to see a shadow pressed against the wall kick out at the dog which was lying almost flat on the ground, hackles raised, still growling and barking.

'I'd advise you to keep quite still if you want to keep your leg in one piece.' Clicking his fingers at the dog, Jake continued, 'Guard, Flossie,' whereupon the dog stopped barking but remained in the crouching position with her eyes fixed on the intruder.

'I weren't doing nothing.' The voice from the shadows was low, wary. 'I watched you come out of the house earlier and I thought you might be Jake Fletcher. I want a quiet word with him.'

'Oh aye?' Jake found himself staring at a shabby, insignificant-looking man, from what he could make out in the darkness. 'And what would that be about?'

'You him? Are you Jake Fletcher?'

Jake held the lamp higher so the light fell full on the man's face. It was thin, the chin covered with grey stubble but it was the eyes that held his attention. They were dark, seemingly black, and they glittered in the light like pinpoints of granite. He was reminded of a rat held at bay. 'Aye, I'm Jake Fletcher,' he said quietly.

'Don't recognise me, do you? Mind, there's no reason you should. You were nowt but a babbie when I left.'

Jake had moved a step closer to the man in order to see him clearly when he'd held the lamp to his face, and now he became aware of the stranger's body odour. It was distasteful, mustily sweet and frowsty; not so much an unwashed smell but something peculiar to the individual in front of him. He didn't think he had ever smelt anything quite like it before. Swallowing hard, Jake said, 'You're trespassing on my land.'

'I know it's your land, lad. Done right good for yourself, haven't you? But then it's in the blood, ain't it? The Fletchers have always known how to look after themselves.' Glancing down at the dog, he added, 'Call it off. I'm no threat to anyone, lad.'

He wasn't so sure about that. 'What do you want?'

'A quiet word, like I said. That's why I didn't knock on the door and announce meself to all an' sundry.'

Jake waited. He wasn't sure if the instant dislike he'd felt for this man was because of the circumstances in which he'd met him or whether he would have felt it anyway, but there was something about the fellow that made his flesh creep.

'Well, see here, it's like this. This might come as a bit of a shock because as far as you know your da died when you was a babbie. That right?'

Jake neither nodded nor replied but remained staring at the man as something in his stomach curdled.

'But they got it wrong, them that said he'd died. It was a mistake, right? Whoever the poor blighter was they pulled out of the dock, it weren't me. I'd

361

skedaddled down south. There were good reasons for me going,' Silas's tongue moved over his lower lip, 'but best I don't go into that. Suffice to say I had to disappear. But I'm your da, lad, that's what I'm saying. Silas Fletcher.'

Jake was standing straight, stiff and tall, and his voice came deep and throaty when he said, 'I don't believe you. My father died over thirty years ago.'

'Aye, well, like I said, there were reasons I had to make meself scarce and them same reasons kept me away. I didn't want to go.' His voice softened, becoming almost fawning. 'What man'd want to leave his wife an' bairn? But I'd have ended up six feet under if I'd stayed, that's the truth of it. And I knew Rose's mam and da'd take you both in, that you'd be well looked after. Aye, I had no worries on that score.'

Jake stared at the little fellow in front of him. He didn't want to believe there was a shred of truth in his story so why did instinct tell him the opposite? And then he realised. The man was the spitting image of his Granda Fletcher. His mam had taken him to see his paternal grandparents once a month until they had died, his grandma when he was eight and his granda a year later. He had hated those visits. His face was hard, his voice equally so, as he denied what his mind was telling him and said again, 'I don't believe you.'

'It's the truth, why would I be lying? Look, I can give you chapter and verse on the Fletcher side of the family.' He reeled off a few facts and figures. 'And after I married your mam, we lived in Hood Street, next to the Murrays. Remember them? Nosy old crow, she was.' He paused, his voice

362

taking on the wheedling note again. 'I know this is a shock, me turning up like this, but you could act a bit more pleased to see me. You like this because of the accident? Your mam filled your head with lies about me, eh? I didn't mean for you to get hurt, lad. I swear it. I didn't mean for no one to get hurt, whatever she's told you about how things were atween her an' me. We were having a row and things got out of hand, that's all.'

Jake's brows came together. Accident? Was this man who was calling himself his father referring to the day he'd pulled an oil lamp on himself?

'Look, when I threw that lamp, it was out of temper. I didn't know you'd put yourself in the way of it. You was just a little nipper, you moved too fast. It was one of them spur-of-the-moment happenings no one could have prevented, whatever your mam's told you.'

A terrible realisation dawned. Jake felt sick with it. His ears ringing, he said, 'You did this to me?' as he touched the side of his face.

There was a long moment of silence broken only by the dog's low growling. His voice less confident, Silas muttered, 'I told you, it was an accident. What did she tell you anyway?'

Jake did not answer this. What he did say was, 'You did this to your son and then you left the same night?'

'I had to, I told you. Besides, I didn't think you'd make it, I didn't think you'd pull through. I'm glad you did, lad, but I couldn't stay around, it was more than me life was worth.'

All his mother had ever told him about his father was a lie. This shifty little individual in front of him was living proof of it. Jake wanted to sit down, his legs felt shaky, but a sixth sense told him to reveal no shred of weakness to the sharp eyes fixed on his face. *His father was alive.* The repercussions of this return from the dead were beginning to dawn, not least for his mother. She couldn't have known he was still alive, she wouldn't have married again knowing. 'My mother...' He had to clear his throat before he could go on, 'She thinks...'

'I was that bloke they pulled out of the water,' Silas finished for him. 'Aye, I know. And the way I see it, there's no reason to upset the apple cart, not with her having wed again and having bairns by this Wood bloke. That'd make them bastards, an' her – well, like I said, I don't want to upset the apple cart. Rose always placed great store by her good name. He's a miner, I understand. Not working though. Must be tight for 'em with just one lad down the pit and another here working for you. You help your mam out a bit, I dare bet.'

Jake said nothing. He just waited. He had no idea what had brought his father back to the north after thirty years but whatever it was, it wasn't to play happy families.

After a few moments, when it became clear Jake wasn't going to respond, Silas rubbed his thumb under his nose, bending forward slightly as he said, 'I don't see meself staying round these parts for long, lad, in case you were wondering, but I had to leave where I was in something of a hurry, you know? Upset a few people. The thing is, it's left me a bit short. I was wondering if you could spare a pound or two to tide me over, me being family an' all and you having this great big farm.'

So that was it. Jake stared into the bullet-hard eyes. A pound or two, his backside. It wouldn't stop at a pound or two.

'Like I said, I don't want to throw a spanner in the works by making meself known to your mam and her other family, but at the same time a man has to live. You understand?'

He understood all right. His father would remain out of the picture if he paid for his silence. He could scarcely believe this was happening. 'How much would it take for you to clear off back to where you came from?'

Silas blinked. 'That's not very nice, is it?' he said mildly. 'Me just having come back an' all. I want to get to know me son a bit, that's natural. Anyway, like I said, there's reasons I can't go back down south for a time. But I give you me word I'll lay low, all right? How about we have a little chat every week about this time out here, eh? That suit?'

Jake had delved into his pocket as Silas had been speaking. Holding out the contents, he said, 'There's thirty bob there.'

'Lad, lad...' Silas sighed, shaking his head, his whole attitude one of sorrowful disappointment. 'It wouldn't be worth the walk from town every week for that. I'll take this for now but come next time we'll be looking at a fiver, all right? No, make it ten. I know you wouldn't want to think your da is going without.'

'I don't have that sort of money to give you each week. The farm holds its own but that's all. My money is tied up in the stock, I'm not rolling in it, whatever you've been told.'

'Look, son–'

'Don't call me that.'

Jake's voice brought Flossie rearing up, her mouth stretched in a snarl. Silas shrank back against the wall of the barn. 'All right, all right, keep your hair on. But ten's me price. It's not going to be forever. Come a few weeks an' I'll be gone.'

Jake ran a hand over his face. In spite of the bitingly cold air, he was sweating. He'd like to knock this little weasel into next weekend and tell him to go to hell, father or not, but how could he? If Silas followed through on his threat and went to see his mam, it would destroy her, it was as simple as that. She'd never be able to hold her head up again. All her scrimping and saving, all she'd put up with through the years would be for nothing. The fact was, his mam was legally married to this man. Dear gussy... 'I don't want you coming onto the farm again, someone'll see you. I'll meet you out on the road next Sunday once it's dark.'

'Anything you say, lad. Anything you say.'

'And if the faintest whisper of this gets out I'll kill you and take the consequences, do you hear me? Like you said, I'm a Fletcher and I know how to look after myself.'

'I know how to keep me mouth shut, don't you fear. And there's no need to take on, I don't want your mam upset any more than you do. Don't forget she's me wife, Jake.'

For two pins he'd beat the living daylights out of him. It took every bit of the self-control he'd gained during the last thirty-three years but he was able to say quite coolly, 'I don't see it that way and I doubt it the law would. You left Sunderland of your own free will and you didn't let my mother know you were alive from the day you left. In fact, you let her believe the opposite. She's not your wife any more than I'm your son.'

'Aye, well, I can see you're a mite put out so I won't argue the point except to say how was I to know they'd pronounced me dead until I come back to these parts? And the last time I heard, a man an' his wife remain wed until they're legally divorced or widowed. Still, we won't put it to the test, eh? We'll keep it nice and friendly like. Best all round. I'll be going then and I'll see you at the weekend, Sunday evening like you said. Oh, an' happy Christmas.'

Jake's body language must have said plenty because Flossie rose to her feet snarling loudly, poised to attack. Jake restrained the dog by touching her head and saying, 'Wait, lass.' To his father, he said, 'I suggest you make yourself scarce before her natural instinct to kill vermin takes over.'

'No need to be like that, lad. I come here in a spirit of reconciliation, it being Christmas an' all, and it would pay you to keep a civil tongue in your head. I don't want no trouble and what's a few pounds to keep everyone happy? I believe in looking after your own, I was brought up that way and that's all I'm asking for. Anyway, I'll be off now but afore I go, I'll just mention I'm not by meself up here. There's a pal of mine who knows where I am and what I'm about and he'd blow the whistle if I went missing. Just so's you're in the picture.'

Long after the small figure had slipped away, Jake stood with his hand on the dog's head in the darkness. The sky had begun to cloud over and the moon had been swallowed up. It was going to snow again, he could smell it, he thought dazedly.

He had done the only thing he could in the circumstances. The alternative was to plunge his mam into a living hell. He nodded to the thought but it was scant comfort. What he would have really liked was to have got chapter and verse from his father as to what had gone on before he left Sunderland and in the intervening years. His father had been fighting with his mam the night he'd gone missing; it was his father who was responsible for the scars he had sustained. Furthermore, this man was not the hard-working husband and father his mother had painted but a character who looked to be capable of anything. Including blackmail. And the irony was, his father had walked out on him and his mam, let them believe he was dead all these years because of some trouble he'd been in, and now he was being forced to pay for the privilege of Silas Fletcher keeping his mouth shut. It would be laughable if it wasn't so serious.

Jake was chilled to the bone by the time he walked back into the house. Hannah was in the kitchen, a pot of tea and a plate of turkey sandwiches on the table. She was slicing a ham and egg pie and she glanced up as he entered, her eyes bright as she said, 'I was just about to come and look for you. What on earth have you been doing?'

He looked at her. She was nineteen years old

and as bonny as a summer's day, but it was her manner and the natural warmth that radiated from her that drew people. He'd seen it time and time again. And she thought his father had been a decent, upright man, like she imagined he was. But he didn't feel decent, not having talked to that man out there who had sired him. He felt dirty, humiliated, less than nothing. 'Like father, like son.' How often had he heard that phrase bandied about? He'd even used it himself when he'd thought about Wilbur and Adam. And now he had seen the stock he'd come from and he felt ashamed. He couldn't ever let her know.

He made himself smile when he said, 'What have I been doing? Having a party out there, what else?'

'Oh you.' She nodded to the table. 'Come and sit down an' have a bite.'

He sat down. He didn't want to eat, all appetite was gone and the bile of bitterness was tart on his tongue. This put the tin lid on any hope he'd had of making Hannah love him, not that it had been anything other than a foolish dream.

But no more dreaming. The stillness of hopelessness settled on him. He was done with all that. No longer would he allow his mind to clutch at fleeting imaginings. He knew what the future held for him now. And come the spring he would make it clear she should go, leave the farm. He'd do it gently but make sure she saw it as being done without sentiment on his part. Her kind heart would baulk at leaving if she thought he wanted her to stay. He had to face the fact that a large part of her affection for him had pity as its foundation, he'd known it all along really. But she had her whole life in front of her and she couldn't waste it forever being housekeeper to such as him. If she didn't want Daniel, there would be someone else for her out there. And he couldn't stand her being around, not now.

'Are you all right, Jake?'

Her voice came to him, soft and concerned, and he glanced up to see her watching him. 'Never better.' He reached out for a sandwich, bit into it and swallowed before he said, 'Just thinking over some plans for the New Year, that's all.'

Chapter 23

'What do you mean, you was up at Jake's place? What the dickens were you doing there?' Wilbur stared at Adam.

'Ssh. Keep your voice down.' The two men were sitting in the bar of the Friendly Tavern in Southwick Road, Adam having invited his father out for a drink half an hour before. Wilbur liked nothing more than a drink on a Sunday evening, not so much for the drink itself but because of the camaraderie that was part of it. On the occasions Wilbur had the price of a gill on him he would make his way to the Colliery Tavern or the Friendly, but he wouldn't do as some did and go in with his pockets empty and his tongue hanging out, waiting for someone to take pity on him. His pride wouldn't let him. Of late he had taken to going round the greengrocers in the market and picking up their orange boxes for a farthing each, chopping them into sticks for firelighters, which he'd tie into bundles with string and sell round the doors in Bishopwearmouth or Hendon at tuppence a go. He always went over the river to sell his wares, he would rather have died than let his neighbours know what he was doing. But tonight his son had asked him out and he was like a dog with two tails.

'Is that where you go sometimes? The farm?' Wilbur's voice was low, and when Adam nodded, he added, 'It's the lass, isn't it? Hannah. You're meeting her on the quiet.'

'What? No, no, nothing like that, I swear it. She doesn't know I even go up there. I ... I just like to see what's going on, that's all. It's easy enough to make sure you're not seen.'

Wilbur's voice held a touch of pity when he said, 'Lad, lad. That's a mug's game. One day you'll be tumbled and what'll you say then?'

Adam shrugged impatiently. 'Look, Da, I've not come to talk about that, just listen, will you?'

'I'm listening, lad. I'm listening.'

'The thing is, for a few weeks now I've noticed an old fella walking that way when I've been on my way back into town. I tried to pass the time of day with him once or twice but he weren't having none of it. He wouldn't even look at me. Kept his head down.'

'It's a free country, lad.' Wilbur took a sip of his pint, smacking his lips.

His benign expression vanished when Adam leant closer, saying, 'That's as maybe, but it's a bit funny when the dead walk, don't you think?'

'What you on about, the dead walking?'

Adam leant back in his chair, enjoying the moment. Then he said, 'Well, what else do you call it when some bloke who's supposed to have been six feet under for the last thirty-odd years turns up alive and well?'

Wilbur stared at his son. 'You feeling all right, lad?'

'Never better. Don't you want to know who he is?'

'Go on then.'

'Silas Fletcher.'

The effect on his father was all Adam could have hoped for. Wilbur had just raised his glass to his lips and now he coughed and spluttered, swearing as beer spilt down his shirt. Wiping his mouth with the back of his hand, he said, 'What the hell makes you think it's Silas Fletcher?'

'I don't think, I know. He looked a nasty bit of work and so today I thought I'd hang about out of sight and just see where he made for. I'd nowt else to do.'

Wilbur looked at his son. Adam and Lily had had a barney to end barnies before Adam had disappeared for the afternoon. He didn't know what was going to happen there. He could see Adam doing for her one of these days, the mouth she'd got on her.

'So I waited till it was twilight and, sure enough, along he comes. But he don't pass the farm. Oh no. He stops and hangs about a little way off, furtive like. And then along comes the lord and master of all he surveys.' This was Adam's new title for his half-brother. 'I could tell straightaway they'd arranged to meet. Anyway, I was in the hedgerow and I edged a bit nearer, keeping me head down. Something changed hands. I couldn't see what. But then I realised it must have been money 'cos Jake says, "I can't keep giving you ten, you must see that. All my money is tied up on the farm in bricks and mortar and the animals." Then the old 'un half laughs, sneering, and tells him he'll have to sell off a few beef steaks unless he wants to watch a touching reunion between his parents.'

Adam paused for breath. Wilbur was sitting as though poleaxed. 'I still couldn't work out what was what at that stage, but then Jake says, "You go anywhere near my mother and I'll kill you, I promise you that," all tough like. And the old 'un says something along the lines that whether he likes it or not he's still his da and still Rose's lawfully wedded husband. Then Jake tells him to sling his hook and the old 'un laughs again, saying he'll be back next week. Same time, same place. And he'd better have what he wants and not a penny short. So,' Adam leant back in his chair again, 'what do you make of that?'

The expression on Wilbur's face was answer enough.

'He's blackmailing him,' Adam went on as though his father hadn't realised. 'Heaven knows where he's been all this time but whoever that poor blighter is in the cemetery with Silas Fletcher on his headstone, it ain't Silas. And that means you're not a married man and the lot of us are bastards.'

'*Don't say that.*'

'Keep your voice down, Da, for crying out loud.'

'I won't have you saying that, you hear me?'

'Aye, aye, all right. I'm sorry, Da. Sit down, man. People are looking. I'm sorry.'

Once Wilbur had sunk back down on his chair, his face red, Adam said quietly, 'I was only saying what folks'll say if this gets out, that's all. Do you think Mam knows it wasn't him they pulled out of the dock?'

'Course she don't know, don't talk such codswallop. Why do you think Jake's paying him off? Your mam's a good woman, a decent woman.'

'All *right*, Da.' Adam glanced round.

'This can't get out.' Wilbur was becoming more agitated by the moment. 'I'll never be able to hold me head up again. Think how some of them jumped-up toadies at the pit would laugh if they found out.' He swore again, softly but vehemently, drops of frothy saliva gathering at the corners of his mouth. 'I can just see a couple of them deputies, Longhurst and Ferry, they'd love this. And the neighbours...' He shook his head desperately. 'This can't get out.'

'Don't take on like this, man. Look, drink your beer and I'll get another pint in while we decide what we're going to do.'

'How serious was Jake about not paying him what he wanted?'

'I don't know. How the hell would I know that? I've told you what I heard.'

'It's no skin off his nose if word gets out,' said Wilbur bitterly. 'He don't live round about no more, he's got the farm and he won't be labelled a–' He couldn't bring himself to voice it. 'Not like the rest of you. I won't have our name dragged through the mire, Adam. I don't care what it takes but I won't have that.'

'Aye, we're agreed on that, Da.'

'I might not have much but I have got me reputation. I'm not like some I could name who have never done an honest day's work in their lives. Hard graft all me life, I've done, and I won't have me self-respect taken away by any man, least of all Silas Fletcher. Your mam let drop the odd thing about him when we was first wed and he was a wrong 'un, all right. All the Fletchers are the same, scum of the earth.'

'He's a skinny little nowt of a man now.'

'That's as maybe, but if he opens his gob too wide we're done for.'

'Then we'll have to make sure he doesn't.'

Wilbur nodded. The angry colour had drained from his face and it was pasty with shock. 'You don't know where he lives, do you?' he asked hopefully.

'No. By the time I'd come out of hiding, he'd scarpered. Jake stood looking after him for I don't know how long and I couldn't risk being seen so I had to wait. Anyway, that's not important. We know where he will be next Sunday, don't we?'

'What it he don't turn up?'

'He'll turn up.'

'There's no reasoning with a man like that, lad. He won't be content until he's bled Jake dry.'

'He could do that and welcome if it wasn't for the danger he is to us. Anyway, I wasn't planning on reasoning with him. What I've got in mind is a sight more physical. You game, Da?'

Wilbur nodded. 'To my mind he deserves everything he's got coming.'

'And more. We're agreed then. Next Sunday you an' I will disappear for a while. We can tell Mam there's a meeting about getting some of the old-timers reinstated at the pit, something like that. There's so many meetings these days about something or other she won't think twice.'

'What about Naomi? She's been to the farm the last two weeks since her an' Stuart packed up.'

'Don't worry about Naomi. I haven't bumped into her yet and I don't intend to start now. She always leaves long before twilight and that's when Fletcher comes. I make sure I watch her go and only come out when it's clear. Sometimes I've been at the end of the North Hylton Road when I've seen Fletcher.'

Wilbur stared at his son. How long had he been spying on the folk at the farm? Months probably. And all the time hoping to catch Hannah with this Daniel bloke. And what good would it do if he did see them together? The lass could take up with whoever she wanted, after all. Rose was right, it was an obsession with Adam; the lass, Jake having the farm, Joe's death and now Stephen working for their half-brother. And if he went to the farm on a Sunday afternoon, where did he go most evenings? Not to the farm, it would take too long to walk there and back. But he was seldom at home these days, that was for sure. Mind, if it wasn't for his fixation on the lass, they wouldn't have caught wind of this other business. Keeping his thoughts to himself, he said, 'How about we let Naomi leave home after we've had our Sunday dinner and give her plenty of time to get to the farm before we start. Then we'll make sure we're in position hidden out of the way when she starts for home again. What if we lose Fletcher like you did today though? What if Jake hangs about again? What if–'

'Enough, Da.' Adam silenced his father with an upraised hand. 'Let's just see how it goes, eh? Play it by ear. All right?'

'Aye, all right, lad.' Wilbur nodded and drained his glass. 'Now, what did you say about another pint? If ever I needed a drink, it's tonight.'

Chapter 24

'What's bothering you these days, lad? And don't say nowt because you haven't been yourself for a while. It's not just me who's noticed it either. Hannah was saying the other day she's worried about you.' Rose stared anxiously at her son over the kitchen table where the two of them were sitting drinking a cup of tea. 'You can tell me, Jake. You know that.'

His mother was the last person he could tell. Staring at her, Jake tried to control the growing resentment and bitterness he felt these days towards the woman who had borne him. He didn't understand how someone like his mam, a good, decent person, could have got mixed up with the type of man he now knew his father to

377

be. She'd lied to him. About everything.

'What was my father really like?' he asked suddenly. They were alone in the house for the first time since Christmas. Lily and Sadie were at her mother's and Wilbur had gone to visit an old friend who recently had had a stroke and was residing in the Sunderland infirmary. The children were due home from school soon and Jake knew if he didn't ask now, the chance would vanish.

'What?' Rose's tea slopped into her saucer.

'My father. I heard someone talking the other day.'

'Someone? Who? What did you hear?'

'That he was something of a wrong 'un. Look, Mam,' Jake leant forward, his eyes angry, 'I'm not a bairn and I've got a right to know what he was like. I know what you've said in the past but I want the truth, all right? Whatever you say won't go beyond these four walls but I want to know.'

Rose's hand had gone to her throat, her fingers plucking at the loose skin. 'It was such a long time ago.'

'Not to me. He wasn't like you made out, was he?'

'Oh, Jake. Don't ... don't keep on.'

'I want to know,' Jake said mulishly.

'Are you sure about that?' Rose bit on her lip. 'Least said, soonest mended. That's what they say.'

'Then they're wrong. I want to hear it, Mam. All of it. I don't want you to keep anything back.'

The kitchen clock on the mantelpiece ticked a full minute away before Rose said, 'No, lad, he wasn't like I made out. He... Your da was a bad man, cruel, violent. You take after my da, not the Fletchers.'

'I want to hear it all. How it was, how he was with you, me, everything. What he was mixed up in, why he ended up floating in the dock. Were there people who were after him for something? Was he in trouble?'

'I don't know that. Truly, lad, I don't. It's possible, more than possible. He gambled, he was in with a bad lot...' Rose gazed helplessly at her son. 'Aye, it's possible.'

'Start at the beginning and don't leave anything out, right up to the night he disappeared and I got burnt. Why did you marry him in the first place? Surely you didn't love him?'

Again the moments ticked by. Rose turned her gaze towards the fire and began talking.

It was twenty minutes before she fell silent and she had told him it all. She had hesitated when she'd reached the part in the story about the last fight and all it entailed, but only for a second or two. She hadn't looked at him once as she had spoken but she had felt his eyes tight on her face the whole time. Now she did meet his gaze. 'I told you what I did because I thought it was for the best,' she said brokenly. 'You had enough to put up with, I didn't want you to grow up thinking your da had done that to you. It was me he was aiming at though, Jake. Bad as he was, he wouldn't have hurt you like that intentionally.'

'But he made your life hell.' He stood up, more shaken than he could express by what he had heard. He put his arms about her, drawing her up from her seat and holding her tightly as she

379

began to cry. Her tears loosened something in him, something that had begun to form a cold hard knot around his heart and as it melted, the old feeling for his mother was restored but with it an understanding that humbled him. All that, she'd endured all that and now that bit of scum was back. What he wouldn't give to shut his lying mouth once and for all. But enough was enough. He'd give his father no more blood money after this last time. It had been eight weeks now and all the money he'd put by for the spring to replace some of the old machinery on the farm had gone. He'd be selling off cattle after this. He'd give him one last payment and make it clear he didn't want to see him again or he'd go to the law. After what his mother had just told him, the little weasel wouldn't want to rock the boat whatever he threatened to the contrary.

'I'm glad you told me.' Handing his mother a handkerchief from his pocket, he smiled at her as she dabbed at her eyes. 'In a funny sort of way it makes this,' he touched the damaged side of his face, 'easier knowing I didn't have a hand in it.'

'Your Granda and Grandma Hedley hated him.' Rose sniffed and blew her nose. 'And there's nothing of him in you, Jake. I've always been glad of that.'

'Did you ever resent me being born? If it wasn't for me you wouldn't have had to marry him.'

'Resent you?' Rose's voice was soft. 'Lad, whenever I've counted my blessings, I've counted you twice.'

The following Sunday was one of those rare days

sometimes found at the end of February. The sky was high and blue, the air crisp and still and the cold winter sunshine a reminder that spring was round the corner. The snow was still thick in places and the ground was frozen, but the birds were twittering madly and sitting preening themselves when Hannah went to fill up the bird table with scraps from the kitchen. Normally a day such as this would lift her spirit, whatever was going on in her life, but since Christmas a greyness had slowly settled on her that no amount of reasoning could shift.

Jake was different. She hadn't been able to put her finger on what was wrong at first, but then twice over the last week or two he'd made some reference to her future and hinted that he didn't see her staying at the farm forever.

She gazed at a couple of sparrows who were making short work of the last of the fruit cake she'd crumbled up for them, but her mind wasn't on the birds. What had changed so suddenly? What had she done? It was the same thought she had had umpteen times since the New Year, and the only thing she could come up with was the peck on the cheek she had given him at Christmas when she'd thanked him for his present. He had seemed a bit strange then, uneasy, wooden even. She had covered her embarrassment at the way he had made her feel by gabbling away about something or other and the difficult moment had passed, but now she wondered if he thought she had been saying more than thank you. Encouraging him. Chasing after him like Farmer Dobson's daughter and Grace Osborne, not that it had done either lady any good.

Had she given herself away? Had he guessed how she felt about him? She thought she had been the same as usual but maybe that brief kiss had set him thinking and this undefinable change in him was the result. It wasn't that he was unfriendly or stand-offish, not exactly, and yet...

She turned and walked slowly back to the house on leaden feet. She couldn't daydream, she had the dinner to see to before she got ready for church. But she couldn't hide from the truth any longer. She had to face the fact that things weren't right. She knew it wasn't her work that was at fault. She rose every morning before six and rarely was in bed before ten o'clock and there wasn't a minute of the day her hands were idle. And if the problem didn't lie with her duties, it had to be her. Her stomach turned over. Jake wanted her to go. He would never come right out and say it, he was too kind for that but she knew it deep inside. She'd just been trying to ignore it. Had he met someone? Someone who might object to him having a young housekeeper? But no, she would know, wouldn't she? He wouldn't keep a thing like that secret. Although... She paused at the kitchen door, her hand on the knob. He made the trip into town each week. He said it was on farm business and she was sure it was, but that didn't mean he didn't have time for other things. He visited his mother, for a start. And then there were the times, more often of late, when he was out riding in the countryside for hours on end...

She shook herself mentally. No more thinking, not now. She only had a few minutes to put the joint in the oven and get dressed to accompany the others to church, and then after lunch Naomi was coming to the farm and she knew her friend wanted a shoulder to cry on. After months of messing Naomi about, Stuart Fraser had finally found himself another lass and broken her friend's heart. The last three Sunday afternoons had been spent sitting in the kitchen listening to Naomi talk and talk, and then mopping up her friend's tears. She didn't expect this one to be any different.

When she had changed into her Sunday clothes, Hannah joined those of the farm folk waiting to be driven to church in one of the farm wagons. Jake was not among them, it was Daniel who was driving the horse and cart. On the occasions Jake attended the Methodist chapel in Castletown, she rode in the horse and trap with him, otherwise she went with the others. She knew from Rose that Father Gilbert blamed Jake for her 'turning', as he'd termed it, but in fact it had been Clara who had first persuaded her to go to the church one Sunday a few months after she had arrived at the farm. It had been a momentous step but after several long talks with the very nice parson, she'd realised she wouldn't burn in hell's flames for attending a non-Catholic church. Furthermore, she much preferred it and she had never gone back to Father Gilbert's church since. Rose had told her all her old neighbours were shocked and no doubt held Jake responsible for her lapse too. When she'd told Jake this he had just laughed and said one more black mark against the 'upstart' was neither here nor there. She had tried to laugh with him but the narrow-mindedness of folk who had known him since a bairn had upset her.

As they came out of church and folk began to gather in small groups to talk to friends they didn't see from one Sunday to the next, Clara drew Hannah to one side. Glancing about her to make sure no one was within earshot, Clara said softly, 'You know anythin' about this man that hangs about on the road of a Sunday evening?'

'Man? What man?'

'Some little fella, accordin' to Frank. He saw him there one night when he was coming back from our George's place. He didn't think nowt of it at first but somethin' in the way this fella was standing about made him check up a while later and he saw the master talking to him. 'They didn't see him, Frank made sure of that, but he got the impression the master weren't none too pleased. Frank being Frank,' Clara wrinkled her nose, 'he made it his business to see if he was there the next few nights and sure enough the next Sunday, there he was. And there was the master a while later. Now you might say it's none of our business' – Clara's tone made it clear she knew Hannah wouldn't dare suggest such a thing – 'but something's not right. And he's turned up every Sunday since.'

Hannah stared into the small, rosy-cheeked face. 'And has Jake met him each time?'

'Oh aye, the master's been there.' Clara had given Jake his title from the day the will had been read.

'I don't know anything about it, Clara. What does this man look like?'

Clara shrugged. 'Don't rightly know except my

Frank says he seems a shifty customer, the sort who'd sell his own grandmother for the right price. Not the sort of man the master'd usually have any truck with, that's for sure.'

Hannah was so taken aback she didn't know what to think. 'Has Frank asked Jake about it?'

Clara looked askance at her. 'Frank can't let on he knows owt. The master obviously wants it kept quiet. That's why I wondered if you knew anything.'

Hannah shook her head. 'And he's a dodgy customer, this man?'

'Let's just say, according to Frank you wouldn't turn your back on him in a hurry.'

'Well, I'm sorry, Clara. I know as little as you do.'

'Ah well, it was worth a try.' Clara bent closer as she whispered, 'Don't let on to Frank I've said owt, he said to keep it atween the two of us but I thought you ought to know.'

It was more likely that Clara's curiosity had become overwhelming. 'I won't say a word.'

'Aye, I know that, hinny. But still,' Clara tilted her head in the birdlike way she had, 'it's a mite funny, ain't it?'

It *was* a mite funny. All the way home and then during lunch, Hannah could think of little else. If her thoughts made her preoccupied, Jake didn't appear to notice, but then he rarely sat at the table any longer than it took to eat his meal these days and the evenings when the two of them had sat in front of the sitting-room fire were a thing of the past. Now, if Jake didn't have work to do in his study he rode his horse rather than sit with her.

385

This day was no exception. After complimenting her on an excellent lunch he disappeared outside.

Hannah had just finished the dishes when Naomi arrived, her broken heart temporarily put to one side by the drama of the news she had to impart. 'Lily's gone back to her mam's and it's for good this time. There's been ructions, I tell you. We've had Father Gilbert round and all sorts. He told Adam to go and bring her back by force if necessary and Adam said he'd rather cut his own throat. Lily's da come round ours and you could hear him and Adam all down the street. Mam was mortified. Lily's accused Adam of carrying on with some lass who lives down by the north dock and she says this lass isn't the first by a long chalk, but because she's a,' Naomi bent close and mouthed, 'you know, a prostitute, Lily says it was the final straw.' She stopped for breath.

'Is it true? Did he go with this woman?' Hannah asked aghast.

Naomi shrugged. 'He says no. He said where would he get the money, but Lily seems dead sure. And I suppose even them women fall in love and do it for free. Adam is very good looking.'

'Good grief.' Hannah sank back in her seat with such a comical expression of sheer amazement that Naomi grinned at her. 'You seem very knowledgable about such things.'

'Comes from working at the jam factory. The things some of them talk about would make your hair curl. I wouldn't dare let on to Mam about half of it. Anyway,' Naomi's face belatedly took on a primness, 'I don't repeat it to anyone. I just listen.'

Naomi was her best friend and yet this was a

new side to her. It was disconcerting. But then life was disconcerting, all the more so of late. Half the time she didn't know which end was up.

Her face must have revealed what she was thinking because now Naomi giggled, flicking back her hair which she'd recently had cut in a short modern bob. It suited her, Hannah thought as she smiled back. It brought an attractive piquancy to Naomi's face which hadn't been obvious before. Stuart Fraser had been mad to treat Naomi the way he had, he'd never get anyone as nice as her again. Her friend was worth ten of him.

Naomi must have begun to think in the same way because now she said, 'So, that's how things are at home. And I'm not going to mention Stuart this afternoon. Mam says I've wasted too much time on him as it is and she's right. How about we go for a walk, lass? Blow the cobwebs away. I did extra time at the factory this week and I don't feel I've seen the light. It's been dark when I left for work and dark when I come home.'

'Suits me.' Hannah was relieved Naomi was more like her old self. Her friend had been miserable on and off the whole time she had been seeing Stuart; the break from him had probably enabled her to see Stuart in his true colours.

As they left the farm by way of the bridle path, Hannah saw Jake in the distance talking to Daniel and his brother. He saw them and waved but made no effort to come and speak as would have been natural considering he hadn't seen his sister for a week.

Blow him then. Pride and hurt tightened Hannah's mouth. She didn't want him any more than he wanted her. And he needn't drop any more of his hints for her to leave. Come the spring she'd apply for other jobs. She had three years under her belt here and plenty of good experience, she'd get something. And then she'd be off. Ignoring the whimper deep inside that this thought brought, she linked her arm through Naomi's and said something silly to make her friend laugh. And she made sure she laughed too, long and loud enough for it to reach the three men. She saw Daniel and John look their way again but Jake didn't turn his head, and this more than anything else caused her to talk and laugh and keep Naomi entertained and her friend's mind off Stuart for the rest of the afternoon.

It was such a beautiful day, they walked as far as Washington, picking their way carefully at times because the snow lay deceptively deep in places and before you knew where you were, it could be up over your boots. By the time they were on the bridle path again and in sight of the farm, the sun was a flaming ball in the sky and night was drawing in. 'You can't walk home in the dark by yourself, perhaps Jake will take you back in the horse and trap.' Hannah put her hand on her friend's arm as they came to the fork in the track which led to the farmhouse in one direction and the labourers' cottages and then the main road in the other.

'Don't be daft, lass. I'll be all right.'

'Naomi, it's nearly dark.'

'It's not dark yet and anyway it's a full moon tonight. I'll be fine.'

Hannah opened her mouth to remonstrate

further but a voice to their left brought both girls' heads turning. 'Hello there.' Daniel approached them, smiling. 'You're usually gone long before this, aren't you?' he added to Naomi.

'We walked further than we intended.' It was Hannah who answered, Naomi appeared to have lost her tongue. Her friend had mentioned in the past that she thought Daniel was attractive, perhaps that had something to do with it.

'Are you going home now?' Again Daniel spoke to Naomi.

She nodded.

'Then perhaps you'll let me make sure you get there safely?'

Naomi had taken on the stance of a rabbit before a fox. 'I... You don't need to do that,' she stammered at last.

'Is that a no?'

He likes her. Hannah stared at Daniel before her gaze moved to Naomi who was blushing profusely. And she likes him. Why hadn't she seen it before? She knew Daniel had long ago accepted that the two of them could be nothing other than friends, and with that acceptance had come an ease between them. This enabled her to say now, 'That would be so kind of you, Daniel. I was just saying to Naomi she shouldn't walk home alone.'

'Absolutely not.' He smiled at Naomi, and Hannah all but saw her friend's knees go weak.

'It's such a long way,' said Naomi helplessly.

'Not at all.' Daniel paused. 'Unless you'd rather go alone?' he added uncertainly.

'Oh no.' Naomi's blush deepened at her forwardness but she had the courage to say, 'No, I didn't mean that.'

'Good.' Again Daniel paused. 'I would have asked before this but I understood from Stephen...' His voice trailed away. He clearly didn't know how to go on.

When Hannah couldn't stand it a moment more, she said, 'Naomi is perfectly at liberty to walk home with you, Daniel. Things have changed recently.'

'So Stephen said today.' Looking straight into Naomi's eyes, he added, 'I didn't know until then.'

Naomi smiled. It was a very sweet smile.

'Goodbye then.' Hannah hugged her friend, trying not to grin like a Cheshire cat. Naomi and Daniel. But why not? They'd be perfect together.

She stood at the branch of the track until they disappeared from view, raising her hand as Naomi turned and waved at the last moment. The sky was putting on a dazzling display of colour, rivers of red and gold and indigo merging to create a spectacle that took her breath away. Somewhere in the shadows a late blackbird sang, the notes pure and melodic as they quivered in the crisp cold air. Suddenly she wanted to cry. She wanted to lay her head against the trunk of the old oak tree in front of her and cry and cry and cry. Compressing her lips, she breathed in deeply. She had nothing to cry about. Jake had taken her in when she had nowhere else to go and he had never said it would be forever. She had to remember that.

Pulling her hat further down on her head, she turned and made her way to the farmhouse.

Chapter 25

'I thought you said Naomi always left before twilight?' Wilbur adjusted his position in the hedgerow, easing his cramped legs. 'If she leaves it much later it'll be dark before she gets into town.'

'She's never been this late before,' Adam muttered. 'That's all I can say. I'm not her keeper, am I?'

The words had barely left his mouth when they heard the murmur of voices and the next moment Naomi and Daniel stepped out onto the road from the lane which led to the farm. Both men crouched down further although there was no chance of them being spotted in their hidey-hole. They watched as the young people walked towards them and then passed the spot where they were concealed, and a few yards on Daniel said something which caused Naomi to giggle, her laugh floating back to them on the cold evening air.

'Who the dickens is that with Naomi?' Wilbur peered after his daughter, narrowing his eyes as the shadows swallowed the two up. 'Seemed very attentive, didn't he?'

'It's Daniel Osborne.'

'Daniel Osborne, Jake's manager? Isn't he the one who's supposed to have his eye on Hannah, according to you?'

'He did have his eye on her.'

'Well, it don't look like it's on her any longer.'

Adam remained silent. There was little he could say.

'Strikes me Naomi's over Stuart Fraser,' Wilbur observed after a moment or two, 'the way them two were looking at each other. Is he well set up, this Daniel?'

'How would I know?'

Sensing this was a conversation his son did not want to pursue, Wilbur settled himself down again in the small hollow they had excavated amongst the old brambles, twigs and hedgerow debris, the leafless branches of the trees forming a dense canopy overhead.

It was only another ten minutes or so before Adam nudged his father. The light was nearly gone now. 'He's coming.'

Wilbur could just make out the figure of a small thin man coming along the road. He was slightly bent over and appeared shrunken, he didn't look to be a threat to anyone. Glancing at his son, he said, 'That's him? Silas Fletcher?'

Guessing what his father was thinking, Adam murmured, 'Don't let outward appearances fool you. I told you, he's dangerous and he's a nasty bit of work.'

They watched as Silas paused on the road just a couple of yards beyond where they were hiding. A minute or two later the tall, broad figure of Jake emerged into the moonlit evening.

'All right, son?' Silas said perkily.

'I told you, don't call me that.' Jake ground the words out as he approached his father.

'You don't want to be so touchy.' There was a

different note to Silas's voice. 'You've got far more to lose than me, or leastways your mam has. How is she anyway, me wife?'

Wilbur's involuntary movement brought Adam's hand hard on his father's arm in warning.

'She's not your wife any more than I'm your son. You relinquished the right to call her that when you took off thirty years ago and let her believe you were dead. And I tell you something else, this lot is the last you're having. I want you gone, back to the stone you crawled out from under down south.'

'I'll go when I'm good an' ready, lad, an' not a day before.' Silas pocketed the bundle of notes Jake held out. 'And if we're name-calling, I'm sure the good folk round your mam's way could come up with a few when they find out she's been living in sin for donkey's years with a brood of bastards to prove it.'

'You make yourself known to her and I'll swing for you.'

'Is that so? Then it seems sensible to me for our little arrangement to go on for a bit longer. Everyone's happy then.'

'Not another penny.' Jake was speaking slowly, quietly, but the menace carried to the two men hidden in the hedgerow. 'She's told me the sort of life you led her. You're not fit to draw breath. So don't push me. You've had a good innings and I've no doubt you will do all right down south but the gravy boat's dried up here. And I'm warning you, you say a word to anyone, *anyone*, and I'll hunt you down and shut your mouth for good.'

'Huh. You're all wind and water, you, like your

Granda Hedley.' Nevertheless, Silas had taken a step backwards away from the towering figure of his son.

'Try me,' said Jake grimly. 'Now get going and keep going.'

There was a long moment when it looked as though Silas was going to say something more but then he turned, putting a few yards between himself and his son, before he said over his shoulder, 'You'll regret this.'

'Not as much as you will if you say one word out of turn.' Jake, too, turned on his heel and disappeared into the lane leading to the farm without a backward glance.

Adam waited a few moments before nudging his father. 'Come on, we don't want to lose him.' He reached forward and picked up a heavy chunk of wood which was a couple of feet long, the remains of a substantial branch of the tree they were beneath.

The frosty twigs and dead grasses crackled under their feet as they emerged onto the road but Silas was far enough away not to hear. Walking rapidly, Adam and Wilbur closed the distance between themselves and the man in front of them. They were some twenty yards away before Silas either heard or sensed them and then he turned his head for a moment before continuing to walk on.

'Hey, don't I know you?' Adam's voice was loud but Silas did not turn his head again or acknowledge he had heard him.

Adam sprinted forward, Wilbur a few steps behind, and when he drew level with Silas, he said again, 'I know you, don't I?'

'I doubt it.' Silas turned his bloodshot gaze on them.

'Oh aye, I think I do. Silas Fletcher, isn't it?' Adam glanced at his father for confirmation and when Wilbur nodded, continued, 'Your son schemed and wheedled his way into the farm up yonder. Isn't that right?'

Silas stopped walking. Warily, he said, 'What's your game?'

'I think it ought to be us asking you that. Let me introduce us. I'm Adam Wood and this,' he thumbed at Wilbur, 'is me da, Wilbur Wood. Name ring a bell?'

Silas said nothing. He waited, peering at them through his rheumy eyes.

'You could do our good name a lot of damage, you know that? But what am I saying? Course you know. That's why you've been bleeding Jake through the eye of a needle, because of my mam. Only now it appears you've got too expensive, right? He's a Fletcher, your son. Sell his own grandmother, or in this case his mother, for a few bob. How much did you manage to get out of him before he decided to tell you to sling your hook and be damned? Only it wasn't you who'd be damned. Just me mam an' da and the rest of the family. How much did he stump up before Jake decided his money was more important than his own mam, eh?'

Silas glanced up and down the deserted road. He licked his thin lips. 'You've got it all wrong.' His gaze flicked over the lump of wood in Adam's hands.

'I don't think so.' Adam smiled. 'But it's good to see you're realising you're dealing, with someone who's got a bit more about him than Jake Fletcher. And you do realise that, don't you? You're scared, aren't you? You're wondering what I'm going to do next.'

'Go easy, lad.' Wilbur's voice was a mutter.

'Go easy? This lump of filth is threatening to drag our name through the mud and you tell me to go easy, Da? It makes me flesh creep to know that Mam was ever wedded to him. Don't it do the same to you?'

'Look, I don't know what Jake's told you but I wouldn't say nowt, I swear it.' Silas gulped in his throat and wet his lips again. 'I swear it.'

'Oh, you won't say nowt. That I can guarantee.' As Adam spoke he swung his body and hit Silas full in the face with the club-shaped piece of wood, knocking off his cap.

Silas gave a hoarse scream as he dropped to his knees, clutching his broken nose which was spouting blood. He crumpled as Adam brought the wood smashing against the side of his head, his mouth frothing red bubbles as he tried to speak.

And then Adam really seemed to go mad. It wasn't Silas Fletcher he was seeing lying curled up on the glistening frosty road but Jake. Jake, who had been a thorn in his side for more years than he could remember. Jake, who had scooped the jackpot while he spent his days grubbing under the earth like an animal for a pittance. Jake, who had killed Joe as surely as if he'd knifed him in the back and who had now taken Stephen too. Jake, who had Hannah waiting on him hand and foot every hour of every day…

'Leave him be, man, that's enough. He's had enough. You'll do for him if you're not careful.'

'I want to do for him.' Adam brushed his father off as though he was swatting a fly before bringing the full weight of the wood whistling down one last time on Silas's hairless scalp.

Silas's body jerked upwards, as though a puppeteer had yanked the strings too hard, and then his legs scrabbled a few times before becoming still and a dark stain flowed out from under his head.

'What have you done?' Wilbur's voice was a whisper in the silence that had fallen. 'By all the saints, lad, what have you done?' He glanced at Adam who was standing motionless, staring down at the figure on the ground. 'What possessed you to go for him like that? We were going to rough him up a bit, you said. Put the fear of God in him so he skedaddled.'

Adam drew in a deep, heaving breath, his hands shaking and the wood hanging limp now. 'He wouldn't have gone. You heard him with Jake. He wouldn't have gone.'

'He's dead.'

'He might not be.'

Wilbur moved closer, making sure he didn't stand in the pool of blood which had spread over the frosty brilliance of the ground like warm honey over bread. He crouched down and put his hand inside Silas's jacket. It was a full thirty seconds before he straightened up and then he continued looking at the body as he said, 'We could go down the line for this.'

'No.' Adam tugged his father away so abruptly Wilbur would have stumbled and fallen but for the younger man quickly steadying him. 'No, we won't. Think, man. No one knows we're here, no one's seen us. And him, look at him. He could be anyone, an old tramp even. There's nothing to trace him to us. There's not a soul'd think he's Silas Fletcher, he's played dead for thirty odd years, hasn't he?'

Wilbur rubbed his hand over his face. 'He's not playing now.'

'He had it coming.'

'Don't talk like that.'

'It's true and you know it. We'd never have known a minute's peace while he was alive. He wouldn't have thought twice about trying to screw us like he's been screwing Jake.' Throwing the piece of wood into the side of the hedgerow, Adam said, 'Empty his pockets.'

'What?'

'You heard me. We can't leave anything on him that might let on who he is.'

'You want his pockets emptied, you do it.'

Adam was about to argue when Wilbur turned away and stumbled a few yards before emptying the contents of his stomach into the ditch at the border of the road. When the bout of nausea had passed and he had wiped his mouth, he turned to see Adam kneeling over Silas, going through the dead man's pockets.

'Look at this.' The moonlight lit up the bunch of notes Adam was counting. 'Jake's been giving him ten pounds a time.'

'That's blood money, it's cursed. Put it back.'

'Oh aye, that'd be bright, wouldn't it? What down-an'-out has this sort of money on him? Think, Da.' Adam stuffed the notes into his trouser pocket along with a tobacco pouch and two or three keys on a rusty ring. When he had searched the body thoroughly, he stood up. As he met his father's eyes, he said, 'Don't look at me like that, Da. I did what I had to do, that's all. And he's scum, you said so yourself.'

'You've killed a man.'

'A man who would have made all our lives a living hell without a moment's hesitation if it suited him. Don't ask me to play the penitent because I won't. I'm no hypocrite, not like him in that farm up there. Now we make our way into town and call in the Friendly for a jar or two, right? We make sure we're seen, not that this could ever be laid at our door. There are a hundred blokes who pass through these days since the slump started, going from town to town looking for work and sleeping rough often as not. But the pub'll be our alibi, just in case.'

'You always meant to do him in.' It was a statement, not a question. 'All this talk of frightening the living daylights out of him with a good hiding was just that, wasn't it? Talk. Well, wasn't it?'

'What do you want me to say?'

'The truth.'

Adam stared at his father. 'He was a Fletcher, Da. The lowest of the low. I don't know if I intended to kill him but the world won't miss him, any more than it would miss that freak he bred. And don't tell me you feel different to me. From a bairn you've told me how Jake threw everything back in your face you tried to do for him. Always thought himself better than us, taking one on the sly, causing trouble and putting the knife in.'

'What about him, Jake? He knows this man was his father. What's he going to say when his body's found?'

'Whatever else he is, Jake's not daft. He'll keep his mouth shut. Why would he pay out good money to make sure Silas remained dead and then say owt? Trust me, all right? Silas'll be buried in an unmarked grave, another homeless vagrant who got done in by persons unknown.'

'It's a mortal sin you've committed the night.' Wilbur's voice trembled.

'Don't come the Hail Marys, not with me. We both know you haven't set foot in a church for years. Besides, God helps those who help themselves. That's all I've done, helped you and Mam and the rest of us. And do you want to know something?' Adam bent forward, the moonlight causing his eyes to glitter. 'I'd do it again if I had to.' He straightened his cap and tucked his muffler into his jacket. 'Come on, we're going to have a jar.'

'You leaving him here in the road? Shouldn't we shove him in a ditch or something? Try and hide him?'

'He'll be found sometime, it makes no odds when.'

Adam walked off, leaving his father dithering. After a few moments Wilbur followed after his son. He walked with his shoulders hunched and his head bent. Suddenly he looked like a very old man.

Chapter 26

The finding of a body on the North Hylton Road caused quite a stir north of the Wear, but nowhere more than on Clover Farm because it was Daniel who discovered it after seeing Naomi home. The police were called and everyone on the farm was interviewed, along with the residents of properties between the outskirts of Southwick and the village south of the farm. No one knew anything. The police who questioned everyone expected as much. Clearly the dead man was a ne'er-do-well of some kind, things of this nature didn't happen to nice folk. Probably of no fixed abode, sleeping rough with others of his kind. Likely there'd been a fight and he'd got his comeuppance. Whoever had done the deed would be long since gone.

Such was the general opinion among the constabulary at the police station in Stoney Lane who were dealing with the event. Things might well have remained thus but for the appearance of a certain Sidney Benson three days later who came forward claiming knowledge of the deceased. The police took notice of Sidney because he was clearly scared out of his wits and worried the person who had despatched Silas might come looking for him. And that person, Sidney said, was the dead man's son. Jake Fletcher. Leonard Craggs was really Silas Fletcher and the same Silas Fletcher had been blackmailing his son for weeks ever since he had returned to the area just before Christmas.

Suddenly what had seemed a relatively un-important murder in the scheme of things, a fight that had got out of hand between vagrants passing through the county most probably, assumed more significance. It aroused not only local interest but reached far beyond the boundaries of the north-east. A man who had been certified dead over thirty years ago returning from the grave, as it were, to find his wife married to someone else with umpteen children by her new husband. And the son, paying the father to keep quiet when he threatened to make himself known and stir up a hornet's nest. As more facts emerged, it appeared the father had been a wrong 'un, mixed up in goodness knows what, but the son was the owner of a fine farm. How had he come by that when he'd been born into mining stock? Something fishy there. One thing was for sure, blood's thicker than water and Jake Fletcher came from bad blood. His own half-brother had told reporters how Jake knocked him about and there were neighbours who bore witness to this. Definitely a violent sort.

Bail had been refused, and when Hannah visited Jake the day before the trial, she was shocked at the change in him. He had insisted on no visitors for the whole of the three weeks he had been held but she had gone to the gaol every day in the hope he would relent and see her. When a kind police-man showed her into the small room where she had to wait, she had sat down with her heart in her mouth, the blood drumming in her ears. She didn't have to wait long. The door opened and there he was, flanked by two burly constables.

'Jake.' She had promised herself she wouldn't cry or in any way make things more difficult for him, but it took all her will not to break down. His clothes hung on him, his face was gaunt and the look in his eyes was that of an animal caught in a trap. 'Thank you for seeing me.'

She had half risen but the kind policeman gently pushed her back down in the chair as Jake seated himself opposite her at the small square table. Without any preliminaries, his voice husky as though it hadn't been used for some time, he said, 'I wanted to ask you to see my mam all right, it's going to be hard for her. She'd be better off at the farm. I've ... made it over to you. I've made a will. It's all legal and above board.'

'Me?' Her eyes widened. And then as the realisation of what he was saying dawned, she said, 'But you'll be coming home soon.'

'Hannah, I didn't kill him.' Jake bent forward, his eyes intent on her face. 'I didn't lay a finger on him, much as I'd have liked to. Do you believe me?'

She hadn't known what to believe up to this point. When the police had arrested Jake he had said not a word. Now, looking into his haggard face, she said firmly, 'Of course I believe you if you say so. But if you didn't do it they'll prove it, Jake. I know they will.'

He shook his head very slightly. 'I'm going to swing for this, Hannah. I can feel it.'

'No.' She leant forward, clasping his hands. 'No, I won't let that happen. But why didn't you tell me? Why didn't you say your father was back and demanding money from you? The papers say he's been in these parts from Christmas. Why didn't you confide in me?'

'I couldn't.' He closed his eyes, opening them a moment later. 'I just couldn't. He was a terrible man, Hannah. I knew he wasn't going to stay around forever and I thought if I paid him enough to keep him quiet no one would be any the wiser. Mam had so much to lose...'

'Oh, Jake.' Her lips were quivering but again she told herself she had to be strong. Now was not the time for recriminations. It hurt he hadn't trusted her but there were more important things at stake.

'But you'll take Mam and the younger ones to the farm? When ... when it's over?'

'But you can't give me the farm. Why not your mother?'

Something flickered in his eyes, the damaged one with the hooded lid almost closing as he narrowed his gaze and turned away. 'My step-father would get his hands on it then and I don't want that. Besides, I want to know ... that you will be looked after too.'

'This is all conjecture anyway because nothing is going to happen to you. You'll be proved innocent, something will come up. They'll find out who really did it. That's what the police do.'

'Hannah, they aren't looking any more. They think they have their man and the evidence is pretty damning. If Clara and Frank think I did it, what hope have I got with people who don't know me?'

'They don't think that, really they don't.'

404

'They've told the police I was meeting my father each Sunday night.'

'They had to do that when it all came out but they don't think you killed him.' Her voice was less convincing than it could have been. Clara and Frank were staunchly for Jake, everyone at the farm was, but she suspected most of them were of the private opinion that he had attacked his father. They didn't blame him for it, she'd heard Isaac Mallard say that even the nicest bloke could be pushed too far, but they did believe he was guilty. *Jake, oh, Jake.* She hadn't slept more than an hour or two each night since the police had come to the farm and taken him away, and she had to force food down her throat. She wouldn't be able to bear it if he was convicted of killing that horrible old man. Her hands still gripping his, she said, 'How are they treating you in here?' He looked awful, worse than awful. He had lost so much weight but it wasn't so much that as the haunted look in his eyes.

Jake made an attempt at a smile. 'Fine. It's the being shut in I can't stand. I've never been able to stand it.'

'Jake, I believe you, I do, but can you think of anyone, anyone at all who would want your father dead besides you?' Realising she hadn't phrased that too well, she added, 'There has to be some-one. I can't believe his murder happened by chance, not on the North Hylton Road on a Sun-day evening.'

'Apart from this crony of his he told me about, no one else knew he was here.' He removed his hands from hers and leant back in his chair, his

405

eyes tight on her face. 'Pretty damning, isn't it?'

'There has to be someone.' She stared back at him, her eyes clear and open. 'You didn't do it so there has to be someone who wanted him dead.'

'Face it, Hannah, I'm scuppered,' he said gently. 'And maybe I'm being punished for what I wished on him. I wanted him dead. From the first night I met him, I wanted him dead but especially after I'd found out the sort of life he'd led my mother before he left Sunderland.'

'You told her he was here?'

Jake shook his head. 'No, of course not. But I asked her about him, made out I'd heard a thing or two. She told me,' he hesitated for a moment, glancing towards the deadpan constable standing by the door of the room, 'he did this.' He touched the side of his face. 'He'd already said as much but I wanted to know everything. I'm not sorry he's dead, Hannah. I can't pretend otherwise. But I didn't kill him.'

'What are we going to do?'

He sat staring at her, his face working, and it was a moment before he could say, 'Thanks for the "we", lass. I thought you'd be—'

'What?'

His head dropped and he murmured, 'Disgusted.'

'Oh, Jake.' She didn't know whether she wanted to shake him or fling her arms round him and kiss him. How could he think that? How *could* he? 'Of course I'm not disgusted,' she said softly.

'Not even knowing what my father was? What I came from? I can imagine what they're saying, Hannah. Like father, like son. Blood outs in the

406

end. I'm right, aren't I?'

She did not answer this because he *was* right. Instead she whispered, 'You came from your mother too, Jake. Don't forget that. And she would be the first to say there's nothing of your father in you. You're all hers and you're a fine, fine man.'

He looked at her then. It was one look, a fleeting second before he lowered his head again but what she read in that unguarded moment stopped her breath. But almost immediately he was on his feet, his voice gruff as he said, 'I don't want you in court tomorrow and that goes for my mother as well. Goodbye, Hannah. Look after everything for me.'

She stood up too, but when she would have moved towards him, the constable behind her put a hand on her shoulder. 'I'm sorry miss. No contact allowed.'

Before she knew what had happened, he had gone.

Outside the building, she stood for some time in the bitterly cold air. February had turned into March in the last few days but the weather showed no signs of improving, the odd snowflake whirling in the north-east wind. She felt unable to move, the screen of her mind replaying the expression on Jake's face before he had stood up.

In spite of the freezing air, her cheeks were burning and she put her hands to them, staring straight ahead as her thoughts spun like the snowflakes. He cared for her. In *that* way. But why had he never said? Why hadn't he let her know? And it wasn't just that he'd never said but he'd actively been pushing her away over the last months, encouraging her to think about leaving the farm. It didn't make sense.

She began walking, not back towards Clover Farm but in the direction of the town. She needed to see Rose. She could make the excuse that Jake had told her he didn't want his mother to come to the court proceedings, not that Rose would take any notice of that. Neither would she. She'd be there. Wild horses wouldn't keep her away.

Why hadn't he *said* something? She racked her brains to see if she had missed something in the past, some gesture, a word, but there was nothing that came to mind. He had always treated her kindly and with respect, but his affection had been that of a brother to a sister. But that look in his eyes hadn't been brotherly. It had been... Again she put her hands to her hot face. It had been everything she could have wished for. Jake, Jake... And he was in prison for something he hadn't done and she couldn't see a way out.

It was beginning to snow more heavily but she stood stock still exactly where she was in the middle of the pavement, her eyes open but her heart reaching out as she prayed, please, please help me. You can't let him die for something he didn't do. All he's suffered in the past and now this. It's so unfair. And I know it was unfair what men did to You so You know how he feels. Show me something. Help me.

'You all right, lass?' An elderly woman dressed all in black paused for a moment, shifting her shopping basket from one arm to the other.

'You're not bad or somethin'?'

'No, no.' Flustered, Hannah said in embarrassment, 'I was just thinking, that's all.'

'Thinkin'? You don't want to be doing that, lass. Gets you in a whole load of trouble, thinkin' does? She chuckled to herself. 'Meself, I've always been a doer an' left the thinkin' to them as has time for it.'

Hannah forced a smile before walking on. Someone had killed Silas Fletcher but who and why? Who even knew he was in town apart from this friend of his and Jake? And who would have anything to lose apart from Jake? He had been trying to protect his mother, she was sure of that. Oh, this was such a tangle but there had to be something that would unravel things. But the court hearing was tomorrow. Her heart began to pound so hard it hurt. And everyone believed he was guilty.

The snow was settling fast and the sky was threatening more to come by the time Hannah reached the top of Wayman Street. She approached the house by way of the back lane although she knew there would still be neighbours who would clock her in and clock her out. You couldn't sneeze in these streets without someone knowing.

Rose answered her knock at the back door, her weary face lighting up when she saw Hannah. 'Come in, hinny. I'm all by meself. Wilbur's gone to his friend's funeral. Oh, I'm that pleased to see you, I can't stop thinking about tomorrow and my lad.'

'I've just been to see Jake and he let me talk to him this time.' Hannah followed Rose into the kitchen which was lit only by the glow of the fire although the afternoon was as dark as late evening. Rose never lit the gas until she had to. Every penny counted.

'He did? Oh, lass.' Rose turned to face her, taking Hannah's hands in her own rough ones. 'What did he say? How is he? I've tried time and time again to see him but he wasn't having any of it. He sent me a letter explaining everything but he was adamant he didn't want me to see him in there.'

'He didn't do it, Mrs Wood.'

'I know that, hinny. My lad couldn't kill a fly let alone a human being, if you can call Silas a human being. I can still hardly believe Silas was alive all these years. He was a wicked man, Hannah. Warped. Unnatural. But what am I doing? Get that wet coat and hat off, lass, and come and sit by the fire while I get a cup of tea.'

Once Hannah had sat down and the tea was mashing, Rose turned and looked at her. 'Why didn't he tell me?' she said quietly. 'All this could have been averted if he'd told me his father was back instead of paying him to keep quiet. I could have told him he was on a hiding to nothing doing that. Silas would have kept on and on until he'd bled him dry. Oh, I know he did it for the best, trying to save my face with the neighbours and all, but now...' She waved her hands helplessly. 'Oh, lass, I'm going barmy thinking of him locked up in there.'

'Me too, Mrs Wood. I can't bear it.'

Something in Hannah's voice made Rose look at her more keenly. 'Do you care for him, hinny?'

she asked softly.

Hannah nodded, her face flooding with colour.

'And him? How's he feel?'

'He's never said anything.' Hannah paused. 'In fact he's been hinting I should look for something else, leave the farm, but today...' She paused again. 'He looked at me in a different way. I don't think he meant for me to see... Oh I don't know, Mrs Wood.'

'Do you want to know what I think, lass? I think he's been fair gone on you for a while but this,' Rose touched the side of her face, 'prevents him from saying anything.'

'But why? He must know I don't care about that.'

'You have to understand something, hinny. You're a bonny lass, you always have been and there's many a lad would look the side you were on if you gave them half a chance. Now my Jake grew up being called the sort of names you wouldn't put to an animal. Bairns are cruel, lass, and there's nothing they like more than tormenting and goading someone more vulnerable than themselves. It's the way of things. I tried to shield him as much as I could but...' Rose shrugged her shoulders. 'And what goes in a bairn's head makes the adult. He's all tough and strong on the outside but inside there's that little bairn crying out to be loved and accepted. But he'd rather cut off his right hand than run the risk of being rejected.'

Hannah stared at Jake's mother. Could that be it? Or had she misread what was in his eyes?

'Now in spite of his scars I think he's a fine figure of a man and he could have been wed long before this if he didn't see himself the way he does. But how you'd break down the barrier he's built for the last thirty-three years I don't know. I don't even know if it's possible, lass, if you want the truth.'

'I'd do it, somehow I'd find a way if I was sure he cared about me, but...' Her voice low, she went on, 'Tomorrow there's the trial.'

'Aye, lass, there's the trial.' Rose's voice broke.

'Oh, I'm sorry, Mrs Wood.' Hannah rose swiftly and crossed to Rose and hugged her tightly as Naomi would have done. 'You sit down and I'll make the tea.'

While the two women drank their tea they talked of what could be done but both knew it was pointless. It was as they were on their second cup that the kitchen door was thrust open and Adam walked in. Acknowledging her son with a nod of her head, Rose said in an aside to Hannah, 'As though things weren't bad enough they're all on short time now. Did you know?' Without waiting for a reply, she added, 'Sit down, lad, and I'll get you a sup. There's one in the pot.'

Hannah had stiffened. She'd read what Adam had said to the *Sunderland Echo* and he had purposely put Jake in the worst light possible. Mindful of Rose's feelings, though, she nodded to him when he said, 'Hello, Hannah.'

'There you are, get that down you.' Rose placed a cup of tea in front of him as he sat down at the table. 'Your da's gone to the funeral, did he tell you?'

Adam did not answer. He took off his cap and ran his fingers through his dark thick hair without taking his gaze from Hannah's averted eyes.

412

Quietly, he said, 'You know Lily's taken the bairn and gone home to her mam's, I suppose.'

Hannah looked at him. Did he really think she cared two pins about that when Jake was incarcerated in prison?

Her face must have conveyed her thoughts because he leant back in his chair. 'I see. Couldn't care less.'

'Don't start.' It was Rose who spoke and her voice had lost the tender quality of earlier and become harsh. 'Not today of all days. Hannah went to see Jake this afternoon and she's upset.'

'Oh aye? They let you in then. Mam's been a number of times and had the door closed in her face.'

'Jake agreed to see me, yes.'

Adam swallowed half his tea, scalding hot as it was, before he said, 'And how is he? The big fella? Cocky as ever?'

Hannah saw Rose's expression but before Jake's mother could say anything, she snapped, 'He's not like that and you know it. You just can't bear that he's made such a success of his life compared to you.'

'Success? Am I missing something here? Forgive me but I thought he was the one banged up in a cell.'

'That's a mistake. He didn't kill his father.'

'No? Well, Sidney Benson says different.'

'Like I said, he's mistaken.'

'And you know, do you? You've got some divine link to the Almighty?'

'Yes I know.' Her eyes flashing, Hannah glared at him. She hadn't realised until this moment how much she disliked Adam Wood. 'I know what sort of man Jake is. He's a good man through and through, he wouldn't do a thing like that.'

There was a moment of profound silence. Then Adam said slowly, his eyes wide and hard, 'So that's it. You and him.' The two women watched him swell with anger before he ground out, 'Well, aren't I the prize idiot? Here was me thinking it was Daniel Osborne when all the time you've had your sights set on a meal ticket for life. And don't tell me it's his good looks that set your heart beating faster.'

'Jake is handsome to me.' Her face white but for two spots of colour burning on her cheekbones, Hannah rose to her feet. 'But he's much more than handsome. He's decent and good and kind, all the things you're not.'

'Decent and good and kind, is he?' he mimicked raspingly. 'So decent and good and kind he decided to do in his own father rather than fork out to keep our good name from being dragged through the gutter. And don't tell me he couldn't afford it. What's ten pounds a week when he's got that farm and the house and plenty in the bank, likely as not?'

Hannah stared at him. Her mind was groping at something, something she knew to be vitally important but couldn't put her finger on. And then it came to her. Slowly, she said, 'Ten pounds a week. You said Jake was giving his father ten pounds a week.'

'What?'

'How do you know that?' Her stomach was turning over.

414

'Everyone knows Jake's been paying him off.'

'Paying him off, aye, but not the amount.'

Adam glanced from Hannah to his mother and then back to Hannah. He shrugged. 'I must have read it in the papers.'

'I've read every word in every paper and no sum has ever been mentioned. There was nothing in Jake's father's pockets when he was found. Not even a handkerchief. Don't you think that's strange?' When Adam said nothing, she went on, 'Well, don't you? And don't tell me you haven't got an opinion about it. You have an opinion about everything. If someone killed Silas to make it look like a robbery then I can understand his pockets being empty, but why would Jake do that?'

'Obvious.' Adam's tongue wet his lower lip, betraying his nerves.

'Is it?' Rose's face was chalk white. 'Not to me, lad.'

'Come on, Mam.' The anger in Adam's voice was forced, both women recognised it. 'What are you saying? That I had something to do with all this?'

Rose sank down on one of the kitchen chairs, and it was Hannah who said, 'Did you?'

'Don't be daft. And course Jake'd empty his da's pockets. That way it looked like some down-an'-out had been done in and there'd be nothing to trace the body back to Jake.'

Hannah didn't take her eyes off Adam. 'You haven't said how you know Jake paid his father ten pounds.'

'I can't remember, all right? And what does it matter? A pound, five, ten, it don't make no difference. Jake killed him and that's that.'

'Jake did not kill him. Sidney Benson himself said in the *Echo* that Jake knew someone was with his da up here, that Silas wasn't alone. Why would Jake kill him and lay himself open to exactly what's happened? But if someone killed Silas who didn't know about the other person, that'd make more sense. You did it, didn't you? Somehow you found out about Silas and you waited on the North Hylton Road and you killed him.'

'I'm not sitting here listening to any more of this.' Adam swigged the last of his tea and stood up, and so did Rose.

'You used to go and spy on 'em at that farm,' she said woodenly. 'You started it a long time ago. And them spots on your coat and trousers, you said there'd been a fight at the Friendly and you and your da had had to separate two blokes.'

'What of it?'

'It wasn't some drunk's blood you got splattered with, was it? It was his, Silas's.'

'You're as bad as her.' Adam made to push past his mother but neither women gave ground and he was forced to remain where he was. Glaring at Rose, he said, 'Ask Da if you don't believe me. We were together that night, first at the meeting I told you about and then in the pub with the rest of them.'

'Your da's not been himself since that Sunday.' It was as though Rose hadn't heard him. Indeed, she was talking as though to herself. 'He said it was a stomach upset but that wouldn't have him walking the floor most nights and looking like death, not after more than three weeks.'

'There was bad beer on that night, several of the lads have had gippy stomachs since. That's all it is. By all the saints, Mam, would I lie to you about this? What do you take me for anyway? And what are you saying now, that Da's part of some conspiracy or other? Just listen to yourself. Look, I know Jake's your son and you're worried to death, that's understandable. But I'm your son too or have you forgotten that?'

'No...' Rose was in anguish. Reaching out and holding Adam's hands, she said, 'Swear to me, lad. Swear to me you know nothing about this.'

'I swear, Mam. On me bairn's life, I swear I know as much as you or anyone else about it. I know me and Jake have never hit it off but do you honestly think I'd set him up?'

'I don't think you purposely set him up,' Hannah said steadily, 'but you didn't know about Sidney Benson. You might fool your mam, Adam, but you don't fool me.'

'Is that so? And this spite couldn't have anything to do with Lily, could it? I've said I'm sorry for that, it was a mistake and believe me I've paid for it, but once she'd fallen for the bairn I had to do the right thing by her. That's something you've never understood, isn't it. Asking me to go away with you, saying we could make a new life together down south where no one would know us. I couldn't do it, Hannah, much as I wanted to. But I told you, it was the bairn, not Lily, that held me. I couldn't abandon my own flesh and blood. Everything was different once a bairn was on the way.'

Rose had pulled her hands free and taken a step

417

backwards as Adam had been speaking, but he had his eyes on Hannah, not his mother.

'You liar.' Her face scarlet, Hannah turned to Rose. 'He's lying. It was him who said all that about going down south, not me. He came to the farm, he said all sorts of things—'

'I came to the farm? And Jake invited me in, I suppose. Or maybe Farmer Shawe did that.'

'It was at Christmas and Jake was here, you know he was, and Farmer Shawe didn't see you.'

'That's convenient. You're a woman scorned, Hannah. That's what this is all about.'

Rose's hand was pressed to her mouth and she looked ill. Hannah wanted to reach out and help her but this was too important. If they convicted Jake, if they found him guilty of cold-blooded murder, he could hang. 'I'm going to the police.' She watched Adam's expression change as she spoke but she refused to be intimidated. 'I shall tell them what you said about the ten pounds and they can check who was at that meeting and what time you and your da arrived at the pub. They'll find out if there was a fight or not.'

'There's no need for that.' The quiet voice from the scullery brought all three heads turning and the next moment Wilbur pushed the door wide open.

'Da, how long have you been there?'

Wilbur looked at his son. 'Long enough.'

'So you heard what she's been saying? What she's trying to pin on us?'

'Not you, Mr Wood. I don't know about you. But I think Adam knows more about Silas's death than he's saying.'

418

'Tell her, Da. Tell her about the meeting and the fight in the pub, she won't take my word for it. Tell her–'

'It's over, lad.' Wilbur's gaze was pitying. 'Accept it.'

Rose looked at her husband. 'Wilbur?'

'Shut up, Da,' said Adam. 'I'm telling you, keep your mouth shut.'

'Lad, you can't talk your way out of this one.' Turning his gaze on Hannah, he added, 'You wouldn't let him, would you?'

'No, Mr Wood, I wouldn't. I'm going to the police.'

'I'm sorry, lass.' Wilbur's eyes moved to his wife. 'It was me who did it. Adam was there but it was me who bashed his head in. Adam tried to stop me but I went sort of mad. I didn't mean to kill him.'

He was lying. Hannah looked into the grey old face that seemed to have aged twenty years in the last three weeks. He was protecting Adam. She'd never been so sure of anything in her life.

'We were just going to talk to him, perhaps frighten him enough for him to take off to wherever he'd been for the last thirty years but it all went wrong. I didn't mean for Jake to get involved but suddenly it was like I was on a runaway horse and I couldn't stop it.'

Rose was leaning against the table for support. 'You killed Silas?' she whispered.

'Aye, I did, and you, lass,' Wilbur turned to Hannah, 'you don't need to go to the law. I'll be going meself in a minute or two but I've a mind to have a last cup of tea first.' He sat down in the

419

armchair by the range and took his cap off. Rose glanced helplessly at Hannah before pouring her husband a cup of tea and taking it to him. 'Thanks, lass.' He looked up at his wife and his face was calm. 'You always make a grand cup of tea.'

'You shouldn't have let them put Jake away, Wilbur. Not my lad. That was cruel.'

'Aye, I see that. I'm sorry, lass. Heart sorry.'

'Da–'

'We'll talk on the way to the police station.' Wilbur cut Adam off quickly. 'All right? Just let me drink me tea first. It's better you come with me now. There's folk in the pub know we were together that night but I'll tell 'em you tried to stop me and none of it was your fault. But what son wants to shop his own da, eh? They'll understand that.'

Hannah sat down at the table, her legs were trembling so much. Rose seemed to have accepted completely that it was her husband who had killed Silas but every word Adam's father had spoken confirmed who the real murderer was as far as Hannah was concerned. She raised her eyes and met Adam's. They stared at each other for some moments and it was Adam who looked away first.

When Wilbur stood up and pulled his cap on his head, Hannah half expected Rose to go to him and put her arms around him or at least see him out but she didn't move until Adam and Wilbur had left the house. Then she went and stood by the window, looking out at the thickly falling snow. 'He would have let my lad swing for something he didn't do,' she said quietly, her back to the room. 'And Jake's been suffering the torments of the damned the last weeks in that place, confined like he is. Wilbur knew that. He knew how bad it'd be with the way Jake is. And then there's Adam. Why didn't he think of Adam being with him before he lost his temper. What sort of father is he anyway?'

Hannah looked at the thin back and the iron-grey hair pulled into a bun against the stringy neck. Believing what she did, she could make no reply to this that wouldn't thrust Rose into worse anguish. 'I'm so sorry, Mrs Wood.'

Rose turned to face her. 'Things haven't been right between me and Wilbur for years but I still find it hard to believe he could do something like this. But it's his pride, you see. He's always been a man who's valued his good name and Silas was going to take that away.' Suddenly plumping down at the table, she laid her head on her arms and began to cry.

Chapter 27

It was nine o'clock the same evening and it had stopped snowing. The world was clothed in startlingly white brilliance that glittered and twinkled like diamond dust. It wouldn't last long, and when the inevitable thaw set in, the slush and mud would be knee high, but for now everything was new and sparkling clean.

Jake stepped out of the police station and walked a few feet before standing quite still. He lifted his face to the sky, taking lungfuls of frosty air before beginning to cough convulsively. The nicer of the constables in there had told him he didn't look well. 'Must be that cold you picked up, along with all the stress and strain you've been under the last weeks but you can go home and rest now.' Rest? he'd felt like saying. When he'd been in hell for three weeks? A hell that kept you tight in a little box where you couldn't breathe or think or feel beyond a desperate panic that was all-consuming. He forced his thoughts to slow down as he continued to breathe in and out. He was free. He wasn't shut in any more. He couldn't give way now.

The sweat was standing out on his forehead like drops of blood. I feel bad, he thought. Oh, I feel bad. His heart was thumping against his ribs demanding air, but breathing made him cough. He hadn't been able to think in there. He had existed in a state of animal panic that had been shaming and degrading and without human dignity. Was he having a mental breakdown? That's what the constable had thought, he'd read it in his face. He'd wanted to ask him why, thinking that, had they continued to keep him trapped in a tomblike, ten-foot wide crypt. But he hadn't. He'd just nodded and smiled, petrified that if he rocked the boat in any way they wouldn't let him out.

He thought her voice was in his mind at first, part of the sickness. And then it came again and he opened his eyes to see Hannah standing in

422

front of him.

'Jake?' Her smile was tentative and confirmed how ill he looked. 'I've got a cab waiting.'

He glanced beyond her and saw the horse-drawn cab at the side of the road. He didn't know how he hadn't noticed it before. He also didn't know how he was going to make the few yards to the cab without passing out. The shivering that had come on and off for the last few days along with the fever was stronger tonight, but he couldn't collapse in front of her. That would be the final humiliation.

'You're not well.'

Her voice was soft, sympathetic, but the pity he fancied he heard worked on him like a shot of adrenaline and he covered the distance to the cab with her at his side.

Inside, she put her hand to his forehead. Her hand was cool. He wanted to grab it and hold on to it but his arms and legs felt leaden. 'You're burning up.' He heard alarm now. 'You need a doctor.'

No, he just needed to get home. He'd crawl on his hands and knees all the way to the farm if he had to. Once there he could rest and he would be all right. He tried to find breath to say this but the coughing was worse, knives twisting in his chest.

When she wrapped a blanket round him he didn't protest. There were words on his tongue. He wanted to know how she was here. How she knew he was being released. But he couldn't speak. Her name was like an intonation in his head, over and over, Hannah, Hannah.

He knew when they reached the farm. He was vaguely aware of Hannah calling Frank and Jack Osborne when his legs refused to hold him up. And then he found himself in his own bed but he couldn't remember how he had got there or who had undressed him.

In the semi-darkness he heard Clara saying, 'Don't worry, lass. The doctor'll be here soon. I think he's got that influenza that's taking 'em down right, left an' centre in the town. The main thing is he's here now, he's home, and all thanks to you, hinny.'

He was home again and he wasn't losing his mind. He felt so ill because he had the influenza. The relief was momentary. His head felt as if it was going to explode and the burning in his chest and back was unbearable. And then the level of pain in his body reached new proportions and he felt himself falling into a fiery darkness where flames were licking at his flesh. And then ... nothing.

'You're looking better this morning.'

'I should do. I've been in this bed four weeks.' Jake smiled at Hannah as she bustled about opening the curtains and then straightening his eiderdown before placing a breakfast tray on his lap.

'Double pneumonia on top of influenza is not something to mess about with,' she said severely.

'No, nurse. Sorry, nurse.'

'Try and eat something today.'

'I will.' It would be a struggle but he'd try to force something down to please her. It was the least he could do considering he owed his life to her. At the time of his release he hadn't questioned why they had suddenly decided to let him go. Strange, but then he hadn't been thinking straight. The sickness in his mind and body had numbed everything else. It had been two weeks, two weeks of raving delirium and terrifying nightmares during which Hannah had barely left his side, before he had discovered the truth.

It had been his mother who had told him the day she and the rest of the family had come to live at the farmhouse and left the town and its gossips for good. Sitting quietly by his bedside, she had talked for a long time and he had been content to lie deep in his pillows and listen. At that stage he had barely been able to open his mouth without it exhausting him.

And yesterday, after a bill of indictment had brought the case to court without delay due to the interest it had generated far and wide, Wilbur and Adam had been convicted of murder. Wilbur had received the death sentence. Adam, life imprisonment, his life being spared due to his father's insistence that his son had tried to prevent both the beating and the fatal blow that had killed Silas Fletcher.

Hannah had attended the two-day trial with Rose and Naomi while Clara had sat with Jake. She had told him beforehand of her suspicions regarding Adam, and it appeared the jury and Judge Grant had similar misgivings. Apparently Adam's defence barrister had been eloquent in his plea it was only fair his client be declared guilty of manslaughter and not murder, but the jury had ignored this. Furthermore, the judge had expressed regret that Wilbur's testimony on behalf of his son made it difficult for him to give the death sentence to both men. Rose had collapsed at the verdict, calling Adam's name, and when Hannah and Naomi had brought her home she had retired to bed.

'How's my mother this morning?'

Hannah looked at him. 'It will take time,' she said quietly.

He nodded. Time. The supposed great healer that made everything easier. Everything except this feeling inside him that was both a curse and a blessing. A curse because it was doomed, it had always been doomed, but a blessing because to be able to look on her face, talk to her, have her near were small snatches of bitter-sweet heaven. 'At least they're both not for the drop. I don't know how she would have taken that, Adam being hanged.'

'But for him to be locked up for the rest of his life, Jake. And don't forget Judge Grant recommended it should *mean* life. Adam's so young.'

'You're sorry for him?' He felt hurt and angry, slighted in some way. Adam had done his best to pin Silas's murder on him. He'd known what he was saying when he had talked to the papers. And then he reminded himself that but for the slim young woman standing looking at him now he could well be in Wilbur's shoes. Nevertheless his voice held a tinge of resentment when he repeated, 'You're sorry he's going to be locked away?'

'No, not really. I think I might have been but for one thing.' She paused and he waited for her to explain. Instead she said, 'But for a mother to see her son imprisoned for the rest of his life, that

426

must be terrible, Jake. That's what I meant.'

He looked down at the tray. It held a bowl of porridge, just the way he liked it, and he knew the covered plate next to the steaming mug of tea would contain eggs, sausage, bacon, black pudding. Without looking at her, he said, 'What was the thing that prevented you? Feeling sorry for Adam, I mean.'

'Don't you know?'

Her voice was soft, gentle. His brow wrinkling, he raised his eyes. 'No, I don't.' He supposed it was Adam's betrayal with Lily but it wasn't like Hannah to bear a grudge under such horrific circumstances.

She stared at him. 'Think about it,' she said at last before turning and walking out of the room.

Think about it? Irritably he pushed the tray onto the bedside cabinet and then reached for the mug of tea. While he sipped it he stared round the room as though it would provide an answer. He couldn't be doing with any sort of double talk, he wasn't well enough. Didn't she know that? He still had a job to keep his eyes open for more than thirty minutes at a time; some days he slept near enough twenty out of twenty-four hours away.

Hark at you. The voice in his head was scathing and his mouth curled in a wry grimace. He sounded like a petulant schoolboy. What was the matter with him, for crying out loud?

Was he still jealous of Adam and the hold he'd had – perhaps still had, deep in the hidden recesses of her heart – over Hannah?

You bet your sweet life he was.

He finished the tea and lay back on the pillows.

He ought to eat something but it'd choke him. How much longer was he going to feel so drained, so mentally and physically exhausted? Dr Stefford had said it would be months, not weeks, before he was fully fit. He wouldn't be able to stand it. He felt so useless, so weak and emasculated. She must despise him. And when he thought of those first couple of weeks when she'd done everything for him... The sound in his throat was tortured. They had never discussed it but however good she was, however kind, it must have sickened her. A man wasn't supposed to crumple like a woman. He knew he had come near to a nervous breakdown after being shut in for all those endless days and nights, the pneumonia brought on by severe influenza was the least of it. And she knew. He had heard his mother and Hannah talking one day when they'd thought he was asleep. A big strong man like him and he'd gone to pieces like a bit lass. Hell, couldn't he at least have kept his pride in all of this? Was that too much to ask?

He glanced at Seamus's commode which Hannah had had brought upstairs to his room once the delirium had finally passed. His nose wrinkled in distaste. It embodied everything his spirit was fighting against. Damn it, whatever Stefford said, he wasn't going to lie in this bed being waited on hand and foot for one more day. He felt sick at what he'd been reduced to. At least before he'd had her respect; now... Again he groaned.

He had managed to reach the wardrobe when he heard her footsteps outside the room. He was hanging on to the wardrobe door with all his might, fighting the spinning faintness which threatened to take his legs from under him. He couldn't move, he knew if he tried to he would either pass out or vomit and neither was an option. She must already look on him as the worst sort of weakling.

The door opened and he heard her exclamation of shock. Then her arms were round his waist, trying to support him as she scolded, 'What on earth are you trying to do, Jake? You're not fit enough to be out of bed, you know that. Come on, come and lie down.'

'No.'

'You must. Look at you. I can't believe you've done this. You'll make yourself ill again.'

He knew he needed her help but he didn't want it. Still hanging on to the door, he said, 'Leave me, I can do it.'

'Whatever you're trying to do, you can't.' Her voice was schoolmarmish, the sort of tone one used to a recalcitrant child. Likely that was how she saw him, not as a man at all.

Grinding his teeth he let her help him back into bed. It was either that or crawl because he didn't have an ounce of strength left in his body. When he collapsed on the bed, he couldn't move for a minute or two. His heart felt as if it was going to burst out of his chest and the drumming in his ears was deafening. Eventually he forced himself to swing his legs up and under the covers and again the slight effort involved was exhausting. He lay with his eyes shut for a few moments. When he opened them she was sitting by the head of the bed, a couple of feet away. If he hadn't been feeling so bad he would have laughed at the expression on her face. 'I know,' he muttered weakly. 'You'd like to tan me backside for being a naughty lad.'

'This isn't funny, Jake. You heard what Dr Stefford said the last time. This could have taxed your heart and you've got to be patient and take things slowly.'

'Take things slowly?' A moment ago, even while he'd been talking, he'd had the desire to drop off to sleep. Now he opened his eyes and glared at her. 'Damn it, how much slower can they be? And I'm not a bairn so don't talk to me like one.'

'Then don't act like one and I won't have to.'

'This is driving me mad. You've no idea.'

'Nor ever likely to have if you don't talk to me and *tell* me how you feel.'

'What?' He had expected sympathy, which was what he had been resenting for the last couple of weeks when it came from her. Now, perversely, he missed it.

'But that's too much to ask, isn't it? Coming from you. Jake Fletcher. The man determined to go it alone no matter who he hurts in the process.'

He was amazed. 'I haven't hurt anyone.'

'I don't count then?'

'You?' He couldn't believe his ears. 'When have I ever hurt you?'

'How long have you got?' She gazed at him, her eyes steady and clear. 'It would take too long to list all the occasions so I'll just take the last months, shall I?' Counting on her fingers, she continued, 'You made me feel like I'd committed an unforgivable sin when I kissed you at Christmas. You've been hinting – and not particularly tact-

430

fully – that you think it's time I left here and found somewhere else to live. You didn't trust me enough to tell me about your father and what he was doing, not even when his body was found not a hundred yards from the lane to the farm. You wouldn't let me see you in gaol until the last day although I'd come every single afternoon since you were arrested. Need I go on?'

There was a taut silence. Outside the window they could hear Jack Osborne calling to someone and then the sound of him laughing, and somewhere in the distance one of the farm dogs barked.

Jake swallowed hard. His throat felt like sandpaper. Part of him was crying out, I haven't got the strength to deal with this now. I can't think straight. I'll give myself away. The other part was horrified she could have been feeling hurt.

She looked beautiful, more beautiful than he'd ever seen her, sitting there with her great liquid eyes fixed on his face. Her face blurred and he swallowed again, looking down at his hands. Quietly, he said, 'It wasn't that I didn't trust you. I didn't want to involve you, that's all. Not in something so unpleasant.'

'What would you have said if I'd done a similar thing?'

'That's different.'

'Why? Because I'm a woman?'

'Yes. No. Oh, I don't know.' He paused. 'But it wasn't that I didn't trust you, I want you to believe that.'

'Then it can only be that you don't think I love you enough.'

He stopped breathing, his eyes remaining fixed

on his lifeless hands on the counterpane. They didn't look as though they belonged to his body. He didn't recognise them. They were too white, too limp looking. His mind was taking refuge in the mundane and he forced himself to respond to what she'd said. She was talking about sister love. He knew that. But this conversation was crucifying him. 'No, I don't think that,' he said woodenly. 'You've always been very kind, very good–'

'So why are you making me behave in such a forward way? It shouldn't be me saying I love you, that I can't live without you and that those three weeks when I thought they might wrongly convict you were the worst of my life. That a world that didn't have you in it wouldn't be worth living in. It's not seemly for me to say all that when you've given me no indication that you feel the same way.'

He couldn't bring himself to look at her. If he did, all this might fade away and he would be forced to recognise his mind – the mind that had played such tricks on him the last weeks – was misbehaving again.

There was a pause which stretched into eternity and then she said brokenly, 'If you want me to leave, I will, once you're better.'

'*No.*' He raised his eyes to her face and what he saw caused his throat to swell and his heart to knock against his ribs. 'But you can't feel like that, not about me.'

'Why?'

'Because I'm–' He stopped. Shaking his head, he said, 'You're young and bonny. You could have anyone.'

'I don't want anyone. Just you.'

'You don't know what you're saying.'

'On the contrary. And before you start thinking this and that, let me make it plain this is no sudden thing.'

Her cheeks were burning with hot colour but her voice was calm, cool even. For a moment he allowed his mind to clutch at the hope that this was no girlish fancy that would evaporate once he was on his feet again and she had stopped feeling sorry for him.

'And the reason I can't have much sympathy for Adam being locked away for good is because he would have happily seen you hang for something he was guilty of.'

So that was it. Reality rushed in. She was seeing him as the injured party, the innocent victim. Not only that but the nursing of the last weeks, when he'd been as helpless as a babe, had brought out her womanly emotions. It would be very different when he was back on his feet and behaving like a man again. Stiffly, he said, 'You don't have to make atonement for what Adam did.'

For a moment she stared at him. Slowly she got to her feet. 'If you weren't so ill I'd punch you on the nose for that, Jake Fletcher.'

A line of red stained his cheekbones as he stared back at her. 'I didn't mean–'

'You're the most patronising, arrogant, awkward, stupid man I've ever come across,' she said slowly and distinctly. 'Why I love you I don't know, but I do and I'm stuck with it. I can't force you to believe me though. You'll have to work through that for yourself. And I'm not going to

433

turn cartwheels trying to convince you either. And now you've made me say this all wrong and spoilt everything.' To his amazement she actually stamped her foot in temper before turning and walking across the room.

She had her hand on the door handle when his voice came. 'Hannah?'

'What?' Her eyes were misty with unshed tears when she faced him.

'Doesn't this,' he lifted a hand to his face, 'repulse you even a little?'

How could she make him understand? What chance did she have of breaking through thirty-three years of aloneness? She didn't know the words to say, she wasn't articulate enough to express all she felt. 'If it was me who had been hurt, would you be repulsed or would you love and respect me all the more for making a good life for myself? I know you won't believe this, but I don't see your scars, Jake. I stopped seeing them a long time ago. To me you're the most handsome man in the world and I mean your whole face when I say that, not just the undamaged side.'

'I ... I find that hard to believe.'

'Try,' she said simply, before opening the door and leaving the room.

Outside on the landing, she stood with her back against the wall, her chest heaving. She wanted to cry but suddenly her eyes were dry, her heart aching. She had said it all wrong. How could she have called him those names? She lifted a hand to her mouth, biting down hard on her thumbnail. She had always known he would never speak first and so she had determined she would tell him calmly how she felt, once he was well enough, and then leave the rest with him. But him suggesting she was offering herself as some sort of compensation for what Adam had tried to do had made her mad. It had been little short of insulting.

She looked towards a shaft of April sunlight slanting across the floorboards at the end of the landing. She walked over to the tall narrow window and peered out. Peter and the twins had already left for the walk into Southwick where they were now attending a new school on the west side of the parish, but to one corner of the farmyard she could see Daniel Osborne and Stephen talking to Naomi. It had been decided Naomi would leave the jam factory and work on the farm. Anne Osborne was getting married in a few weeks and Naomi would take her place in the dairy. Enid had already offered to train Naomi up. Naomi was getting on well with Daniel's mother, something she herself had never done. As she watched, Daniel lifted his hand and brushed a strand of hair from Naomi's cheek.

Hannah turned abruptly. Naomi and Daniel. Anne getting married. Florence expecting another bairn. Even Grace Osborne had just started walking out with a lad from the village. For a moment envy swamped her. It was all so easy for them.

She stared down at her chewed nail. Jake had never said he loved her. What if she'd misread that look in his eyes at the police station? But then she reminded herself it had been her name he had muttered in the midst of his delirium, not just once but many times. And she loved him. No one else would do.

Moving her head impatiently at her thoughts, she made her way downstairs. She had too much to do to stand mooning, as Clara would call it. Dear Clara. She had been a rock the last weeks. She had already made it her business to make a friend of Rose, chivvying Jake's mother along as best she could when Rose's despair had threatened to overwhelm her.

Pausing outside the kitchen door, Hannah took a deep breath, composing her face before she pushed the door open. Rose was sitting at the kitchen table drinking a cup of tea. Glancing at Hannah's empty hands, she said, 'I thought you went for his breakfast tray?'

'He hadn't finished.'

'But he was eating something? That's a good sign.'

'I'm not sure if he'd had anything.'

Rose looked up into the face of the girl she thought of as a second daughter. Her voice changing, she said, 'What is it? What's happened now?'

'Nothing.'

'Something's wrong. Is he worse?'

'No, no. He's fine. Well, as fine as he was yesterday anyway.' Hannah plumped down on a chair. 'It's just – oh, I shouldn't be bothering you, you must be feeling awful. You've enough on your plate.'

'Lass, I've had plenty on my plate, as you put it, since my Joe died and I'm going to be feeling awful for a long time. Every time I think of my lad locked up in that place, in fact. But that don't mean life don't go on. It went on after Joe and it'll go on now, that's the way of it. Wilbur...' Rose paused. 'That's going to happen and I can't do nowt about it. The good book says an eye for an eye and God won't be mocked.'

Hannah nodded. She always felt acutely uncomfortable when Rose talked about Wilbur but there was nothing she could say or do. Wilbur insisted he'd been the one to deliver the fatal blow. Adam had not challenged this and certainly it was more acceptable to Rose that it was her husband and not her son who had murdered Silas. Hannah knew that her suspicions were something she would have to live with, shared only with Jake.

'So what is it, hinny? What's upset you?'

'You remember the day I came to see you when we found out about Wilbur and Adam, when I said how I felt about Jake? Well, I told him this morning that I loved him. I should probably have waited a while. It ... it didn't go well.'

'Oh, lass.'

'But I do love him, Mrs Wood, and I'm not going to give up.' As she spoke, Hannah's voice gathered strength. 'And he would never have said anything to me, you know that yourself.'

Rose nodded. 'That's for sure.' There was silence in the kitchen for a moment; then Rose said, 'I want you to know this, lass. However things turn out in the future, I want to say this now. I think of you as one of my own, I always have, and I'm for you come hell or high water. Just so you know.' She paused. 'What are you going to do?'

'Carry on as before.' A voice inside her head said, can you? Do you really think you can pretend this never happened and just act normal? She answered it by saying out loud, 'I'm going to

437

let the next move come from him and if he chooses not to say anything...' She shrugged. 'I can't do more, Mrs Wood.'

'No, I see that, lass.'

'But thank you, for what you said about being for me.'

'What will be, will be, hinny. Take comfort in that.'

Hannah smiled at Jake's mother. What will be, will be. Did she believe that? Not altogether, no. Many a time since coming to the farm she'd heard Clara say that it was all very well to pray to God to bring you into His harbour of blessing in times of trial and turmoil, but He expected you to do your bit and row the boat as well. Well, she'd done her bit of rowing, she'd pointed the boat in the right direction; where it ended up wasn't down to her any more.

Chapter 28

It was a week later and the last seven days had not been easy ones for Hannah. Outwardly she had appeared the same, inwardly she could feel herself shrivelling a little each day. She had been true to the promise she had made herself in the kitchen that first day and the next time she had gone into Jake's room she had acted as though all they'd talked about was the weather. And so it had continued. Somehow she had managed to chat and laugh and carry on as normal but the price was crying herself to sleep each night and this feeling that she was diminishing in the core of her. It was about the third day that it came to her that she was experiencing a taste of what Jake had endured all his life, and with the knowledge came a new understanding of the man she loved.

The knowledge provided no answers to the situation she now found herself in. Maybe there were none. And so day followed day as she continued to play the part allotted to her.

She didn't know what to do. What *could* she do? she asked herself, as she ran one of the sheets she had washed that morning through the mangle in the wash-house. She couldn't beg and plead. He had been pleasant enough since she had spoken but with a cool reserve about him. He was holding her at arm's length. Perhaps she *had* got it wrong. Perhaps he didn't love her as a man loves a woman. Perhaps he cared for her only in the same way he cared for Naomi. She didn't know any more. All she did know was that her declaration had made it impossible for her to stay once he was well.

The last of the sheets done, she straightened her aching back. She had been in the wash-house since eight o'clock that morning and it was now eleven but the poss tub was finally empty, the clothes mangled. All that remained was to peg everything on the two long lines at the side of the farmhouse where they caught any wind, and it was a fine drying day. It was cold but the sky was high and the sun was shining and there was enough wind to ensure come evening everything would be dry.

She had left Rose in charge of preparing lunch and baking some bread and cakes in the kitchen, but as she left the wash-house with the first of the three baskets of clothes to be hung on the line, she saw Jake's mother hurrying towards her. The expression on Rose's face was enough for Hannah to drop the basket.

'Come quick.' Rose did not shout; on the contrary, her voice was low but urgent. 'He's up.'

'Jake?'

'Aye, who else?'

They reached the kitchen door and Rose clutched at Hannah, preventing her from entering the house. 'I heard a commotion a few minutes ago and there he was, staggering down the stairs. How he didn't go from top to bottom, I don't know. And he's dressed.' Bending her head still closer, she murmured, 'I think he's gone round the bend, lass. I do straight. When I asked him what he was doing he said he's resuming his rightful place in the house. Just like that. That's word for word. And then he made his way into his study. I went to the door to see if I could help and he told me to come and get you. Wouldn't let me say another word. Just kept repeating for me to get you. All this has been too much for him. We'll have to send for the doctor.' Opening the door, Rose let Hannah precede her into the kitchen, saying, 'Do you want me to come with you?'

'No, no, it's all right.'

'What if he collapses?'

'Then I'll call you.'

'I couldn't believe my eyes when I saw him.'

Again Rose was clutching at her. 'And I thought he was getting better an' all. Lass, I couldn't stand something happening to another of my lads and that's the truth, it'd finish me off. First Joe dying and Adam as good as–'

'Nothing's going to happen to Jake, Rose.' It was the first time Hannah had called Jake's mother by her Christian name but both women were too upset to notice. 'And he *is* getting better. Just the fact he's up and downstairs proves that.'

'You haven't seen him,' said Rose darkly. 'He looks like death warmed up and there's something in his eyes... He's not well.'

'Let me have a word with him and then we'll decide what to do, whether to send for Dr Stefford or not. All right?'

'Aye, all right.' Rose followed Hannah into the hall, saying, 'I'll wait out here and you call if you need me, lass.'

'She won't need you.'

The voice from the study caused the two women to look at each other and Rose to remark drily, 'There's nowt wrong with his ears anyway.'

Hannah stood in the doorway of the study looking at the man seated at the desk. She could see what Jake's mother had meant. He did look like death warmed up.

Jake stared back at her for a moment and then said, 'Shut the door please, Hannah.'

She did as she was told but didn't venture further into the room, not until he said, 'Come and sit down. I won't bite.'

Slightly reassured at the normality of his voice, she took the seat he'd indicated on the other side of the desk. 'You've frightened your mother to death.'

'Have I? I'm sorry about that. I was hoping to be down here and established before anyone knew but she's always had cuddy lugs.' He smiled but she could see it was an effort.

'You shouldn't be up. Dr Stefford said—'

'Damn Dr Stefford.' And then he waved his hand. 'No, I shouldn't say that, he's been very good, but one more day in that bed and I would have been climbing the walls, Hannah. Believe me. It was of vital importance I came downstairs.'

'Why?' She glanced at his desk. 'There's nothing that can't wait when getting up too early could put you back weeks or worse.'

'It won't put me back. It will be the making of me. And as for the reason I had to be dressed and myself again...' He stood up and walked round the desk. Dropping onto one knee, he said, 'If you think I was going to do this lying flat on my back then you're wrong. Hannah, I love you with all my heart. I don't know how you can love me but I believe that you do. You will never know what you mean to me. If I tell you every day for the rest of our lives, it won't be enough.'

And then he flung aside what was obviously a well-rehearsed speech, stood up and drew her into his arms. 'Tell me, tell me you love me,' he murmured. 'Say it.'

'I love you.' Her voice was dazed, she felt dazed.

'And you're sure? You're sure you want a fellow like me?'

Her reply was smothered as he took her lips, holding her so tightly against him she could feel

442

the thud-thud of his heartbeat as they swayed together in what was no gentle embrace but a desperate desire to merge. When his lips left hers, they travelled the whole surface of her face in wonder before returning to her mouth, his husky mutterings unintelligible but filled with a desire that needed no translation.

When eventually he raised his head, she would have fallen but for his arms holding her. They were both breathing hard and it was a moment before he whispered, 'I am a brute, forgive me. I had a speech all ready, I was going to woo you so gently.'

For answer she stood on tiptoe and slipped her arms round his neck, her eyes shining as she pulled his head down to hers and took his mouth with a touchingly inexpert hunger which said more than any words could have done.

When they next parted, he lifted a hand to her face, tracing a path to her mouth as he murmured, 'I love you.'

'And I you.'

'You'll marry me?'

'Yes, oh yes.'

'I promise you I'll make you happy. Anything that is in my power to give you will be yours.'

'I only want you. I've only ever wanted you.' She cradled his handsome marred face in her hands. 'Just keep loving me. That's all I ask.'

Epilogue

Hannah and Jake were married six months later at the little parish church in Castletown. It was a quiet affair in view of the events which had occurred earlier in the year, but everyone agreed Hannah was a beautiful bride in her gown of ivory antique lace. Her aunt and uncle were abroad at the time of the wedding and Miriam had never been in touch since the day Jake had put her on the train for London. Hannah wasn't sorry about any of this. Jake's family were her family now, along with the folk at the farm. She didn't need anyone else.

They held a feast in one of the barns at Clover Farm after the ceremony Rose and Naomi and the other women had decorated it from top to bottom with garlands of wild flowers and ivy, and Daniel and John were in fine form as they struck up tune after tune on their fiddles so the assembled guests could dance the night away. Even Rose joined in when Stephen asked his mother to partner him in a barn dance, the sadness that sat on her like a cloak these days lifting briefly.

Jake had had a new wing built to the farmhouse in the last months and this now housed his mother and half siblings. This arrangement suited all parties well. It meant Rose felt she was mistress of her own home again, the wing having a separate front door along with a small kitchen, sitting room and three bedrooms. For Jake it meant he and Hannah could start their married life together with a greater degree of privacy.

Now, as the company formed in lines to begin the Gay Gordons, Jake drew Hannah to one side. 'Come and walk with me in the moonlight a while,' he murmured, his arm round her waist.

Hannah nodded, smiling as they left the noise and merriment and whirling throng of dancers. Nature had conspired to present them with a magical evening. The harvest moon was riding high in the sky and the air was surprisingly mellow for late September, a hundred scents from sun-warmed fields and hedgerows heavy in the still air. Not a breath of wind stirred the grasses and wild flowers at their feet as they walked along the bridle path wrapped in each other's arms.

The harvest had been completed the week before and as they turned off the path into one of the fields, haystacks rose like watching sentinels against a background of star-speckled slate-blue sky. Jake drew her down onto a seat of baled hay. Lifting her left hand to his lips, he kissed her wedding ring before murmuring, 'You're mine,' a note of wonder in his voice.

'And you are mine.' He looked magnificent in the moonlight. The white full-sleeved shirt he was wearing was open at the neck, his formal jacket having been discarded during the dancing, and his black trousers fitted tight against his thighs. Hannah thought he had never looked so handsome.

'I'm the most envied man in the county, do you know that? What does she see in him? That's what they're all saying.'

445

There was love in his embrace and love in his words, but underneath she sensed the silent need for reassurance. It didn't happen so often now. Over the last months since they had been betrothed she had made him talk to her, patiently persuading him to open his heart and mind. He was a complicated, enigmatic man but the more she understood him, the more she appreciated what a fortunate woman she was. 'Only the men would say that,' she said softly. 'The women would know exactly what I see in you because they see it too.'

He smiled. Lifting his hand, he traced the outline of her mouth with one finger.

For a moment the memory of that other night so long ago when she had loved under the harvest moon intruded. The promises made then had melted away in the light of day. They had been unsubstantial and without weight, fragile and fanciful dreams. But this, this was real.

'I love you,' she said softly, reaching for him.